NOTHING
SO
GLORIOUS

(Cris De Niro, Book 5)

ALSO BY GERARD DE MARIGNY

CRIS DE NIRO

ARCHANGEL

What readers are saying of ...
THE WATCHMAN OF EPHRAIM (Cris De Niro, Book 1)

"For a real page turning thriller with twists and one which keeps the reader hooked, read this book."
beckvalleybooks

"The Watchman of Ephraim," was a ride. I loved every minute I spent with the story and characters. I found myself getting choked up with the description of the events of 9/11. I was totally drawn into the story and couldn't put the book down."
Daniel N. Wallace

"Just finished reading "The Watchman of Ephraim" and I must give a very enthusiastic "WOW!" Gerard de Marigny has crafted a very exciting and engrossing story of international espionage with vibrant, fully-developed characters whom the reader connects with. Throw in a few exotic locales and you have a totally worthy successor to either James Bond or Jack Ryan. Read it -- you won't be disappointed."
Musicman

What readers are saying of ...
SIGNS OF WAR (Cris De Niro, Book 2)

"An action-packed, patriotic read that held my interest from start to finish."
Francie VW

"The part that I loved most about this book, as well as this series, is that the author has taken the time to research the military, the government, the weapons, the many different locations, technology, etc."
James Mathis

"Heart-stopping action, impossible decisions, a touch of romance, suspense, betrayal and courage set the tone for this thrilling installment in the Cris De Niro series. Gerard de Marigny writes with flair and attention to detail, ensnaring the reader in his web from the first page. If you enjoy political thrillers jam-packed with action and extraordinary characters, you won't want to miss Signs of War!"
Wendy L. Hines "MindingSpot"

What readers are saying of ...
PROJECT 111 (Cris De Niro, Book 4)

"... Another home run on a well executed story that has plenty of suspense, action, thrilling moments. The story unfolds in a well paced story line that at the end, you are left wanting the story to continue. I am a big fan of de Marigny novels and look forward for more to come."
Robert "Robear" (*Amazon* Review)

"If you enjoy Thor, Flynn, Silva, Coes, or any books in this genre, you'll love this series! The depth of the characters is so well done, you get hooked from the first page on. I'd recommend reading the books in order. Not that they don't stand on their own, they do, but the way the author builds upon each character really engages you in their lives. Love the patriotism, attention to detail and story-lines! Keep 'em coming!!!"
Barb (Amazon Review)

"This book was a delight to read ... The development of the main characters is great and believable. I like how everyone that is connected to Cris becomes family to him, even the Russian prisoner. I enjoyed the little bits of humor every now and then ... I like how the author references actual events that happened in the real world in this book ... This was a great book."
Bobmandingo (*Amazon* Review)

.

NOTHING *SO* GLORIOUS

GERARD DE MARIGNY

(Cris De Niro, Book 5)

JARRYJORNO PUBLISHING

HENDERSON

Published by JarRyJorNo Publishing
Henderson, Nevada

Edited by Lisa de Marigny

ISBN: 1495215644
ISBN-13: 978-1495215643

Library of Congress Control Number: 2014900865

1 2 3 4   14 13 12 11

This is a work of fiction. Names, characters, places, and incidents either are the product of the author's imagination or are used fictitiously, and any resemblance to actual persons, living or dead, businesses, companies, events, or locales is entirely coincidental.

While the author has made every effort to provide accurate telephone numbers and Internet addresses at the time of publication, neither the publisher nor the author assumes any responsibility for errors, or for changes that occur after publication. Further, the publisher does not have any control over and does not assume any responsibility for author or third-party websites or their content.

In memory of Vince Flynn.
Prayers for his family.

Cris, Mugsy, Scipio, and Gerard will miss checking in with Mitch Rapp.

"I can take a lot of crap from people, Valerie, but one thing I can't stand is a lack of gratitude. I'm one of those guys on the beach getting shot at, trying to do the right thing, risking it all for love of country, duty and honor. Words that mean nothing to you. I've been there and you haven't." (Executive Power, page 74)

"Vince Flynn was one of the greatest writers of our generation.
He will be missed. R.I.P. Vinnie."
(Gerard de Marigny)

There is nothing so glorious nor more wide-spread than the unity of mankind, that partnership and sharing of interests, that dearness of the human race, which has its origin at birth, because parents love their offspring, and because the whole family is bound together by marriage and by parenthood. This sentiment gradually spreads beyond the household, first to blood relatives, then to relations acquired by marriage, then to friends and later to neighbours, then to fellow-citizens and to those who are allies and friends in public life, and finally comes to embrace the whole human race.

— Marcus Tullius Cicero
De finibus bonorum et malorum
(On the Ends of Good and Evil)

Continued thanks to my ever-growing group of friends on my website, Twitter, Goodreads, Facebook and LinkedIn …
I'm very grateful for your friendship and support!

Thanks also to David Vandagriff (Passive Guy), Dean Wesley Smith, Kristine Kathryn Rusch, Robert Bidinotto, Stephen England.
You have all taught me, motivated me, and kept me informed.

Special mention and continued gratitude to my dear friends, Executive Producer Philip Norbert of Downtown Films, Jay Nemeth of Flightline Films, John McClain/Dog and Pony Studios, screen and stage actor extraordinaire Elijah Alexander/audiobook narration, Cinematographer Brad Hill, David Nicholls/LinkedIn Aspiring Writers Group, and newest member of "Team De Niro," Sarah Gardner.

Very special mention, respect, and appreciation to dear friends and rock music legends Jeff Glixman and Phil Ehart. Cris and I are humbled by your friendship, mentoring, and all of your efforts on our behalf. Also to Executive Producer Tom "Swanie" Swanson for your blessed vision to bring Cris & company to the big screen.

Eternal thanks to my wife Lisa and my sons Jared, Ryan, Jordan, & Noah. Your faith and support are my greatest blessings.
All my hopes …

All praise to Him!

NOTHING
SO
GLORIOUS

(Cris De Niro, Book 5)

CHAPTER 1

Cris De Niro opened his eyes at the sound of his youngest son's voice.

De Niro watched as twelve year-old Louis paced the room while he talked on the phone, "Hello ... hi, I would like to order room service please."

De Niro noticed his oldest, Richard, sprawled across the opposite side of the bed the three of them shared, with his head under a pillow, still sound asleep.

Louis read from the room service menu he laid on a chair, "We would like scrambled eggs, turkey bacon, organic chicken sausage, house smoked salmon, bagels, pancakes, Belgian waffles, French toast with maple syrup, charcoal grilled skirt steak, lamb sausage, a fruit plate, wheat toast, orange juice, and coffee ... please."

"For how many?"

Louis started counting on his fingers, "Um, for eight people … enough for eight people please, oh, and one apple fruit smoothie … for me."

There was a pause. Louis frowned and looked back at his dad, "Hold on, I'll put him on."

De Niro took the phone with a raised eyebrow and covered the receiver with the palm of his hand, "Are you sure you ordered enough food? I think you just ordered the whole menu."

"No, I didn't," Louis replied with a big smile, "I left off all the pork items and anything I couldn't pronounce."

De Niro shook his head, removing his hand, "Hello, this is Cris De Niro. That's quite all right; my son Louis is learning how to order room service … Lord, help me."

There was laughter on the phone.

"Just bring everything up, to be served buffet style … for eight … and don't forget the coffee."

De Niro tossed the phone back to Louis as he got to his feet and stretched. The familiar knock of a *shave-and-a-haircut* emanated from the suite's door.

"That's Mr. Vin, Karl, and Spiro. Let them in. I'm gonna jump in the shower. Your Uncle Mugsy and Scipio should be here soon too. Make sure you tell them you already ordered enough food for an army."

Wearing only pajama shorts, Louis padded to the door, "Who goes there?"

"Louis, open the door." The voice belonged to the leader of ARCHANGEL's *Michael* squad, Vin Rigoni.

ARCHANGEL was the paramilitary arm of The Watchman Agency. It was structured like a Navy SEAL team, composed of three squads - *Michael*, *Gabriel*, and *Padael*. Each was commanded by a Chief – in addition to Chief Rigoni, Karl De May of *Gabriel* squad, and Spiro Pescalitis of *Padael* squad.

All three were former Warrant Officers in the United States Marine Corps, though Rigoni outranked them by grade. De Niro and his brother-in-law, Captain Louis "Mugsy" Ricci, USN SEALs (Ret.),

President of The Watchman Agency, honored Rigoni's seniority in rank by placing him tactically in charge of all three squads.

Rigoni reported directly to the former Army Delta Force legend known simply as Scipio. Scipio was—by title—The Watchman Agency's Vice President of Operations, but he embraced only one component of the job description – head of ARCHANGEL.

Upon taking command of ARCHANGEL, Scipio immediately assigned Rigoni an additional duty bestowed to him as an honor – bodyguard of the founder, Cris De Niro. When not on his ranch in Henderson, Nevada where he was guarded by his head gaucho, Martin Fierro, wherever De Niro went, Rigoni accompanied him. Likewise, whenever De Niro's sons left the ranch, Scipio assigned De May and Pescalitis to guard them.

Louis grinned, "What's the password?"

"The password is – I'm gonna hang you upside-down outside the window if you don't open this door."

Louis smiled, "That's not it."

"The password is," this time it was Spiro Pescalitis's voice, "I won't tell Richard it was you who hid his cell phone."

Louis swung the door open, "That's not fair. You have no proof!"

Rigoni patted him on the head as he entered, "The proof is in the fact you opened the door, young man."

Louis closed the door and followed them, "Don't tell him, okay. *He'll* hang me upside-down outside the window."

Rigoni headed to the bedroom. Louis called to him as he took a seat between Pescalitis and De May, "My dad is taking a shower and I ordered food."

"You ordered food?" asked De May.

"Don't worry, I ordered enough."

The giant, muscle-bound man looked relieved, which made Pescalitis add, "He was worried he'd have to settle for a human-sized portion."

Rigoni returned from the bedroom, "Your brother is still sleeping?"

"Yeah, he was up all night playing *World of Warcraft* and chatting with his *girrll-friend*."

Rigoni returned a stern look, "Your dad knows about this girl?"

"Relax Riggy," replied Pescalitis, "Mr. D knows."

There was a knock at the door. De May answered it. Wearing brown gabardine trousers and a matching jacket, with a buttoned striped shirt, Mugsy Ricci shook De May's hand, "Good morning, gentlemen."

Rigoni replied for them as Pescalitis waved his hand in a mock salute, "Good morning, Captain."

Louis made a beeline to his uncle. Ricci patted his head, "Where's your dad?"

"He's in the shower."

Ricci looked around, "Where's your brother?"

"He's still asleep."

There was another knock at the door. This time, Ricci answered. A small man dressed entirely in black flashed a slight grin. Ricci offered his hand, "Good morning Scip."

"Hello Captain." Scipio took a few steps and scanned the room, "So if it isn't Mo, Larry, and Curly."

Rigoni walked over with his hand extended, "Morning boss."

De May opened the door and peaked into the hall.

Scipio noticed, "Looking for the breakfast wagon, big guy?"

"De May took a step out into the corridor and took a few deep breaths, "Mmmm, something smells good. If the food doesn't come soon, I'm gonna start knocking on doors."

Pescalitis pulled a banana from the complimentary fruit basket and tossed it, "There, that should hold you. Nothing like feeding a banana to a—"

"Very hungry man," De May cut him off. "Can I help it if I have a fast metabolism?"

Ricci and Scipio raised their eyebrows.

Rigoni added, "My wife is on a new diet plan. She was telling Karl all about how metabolism affects dieting."

Pescalitis chimed in, "Yeah, now every other sentence of his has the word 'metabolism' in it."

De May pushed the last of the banana into his mouth and shrugged his shoulders. He flung the peel into a pail near a cherry desk, situated in a corner of the suite outside the master bedroom. The corner was fashioned as a makeshift office, complete with dark cherry walls and a ceramic floor.

Pescalitis turned on the 50" plasma screen TV and took a seat on one of two opposing sofas. De May plopped himself down on the other one.

Reporter Kelly Wright of the Washington, D.C. Fox News bureau appeared on the screen. A picture of an Oriental woman appeared in the background. Pescalitis turned up the volume, *"… was the South Korean President's first visit to the United States since being elected with 51.6% of the South Korean vote, back in December.*

"President Park's visit came on the heels of increasing rhetoric and threats by North Korean leader Kim Jong Un and other North Korean statesmen following the joint U.S. and South Korean military exercises that begun last month."

Pescalitis shook his head, "Someone should put a bullet in Kim Jr.'s forehead," alluding to Kim Jong Un, the son of the former—and equally maniacal—Supreme Leader of North Korea, Kim Jong-il.

Rigoni leaned over the back of the sofa, "Better make sure someone takes his finger off the button first, just in case he spasms and launches a nuke."

"There's talk they have ICBMs and they're targeting five American cities – L.A., New York, D.C.—"

Scipio approached, "Nah, their longest range missiles are *Musudans*, with only a range of 1,800 miles. Not enough to hit us."

"But enough to strike South Korea and Japan," added Ricci.

"I wonder what the President told the new Madam President of South Korea," said Rigoni. "She sure has a lot on her plate."

"It's like having a complete maniac running Mexico … and with them armed with nukes pointing at us," said Pescalitis.

De May was the first to jump at the sound of knocking. He opened the door and offered a dramatic gesture of welcome to the convoy of waiters pushing room service carts, "You can set it up there, next to the dining room table."

* * * * *

Cris De Niro stepped out of the bathroom still brushing his teeth. He was wearing navy chinos, a Brooks Brothers *BrooksCool* triple check sport shirt, and Peal & Co. Cavalry Chukka ankle boots.

He walked over to the bed, took hold of his son's leg and shook it gently. Richard didn't stir, so he grabbed his ankle and tugged it. The soon-to-be 14 year-old responded with a grunt and a moan, with his head still hidden under a pillow.

"Up and at 'em, son."

Richard didn't move.

"Boy oh boy, I thought the aroma of breakfast would have your mouth watering."

"I'm not hungry," his son mumbled with annoyance.

"Well, you better get up and get some food before Karl eats it—"

"I said I'm NOT HUNGRY!"

"Hey … easy …." De Niro paused, "It's no big deal. Do you want me to save something—?"

Richard pulled the pillow from his head, "How many times do I have to tell you, I'm not hungry?!"

De Niro stared back at the agitated teenager, "What's the matter with you?"

"Nothing …."

"You were up late last night, why don't you—"

"I said I'm not hungry!"

De Niro bit his tongue before replying, "I was going to say, why don't you go back to sleep for awhile. I have to sit in on this meeting. It should take about two hours – more than enough time for you to get some more sleep, shower and get dressed. As soon as the meeting breaks we can leave for—"

"I don't want to go!"

"… The Smithsonian. Since when don't you want to go to the Smithsonian?"

"Since forever, I never wanted to go to there."

De Niro's stomach tightened. Over the course of the last year, he detected a change in Richard. His wife, Lisa flashed into his mind.

Our little boy is becoming a young man, my love, and I'm scared to death! I need you … he needs you.

He smiled and tried to lighten his tone, "How could you know you never wanted to go there, if you've never been there?"

"Because it's boring and for babies and I don't want to go!"

"You think the Smithsonian Institution is boring … and you haven't even been there? Richard, what's the matter?"

Richard buried his head under the pillow, "Nothing! I just don't want to go, and I'm not hungry. I just want to be left alone."

De Niro stood there trying to think of what to say. It was times like this his heart ached for Lisa.

Over 11 years passed since his wife perished in the North Tower of the World Trade Center, on that beautiful September morning, taking their unborn son to the grave with her.

While others seemed to get on with their lives, remarrying and coping with their loss, De Niro couldn't. Time healed wounds for others, but for him it was the measurement of his loneliness. Without the love his life, he felt a piece of himself missing. Even their sons, Richard and Louis, didn't fill the void created by her death.

We were supposed to grow old together. We were supposed to live on after the boys grew up and moved on with their lives … and what about now? Richard is going through puberty and I have no idea what to do or say. I can feel … he needs his mother.

De Niro felt tears welling in his eyes.

I miss my wife … and my little boy.

Damn those terrorists! Damn myself for not getting there sooner to rescue her!

De Niro tried to prevent his voice from cracking, "We don't have to go to the Smithsonian, pal. Another place your mom used to love is—"

"And another thing, I don't care what my mother liked, I'm NOT HER, okay?! You're always trying to get me to like what she liked … always telling me, 'mama liked this, and your mama liked that. Well, I never knew her, okay, so stop telling me what she liked!"

His son's words struck his chest like a sledgehammer.

"Now leave me alone!"

De Niro wiped a tear away, when he noticed someone was standing behind him in the doorway.

"I just wanted to tell you that breakfast is here," said Scipio.

They locked eyes for a moment.

De Niro blinked the rest of his tears away. He patted Scipio on the shoulder as he passed, "Thanks."

Scipio lingered.

Richard waited until he was sure his dad had gone to lift his head. He was startled to see the small man in black standing right next to the bed peering down at him.

"Scipio ... what are—?"

"You know," Scipio cut him off, "I don't like kids. Personally, I was never a kid. Even when I was young I didn't like kids. I mean, in my book most kids were crybabies or spoiled brats."

Richard sat up and wiped the sleep from his eyes, "What are you talking about?"

"I'm talking about spoiled brats. And you know what spoiled brats grow up to be ... pricks."

Richard's eyebrows lifted.

"And it may not be Biblical, and your dad may not agree, but to me, once a prick always a prick."

"Scipio, are you saying that I'm—"

"A prick ... no, you're still just a spoiled brat, not mature enough yet to be a full-fledged prick."

The boy's face flushed with anger, "I'm not spoiled!"

Scipio grinned, "Not spoiled, huh?" He changed to a mocking tone, "'*I'm not hungry ... how many times do I have to tell you! I don't want to go to the Smithsonian Institution ... it's boring! I never knew my mother!'* Give me a break!*"

Richard sat on the edge of the bed, "You were listening? You had no right-"

Scipio went on, "Listen to you. You sound like Veruca Salt from *Willie Wonka and the Chocolate Factory*."

"Who ...?"

"The spoiled rich girl, and you know what, even she was brighter than you. Richard, my boy, anyone that calls the Smithsonian Institution boring is an idiot. And the fact that you've never even been there makes you an ignorant idiot."

Richard's eyes reddened.

Scipio didn't let up, "Yeah, I know, you lost your mom in the Twin Towers on 9/11, but come on … you just admitted that you don't even know the woman. I didn't either, by the way, though I've heard a lot about her."

Scipio hunched down to look the boy in his eyes, "From what I can tell she was one hell of a person, and from what your dad told me, she was the best - the best mom in the world to you and your brother, and the best wife in the world to him.

"The thing is … you didn't know her, so how can you miss her?"

"I miss her! I miss her a lot!"

"You do, huh … really? I thought you told your dad you didn't even know her?"

"I knew her," tears rolled down Richard's cheek. "I knew her, okay! I remember when she used to play with me. I remember her laugh and her smile. I remember she used to dance with me …." His voice trailed off.

Scipio put his hands on the boy's shoulders. Richard hugged him, weeping like a little boy.

Scipio held him tightly until he felt his emotions subside. Then he broke the embrace.

"You know Richard, you only knew your mom a few years and those years you were just a tot … and see how much it still hurts?

"Think how much more it hurts your dad. That was his soulmate. You don't know what that word means yet. Hopefully someday you will. I can't explain it fully, but let's just say it's like having a best friend times a billion."

Richard wiped tears away with the palm of his hand.

"I heard you have a new friend."

Richard squinted, "How do you know about her?"

Scipio chuckled, "It's my business to know."

Richard let his body collapse back down to the bed, "Yeah, well she probably won't be my friend anymore. I haven't been able to contact her since we flew here. I can't find my cell phone and I didn't take my tablet."

Scipio stood up and started for the door. He turned before walking out, "You miss her don't you?"

"Well, I haven't actually met her. We just talk a lot by phone while we play games online … but yeah, I miss her."

"Then can you imagine how much your dad misses your mom? He loved your mom and he can never talk to her again."

Richard wiped another tear from his eye and nodded.

"Maybe … just maybe you should cut your dad a break, okay?"

Richard nodded, "Okay."

Scipio winked and walked out then popped his head back in, "And oh, are you sure you looked everywhere for your phone?"

"Yes, I'm sure, what do you think—"

"Absolutely positive you looked everywhere?"

Richard furrowed his brows, "Scipio, I'm sure!"

"Even under your pillow?"

"Under my pillow …? I slept with my head—"

He stopped in his tracks, lifted his head, and tossed the pillow aside. Lying underneath was his Big-Brutha™ Droid Razr M phone.

"No way …!" Richard turned, but the small man in black was gone.

Scipio walked behind Louis who was busy eating his breakfast and whispered in his ear, "I returned Richard's phone."

Louis whispered back, "Thank you. You saved my life."

De Niro approached. They spoke in a low tone so the others wouldn't hear, "How is he?"

"He's okay. He's just going through his teen metamorphosis."

"He said he's not his mother, but you know something, he's more like his mother than he knows. She would have said the same thing to me. I didn't realize I was doing that to him."

"Doing what?"

"You heard him. I keep trying to make him do things that his mother and I enjoyed."

Scipio shook his head then let a smile appear, "Cris, you haven't done anything but be the best dad to both your boys.

"What Richard is going through is all about him, not you. One of you has to realize that. Since you're the dad, that means you have to."

De Niro stared into his eyes a moment before cracking a smile, "I wish she was here. You'd like her a lot."

"I like her a lot already. Now sit down and have some breakfast so we can get this meeting done and you and the boys can enjoy the Smithsonian."

De Niro's eyes sparkled.

There was another knock at the door. Rigoni answered. Two large Korean men wearing black suits with white buttoned shirts and black ties stood with their hands folded in front of them. Rigoni noticed holstered pistols protruding slightly from just under their armpits.

Before he could utter a word, the two men parted to allow a much shorter man, also dressed in a black suit, but wearing a black buttoned shirt with no tie, to approach him. Though he presented a quiet demeanor, Rigoni detected an intensity radiating from him.

He reminds me of … the Asian Scipio, right down to his size and style of dress.

The small man revealed no emotion in his face. Like the two larger men, he kept his hands folded in front of him, "Good morning, is Mr. De Niro available?" His voice was soft but forceful, with a definite Asian accent.

"Who should I say is—?"

From behind the man an elegantly-dressed Korean woman, looking a bit younger than her 61 years, walked up beside him. The man bowed his head and remained silent.

After a moment of hesitation, Rigoni snapped to attention, a reflex from his Marine Corps days, "Please come in, Madam President."

CHAPTER 2

PRESIDENTIAL SUITE – EAST WING
THE FOSTER LAFAYETTE
WASHINGTON, D.C.
6:30 AM (LOCAL), FRIDAY, MAY 10, 2013

Everyone in the room including young Louis rose from their seats as President Park Geun-hye entered. She was immediately halted by the small man. He spoke to her briefly in Korean before addressing everyone.

"Gentlemen, I am Colonel Cho Jung-woo, of the Presidential Security Service of the Republic of Korea. I'm in charge of her Excellency President Park's security detail. If you don't mind, I would like to have my men perform a room sweep, and I would ask your permission to allow them to search each of you for weapons.

"Search us for weapons … do we get to search you too?" sniped Pescalitis.

"Stand down, Chief," ordered Mugsy Ricci, none too kindly. Ricci and De Niro walked over. De Niro tipped his head before offering his hand.

President Park took it in hers and shook it firmly, "Mr. De Niro, I apologize for barging in on you like this."

"Not at all, your Excellency and please, call me Cris."

"Thank you Cris. Would it be okay if we appease my chief of security? Colonel Cho is already upset with me for this impromptu visit. I'm afraid he will never forgive me if he is not allowed to do his duty."

"That's quite alright. Gentlemen, if you would, please accommodate Colonel Cho." De Niro nodded to the Colonel, who returned the nod before addressing the room again, "If everyone would please remain standing, my men will make this inconvenience as brief as possible."

The Colonel gestured to his men and they immediately began frisking everyone. Colonel Cho walked over to young Louis and winked to De Niro before turning to the boy again, "Please place your hands on your head."

Louis couldn't suppress a smile as he complied. Colonel Cho mock patted him on his waist, "What is your name?"

"Louis."

"Well Louis, do you have any weapons concealed?"

"No sir."

"That is a good boy," the Colonel winked again at De Niro before walking over to the bedroom. He stopped before entering.

De Niro followed him over, "My oldest son is in there, Colonel. Let me call him out."

"No need Dad," Richard walked out wearing only the pair of jeans he slept in.

Colonel Cho pointed to the room with impatience, which resulted in one of his large men almost running inside. After a minute the man came out and nodded once.

Colonel Cho walked over to De Niro, "Again, my apologies for this inconvenience. If you would, please ask your men to remain in the dining area while Her Excellency speaks with you in private, here in the living room."

Mugsy heard the request and corralled everyone around the dining room table while Colonel Cho escorted President Park over to one of the sofas. De Niro took a seat beside her.

Colonel Cho bowed his head, "The room is secure, Your Excellency."

"Thank you Colonel, Mr. De Niro … Cris, the reason I'm here is …," she glanced at Cho, "delicate and time-sensitive, perhaps even imperative."

"May I offer you a cup of coffee, Ms. President?"

President Park flashed a quick smile, "Thank you, I would."

De Niro turned, "Mugsy, bring over a pot of coffee and cups and join us please."

He turned back, "If you don't mind, I think the President of The Watchman Agency should sit in."

Mugsy walked over carrying a coffee service. Colonel Cho stepped in front of him.

"It is okay, Colonel. I'm sure Mr. De Niro isn't trying to poison me."

Colonel Cho didn't move. He started to protest in Korean.

"Colonel, we are guests here. It is rude not to speak English. I said it is okay. Now you can wait in the next room, or join us if you behave yourself."

Colonel Cho stared back at her for a moment with fire in his eyes before taking the tray from Mugsy, "Once again, I apologize Captain. Please, allow me."

The Colonel set the tray down and began pouring coffee. De Niro and Mugsy both noticed him taste his before handing the President her cup. He then took a position standing with his back to the bedroom.

President Park took a long sip before setting her cup down, "I tease Colonel Cho, but he really is the best at what he does."

The Colonel nodded his head slightly in appreciation.

"He also has reason to be so cautious with me. I only became President at the end of February and there have already been innumerous threats against my life. You gentlemen might also be aware of what happened to my father?"

"Your father was Park Chung-hee, third President of South Korea," replied De Niro, more for the benefit of Ricci. "He was considered by many as one of the most important and influential leaders in Korean history. He was assassinated in 1979."

"You are knowledgeable of my country's history. So you see, my concerns are justified," Colonel Cho interjected.

"Park Chung-hee was assassinated by Kim Jae-gyu, the chief of his own security services," Scipio's voice came from behind the Colonel.

Startled, in one motion and with blinding speed Colonel Cho spun around and placed the barrel of his pistol against Scipio's temple.

Scipio smiled as he continued, "That would be the same position you hold, Colonel."

Mugsy began to rise but De Niro held his arm, "Your Excellency, Colonel … allow me to introduce you to the Vice President of Operations of The Watchman Agency, Scipio."

"Apparently the room was not quite as secure as you thought, Colonel," replied President Park with a hint of sarcasm. "Put your gun away."

Colonel Cho held his pistol against Scipio's head for several seconds before withdrawing and returning it to its concealed holster, almost as fast as it was drawn, "Apparently not, Your Excellency." He shot a fierce glare at the large bodyguard who made the room search.

"Please … Scipio, your name is?"

Scipio winked at the Colonel before passing him, "Yes, Your Excellency, like the Roman general who was my namesake."

"Best known for defeating Hannibal at the final battle of the Second Punic War at Zama," replied Colonel Cho. "A feat that earned him the agnomen 'Africanus', and the nickname "the Roman Hannibal", as well as recognition as one of the finest commanders in military history."

"Among other expertise, Colonel Cho is also a historian," added President Park.

"And what other expertise do you possess, Colonel?" asked Scipio.

"The Colonel is a martial arts expert, weapons expert, and counter-terrorism expert, as well as security expert," President Park answered for him.

Scipio stepped up to the Colonel. Both men were of identical stature, "I would be honored to see the Colonel's martial arts prowess. If it's on par with his security ability, I'm sure it'll be something to see."

Colonel Cho matched Scipio's grin, "I would be honored to give you a demonstration some time."

"If you gentlemen are finished introducing yourselves," De Niro interrupted, "perhaps we can allow Her Excellency to continue."

The men remained toe to toe until Colonel Cho lifted an eyebrow and extended his arm, "Have a seat."

De Niro shook his head, "Please, continue Ms. President."

"Three days ago I met with your President Obama. Among other things, I told him of a situation that has arisen … perhaps an opportunity."

"Or a trap, with respect, Your Excellency," added Colonel Cho.

She looked at him and nodded, "Yes … or a trap. There is no way to be sure except to …." President Park looked down at her lap.

"Except to what, Excellency?" asked De Niro.

President Park exhaled audibly, "Except to infiltrate into North Korea to investigate. Let me explain.

"One month ago, a North Korean soldier defected to South Korea carrying a most unusual—"

"And suspicious," Colonel Cho cut in.

President Park nodded impatiently, "And suspicious message, signed by a sojang—"

"Excuse me, a what?"

"A North Korean general," replied Scipio.

"A North Korean major general, to be precise," Colonel Cho corrected.

De Niro nodded, "Please continue Excellency."

"The sojang's name is Kim Gil-su. He was adjutant to one of North Korea's most infamous generals, recently promoted to Taejang rank." The President looked to Colonel Cho for clarification.

"Taejang is equivalent to your General of the Army or Fleet Admiral."

"His name is Kang Kum-Sok." She looked to Colonel Cho to continue.

"The soldier—who has been traced back to a unit stationed hundreds of miles away from Kim and Kang— launched his plan near the South Korean-financed industrial complex, in the North Korean border town of Kaesong.

"At noon, on the day in question, and in broad daylight, the soldier apparently shot a platoon and company commander before crossing the western side of the Demilitarized Zone (DMZ)."

"You're saying this soldier just shot these commanders then walked across to South Korea?" Scipio asked with skepticism.

"That is exactly what I am saying," replied Cho. "After shooting them, the soldier used a bullhorn to warn the South Korean border guards of his intention to defect and walk across the DMZ.

"His method of defecting was not unique. This past October, another North Korean soldier did precisely the same thing, right down to using the bullhorn.

"The fact that there was nothing remarkable about this soldier's record or any known connection between him and General Kim would have made this whole thing highly suspect. But, it is very unlikely a soldier of his lowly rank would have even known about the previous soldier's defection, let alone the exact details. Yet, he copied it precisely – location, choice of targets, time of day … even the use of the bullhorn. Only a general of Kim's rank or higher could have known those particulars."

President Park took over, "Our interrogation experts have been grilling the soldier for the past month, as well as using every means at our disposal to verify the authenticity of the handwritten message he was carrying. Their conclusion is that—despite the extraordinary nature of his defection—the soldier's defection is real, the message from General Kim is real, and so are his allegations."

De Niro tilted his head, "Allegations?"

Once again, President Park looked at Colonel Cho. De Niro wasn't sure whether she did so for support or because the two contended over whatever it was she was about to say.

"The soldier maintains that he defected to save his country. He stated that he never met General Kim or General Kang. He also stated that he was given the written message—which was sealed in an unopened envelope—from the leader of an underground group … one that is plotting the overthrow of Kim Jong Un and his regime."

"Save … how?"

The President kept her eyes locked on Colonel Cho, "The soldier was told that the contents of the message must be delivered to a high-ranking South Korean official to stave off a terrible war that will annihilate the North Korean people. Our experts are sure he believes what he was told about the message. They also believe that the soldier knows nothing of what the message says or who signed it."

"And what does this message say?" asked De Niro.

"As I've said, the message is handwritten and, as far as our experts can tell, written and signed by General Kim himself. In it, the General accuses his former superior, General Kang of … preparing to launch Musudan missiles at our second largest city of Busan, on the southeast coast."

"Aren't those the missiles that North Korea just withdrew from the coast?"

"Yes. Their timing for withdrawing them was uncanny, just one day before I met with President Obama."

"Then the threat no longer exists?"

"That is what your President and his staff believe."

"But not what you believe?"

"I do not know what to believe, Cris, but my feeling is this - General Kim would have known about the pending withdrawal of the Musudan missiles from the coast even when he wrote the message. And he would not have risked so much sending it, if he did not think that the threat still existed after the missiles were withdrawn."

"Those missiles were on mobile launchers," added Mugsy. "It's possible that Kang could have moved them to another location and may still be able to fire them."

"Does it mention whether the missiles carry nuclear warheads?" asked Scipio.

"It does not," replied President Park.

"Busan … why there?" asked De Niro.

President Park nodded again to Colonel Cho.

"Our experts believe it is because the Musudan has an effective minimum range of around 650 kilometers, about 400 miles. Even if Kang launches from their northern-most nuclear test sites, Busan is the only major target far enough away to fall within the missile's minimum range. They also need a major target to keep within the missile's CEP ... its circular error probability of about 1.5 kilometers. That means the Musudan has about a 50% probability of hitting its target within 1.5 kilometers."

"Why go to all that trouble to launch the mid-range Musudans when he could much more easily launch his short-range arsenal?" asked Scipio.

"We believe the reason to be keeping the nuclear threat in play," replied President Park. "The Musudan is the missile that the world believes the North intends to equip with a nuclear warhead, but your point is valid."

"Nuclear ...," replied Ricci, "Excellency, with respect, our intelligence has all but verified that North Korea does *not* pose a credible nuclear threat, at least not one of nuclear *missile* capabilities."

"So have ours, but that does not rule out the possibility that General Kang could launch conventional warheads at Busan."

"The BM25 Musudan is capable of delivering a single warhead with the potential payload of just over one ton of high explosive," added Colonel Cho. "On its own, one Musudan missile with a conventional warhead could level a structure and perhaps kill hundreds. General Kim asserts that General Kang has the ability to launch two Musudan missiles, as well as several other short-range missiles, all with the range to hit Busan. The short range missiles could also hit any point in between."

President Park continued, "By themselves the missiles would do horrendous, but most likely, not catastrophic damage. However, our response and that of the United States would very possibly be to launch a full-range attack against the North. General Kim states in the message that - that is exactly what General Kang wants ... to provoke us and the United States into military action. Even one missile launched at a strategic target could provoke a major conflict."

"But why ...?" De Niro touched his fingertips together in

thought, "Common belief is that Kim Jong Un and his cronies know the gig is up for them if a confrontation erupts. They must know they can't achieve victory against the south. So what could be gained—?"

"Excuse me, Mr. De Niro," Colonel Cho interrupted, "but also according to General Kim in the message, the Supreme Leader of North Korea is unaware of General Kang's plans. Our intelligence agency has at least confirmed that, for the last year, there has been a power struggle between Kim Jong Un and his followers, and a number of high-ranking generals, of which, General Kang is believed to be the leader."

"Lord, help us all if a North Korean General has gone rogue," Ricci thought out loud.

De Niro considered the implication, "If that's true, what does Kang and his cohorts gain from provoking a war between North and South Korea … a war that the North cannot possibly win?"

"Here is where General Kim's claims transform from the unbelievable to the unfathomable, replied President Park. "He claims that General Kang is plotting with an unknown, high-ranking South Korean official to bring about a North Korean defeat, and following … a military coup of my government."

Scipio thought out loud, "That would create—"

"A unified Korea under a new leader, and one that would have the support of both militaries," Colonel Cho finished his thought.

There was silence.

De Niro reached for the pot of coffee, nodding to the President first and then to the men. All of them shook their heads before he poured a cup.

"Your meeting, Excellency, with President Obama … can you tell us how it went?"

"Yes, with the President was Secretary of State Kerry, the Director of National Intelligence, the Chairman of the Joint Chiefs of Staff, the Director of the CIA, the Defense Secretary, and the Director of the Defense Intelligence Agency.

"After listening to what I just told you, your President conferred with his staff. I was disappointed when he told me that, for now, your country cannot … or will not take part in any investigation that would involve sending human resources into North Korea.

"Apparently, the President and his advisors believe the plot to be preposterous and the message to be misdirection intended to provoke us and your country into initiating some type of military action. He went as far as to ask for my pledge not to take any action that could lead to an escalation in this conflict."

"President Obama is most concerned with the world's view of our nation's actions," offered Scipio.

"Is not South Korea part of that world view?" replied Cho.

De Niro sipped his coffee and paused, "Under the circumstances as you explained them, Ms. President, I think you can understand why President Obama can't pledge more support at this time, but I'm sure our government is looking into—"

"There is no way anyone can look into this situation without entering North Korea." President Park cut De Niro off tensely.

The room fell silent again for over a minute.

"I apologize, Mr. De Niro."

"Please Excellency … Cris, there is no reason to apologize."

Some of the tension appeared to vent from President Park. She nodded quickly smiling softly.

"You are too kind … Cris. I'm afraid the intensity of this state of affairs and the stonewalling from your government is beginning to affect me. While some people react to threats with fear, I react with anger. In my new position, I cannot afford to react with anger."

"Especially since it appears that's exactly how your enemy wants you to react," replied Scipio.

Colonel Cho nodded to Scipio.

"I will not give them that satisfaction," replied President Park. "But, I will also not stand down while some North Korean madman attacks a city of 3.4 million citizens. And I don't like feeling like a puppet having my strings pulled by anyone from the North … or from the West."

De Niro remained quiet. President Park examined him for a long moment, "I appreciate that you did not ask if we have a plan."

"I wouldn't want to place you in the uncomfortable position of having to tell me to mind my own business."

President Park smiled, "Especially after barging in on you like this, and after I discovered that you gave up the Royal Suite to accommodate me. The hotel manager informed Colonel Cho, who told me just before we barged in. I hope I haven't inconvenienced you and your sons."

"Not at all, Excellency. As you can see, this suite is more than adequate."

"But it only has one bed," remarked Richard, from just behind the couch.

"And Daddy snores," added Louis who appeared next to him.

De Niro looked over his shoulder and sighed, "It is I who should apologize, Excellency, for the behavior of my children …," he turned, "who know it is rude to eavesdrop!"

President Park failed to suppress a giggle, "That is quite all right. What they might have overheard so far is nothing more than, in the words of your President, 'unsubstantiated intelligence from a precarious source.' Besides, I am not concerned with your children, or the rest of the men in the room, for that matter. I am concerned only with the leadership of North Korea."

"Nevertheless," Mugsy Ricci addressed the boys, "whatever may have been overheard in this room is strictly confidential. Have I made myself clear?"

The replies were in unison, "Yes, Uncle Mugsy."

"In any case," replied De Niro, picking up where they left off, "I also didn't ask because I assume you're already devising some plan of action … one in which you would like to involve my firm, or you wouldn't be here."

President Park glanced again at Colonel Cho. The Colonel remained stoic, but De Niro and Scipio could read his eyes.

He doesn't want us involved.

"That is precisely why I'm here. General Kim stated that General Kang plans to launch the missiles sometime in the next 30 days. After that, the missiles will be removed from the mobile launchers and Kang will lose the ability to fire them, which is why something must be done now. Your president and his staff do not fully appreciate the urgency of the matter."

"If General Kang's missiles were pointed at Washington D.C. or New York, I believe they would appreciate the urgency," Colonel Cho added.

President Park shot a fierce glare at the Colonel. Colonel Cho lowered his head.

De Niro broke the tension, "Perhaps you could tell us your plan."

President Park looked over De Niro's shoulder, which prompted him to glance at his brother-in-law, which signaled Mugsy Ricci to jump to his feet and head into the dining room.

"Riggy, why don't you take everyone downstairs to the lobby and let the boys buy something from the souvenir store."

Richard and Louis jumped out of their seats and raced into the bedroom, to the delight of the President and the embarrassment of De Niro. They emerged less than a minute later with Richard wearing a wrinkled t-shirt, socks and sneakers, and still wearing the jeans he slept in.

De Niro called to them before they reached the door, "One souvenir each, understood?"

Neither boy turned around, but both mumbled, "Understood."

When they all left the room, the large Korean bodyguards shut and locked the door, with one remaining outside the suite and one inside.

"They are good boys," remarked President Park. "I know of the loss of your wife and how difficult it must be for you to raise them on your own."

De Niro paused, "They take after their mother I'm pleased to say." Then he leaned in, "Tell us Excellency how may we be of service to you and South Korea?"

President Park nodded, "As I mentioned, your president asked for my word not to take provocative action. It is imperative for South Korea to keep good relations with the United States, especially at this critical time, so I had to commit.

"However, since I am the leader of my country, one can interpret President Obama's request to mean for 'South Korea' not to take any provocative action. That was my interpretation, and so my pledge extends only to South Korea not taking action.

"But wouldn't your solicitation of my firm's services also be construed as actions taken?" asked De Niro.

"You misunderstand the purpose of this visit," replied President Park. "We are not here to solicit you; we are here to implore you to take your own actions."

"Excellency, The Watchman Agency is a counter-terrorism firm. Our mandate is to protect American citizens."

"Cris, there are over 28,000 American troops presently stationed in South Korea. And although there is no longer a US military base in Busan, there are four Department of Defense facilities based there, not to mention that many of your Navy servicemen and their families live there.

"If General Kang launches missiles at Busan, there is a strong possibility that at least some of those servicemen and their families will be harmed or killed. Yet, the loss of American lives from the initial attack will pale compared to the amount of casualties from the inevitable ensuing confrontation.

"Are not the Americans in South Korea citizens worth protecting?"

De Niro leaned back in his chair with his fingertips touching. He thought in silence during which no one spoke.

"If I did assign my people, how much support could we expect from your government, given the pledge you made to President Obama?"

Yet again, President Park glanced at Colonel Cho before replying.

She obviously respects him. It's a wise leader who can check her ego and look for council from subordinates, especially ones with differing opinions.

"Very little, I'm afraid, and none directly."

"Yet, that is not to say that certain patriotic South Koreans will not offer their support on their own," added Colonel Cho, "present company included."

De Niro, Ricci, and Scipio understood.

De Niro leaned in, "If I may ask an obvious question, Ms. President?"

President Park nodded.

"Since this General Kang is allegedly working without the knowledge of his leader, can't you just bring it to Kim Jong-Un's attention somehow? Perhaps just raising suspicion about Kang would be enough for Kim to have him investigated."

"I wish it would be that easy, Cris, but I am afraid Kim Jong-Un would never listen to reason. Even if we had conclusive proof of General Kang's treachery, which we do not, Kim would never accept it coming from us. We would have to divulge that it was General Kim who wrote the letter, and then they would interrogate and execute him and his family."

De Niro nodded understanding, "What about having the Chinese try to convince him? I'm sure they wouldn't want a war on their border, and I would think if Kim would listen to anyone it would be the Chinese."

"Don't be too sure that the Chinese wouldn't want a war, Mr. De Niro," replied Colonel Cho. He looked at President Park for permission to continue. She nodded slightly.

"The truth is that North Korea is the vicious dog China raised that has become like a rabid animal. It no longer acts like China's obedient pet. The Chinese tolerate their rabid dog as long as he snarls and barks facing south.

"However, we believe if China ever discovered a North Korean general was planning a coup that could unite all of Korea, they might endorse it. Perhaps, even help Kang carry it out with the intention of making the unified Korea, under Kang, their new obedient dog."

"Now you see why we are here, Cris?" added President Park.

"Exactly what would be our objectives, Ms. President," asked Ricci.

"I will defer the answer to that hypothetical question to Colonel Cho, who has more expertise in the area of tactics."

President Park stood, prompting all the men to stand, "You must excuse me, I am meeting with the First Lady in less than 30 minutes and I do not want to keep her waiting. She is hosting breakfast at a local school to introduce me to her program against childhood obesity.

"If the people of North Korea ever heard of such a thing – that

America's children suffer from eating too much food, while their children starve – I believe they would overthrow Kim Jong Un and his evil regime in an instant. That is why the people are kept in ignorance.

"In any case, I leave you in Colonel Cho's capable hands. Good day, gentlemen. Cris, would you mind walking me to the elevator?"

"It would be an honor, Excellency."

The large bodyguard standing at the door hastily opened it as President Park approached. De Niro and she walked down the corridor in silence until they reached the banks of elevators. One was already being held for her.

President Park spoke softly, "Cris, I must ask that whatever you decide from this point forward, I cannot know of any of your actions. What is the term … plausible deniability?"

"Understood, Excellency, but you don't even want to know my decision?"

President Park stepped onto the elevator and smiled, "It is spoken that you are a man of faith. I trust that you will do what is right."

CHAPTER 3

PRESIDENTIAL SUITE – EAST WING
THE FOSTER LAFAYETTE
WASHINGTON, D.C.
8:00 AM (LOCAL), FRIDAY, MAY 10, 2013

De Niro re-entered the suite and called Mugsy Ricci, Scipio, and Colonel Cho over to the dining room table. By orders of Ricci, Scipio fetched a box from a closet that contained tablet computers loaded with The Watchman Agency's Big-Brutha™ data management and communications system.

Big-Brutha was the creation of the firm's über-nerd Chief Information Officer (CIO) John "Johnny-F" Francis. Francis—a childhood friend of De Niro's—went on to become the multi-millionaire founder of several high-tech companies in Silicon Valley, predominately in gaming, and later, in the homeland security industries.

Their friendship and the tragedy of 9/11 prompted Francis to offer his expertise to De Niro's burgeoning counter-terrorism firm. De Niro graciously accepted, and immediately appointed the brilliant and often eccentric Francis, CIO, backing him with a virtually limitless budget, all flowing from De Niro's personal finances.

Big-Brutha™ became the first of Francis's achievements for the firm. He followed with the design and construction of *The Coyote's Den*, the underground headquarters for The Watchman Agency's paramilitary group, ARCHANGEL, located on De Niro's sprawling ranch, *Estancia De Niro*. He also designed all of the electronics aboard De Niro's *Warbird*, a converted 747-8F, the freighter version of the famous Boeing 747, transformed into—as everyone referred to it— "a flying NSA."

The men took seats at the table. Colonel Cho looked down at the tablet in front of him.

"It's loaded with our firm's data management system, Colonel," Ricci demonstrated. "The DMS is also loaded on the cell phones of every member of the firm. Everyone is given tiered security access, allowing them to update, add, modify and delete information, keeping us all on the same page and current.

"Impressive."

"If we decide to move forward, you'll be assigned one of our phones for the duration of the mission."

Ricci held his hand up to call the meeting to order, "For purposes of this discussion and possible operation, everyone present will be given operational clearance to November-Kilo 051013."

He turned again to Cho, "That's where you'll find all data regarding the mission in Big-Brutha™. Also, in the 'Communications' app, you'll be able to contact anyone with operational clearance on a secure channel."

Cho nodded his understanding.

De Niro started, "I asked about what our objectives would be, Colonel."

All eyes turned to Cho, "First I will state an overview, so that everyone is clear on what needs to be accomplished. Afterwards, you may ask questions and I can go into more detail."

Cho looked around the table until he saw each man acknowledge before continuing.

"The ultimate goal is to ascertain if General Kang ... or General

Kim is indeed planning to launch missiles at Busan. I want to make it plain from the onset that I believe there is as much a chance that General Kim is the culprit as General Kang."

De Niro and Mugsy raised their brows with surprise while Scipio raised his in doubt.

Cho continued, "The objectives are, in order: 1-to enter North Korea; 2-to make contact with the leader of the anti-Kim Jon Un cell; 3-to make contact with General Kim; and 4-to locate both General Kang and/or the Musudan missiles and render both or either harmless. Questions?"

Ricci folded his arms in front of him, "Before we get to your assertion about General Kim, let's start at number one, how exactly would we enter North Korea?"

"We must enter via China. We must fly—"

"Wait, why via China?" asked De Niro.

"We know the missiles are located in the far north. Movement within North Korea is difficult, especially in the southern part of the country near the border. We will have to cross somewhere along the northern stretch of the border between North Korea and China.

"We will utilize the North Korean brokers to smuggle us across the border and then guide us in country. Crossing in the north will leave us with a much shorter distance to the location of the missiles, which is also where General Kang and Kim will most likely be."

"Brokers …?"

"There are some entrepreneurial North Koreans that have escaped into China. Instead of leaving, they saw an opportunity to become rich smuggling goods into, and people out of North Korea. In our case, we will simply hire them to smuggle us in and out."

"And what if they don't want to smuggle us in and out?" asked Scipio. "If I were them, I wouldn't jeopardize my lucrative business, not to mention my life, smuggling Americans and a South Korean into the motherland."

"If we can't hire one, there are other ways we can persuade them to help us. For instance, the Chinese government doesn't actively pursue these brokers, preferring to accept bribes and turn a blind eye. But if someone anonymously threatened to tell the North Koreans about that set up, NK would demand that they be rounded up and sent home."

"I can imagine what would happen to the brokers then," replied Ricci.

"They would be shot and their families would be imprisoned," replied Cho, matter-of-factly.

Everyone remained silent.

"Moving on to number two," Scipio broke the silence, "what's the use of meeting up with the anti-Kim Jong-Un folks?"

Cho continued, "The dissidents already have an established underground. They pose no real threat to Kim Jong-Un or his regime, but they could be helpful to us in terms of safe lodging and access to resources once we are in country.

"According to the soldier, it was the leader of one of those groups that gave him the message, so we know they have some connection to General Kim. And General Kim also mentioned in his message that someone in the anti-Kim coalition has some sort of regular access to General Kang. We might be able to use that to get close to Kang."

"Did General Kim mention any exact locations in his note where we can find the dissidents, or General Kang or the missiles, for that matter?" replied Scipio.

Cho shook his head, "He provided the location on the coast where the Musudans had been positioned when the North Koreans were saber-rattling. Undoubtedly, that is where they and General Kang were located when he wrote the note … and presumably why he wrote it in the first place.

"But since then, we all know, in keeping with the North's pattern of threatening and later backing off that the missiles have been moved off the coast."

"So, you're saying we have no idea where the missiles or General Kang are now. Then where are we supposed to start?"

"After interrogating the soldier further, we were able to get him to tell us where he was given the note. It was at an abandoned warehouse on the outskirts of a small industrial town, just outside of Hyesan. Hyesan is a North Korean border city in northern

Ryanggang province. We had the soldier show us exactly where the warehouse is on a map, so we have the coordinates.

"The soldier's family lives in the town. He was visiting them when the head of the dissident cell made contact with him."

Scipio brought it up on a map that appeared on everyone's tablet, "You can move the map around with your finger, Colonel."

Cho nodded, "The cell of this dissident group uses the warehouse as its headquarters."

"That looks like a pretty remote place to have as a base," replied Mugsy.

"You are correct, Captain. The town and indeed, the entire county are located in a high, mountainous area. However, the county is dominated by the lumber industry, which gives them access to the Paekmu Line railroad, as well as a number of roads. So, it is not totally isolated.

"And there is something else," Cho moved the map with his finger. He zoomed in and marked what looked like a barren area. "Approximately 40 miles east of the town is the location of the Punggye-Ri Nuclear Test Site. You might remember that as the site of the last three North Korean underground nuclear tests."

"You couldn't tell from the map," said De Niro.

"A trained eye could," replied Cho, with a touch of smugness. "If you recall, General Kim stated in the note that the dissidents had a member that made regular contact with General Kang. Well, the road between the industrial town and the coastal city of Chongjin passes within 6 kilometers of Punggye-Ri. And there is also an underground rail line that leads directly from the town into the facility."

"So, you think General Kang is headquartered at Punggye-Ri," replied Mugsy. "What about the missiles?"

"I suspect if General Kang is intending to fire those missiles, he will keep them on the mobile launchers and he will want them as near to him as possible. Keeping them at the test site can be easily explained as necessary for testing."

"But Colonel, you said you believe General Kim—"

The Colonel raised his hand to cut Mugsy off, "Captain, General Kim is General Kang's adjutant, which means he would have no way of directly controlling the missiles except by manipulating General Kang's authority over them. If I am correct about him, he would come up with a way to keep the missiles mobile and near Kang. That would give him functional control over them until the time comes to fire them."

"Then what?" Asked De Niro.

"If you are asking if General Kim has the ability to fire those missiles himself … he does not. However, with his position, it is entirely possible that he could gain possession of the launch codes in a variety of ways.

"In any case, regardless of which general is the conspirator, I believe we will find General Kang at Punggye-Ri and I strongly believe the missiles are being kept mobile and concealed somewhere at that facility."

"If you feel so strongly that way, why don't we just head to where you marked the map?" asked Mugsy.

"Nuclear test sites, as you may know, are very large and mostly concealed deeply underground. I marked the location where my country believes Punggye-Ri exists, based on our detecting one access point and triangulating seismic readings after each blast. But that access point, which was a tunnel entrance, has since vanished.

"Even if we go to the exact coordinates of the ground zeroes for each test, we probably still wouldn't find an entrance into the facility, never mind the missiles themselves. And we simply don't have enough time to look.

"No. We need to be directed into the facility, hopefully by the dissident. Besides, we need the dissidents to tell us where we can find General Kim."

"But you said Kim is General Kang's adjutant. If Kang is headquartered at Punggye-Ri, wouldn't we find General Kim there too?"

"Not necessarily. As General Kang's second-in-command, among other duties, General Kim is Kang's liaison to Pyongyang. We know from our spies in the Capital that Kang hasn't shown his face there in a long time, while Kim is there at regular intervals. He has also been spotted at several other locations throughout North Korea, so the only way for us to find Kim will be through the dissidents."

"That is, if he intends to be anywhere near Kang and the missiles going forward," replied Mugsy. "If you're wrong about him Colonel, he may use his ability to travel to stay the heck away from both."

"I don't think so. If I'm correct then General Kim will have to remain as close to Kang and the missiles as possible, in order to get the launch codes and fire them. But if not, then I believe General Kang will make sure his adjutant is with him when the time comes, just to keep an eye on him."

There was a pause. Scipio shot a glance that only De Niro could see and perceptibly shook his head.

Mugsy finally spoke, "Your number three is making contact with General Kim, did he ask for contact to be made with him in his message?"

"He did not," replied Cho.

"Do you think it's wise then to—"

"I will be frank, Captain," Cho cut him off, "I do not believe General Kim's message, at least, not his reason for sending it, or his accusations about General Kang."

"But you said yourself that your experts thoroughly vetted—"

Cho cut Ricci off again, this time by holding up one finger, "Correction, Captain I said, 'to the best of our abilities.' We are reasonably certain that the message was written by General Kim, but even if it was, we cannot be certain that what he wrote is true."

"What purpose would it serve, Colonel, for Kim to send such a message, if the message is bogus?" asked Scipio.

"Bogus … ah yes, I know this word," said Cho. "My personal opinion is that General Kim might in fact be hatching a plot for *him* to take control of a conquered North Korea.

"Think of what would happen … what their madman leader would do if Americans and South Koreans were caught in North Korea and it was discovered that they were there to murder the highest ranking North Korean General."

"What exactly do you think would happen, Colonel," asked Scipio.

De Niro caught a hint of skepticism in Scipio's tone.

Cho grinned slightly at the challenge, "I think it is reasonable to believe that the madman Kim Jung-un would attack the South and perhaps other U.S. allies like Japan too. He would have to, you see. His own people, especially the military would demand it, and he would also stand to lose face with the world if he didn't attack.

"That attack would demand a counter-attack, and the counter-attack, a counter-attack. North and South Korea would soon be locked in an escalating conflict, neither of which could stop short of victory or defeat.

"Inevitably, North Korea as we know it would be destroyed and with it, the present regime. In its ashes, it is plausible that General Kim could rise as the new leader."

"What about General Kang?" Scipio pressed.

"As leader of the North Korean army, General Kang could be saddled with a war crimes tribunal," replied Cho with impatience.

De Niro watched as Scipio sat back in his chair. *I don't think he believes one word of what Cho is saying.*

Cho continued, "All that I have stated is plausible, but what is also plausible is – a subtler and more cunning scenario."

Cho looked from man to man, "If I am correct, General Kim could accomplish all this without taking control of the missiles. All he would have to do is lead us into a trap and then capture and hand us over to Kim Jong-Un."

Mugsy shook his head vigorously, "You lost me Colonel. You just explained how you think General Kim could take control of the missiles and launch them and now you're saying he doesn't even need to."

Cho looked unconcerned, "Obviously, Captain, General Kim would have to have contingency plans in case he doesn't capture us.

"Personally, I believe that we will only have to accomplish the first three of the objectives I laid out. Once we get to Kim, we will be able to prove that he is the one behind all this."

"How …?"

"Captain, while your country needlessly concerns itself with the humane treatment of persons of interest while being interrogated, my country does not. I assure you that I will be able to compel General Kim to confess relatively quickly."

Mugsy's tone became more stern, "I believe my country is more concerned with the efficacy of any confession coerced with torture than the actual use of it Colonel, but let's say you can make him confess. What then?"

Cho took a gold cigarette case out of his breast pocket. He looked at De Niro, "May I?"

De Niro nodded pushing an ashtray in front of him.

Cho took time to light his cigarette, taking a deep drag and exhaling before replying, "We kill him."

"Kill him?" Ricci leaned toward Cho. "Colonel, we better be damn sure we're killing the right North Korean General, or the other guy could still launch the missiles at Busan."

"We would have no choice except to kill him. We could not simply leave him in his position, and we would not be able to hand him over to anyone in North Korea, including the dissidents. Kim would be missed and searched for relentlessly. Nor would it be practical to attempt to smuggle him back into China with us. The Chinese turn their eyes from smugglers and brokers, but they would not do so from a North Korean general."

"And what if General Kim doesn't confess," asked Scipio. "What if he maintains his allegations against General Kang are true?"

Cho took another drag and exhaled. He stared at Scipio through the plume, "Then we continue to the fourth objective. We locate General Kang and/or the Musudan missiles and render both or either harmless."

The room went silent. Colonel Cho looked unconcerned with Mugsy's expression of bewilderment.

"You left one objective out, Colonel," asked De Niro, changing the focus of the discussion.

"And what objective would that be, Mr. De Niro?"

"Did you forget about the high-ranking South Korean official General Kim mentioned in the message?"

Cho took another deep drag, before snuffing out the cigarette. He replied with a tolerant tone while looking at the ashtray, "I did not forget, Mr. De Niro, I simply think it will be a waste of time."

"A waste of time?"

"Yes. I do not believe you fully understand the feelings those in our military have for the North Koreans. The hatred we feel towards their leaders."

"The message didn't specify 'military,' General. If I remember correctly it said, 'high-ranking official'"

"Mr. De Niro, the message also stated that this official would help to bring about a military coup. Really, only a high-ranking military officer could do that."

"Point taken. By the way, can we see this message from General Kim?"

"I'm afraid that would be out of the question. In order to show you the message, it would involve removing it from our intelligence services. That would attract attention. Questions would then be asked, questions that President Park would be forced to answer. This is not acceptable. You do understand?"

De Niro nodded, "I do. Getting back to my question, why shouldn't we also investigate the South Korean connection?"

"Because, Mr. De Niro, I cannot be in two places at once. My presence in North Korea is absolutely necessary."

"Colonel, your presence in North Korea may be necessary, but mine isn't."

"If you are referring to Captain Ricci and Scipio, I will need them in North Korea."

"Actually, I was referring to myself, Colonel."

"You …? With respect, Mr. De Niro, I have read all of the intelligence my country has on the members of your firm." Cho nodded towards Ricci and Scipio, "These men are professional soldiers and counter-terrorism experts. You are not. Is that not correct?"

Finally, the Colonel expresses his true feelings towards me.

"Colonel," Ricci replied for him, "speaking as one of the counter-terrorism experts you mentioned, I'll vouch for my brother-in-law."

"I'll second that," added Scipio, with a raise of his hand.

De Niro nodded to his men, "I appreciate the vote of confidence. Besides Colonel, I wasn't expecting to go it alone."

"Mr. De Niro, as President Park explained, there can be no

connection between you and your people, and our government." He forced a smile, "I simply could not allow a group of your people to go around interrogating our top Generals."

"Colonel, I didn't say anything about a group or about interrogating anyone … you did," replied De Niro. "In fact, I had only two people in mind to accompany me, the CIO, and the Vice President of Intelligence of The Watchman Agency."

De Niro winked at his brother-in-law Mugsy, who just happened to be engaged to The Watchman Agency's VP of Intelligence, Michelle Wang.

De Niro continued, "As far as our cover, there doesn't need to be a direct connection between us and your government. In fact, I've been seriously considering opening a manufacturing plant for electronic parts in South Korea."

Colonel Cho looked confused.

"Your country's intelligence on Cris De Niro *did* mention something about him being one of the richest human beings on the planet, didn't it, Colonel?" teased Scipio.

Cho remained silent for almost a minute. His only body movement was the blinking of his eyes. Finally, he bowed his head with a tense grin, "Very well, but as I stated, my government can have no direct involvement with you, nor can we offer you support of any kind. Is that understood?"

"Completely," replied De Niro.

"Are there any other questions, gentlemen?" asked Cho. When no one replied, he stood up, "Then I will take my leave."

"Colonel," Ricci handed him the tablet on the table in front of him, "as I said, since it appears that we're moving forward, this is yours."

Cho stuffed it into his breast pocket, blinking with gratitude.

"One more thing, Colonel," De Niro walked to the door with him. "Among your generals, do you have any suspicions of who could possibly—?"

As he did to Ricci, Cho cut De Niro off, "I do not."

Cho exited the suite but stopped in the corridor. He turned back to De Niro, "Come to think of it, there is only one general who

would have the ability to successfully carry out a military coup …
Daejang Jeong Seung-jo. He is Chairman of the Joint Chiefs of Staff
and Chief Director of the Joint Defense Headquarters. Daejang is
equivalent to your 4-star general."

"Thank you, Colonel," De Niro replied with a slight bow of his
head.

"A word of advice, I would tread very lightly around, Daejang
Jeong. He is a very powerful man, many believe more powerful than
even our new president."

"Understood. Thanks again, Colonel."

"Good day, Mr. De Niro. Tell your men I will be in touch soon,
via your spy phone."

De Niro closed the door.

"Our spy phone?" said Ricci who had been standing just out of
sight with Scipio. "I get the feeling Colonel Cho doesn't trust us."

"And I get the feeling Colonel Cho is lying through his teeth,"
added Scipio. "All that convoluted crap about General Kim sounded
like a giant smoke screen to me."

"A smoke screen … hiding what?" asked De Niro.

"Cris, all I can tell you is that in the field the primary reason to use
a smoke screen is for self concealment."

"I admit, he confused the heck out of me," added Mugsy. "It was
like he was trying to finger General Kim while still keeping General
Kang in play."

"I got the same feeling," replied De Niro, "but not just finger
Kim, he said 'kill him.'"

Scipio scratched his chin, "And Colonel Cho knows better than
that malarkey he spouted about torturing a confession out of Kim.
South Korea utilizes the same interrogation methods as we do. He
knows a proper interrogation is more an exercise in psychological
manipulation than physical torture. It sounded more to me like he
just wanted a reason to kill him."

"But why?" asked De Niro.

Scipio exhaled audibly, "I don't know. I just don't know. I normally
can size up a person – good guy or bad guy – pretty quickly, but I
can't with the Colonel."

"You said you think he's lying through his teeth."

"I did say that, but that doesn't necessarily mean he's playing for the other team. We need to find out his reason for lying."

De Niro nodded slowly, "I'll call down to Rigoni and tell him to keep an eye on the boys for awhile. Meantime, let's the three of us head over to The Watchman. Mugs, call ahead and have Michelle, Johnny-F, and Karla meet us in the conference room in 30 minutes."

"On it," replied Ricci as he put his cell phone to his ear.

De Niro walked over to one of the floor-to-ceiling windows and gazed out to a spectacular view of the city's skyline. Scipio followed.

De Niro addressed the small man dressed in black without turning around, "What did you think of the Colonel telling me about Daejang Jeong?"

"If ever a finger was pointed," replied Scipio.

De Niro nodded, "I thought the same thing."

"The Colonel was absolutely honest about one thing though, Cris."

De Niro turned, "What's that?"

"Daejang Jeong is a very powerful man. If he discovers that you're investigating him, you can find yourself in a world of trouble. Remember, Mugsy and I won't be anywhere near to protect you. And if Jeong *is* conspiring with Kang, you, Michelle, and Johnny-F could find yourselves floating face down in the Han River."

De Niro stared back a moment before patting Scipio's shoulder, "Coming from a counter-terrorism expert, I'll keep that in mind."

CHAPTER 4

EXECUTIVE CONFERENCE ROOM - ALPHA
THE WATCHMAN AGENCY
ARLINGTON, VIRGINIA
10:00 AM (LOCAL), FRIDAY, MAY 10, 2013

Cris De Niro, Captain Louis "Mugsy" Ricci, USN SEALs (Ret.), and Scipio entered the firm's main conference room. Already seated were CIO, John "Johnny-F" Francis; VP Intelligence Services, Michelle Wang; VP Government Relations, Karla Matthews; and Mugsy Ricci's Executive Assistant, Debbie Lynch.

Designated Executive Conference Room – Alpha, with the help of their Uncle Mugsy, De Niro's sons surprised him by having the room redesigned to resemble, almost identically, the conference room aboard the fictional *Starship Enterprise*. In fact, many that worked for De Niro noticed the resemblance between their boss's inclusive, "get-your-subordinate's-opinions-first-then-make-your-decision leadership style and Captain Jon-Luc Picard's.

Knowing his brother-in-law was an avid *Star Trek* fan, affectionately known as a "trekkie," was only part of the reason

Mugsy agreed to the makeover. The other reason was that after studying the layout of the Enterprise-D's conference room and futuristic conference table, both Mugsy and Johnny-F were impressed with the utility of the design.

The space was ergonomically laid out, as was the long, slightly curved table and contoured cushioned chairs. Everything about the room and table were both functional and comfortable. The table in particular, with its bull-nosed mahogany trim encasing a black acrylic table surface with built-in touch-screen monitors, really impressed the über-nerd Francis.

Coffee and tea was set up on a table at the far end of the room. Alongside were two baskets, one filled with fresh bagels that were still warm from the oven and the other was filled with freshly-baked pastries and turnovers. In front of the pots and baskets were a creamer and small bowls filled with butter, cream cheese, and marmalade. To the side were bottles of water and a pitcher of orange juice.

In addition to being the most professional executive assistant, the people in the room considered Debbie Lynch to be the most considerate. They were all aware that she went out of her way to make sure the coffee was Mr. De Niro's favorite, a Jamaican blend, the favorite of the last five U.S. Presidents; the pastry was from her boss Captain Ricci's favorite bakery; a specific brand of chai tea was an addiction of Michelle Wang's; and the orange juice was something she noticed the reclusive Scipio enjoyed.

The turnovers were a special treat for John Francis. Francis once told her about the apple turnovers that his mother used to make when he was a kid and how much he loved them. Lynch found out that Francis's mother had passed away years ago, so she enlisted De Niro's help to get the recipe from another of Francis' relatives. Francis's jaw dropped open the first time he smelled the familiar aroma in the conference room. Lynch talked Mugsy's favorite bakery into following Johnny-F's mother's recipe. Since then, she made sure to order some every few weeks. As for Karla Matthews, the tall, stately African American woman seemed to enjoy everyone else's favorites.

With the exception of De Niro and Mugsy, the executive staff helped themselves then took a seat. Customarily, as President of the firm, Mugsy Ricci would sit at the head of the table, but he deferred that honor to De Niro whenever his brother-in-law visited.

De Niro allowed some time for everyone to enjoy their brunch and small talk. He noticed the two love birds, Mugsy and Michelle, sitting next to each other, talking and smiling as two people in love do. They had thrown their engagement party on De Niro's ranch and loved it so much that they asked him if they could get married there. De Niro felt honored. He was excited for both of them. As he watched them, his thoughts drifted to his wife.

I remember when Lisa and I sat like that. Just beholding the radiance of Lisa's smile used to captivate me. She sometimes thought I wasn't paying attention to what she was saying. She was right, her lips would move but her beauty left me deaf and dumb.

He took a deep breath and held it before exhaling and allowing one last thought of his wife.

I love you, babe.

Mugsy caught his brother-in-law looking at them. De Niro winked and smiled before calling the meeting to order.

"As you all probably know by now, this morning the new leader of South Korea, President Park Geun-hye paid a call on us."

Mugsy broke in, "I've already given operational clearance to John, Michelle, and Karla to November-Kilo 051013."

De Niro nodded, "Very good, thank you Mugsy. Have the three of you had time to read it?"

"I have," replied Karla.

"So have I," replied Michelle.

Francis held up one hand as he shoved the last of an apple turnover into his mouth. He tried to swallow it as quickly as he could.

"Sorry … I can't stop eating these things. Debbie, as CIO do I have the authority to give you orders?"

"Yes, sir, you do."

"Then this is an order. No more turnovers! Since you started ordering these things, my belt is barely buckled on its last hole. Have I made myself clear?"

Lynch smiled, "Crystal, Sir."

"Well then … that's better."

"John … have you—"

Francis held his hand up cutting De Niro off, "I'm sorry, Cris. I just want to clarify to Debbie, when I said, 'no more turnovers,' I was really only referring to not bringing them in every week."

"But I don't bring them in every week."

"You don't … are you sure?"

Lynch tried to hold in her laughter, "Yes, Mr. Francis, I'm sure. I only bring them in every three or four weeks, when I stop for Captain Ricci's pastries. He has a rule against my ordering them more than once a month."

"That rule came from me," Michelle raised her hand. "Captain Ricci needs to lose 10 pounds before our wedding to make room for the 10 pounds he's bound to gain on our honeymoon cruise."

Everyone laughed.

"John …," De Niro spoke up again, but again Francis held up his hand, "Just a sec, Cris." He turned to Lynch again, "You only order these once a month?"

Lynch nodded her head jovially.

"Then why the heck is my belt so tight?" he thought out loud.

"Could be those Taco Bell runs you make twice a day," replied Karla.

"Or the bagel runs," added Michelle.

"Or the—"

Francis made a slashing motion with his hand across his neck to everyone, "Okay … got it! Thanks everyone. Wow, I didn't realize my dietary habits were such a fixation with everyone around here."

De Niro looked like he was about to speak when Francis held up his hand one more time, "Sorry Cris." He turned to Lynch again, "You know what Debbie, in light of new evidence, I'm rescinding that last order I gave you. I'll cut my Taco Bell runs down, so no reason for you to stop picking up the apple turnovers."

The women held in their laughter. Mugsy dropped his head and shook it. De Niro flashed a tired smile.

"You were saying, Cris?"

"Actually, I was asking … if you--"

"Read the file, I did."

De Niro glanced at Mugsy, who again shook his head.

Francis continued, oblivious, "Question … do you really want to open a manufacturing facility in Seoul? I only ask because it's not a bad idea.

"I was actually looking into opening up a manufacturer of some of my high-tech toys for the U.S. military there a few years ago.

"A couple of takeaways from my diligence – As of '06, South Korea became the 12th largest economy and trading partner in the world. They have a highly-educated population and workforce. If I remember correctly, over 82% of their young people are enrolled in college, seven per cent of the country's entire GDP is spent on education, and nearly three quarters of South Koreans undertake postgraduate-level study.

"And over the next few years, the South Korean economy is set to make the 10th-largest contribution to world growth. That's as much as the U.K. and more than Italy or France."

De Niro had to chuckle, "Leave it to you, John, to keep all that information in your little grey cells and ask that question first. The answer is … perhaps, and I'm taking you specifically so that you can continue your investigations in that area. But please don't forget our primary objective. We're there to investigate Daejang Jeong …," he looked at Scipio, "preferably without us ending up face down in the Han River."

Francis looked down frantically at his view screen, "Face down … in the Han River? Cris, I didn't see any mention of that!"

"Let's just say that's a real possibility if we're not careful. Speaking of careful, Karla, I'll need to meet with a few of their ministers – of finance, business, and unification, off the top of my head, to keep up appearances. Can you manage that?"

"I can set up those meetings. I'd like to add a few points of my own to John's. It'll be important for you both to understand some of the etiquette of doing business in South Korea and generally, their culture.

"For instance, corruption remains an issue there. For purposes of commerce, there are still many cases of bribery and corruption among their public officials. So don't be surprised if they make veiled allusions to anything under-the-table.

"Also, Korean is the official language of business in South Korea. However, English is widely spoken by their senior business figures and government officials. It wouldn't be unusual for high-level business meetings to be conducted mainly in English, but they would appreciate it if you use their language whenever possible.

"And when you speak in English, remember to talk slowly and repeat any key points. In order to save face, Korean hosts won't necessarily let you know if they don't understand something. You really should have an interpreter, particularly if you're considering leaving Seoul, and all important written documents need to be translated in Korean."

"Good to know, thanks Karla," said De Niro, "Michelle, how's your Korean?"

"I studied both Japanese and Korean in school. Truthfully, my Japanese is better, so I'll cram some Korean language studies into our flight there."

"Do that. I don't want to use an outside interpreter. Hopefully, like Karla mentioned, the high-ranking officials will all be able to speak English, but we need to be able to understand them when they switch back to Korean."

"Well, fortunately, I can understand the language more than I can speak it, but I'll brush up on both."

"Good," De Niro turned back to Matthews, "Karla, we need some way … some reason to come in contact with Daejang Jeong … something like a state affair or dinner."

She tapped onto her view screen, "I'm checking the General's public affairs calendar. It looks like the only public affair he'll be attending is South Korea's Memorial Day ceremony on June 6th. They hold it in the National Cemetery in Seoul. There'll be a state dinner after the ceremony. I can get you invited to both."

"That'll have to do then, but June 6th is almost a month away. According to General Kim's note, General Kang is intending to launch the missiles in the next 30 days."

"June 6th is 27 days away," Scipio did the calculation for everyone.

De Niro nodded, "We'll just have to hope you, Mugsy, and the Colonel are successful. Meanwhile, Karla, set up our itinerary for Michelle, John, and me to arrive in Seoul the week before."

Mugsy turned to Debbie Lynch, "Debbie, take care of their travel and lodging needs. Contact Duke O'Rourke and tell him that he and Charger will be needed to fly Mr. De Niro, Michelle, and John to Seoul on the QSST ...," he turned to De Niro, "when do you want to arrive, the 31st?"

De Niro's face turned red. Most of the people at the table had no idea why.

"Sorry, Cris, how about June 1st?"

"June 1st is fine," replied De Niro, as he stood and headed for the door. "Let's schedule another meeting right after you hear from Colonel Cho. We'll finalize everything then."

"That probably won't be until sometime next week," replied Karla. "President Park is scheduled to be returning to Seoul on Monday morning for a meeting with the Japanese Prime Minister. That means the President and her entourage have to depart Washington no later than sometime Sunday morning. It's a 14-hour non-stop flight and Seoul is 13 hours ahead of D.C. time.

"The rest of President Park's activities while here are all public functions, so, her security chief will have his hands full until they return home."

De Niro nodded, "The Colonel said he'd be in contact soon though, so let's be ready on our end. Meantime, I'll be busy for the rest of the day. The boys and I will be returning home tomorrow morning. Anyone that wants to hitch a ride on *Peregrine* with us is welcome."

Peregrine was De Niro's $80 million supersonic jet, more precisely, *Quiet Supersonic Transport* or QSST. It could fly twice as fast as any commercial or executive jet without causing a sonic boom.

Scipio raised his hand, "Save me a seat."

"Me too," added Francis.

"Michelle and I might as well tag along too, replied Mugsy. "We can stage from the *Coyote's Den.*"

"Then with the three stooges, that makes 10," Scipio quipped with a grin, referring to Rigoni, De May, and Pescalitis.

"Can't blame any of us Cris," added Francis, "who would pass up a flight on that beautiful bird?"

Before De Niro was out of earshot, Scipio called out, "Have a good time at the Smithsonian with the boys."

"Meeting adjourned," said Mugsy.

No one moved.

"What was that about May 31st?" asked Scipio.

Mugsy tapped a button to shut his viewscreen then sat back in his chair. He rubbed his eyes then stretched, "May 31st was my sister's birthday."

Mugsy rose from his chair, "It's funny. Birthdays were never a big thing to my sister or Cris. Something about how God's people didn't celebrate birthdays in the Messiah's day, only the pagans did."

"Actually, that's true," added Francis. "The celebration of a person's birthday has pagan origins."

Mugsy stopped at the door, "Yeah, well, since 9/11, Cris has spent every May 31st with his boys … and only his boys."

"I always wondered about that," replied Francis.

Scipio patted Francis on his back as he passed, startling him. He was biting into an apple turnover, "These are pretty good, John, kudos to your mom."

Francis waited for everyone to leave the room before grabbing the last turnover and stuffing it into his jacket pocket.

CHAPTER 5

PUNGGYE-RI NUCLEAR TEST SITE
KILJU COUNTY, NORTH HAMGYONG PROVINCE
NORTH KOREA
6:00 PM (LOCAL), SATURDAY, MAY 11, 2013

The footsteps of Sojang Kim Gil-su echoed down the man-made tunnel as he made his way to the control center of the underground nuclear test site. Every 50 meters a pair of guards would snap to attention and salute as he passed. He didn't acknowledge any of them.

Upon reaching the steel doors of the control center, the squat middle-aged Sojang placed his identification in front of the scanner. It took a few seconds before a buzzer was heard, signaling that the guard behind the bullet-proof glass authenticated Kim's identification and had released the locks to the door. Sojang Kim—equivalent to a two-star (major) general in the U.S. Army—waited while another guard pushed open the door and stepped to the side, saluting.

A tall, thin sangjwa, equivalent to a U.S. Army colonel was waiting to escort him inside. The sangjwa saluted crisply, but once again,

Kim showed no sign of acknowledgement. Neither man spoke as the Sangjwa lead him down an impeccably cleaned and polished, but otherwise drab set of corridors leading to another set of doors. Upon reaching them, the Sangjwa knocked twice in quick succession, before pushing the door open. He came to full attention and held his salute.

Sojang Kim entered behind him, walked across the finely furnished large office and came to attention in front of the massive desk at which Taejang Kang Kum-Sok was sitting. With the equivalent rank of an American Army 5-star general (General of the Army), the mid-50's Taejang never looked up as he slurped a spoonful of *chueotang*, also known as Mudfish, a thick soup made with Loach.

The North Koreans considered chueotang a desirable and healthy meal. In order to prepare it properly, the fish had to be added to the boiling water while still alive. Kang had a chef from the local village given a security clearance so he could enter the test site.

With Sojang Kim standing at attention just in front of the desk, and the tall sangjwa still standing at attention and saluting near the door, Taejang Kang took a few more loud slurps of his mudfish soup before addressing them.

"Leave us, Sangjwa and I do not want to be disturbed while the Sojang is with me."

"Yes, sir!" barked the Sangjwa as he lowered his arm and hurried out of the office, closing and locking the door behind him.

Kim waited to hear the click of the lock before addressing Kang, "Sir, did you think it wise to call me here. I thought you said—"

Kang held his hand up, "Circumstances dictated that this meeting was required. As for confidentiality, we can speak here without possibility of being overheard. The walls are over three meters thick and lined with lead, as are the doors, to protect from any nuclear radiation, and I have already had the room swept for listening devices."

Kang paused before continuing. Kim remained silent doing his best to conceal his anxiety.

"What news do you bring me, Gil-su? Is our fearless, spoiled-boy leader planning to spout out any new empty threats against the Americans or our weak siblings to the South?"

"None that I know of, Sir."

Kang stared intensely at Kim, "You mean to say that you visited Pyongyang and came back with nothing to tell me? How can that be?"

"Simply that I did not spend much time in our Capital. I had to take care of some business in Wonsan."

"I know about your trip to Wonsan," Kang wiped his mouth on a linen napkin before tossing it over the soup bowl and rising from his seat.

He took a cigarette from an ornate golden box on the desk, placed it between his lips, and waited for Kim to light it. Kim obliged using a matching golden ornate lighter next to the box.

Kang took a long drag from the cigarette as he continued to stare at Kim, who stared back in silence.

"In fact, you have taken several trips in the last few months, some made sense to me, but a few were to remote outposts. Perhaps, Sojang, you can enlighten me as to the purpose of those trips?"

Kim looked unshaken, "Permission to speak freely, Sir?"

Kang nodded by blinking.

"I was not aware, Taejang, that I was under suspicion, especially by you. Have I given you any reason to place me under surveillance?"

Kang pounded his fist onto the desk, "I am Taejang! I do not need a reason to take actions that I deem necessary."

"So then you deemed spying on me necessary?"

Kang stepped face-to-face with Kim, "That is quite enough, Sojang. You have taken too much liberty with your permission to speak freely."

Kim stared back for a moment before lazily straightening his eyes and coming to attention.

Kang pressed closer, almost nose-to-nose, "You know what is at stake. I brought you into my confidence because you have always been a loyal officer to me."

"I serve our country, Taejang."

"Of that, I am sure, and you have served The Democratic People's Republic well. But in these times, our country requires more than service to survive."

Kang's face became fierce, "I will not repeat myself, Sojang. Answer the question."

Kim let his eyes drift to meet Kang's, "The purpose of my trips was to personally meet with some of our field grade officers, especially the ones stationed in strategic locations that I had never met before."

"Go on."

"With the time closing in, I thought it would be important to know which of the higher-ranking officers we might want to keep out of harm's way when the hostilities begin. One's that we might count on when the current regime falls."

Kang frowned dismissively, "We discussed who—"

"With respect, Sir," Kim interjected, "discussing the metal of a man can be done from a distance; but deciding a man's loyalty can only be done by looking into his eyes. Do you not agree?"

Kang studied Kim for another moment before cracking a small grin, "Indeed, the eyes are the windows to the soul. Your intentions seem reasonable, but your decision not to advise me was impertinent."

"I was only following your orders, Taejang, no unnecessary contact or communication between us until the action is taken."

Kang nodded slowly, "Perhaps your definition of what is necessary and what is not is different than mine, Gil-su."

He's calling me by my given name again, thankfully!

"Besides, we both agreed … having you spend as much time as possible in Pyongyang is prudent, so you can keep an eye on the spoiled brat and his court of fools."

"And I have. The trips I took were only day trips. I believe they actually helped to avert any notions the inner circle might be forming about my extended stay in the Capital."

Kang nodded in understanding, "And you have nothing to report?"

"Nothing of any consequence except that I've confirmed with a few of them that they have no intention of ordering the deployment of the missiles in the near term. And you will be pleased to know that your ruse worked. It seems no one in Pyongyang is aware that the missiles are still armed and loaded on the mobile launchers."

Kang stood silent for a moment before inhaling the last of his cigarette and snuffing it out.

"I hope you understand, my old friend, the reasons for my caution."

"May I speak freely once more?"

Kang gave a curt nod.

"I can understand caution Kum-Sok, but not doubting my loyalty or calling into question my actions. I have served alongside you for many years. In all those years, have I ever given you reason for pause?

Kang didn't reply right away. Instead he reached out and patted Kim's shoulder.

"You have not, my old friend. Nevertheless, my vision for the future of our country is too important, and the time to bring it to fruition too close to take anything for granted … even old friendships."

Kang began pacing slowly.

"A pampered prince now controls our fate. A spoiled brat surrounded by an inner circle of idiotic sycophants who think the answer to every provocation from the Americans is to detonate another atomic bomb or test another ICBM."

"Then they make foolish, toothless announcements to the world … that the war with the South has commenced again … that Japan will suffer if they interfere … that we can attack Hawaii … even California!"

Kang stepped back shaking his head, "All the while the spoiled brat and his inner circle of pompous baboons know full well that they could never strike anyone without risking their lavish lifestyles … their palaces and cars and yachts.

"Meanwhile, the imbeciles are blind to what is happening to our culture. For over 60 years, we have been able to shield our citizens from the corruption of the outside world. In that time, we have raised generations of loyal citizens who would give their lives to protect our government.

"Yet, their loyalty was based on the purity of our message … one message heard by all. One message, that our country is Heaven on

Earth, and that our leader is our god."

Kim noticed that Kang stopped pacing and looked like he was falling into a trance. Kim stood in silence and waited.

Kang finally glanced at him. He looked lucid again, "Over 60 years we have promoted that lie with impunity. That was possible because there was no questioning the veracity of our message. There was no rebuttal, no dissenting opinion. How could there be? Without connection to the outside world, our countrymen had no way of knowing ... what is that American expression? That the grass is greener on the other side?"

Kim nodded, "But that term is used to describe the misconception that others have it better than we do."

"In our case though, the grass is not only greener on the other side, but the food is more plentiful, the pay is more lucrative, and the opportunities endless.

"We used to have the ability to draw the universe anyway we liked, and teach that science to our masses, but technology, the global media, and the internet are changing that. They are using balloons to fly over our border and drop Christian Bibles!

"In time, our people will learn that their cousins to the South are not starving or poor. That they are well-fed and live in luxury, and that the Americans don't eat North Korean babies.

"When they learn those truths they will be shocked, and then they will become angry at the ones who told them those lies. That is how revolutions begin. And in revolutions, all senior officials like you and me are usually put to death, imprisoned, or exiled."

Kang walked over to a credenza, opened it, and retrieved a bottle and two glasses.

"Our lies are no longer sustainable. And it's not just our lives at stake, but our national identity. Think of it Gil-su ... if our people overthrow the spoiled brat's regime and rid themselves of all of our country's senior officials. Who will fill the vacuum of leadership? The peasants ...? The farmers ...?"

Kang opened the ornate white bottle and poured the yellowish-brown liquor into both glasses. He handed one to Kim and tapped the glass with his. Kim brought it to his nose. He thought the liquor had the aroma of a munbae tree, a type of pear tree.

"No. More likely, our allies to the North would infiltrate, under the guise of restoring order, but make no mistake, once the Chinese take control, they will not relinquish it.

"There is also the possibility that our cousins to the South would seize control, with the help of the Americans. In either case, the Korean national identity would be forever lost, replaced with a Chinese or American one."

Kang raised his glass and examined it, "Can you tell what type of liquor this is without tasting it?"

Kim put it to his nose again, "Of course, it is Munbaeju. One can tell just from its aroma."

"Yes indeed, it's named for its aroma, but did you know that it is not made from Munbae at all. That is merely smells like the pear?"

"I didn't know that."

Kang held his glass up high and turned it slowly, eyeing it thoughtfully. Kim looked on in confusion.

"In 1986, South Korea designated Munbaeju as their Intangible Cultural Property No. 86."

"I do seem to recall …," replied Kim, "didn't they use Munbaeju for the toast at the North-South Korean Summit in 2000?

Kang nodded, "But were you aware that Munbaeju was brewed for the first time in Pyongyang? It's been brewed for generations in Pyeongan-do, but the South Koreans take credit for it to the world.

"Despite that, this liquor is a symbol that the North and South are inexorably tied together.

"I have tasted many liquors of the world and none taste like Munbaeju. It is unique. One smells its aroma and tastes it and doesn't say it is of the North or of the South. They simply say, 'it is Korean.'"

Kang put the glass to his lips and sipped. Kim followed his lead.

"It is time we too remove the terms north and south when we speak of Korea."

Kim kept pace making sure to finish his glass when Kang did. They drank in silence. After taking his last sip Kim spoke up, "Speaking of time, you haven't told me yet exactly when you're planning to launch the missiles."

Kang walked back to his desk and took a seat. He removed another cigarette from the golden box and this time lit it himself.

"You will know soon enough. For now, return to Pyongyang and resume your surveillance. It is imperative for me to know if the spoiled brat or his minions are planning to pay a visit here.

"As soon as his father died, Kim Jon-un stripped me of my power and prestige and exiled me to this cold, barren wasteland. The fat, little prince always felt my loyalties to his father were a threat to him. Jong-il was my closest friend, but he loved his son. It is too bad he loved his son more than his country."

Kang sat staring down at the desk puffing his cigarette. Kim decided that he was dismissed and started for the door. When he reached it, Kang spoke again, "No more surprises Gil-su, understood?"

"Yes, sir."

Kim let himself out of the office. The officer that led him in was sitting outside waiting to lead him back out.

Once in the car, Kim told his driver to head for the airport, before raising the glass separator. Only then did he allow himself to tremble. He removed his cap and loosened his tie, then reached for a flask of American whiskey he kept with him at all times. He unscrewed the cap and gulped down half of its contents before coming up for air.

The amber liquor didn't serve to stop his trembling.

CHAPTER 6

THE *COYOTE'S DEN*
ESTANCIA DE NIRO
HENDERSON, NEVADA
4:00 PM (LOCAL), SUNDAY, MAY 19, 2013

At the "CommSec," short for Communications & Security station, Karl De May, the tall, muscle-bound squad leader of ARCHANGEL's *Gabriel* squad hunkered over the control panel. He was summoned there by an instant message sent from Scipio, via Big-Brutha™. The message simply read, "Ding-dong."

There was only one way to gain entry into ARCHANGEL's covert underground headquarters from the ground. For members of The Watchman Agency and ARCHANGEL, their Big-Brutha™ devices had a thumb-activated app that emitted a micro-wave radio beacon. A small hidden receiver was programmed only to accept signals originating from five meters in front of the flawlessly camouflaged entryway to the facility.

The beacons themselves were actually encrypted bursts of data, in this case high-resolution thumbprint scans. The thumbprint was instantly analyzed by ARCHANGEL personnel at the CommSec station, who also visually identified the visitor using several micro HD cameras. If confirmed, a giant hatch, as big as a bus, rose from the desert floor allowing entry.

If the thumbprint and visual identification weren't confirmed, or if someone just happened by in front of the entrance, a number of things could happen: ARCHANGEL guards could appear from nearby hidden security portals to question and subsequently escort the trespasser off Mr. De Niro's property; trespassers could be taken into custody; tranquilizer darts fired from mini-cannons concealed in nearby shrubs could incapacitate a person or curious animal; or if the trespassers were considered hostile, up to four HITROLE® Light Remote Weapon Stations (RWS) (5.56mm, 7.62mm, 12.7mm machine guns, and 40mm automatic grenade launcher) could deploy, springing up from the ground within seconds to reign hellfire upon them.

Each weapon station utilized a modular sighting system including a Day TV camera, an IR camera for night vision, and an eye safe Laser Range Finder (LRF). Both the sighting and firing systems were computer assisted and operated from the CommSec station through a multi-function display and joystick. The gunner was supported by a Fire Control Computer (FCC) with ballistic and cinematic computation as well as an auto-tracker.

Scipio's clowning message wasn't necessary, as much as it was a "head's up" to *Gabriel*'s squad leader that the big chiefs were on their way in. He had texted De May a few minutes before that De Niro and the others were on their way from the main residence, and that he was cutting his afternoon of target practice short to head back in and join them.

Before getting to the CommSec station De May briefed his counterparts, Vin Rigoni and Spiro Pescalitis. Rigoni headed right for the main conference room to activate all of the Big-Brutha™ communication and information management systems, while Pescalitis hurried over to the access corridor.

The access corridor, a 20-foot wide by 80-foot long tunnel, began at ground level outside, and ended 40-feet underground. To accommodate horses, the floor of the corridor was composed of a special hardened rubber, which could also take the abuse from wheeled-vehicles like quads. The distributor of the material also assured that heavier vehicles could roll over the material without damaging it, but that would probably never be tested. The *Coyote's Den* was located in a very rugged desert area 10 miles from De Niro's main residence. The terrain was too rough for most vehicles and too narrow at points through jagged rock formations for larger all-terrain vehicles.

There were no markings of any kind pointing to *The Den*'s location, and no roads that led to it, only dirt trails. None of the estancia's staff, save De Niro's Executive Assistant William Bret and his head gaucho Martin Fierro even knew of its existence.

Other than De Niro's stable of horses, the only ground transportation that could safely reach *The Den* were trail bikes and quads. From the main residence, by horse it took 30 minutes, and by trail bike or quad it took about half that. Today though, De Niro decided to take the fastest form of transportation, via his new Sikorsky S-76D™ helicopter, which could make the trek in under four minutes.

Once confirmation was made that the small man dressed in black sitting on the green *Artic Cat Mud Pro 700* quad was indeed Scipio, De May placed his hand on the CommSec duty officer's shoulder.

"Let the boss in, Peterson."

A button on the touch screen was depressed, followed almost instantly by the faint mechanical sounds of the access door linkage, and then the echoed roar of the compact all-terrain vehicle.

Scipio pulled up next to Pescalitis and handed him his helmet, "Do me a favor Spiro, lock my rifle up, and then park the quad."

"Aye, boss."

Scipio headed straight over to the newly-installed helipad door control station. A technician he didn't recognize was already manning the controls. Rigoni joined him and answered his boss's question before it was asked, "He's with the company that designed and installed the doors. Part of the fee we paid them also paid for a tech's on-site services for the first 30 days, just to work the bugs out."

Scipio noticed that the technician was listening. He winked at

Rigoni, "Understood, but be sure to dispose of his body where no one will find it after the 30 days are up."

Rigoni couldn't hold in his laughter at the technician's look of shock.

"Good afternoon Archangel Ground, November-three-niner-one-five-tango requests landing clearance and access to helipad." Charger Miller's voice crackled through the station speakers.

The technician didn't move.

Rigoni leaned down and spoke softly into the frightened man's ear, "Perhaps you should let them in or my boss might make me dispose of you right now."

This time Scipio chuckled as the technician almost jumped out of his seat, depressing touch screen buttons and speaking into his headset mic, "November-three-niner-one-five-tango, Archangel Ground. You are cleared for landing, Sir. Stand by for helipad access."

* * * * *

Captain Douglas "Charger" Miller, USAF (Ret.) was piloting the sleek thirteen-passenger, double-engine chopper. The "76" could cruise at up to 178 mph with a ceiling of 9,700 feet, and a range of over 441 nautical miles. Onboard joining De Niro were Colonel James "Duke" O'Rourke, in charge of De Niro's fleet of aircraft, Michelle Wang, Mugsy Ricci, and John Francis.

Over a week had passed since Colonel Cho said he would be in touch. It was decided that the best place for everyone involved in the upcoming mission to wait would be on the estancia. They would inevitably stage from *The Den*, so it made sense. Mugsy and Michelle had been "living in sin," as De Niro gibed, in the main guest house, while Francis took residence in smaller guest quarters next door.

Duke and Charger lived in private homes built for them and their families in a quaint "village" located on the estancia, not far from De Niro's home. At first, De Niro constructed the village for the estancia's staff, but he eventually offered homes there to other employees on his payroll as well. ARCHANGEL's squad leaders lived there, as well as all of their senior officers.

It was something he and Lisa always wanted, to allow the people that worked for them to enjoy some of their blessings. After she died, De Niro decided to follow through with that vision. He knew that would have made her overjoyed and that brought joy to him.

De Niro hired an architect and had her design the village to emulate ones near the coast of Southern Spain. Not only did De Niro build the estancia staff homes, but the village also included a main pool, a recreation building, and a small schoolhouse staffed by a full time teacher for their children. The estancia staff was so impressed with their *pueblito* they named it "El Paraíso," The Paradise.

Scipio was the only executive to pass on the offer to live in El Paraíso, choosing instead to call the *Coyote's Den* his home. De Niro didn't consider it a slight. He knew the seclusion of *The Den* was ideal for a man that spent most of his life as a lone wolf.

Other than Scipio, the rest were at the main residence when Scipio received the call from Colonel Cho. They were invited by De Niro to partake in the Italian tradition of "Pasta Sunday." That is, on Sundays in Brooklyn, where De Niro grew up, all the Italian families ate an early multi-dish dinner and the main course was always pasta. De Niro cooked the sauce (if meat was added, it was called 'gravy') himself, the recipe taught to him by his mother.

The 76's cabin was very comfortable and relatively quiet, enough for everyone to speak easily over the redundant din of the rotors.

"I'm glad the Colonel called after we finished dinner," replied Francis. "You make the best pasta, Cris."

"I didn't think you could find the pasta with all the mozzarella you covered it with," replied Mugsy.

"That mozzarella was to die for … and the antipasto and the fresh-baked bread …." Francis rubbed his stomach.

"Arturo and Aurelio were responsible for all that. They actually made the cheese from scratch and learned how to bake artisan bread," replied De Niro, referring to his Mexican chefs, who were brothers.

"I just wish the Colonel would have called a little later," added Michelle. "I was so looking forward to Aurelio's tiramisu."

They heard Duke O'Rourke's voice come over the cabin speakers. He was sitting with Charger in the cockpit, "We're about to set down. Please fasten your seat belts."

Francis complied straining his neck to look out the window, "Can't wait to see the tripped out James Bond chopper pad doors open."

On cue, everyone sitting near the cabin windows watched in awe as, directly below them, a 60-foot by 50-foot rectangular patch of desert floor appeared to sink a few feet before splitting apart. Within a minute, a hole appeared just large enough for the 76 to lower into. With precision, Charger did just that, landing dead center inside a circular helipad branded with the ARCHANGEL emblem. The immense leafs began closing even before the chopper touched down.

The 76's cabin door opened and everyone exited as the rotors winded down – Francis first, followed by Michelle, Mugsy and then De Niro.

Scipio and Rigoni met them half way then took the lead guiding them to the conference room. Everyone took a seat.

A cam-window of Karla Matthews beamed from The Watchman Agency in Arlington appeared in the upper right-hand corner of all the monitor screens. Everyone exchanged greetings before Scipio started, "Nice touchdown, Charger. How was it?"

"Like threading a needle with a six ton chopper," he replied.

"That was so cool," added Francis. "I was humming the James Bond theme the whole way down. You know what we should do - we should buy Cris a cat he could pet while he sits at the end of the table."

"I was thinking more along the lines of a shark tank we could use to dispose of eccentric CIO's," replied Mugsy.

Everyone laughed.

"I thought we'd see more people here," said De Niro. "Trouble staffing?"

"Not staffing, Mr. D," replied Rigoni, "we can find people, but, with respect to Capt. Ricci, back in Arlington, H.R. is a mess. Background checks are taking forever, not to mention drug testing results, and Kolbe® MOs …."

From a business perspective, based in Arlington, Virginia,

The Watchman Agency was technically the parent company of ARCHANGEL, which meant it handled administrative functions for the paramilitary unit. One of those functions was legal services, which included human resources.

"Riggy's right, Cris," added Mugsy. "We haven't replaced the head of our legal since Les. My Executive Assistant Debbie Lynch is doing the best she can, trying to maintain some oversight, but without a department head, things are falling apart. That's my fault. I wanted to talk to you about possibly hiring that attorney we used in Chicago, Ike Aljure."

Les Pastak was the former head of the legal department. They inherited Pastak from the failing counter-terrorism firm that De Niro purchased in order to start The Watchman Agency. After becoming embroiled in a conspiracy hatched by Iranian terrorists, Pastak disappeared. Although his body was never found, he was presumed dead at the hands of the terrorists.

Ike Aljure was a sharp, young African American attorney that Cris De Niro hired to represent a man named Rodolfo Jiménez. Jiménez had come to De Niro to ask for help after his granddaughter was slain by a notorious Chicago street gang.

A hero of the Korean War, the old man Jiménez had taken his vengeance out on several members of the gang before De Niro could send men to his aid. De Niro immediately contacted a top law firm in Chicago to dispatch counsel to protect Mr. Jiménez from possible prosecution. They sent Aljure. He was subsequently successful in keeping Jiménez out of jail.

"Mugsy, The Watchman is your company to run. If you think he's the man for the job, make him an offer."

"I'll do that."

Only De Niro noticed his brother-in-law's look of embarrassment.

Scipio brought up a map of Korea and part of southeastern China on the room's monitors, "As most of you know, about 15 minutes ago I communicated with Colonel Cho via Big-Brutha™. He explained to me that although it took longer than anticipated, he's made most of the preparations for our incursion into North Korea.

"Originally, we were to fly from Seoul into Beijing, but he's secured seats for Mugsy, me, and him on Korean Air flight 831 which lands in Shenyang. Shenyang is over 400 miles closer to our border-crossing point, which should help make up for some of the lost time."

"What day do we leave?" asked Mugsy.

"Friday, May 24th." Once there, he said we have to make our way to Ji'an, a Chinese town very close to the North Korean border. That's the town the broker is supposed to be working from."

"What preparations has he made, and what took him so long to book a commercial flight?" asked Mugsy.

"I asked him the same questions. According to the Colonel, he had to locate and confirm where this particular broker would be. He explained, as part of their business, these brokers continue to move back and forth from different towns and villages along the border when they're not traveling into North Korea itself.

"Supposedly, this broker will be returning from North Korea to Ji'an with a new batch of defectors on the 24th. He's supposed to be meeting with smugglers, based in Thailand, that'll take the defectors the rest of the way into South Korea. After 'rendering them harmless', as he put it, we're to pose as those smugglers."

"And who supplied him with that intel?"

"Cho said a contact within the Chinese National Police Agency. Apparently, the Chinese authorities only turn one blind eye to these brokers. With their other eye, they keep tabs on them."

"So, the Chinese know we're coming?"

"No. At least that's what the Colonel told me. He said he told his Chinese contact that he was making inquiries into the broker as part of a routine investigation concerning a recent North Korean defector."

Rigoni shook his head, "Rendering Thai smugglers harmless in China, and then posing as them to a North Korean broker … the whole thing sounds pretty hinky."

"I agree," added De Niro. "If force is needed, I think we should be sending in more men."

"De May, Pescalitis, and I volunteer," replied Rigoni.

"Would be great to have some authentic Chinese food," added

Pescalitis. "Whaddaya say, Captain?"

"Unfortunately, that's out of the question," replied Scipio. "I took it upon myself to ask Colonel Cho if we could add Mo, Larry, and Curly to the flight. He declined, stating that it would be—quote—*unnecessarily risking discovery by the Chinese*—unquote. According to the good Colonel, the less of us there are, the easier it'll be for us to remain undetected by both the Chinese and the North Koreans."

"Excuse me for asking," Michelle spoke up with apprehension in her voice, "but aren't *we* running this rodeo?"

"We are, Michelle," replied De Niro, "but I'm afraid Colonel Cho gets to set the rules. Still, it's your call, Mugs. You decide if we're in or out on this one. Just keep in mind … from the time you land in China, if anything goes wrong, we won't be able to send help, at least not right away. And compared to China, rescuing Scipio from that Iranian prison was a cake walk."

Mugsy glanced at his fiancé before replying. She shook her head slightly but sternly.

"Sorry, my love, but I think the stakes are too high for us not to go in."

Michelle stared back at Mugsy with misty eyes.

De Niro broke the silence, "Scipio, what are the next steps?"

Scipio nodded to Mugsy. It was his way of telling him that he made the right decision, "The next steps are … we have to get ourselves to Seoul as soon as possible. Colonel Cho said he'll take care of our phony identification once we're there."

De Niro nodded, "Duke, how quickly can you get my brother-in-law and Scipio to Seoul?"

"Six hours, and that includes a fuel stop in Hawaii."

"If we left 8 PM tonight, what time would that put us into Seoul with the time difference?"

O'Rourke pulled his cell phone from his pocket and started tapping, "If we depart at 8 PM, we can touch down in Seoul tomorrow, noon time, their time."

"Good, make preparations. John, will we have any trouble communicating with them once they're in China and North Korea."

"Via Big-Brutha™, not at all. Our encrypted satellite link covers all of Southeast Asia. And since January, North Korea has eased restrictions on foreigners making cell calls. You're now able to call most foreign countries, foreign embassies, and international hotels in Pyongyang using a WCDMA-compatible mobile phone, one you can bring into the country. So, they won't even stick out if they use their phones in public."

"Good to know," De Niro turned to his monitor screen, "Karla, is everything set for our trip?"

Karla replied from the monitor screens, "Just about. I've made reservations for you, John, and Michelle at the Foster Lafayette Seoul, and I've already confirmed several meetings between you and a few high-ranking government officials who handle business development, labor relations, and transportation and logistics."

"What about the Memorial Day ceremony and state dinner that follows?"

"I've contacted the necessary people, just waiting to hear back from them."

"Are you anticipating any problems?"

"I'm not, but if I do run into trouble I'll be able to cash in on some favors I'm owed from friends at State. I'll have confirmation before you depart for Seoul. I assume you'll be flying there on *Peregrine*?"

De Niro turned to Francis, "John, how are you doing with the installation of the mini-drone control station aboard *Warbird*?"

"The installation team finishes their work next week. Then I scheduled a testing team to run it through its paces over the next couple of weeks."

"It may give us an advantage to have *Warbird* there with mini-drone surveillance capabilities."

"I could expedite the testing phase a bit, but without a full evaluation, I can't make any reliability promises."

"Fair enough, but make it so. Duke, when you and Charger get back, I'd appreciate it if you'd both sit in with the testing team. I want you to get a working familiarity with the ins and outs of drone deployment."

"Why just them?" replied Francis. "Cris, we're not talking

Predators and Reapers here. These are mini drones, many the size of your hand. You don't need pilots to operate them. In fact, I'm putting the finishing touches on an app that'll allow anyone to deploy and control them remotely from any double-B device. That is, with the proper security access."

"In that case, you, Michelle, and I will also sit in."

Francis rubbed his hands together, "I'm looking forward to it. I even took the liberty of inviting your boys to learn how to fly them."

De Niro stared back but didn't reply.

Francis shook his head with a grin, "Cris, no offense, but I would bet that the boys could fly these things better than you and I … even better than Duke and Charger. After all, controlling them is more akin to playing a video game than it is flying a real aircraft."

"I don't doubt that, but just in case, make sure none of them are armed. After watching Richard and Louis play Starcraft®, no one within the drone's range would be safe," De Niro winked, "including us."

The room filled with laughter from everyone except Michelle.

De Niro pressed his palms on the table as if ready to stand, "If there's nothing more …?"

"Any more questions," Mugsy added.

There were none.

"Class dismissed," replied Mugsy.

As everyone filed out of the room, De Niro approached Mugsy, "Stay for a moment."

As she exited, Michelle looked back at Mugsy as if she wanted to talk to him.

De Niro waited for everyone to leave, "Mugs, what was that all about with hiring a new head of legal?"

Ricci's face turned a shade of red, "That's on me Cris. I just dropped the ball."

"I know, but why?"

"Truth be told … I don't have any real experience dealing with lawyers, let alone hiring one. In the SEALs, we had JAG. My relationship with them had always been … I stay out of their way and they stay out of mine.

"I tasked Debbie with finding potential candidates and vetting them, but when it came time for me to meet with them, I felt like they were interviewing me for a job. To use a naval term, I felt out of my water.

"I thought it might be a good idea if you met with them instead."

"Mugs, when I hired you to become president of the firm, I did so with full confidence in your ability to make staff decisions."

"And I understand that Cris, and sincerely appreciate your confidence in me. I guess I just ... to be completely honest, I really don't like lawyers. As a breed, I think they're heartless, soulless, arrogant billable-hour parasites."

"Woo, Mugs. Where did that come from? For a guy that just told me he had very little contact with lawyers—"

"I meant personal one-on-one contact."

De Niro stepped up to him and put a hand on his shoulder, "Am I missing something here?"

"Did my sister ever tell you about our dad?"

De Niro thought about it, "She did. She said he was a salesman for a trucking company and he died of a heart attack."

"Did she tell you what he did before becoming a salesman?"

"No, she didn't."

"Our dad used to own his own trucking company, Ricci Trucking. It was a small LTL carrier based in South Philly. That is until one day when this couple apparently got hit by one of my dad's trucks. The driver denied hitting them. In fact, he said this guy and girl walked up to the front of his truck when he was stopped for a light, rubbed their sides against the grill, and then proceeded to fall on the ground screaming bloody murder.

"But to the driver's disbelief, this lawyer walks up and says he saw the whole thing. He said he saw the truck hit them.

"Next thing you know, my dad gets a lawsuit served on him. The lawyer was suing my dad's company for $250,000 back in the days when that wasn't chump change."

De Niro rubbed his chin, "I'm surprised Lisa didn't tell me anything about that."

"She was young, very young. We both were."

"What happened?"

"What happened? The lawyer drew the case out. The longer he did the more money my dad had to pay his lawyer, until he reached a point where he was no longer able to pay. He ended up settling for $100,000, which his insurance carrier paid and immediately after, dropped the coverage on my dad's fleet.

"He shopped around for a new provider, but the only coverage he could find was too expensive. Within 90 days of that settlement, my dad had to close the business he built up over 20 years. If it weren't for his making friends with a competitor, who eventually offered him a sales position, we literally would've been thrown out on the street."

The two men were quiet while Mugsy regained his composure. He finally managed a small smile, "Since then, I never trusted a lawyer I couldn't toss off a bridge, preferably with a mill stone tied around his neck. I know ... not too Christian of me."

De Niro squeezed his brother-in-law's shoulder with a wink, "Woe to you lawyers also! For you load people with burdens hard to bear, and you yourselves do not touch the burdens with one of your fingers."

"Amen to that ... who said that?"

De Niro patted his back then walked to the door, "You really need to study your Bible more. As for young Mr. Aljure, you already met him in Chicago, what did you think of him?"

"He seemed like a nice enough guy but again, I didn't get in his way and he didn't get in mine."

"Well, when you get back, call him in and talk to him. You don't have to know the law ... you just have to know the man."

"I'll do that."

De Niro took a step out then turned again, "Oh, and Mugs. If things don't work out, stay away from bridges."

Mugsy chuckled heading for the door. He ran into Michelle at the doorway. She pushed him back into the conference room.

"Mugs, I want you to answer a question and I want you to answer it honestly, understand?"

Ricci put his hands on her shoulders, "Honestly, I'm not sure I know what that—"

"Mugsy …!"

He kissed her cheek, "I'm teasing."

"And I'm serious."

"Okay … shoot."

"If our roles were reversed and it was you going with Cris to South Korea and me going with the Colonel to North Korea, would you have still thought … how did you put it '… *the stakes are too high for us not to go in?*'"

He didn't reply right away, "Yes, I would have."

She broke out of his grasp, "You're such a liar."

"Hey … you asked me and I told you."

"And I don't believe you."

She turned her back on him but he twisted her around to face him, "Hey, what's this with not believing me? I could take it personally, you know."

She crossed her arms and turned again, "That's exactly how I meant it."

This time, he tried to slip his hands around her waist, but she moved away.

"Michelle, what's the matter? I can understand your being concerned for me—"

"Concerned for you, is that what you think this is all about?"

"I'll be honest … I have no idea what this is all about! I wish you would tell me."

"It's about double standards. There is no way you would let me go on that mission, not with all of the uncertainties and risks, not to mention the precarious Colonel Cho. Yet, I can't stop you from going."

"That's right, you can't, and that has nothing to do with double standards. It has to do with chain of command."

She turned quickly, "Well you can shove your chain of command … I'm out of here!"

She rushed out of the room. Mugsy followed after her but stopped just outside the conference room. He called to her, "Out of where?! Michelle!"

She disappeared around a corner. Mugsy looked behind him and saw Scipio standing there.

His hands were folded behind his back, "Is this a bad time?"

Ricci turned back in Michelle's direction, "I guess not."

Scipio walked next to him but said nothing.

Mugsy finally spoke up, "It's ironic Scipio. Men like us can face down an army of bad guys, but one woman can bring us to our knees."

"Not just any woman, Captain. Michelle isn't just any woman."

Ricci turned to face the small man dressed in black, "You're right about that." He managed a smile, "What can I do for you?"

"We haven't discussed weapons."

"You're right, we haven't. Traveling to China by a commercial airline and then having to hoof it back and forth from there to North Korea, conventional weapons are out of the question. You have ideas?"

"I do, but before I go on about them, let me make a few phone calls and see what I can scrounge up. I'll figure something out before we board *Peregrine*."

"Very good."

Scipio left Mugsy standing there. The Watchman Agency's President started in the direction of his fiancé, hesitated and then headed in the other direction.

CHAPTER 7

INCHEON INTERNATIONAL AIRPORT
JUNG-GU
INCHEON, SOUTH KOREA

12:45 PM (LOCAL), MONDAY, MAY 20, 2013

Mugsy Ricci and Scipio stood in Cris De Niro's bedroom cabin in the rear of *Peregrine* naked from the waist up. The supersonic aircraft had just touched down at Incheon International Airport, South Korea's largest and the primary airport serving the Seoul National Capital Area.

Mugsy peered out the cabin window, "This is one big airport."

Scipio handed him what looked like a body-fitting t-shirt but it had small flat compartments sewn into it on its sides, just under the armpits, "You've never been to South Korea?"

"I have, but years ago. Back then, there was only Gimpo International."

"Gimpo is mostly only used for domestic flights now, and shuttles to China, Japan, and Taiwan. We'll be flying to China from Gimpo."

Mugsy peeked out the cabin window again, "I can see why they changed their domestic flights to this airport. It's very impressive."

"This airport is one of the largest and busiest airports in the world," replied Scipio, as both men donned the t-shirts. "For the last seven years, it was rated the best airport worldwide by an international airport council."

Mugsy looked at himself in a mirror, "You know something Scipio … you're just a regular fount of knowledge."

"You'd be surprised what you can learn from the in-flight magazine."

"Well then sage, explain to me again how these overly-tight, uncomfortable t-shirts are gonna help us smuggle your secret weapons past airport security?"

Scipio walked over and carefully slipped what looked like 8" steel blades with no handles, one into each of Mugsy's side compartments.

"Hang your arms normally."

Mugsy complied looking into the mirror, "Not bad, I can barely see them already without even putting my shirt on."

Scipio slipped identical blades into his side compartments then handed Mugsy a buttoned shirt and jacket before putting on his own.

"To answer the question you were about to ask, the blades are made of zirconium dioxide, also known as zirconia … a ceramic. They're produced by dry pressing zirconia powder and firing them through solid-state sintering. The resulting blade is sharpened by grinding the edges with a diamond-dust coated grinding wheel. Zirconia happens to rank 8.5 on the Mohs mineral hardness scale. To compare, hardened steel ranks 7.5 to 8, and diamond ranks 10, so the very hard edge never needs to be sharpened.

"As you're well aware, ceramics aren't seen by conventional metal detectors."

"So that's it? That's all it takes to sneak a knife past metal detectors?"

Scipio finished buttoning his shirt and slipped his arms into his jacket. Mugsy noticed the shirt Scipio handed him was white and the jacket blue, but he was wearing all black.

After adjusting his sleeves then nodding approval to himself, Scipio finally replied, "Not exactly. Ceramic blades may be detected by extremely high frequency scanners, like millimeter wave scanners and X-ray backscatter scanners, hence the need to conceal the blades as close to the sides of our bodies as possible.

"Remember to walk quickly through the body scanner, but not too quickly or they'll make you walk through it again."

Mugsy picked up one of two pens on the table and wiggled it, "What about these … do they explode?"

"No, they don't explode. They're normal metal-cased Parker pens, but with the addition of poison needles that deploy from the tip. Click to write, or simply twist the upper part of the shell to kill."

Mugsy examined the pen then clicked it a few times, "And where do we carry these?"

Scipio straightened the lapel on Mugsy's jacket before picking some lint from it, "Even in tense circumstances, one should never let oneself go."

He stepped back and demonstrated holding the pen tightly in his closed fist, "We carry the pens in our hands like so. When walking through the scanner, make sure to move the hand with the pen in it faster than your body passes through. Just swing your arm in front of you.

"The scanners use a metal ratio that sets off the alarm. In other words, once the scanner detects a certain percentage or ratio of metal on a person, the alarm is sounded. So, the trick is to try and pass the pen through the scanner's ratio-analyzing software slightly before the rest of you passes through, thus keeping your metal ratio low."

"And what happens if the alarm does sound?"

"Then you calmly hand them the pen in your hand and hope they don't twist the top."

"And what about the blades?"

"We carry them on our sides because, in a pat down, security officers tend not to want to overly touch the sweaty armpits of strangers for eight-hour shifts."

Mugsy grabbed their luggage, one small bag each, and both men started towards *Peregrine*'s main cabin.

"I won't ask how you know so much about sneaking weapons through airport metal detectors. I'll just assume that's part of Delta

Force's advanced training program."

Scipio smiled, "Not exactly, but you'd also be surprised what you can learn on YouTube nowadays."

Duke O'Rourke and Charger Miller stepped out of the cockpit. The men shook hands.

"Make sure you don't miss the return flight," O'Rourke called down as they descended the airstairs. "We don't give discounts to one-way passengers on this airline."

A grey Hyundai sedan was waiting for them at the bottom of the stairs. Out of it, a middle-aged, average-sized Korean dressed in a dark suit approached them. He appeared to be unsure of whom to address and finally settled on Mugsy.

He spoke in Korean-accented English, "Captain Ricci?"

"I'm Ricci."

The man extended his hand to Mugsy first and then Scipio, "I am Soryeong Han of the Presidential Security Service, of the Republic of Korea. Welcome to Seoul gentlemen."

The Soryeong, equivalent to a U.S. Army major, held his arm out, "Please, Daeryeong Cho has made arrangements for you at a hotel downtown. I will take you there."

"Actually, our firm already made reservations for us at another hotel, the Foster Lafayette."

Both men noticed the Soryeong's face flush. His tone became stern, "Daeryeong Cho instructed me to take you to the hotel he—"

"If it's a problem, we'll just catch a cab, but we're going to the Foster Lafayette. Tell Cho he can reach us there."

Mugsy and Scipio walked past the confused man and made it a few feet before he turned and called to them, "Captain, one moment please. I ... will take you to your hotel, but Daeryeong Cho requests your presence this afternoon, at the Song Jook Heon restaurant."

"Song Jook Heon, okay, what time?"

"He asks if 1:30 PM would be convenient."

Mugsy looked at Scipio who just shrugged his shoulders slightly.

"You can tell Cho that we would be happy to meet him at Song Jook Heon at one-thirty. That is, if we can get through customs and to our hotel with time enough to get there."

"Daeryeong Cho sent me here to ensure that you will not have to go through customs. I assume neither of you are carrying any weapons?"

Scipio pulled his pen out and clicked it, "Just my pen and my smile and I only use the latter to slay the ladies."

Han looked shocked until Scipio winked. He let out a relieved chuckle.

The men slipped into the back seat while Han went to the trunk to place their luggage inside.

Mugsy shot an irritated glance at Scipio, "Just your pen and your smile?"

Scipio beamed, "Our friend Han looked like he was gonna have an ulcer when we said we weren't following Cho's instructions to the letter. The Colonel must be a scary character when he's disobeyed. I wonder what he'd do if he was crossed. In any case, I just wanted to lighten the air a bit. No need in our making enemies in both Koreas."

* * * * *

Daeryeong Cho Jung-woo entered the lavish State Reception House. It was located on the magnificent grounds of the executive office and official residence of the South Korean head of state, the President of the Republic of Korea.

Instantly, Soryeong Han marched over and snapped to attention, "Daeryeong!"

Cho merely looked around with his hands folded behind his back, "Have you followed my instructions?"

"Yes, sir, I have, but with one exception."

"Exception …?"

The officer blinked nervously, "Yes, sir, per your orders, I personally drove to the airport to pick up the Americans, but they insisted on being taken to a hotel of their choice."

"Insisted … which hotel?"

"The Foster Lafayette. It is located—"

"I know where it is located, Han, and what of our meeting arrangements?"

"Captain Ricci said that he and the other gentleman would be happy to meet you at the restaurant you requested, Song Jook Heon at 1:30 PM."

"Very good. Arrange my transportation to Song Jook Heon. Have a car waiting for me outside in 15 minutes. You will drive and wait for me while I meet with the Americans."

Han snapped to attention again, "Yes, sir."

"And Han, as I said, you are to tell no one about these men, absolutely no one, do you understand?"

"Understood, Sir!"

CHAPTER 8

SONG JOOK HEON RESTAURANT
SEOUL, SOUTH KOREA
2:00 PM (LOCAL), MONDAY, MAY 20, 2013

Sitting around a table covered with small white bowls filled with an assortment of *hanjeongsik* dishes were Colonel Cho, Mugsy Ricci, and Scipio. Many of the bowls were empty or near empty.

Cho used chopsticks to move a succulent chunk of steamed beef from a ring-shaped metal tureen to his plate. He did the same with the wide noodles underneath the beef chunks.

"This is delicious," remarked Mugsy, "though I'm not exactly sure what it is."

"You have grilled abalone with pan-fried ginkgo berries, duck patties with a hint of ginger, and codfish dumplings with egg white foam, on your plate," replied Cho.

"Well, it's all exquisite, Colonel, my compliments to the chef."

"I shall pass your compliments onto him."

"And you, Mr. Scipio, have you enjoyed your meal?"

"It's just Scipio, Colonel, and yes, I have. I've always enjoyed hanjeongsik."

"Hand-jong-what?" inquired Mugsy.

"*Han-jeong-sik* is how it is pronounced, Captain. It means traditional Korean food. It describes both the dishes themselves and the way they are served all at once."

"Well, I can tell you that even my Italian grandmother would be proud of this spread," replied Mugsy. "There has to be thirty bowls on this table."

"Your grandmother enjoys Korean food?"

Scipio hid a chuckle behind his napkin, "No, Colonel, I doubt Captain Ricci's grandmother ever tasted Korean food. He was referring to the fact that Italians are known for serving multiple dishes for dinner."

"Ah, I see."

"I'm sure there would be a revolt if the North Koreans ever discovered this hanjeongsik," replied Mugsy.

Colonel Cho motioned to the waiter standing behind him. He said something in Korean before the man took off, "Actually, Captain, hanjeongsik is not exclusive to South Korea."

He sipped his tea before continuing, "Korean cuisine is one of the things that have remained the same after the split of our country. There are several restaurants in Pyongyang that serve excellent hanjeongsik. Unfortunately for our northern cousins, only tourists get to enjoy it there."

"Have you?" asked Scipio as he blew on his tea.

"Have I what … enjoyed hanjeongsik in Pyongyang?"

Scipio only stared back over his cup.

"Yes, as a matter of fact I have. In 2005, I was sent to check on the safety of our citizens after the Hyundai Company came to an agreement with the North Korean government to open up more areas to tourism."

"I see," replied Scipio setting his cup back down.

Two waiters walked over and removed the bowls on the table, followed by a third who set rice down and a variety of *jeotgal* and *jangahjji* (salted fish eggs and anchovies). All three men indulged.

Mugsy finally pushed back from the table rubbing his stomach,

"That was absolutely delicious."

Colonel Cho spoke into the headwaiter's ear. Instantly, he and the other waiters removed everything from the table and cleaned it. A fresh pot of tea and cups were then placed, before the entire restaurant staff disappeared. It was then Scipio noticed, though there were other customers dining when they first arrived, the restaurant was now completely empty, except for them.

Colonel Cho filled each of their cups, "All arrangements have now been made. Friday, our flight departs at 8:10 AM. I will send a car for you at 6 AM. Please make sure to pack your luggage as any tourist would."

"And by that you mean?" asked Mugsy.

"That means with no secret compartments or weapons hidden inside. I suspect the Chinese will be quite thorough in checking your bags, especially in that part of China, so close to North Korea."

"But not your luggage?"

Cho grinned, "They will certainly check my luggage too, but perhaps not with the same attention to detail."

"What will we do for weapons?" asked Scipio.

Cho's grin remained, "We will not carry any weapons with us."

Mugsy pressed, "But once we're on the ground in China, can't you make arrangements for us to get weapons?"

Cho took time to sip his tea, "Gentlemen, the less attention we attract in China, the better. Right now, the only communications I've had with people there has been in line with our cover. Remember, we are travailing under the guise of a group based in Thailand interested in possibly helping some North Koreans defect. Asking for weapons would cause unnecessary suspicion."

"Unnecessary? What about your idea with the broker, to compel him to help us? How are we supposed to *compel* him without weapons?"

Cho finished his tea then looked at his watch, "Captain, I said we would carry no weapons, nor ask for any, but that does not mean we will not have any weapons. Now, I am afraid I am going to be late for my workout, unless I leave now. Would you like to accompany me?"

"We would, but not today," replied Scipio, jumping in. Mugsy noticed.

"Very well, how about Wednesday? It will be the last time I will work out before we leave."

Scipio glanced at Mugsy, who replied for them, "Wednesday is fine.

"Very good, the Colonel stood. "I will have a car meet you at your hotel at 1:30. Do you have transportation back to your hotel now?"

"We do," replied Mugsy. "Thank you, Colonel."

Colonel Cho bowed slightly then turned for the door. Mugsy waited for him to leave before raising his brow at Scipio, "What was that all about? Why couldn't we make it today?"

"Because I want to check something first," Scipio motioned to the waiter. "Could you call us a taxi, please?"

The man nodded and headed for the hostess stand.

Mugsy scooped more rice and anchovies onto his plate, "Where are we going?"

"Back to the hotel."

"This food was really incredible. Can we get Korean food like this back in the States?"

"I know of a few places in New York, but haven't found any in Vegas yet … not this authentic."

Mugsy scraped the rest of what was on his plate onto a spoon and ate it, "You obviously picked up on something I didn't."

Scipio leaned in and spoke softly, "I'm not sure, but I think the good Colonel was lying about his reason for being in Pyongyang."

"What makes you think so?"

"I remember reading something about that agreement Hyundai worked out with the North Koreans back in '05. It was all about opening a couple of areas to tourism. As I recall, one of those areas was Baekdu Mountain and the other was Kaesong."

"So?"

"Well, neither is anywhere near Pyongyang. Baekdu Mountain is on the northern border with China and Kaesong is over 80 miles away, I think."

"80 miles isn't that far. He could have driven that and back in one day."

"It's not just the distance. In North Korea, visitors aren't allowed to travel outside their designated tour areas without North Korean guides. Somehow, I find it very doubtful that a South Korean Colonel was given permission to travel to Kaesong, let alone Pyongyang.

When we get back to the hotel, I'll contact Karla. If anyone can find out about it, it's her."

Mugsy nodded, "And what if he is lying, where does that leave us?"

Scipio finished the tea in his cup, "It leaves us with a South Korean Colonel that either lied about eating in Pyongyang, or lied about his reason for being in Pyongyang in the first place. Then the question I have is, if he's lying, do we go on this mission with him?"

Mugsy stood up and stretched, "Before I answer that, I'd like to do a little research of my own, on Colonel Cho's past ... see if there's any North Korean connection. I'll say this though, without smoking-gun evidence that he's playing for the other side, we'll have to go."

He looked around the restaurant, "This was an excellent place. I'd like to take Michelle here when we get back."

Scipio poured some more tea and handed a cup to Mugsy, before holding his up, "Here's to getting back."

CHAPTER 9

MAIN RESIDENCE
ESTANCIA DE NIRO
HENDERSON, NEVADA
8:00 PM (LOCAL), TUESDAY, MAY 21, 2013

Michelle Wang and Cris De Niro sat on the sweeping back porch of De Niro's home watching his sons, Richard and Louis toast marshmallows over a large fire pit. Richard walked over and held a stick out to Michelle, while Louis did the same to his dad. The marshmallows on both were still aflame.

William Brett, De Niro's former butler, now his personal assistant hurried over with two plates and forks.

"Master Richard, give that here, please!"

The old British gentleman quickly took the sticks and waved them about until the flames went out. Then, using one of the forks, he slid the marshmallows off the end of them and onto the plates.

Shaking his head in dissatisfaction, he placed the plates down in front of Michelle and De Niro.

"I apologize. They appear to be rather burnt."

"William, they're supposed to be eaten off the stick," cried Richard.

"A gentleman does not hand a lady a stick with a blazing confectionary impaled on it."

"Actually, William, Richard is correct," said De Niro. "It's one of those quirky American customs."

"And what quirky American custom would that be, Sir, the custom of setting a lady's face on fire?"

Everyone laughed except William.

Michelle forked the blackened marshmallow into her mouth, "Mmm … I haven't had a toasted marshmallow in forever. Thank you Richard, and thank you William for dousing the flame."

"Not at all, Madam."

Louis came running over with three more sticks, each with burning marshmallows on them. He handed one to his brother and one to William, "Here William … try one."

William watched as the boys blew theirs out before devouring it right from the stick. He did his best to mimic them.

"Well, what do you think," asked Richard as he took the bare stick from him.

"It is actually quite tasty, though I don't see the reason why they must be eaten off of a stick.

"Can I get anyone anything else? If not, I would like Master Richard and Master Louis to follow me back inside the house so that they may finish their homework."

"Good idea," replied De Niro. "Boys, say goodnight to Michelle."

"Dad, you don't need to tell us to say goodnight to people anymore," replied Richard.

Both boys said, "Goodnight Michelle," in unison.

"Goodnight boys."

She watched them disappear into the house.

De Niro held a small coffee pot up, "Would you like some? It's decaf."

"Yes, please."

He poured two cups and handed one to her.

She sipped it gazing out to the resort-sized pool. The water looked like glass, with lights dancing on the surface.

De Niro remained quiet. He knew she had something on her mind, but decided not to ask. After a few minutes of silence, Michelle turned back to him, "Cris, may I ask you something?"

"Of course."

"It's of a personal nature."

De Niro sipped his coffee then set the cup down on a saucer, "Michelle, you're soon to be my sister-in-law. If you haven't already noticed, Italian families are close-knit. You can ask me anything."

She smiled, and moved closer to him, "Chinese families are close knit too, but not in the same way. In fact, I wouldn't ask anyone in my family what I'm about to ask you."

"Uh-oh," De Niro teased, hoping to lighten the moment. Instead, Michelle's face became serious.

"When you and Lisa had Richard … I mean, when you two decided to have kids … if you did decide … I mean if it was a conscious decision …," she paused. "I'm not making sense."

"Take your time."

She sipped her coffee and tried again, "I guess what I'm trying to ask is, did you plan to have Richard?"

"You mean did we plan to have a baby, when we made Richard? You can't really plan to have a particular child, you know."

Michelle noticed his smile and finally returned one, "I think I know at least that much about making children. Yes, that's what I meant."

"Well then, you know more than we did. I remember talking about kids on our very first date. I told Lisa I wanted to have four kids because the family I grew up next to had four. I thought it was so cool how it was always like a party when they were together."

"Four … what did Lisa say?"

"She blew my mind. She said, 'Me too, I've always wanted to have four kids.'"

"Really … wow!"

"Wow is right. I didn't think women nowadays would want that many kids, let alone a career-minded woman like Lisa. But, that's what she said."

"Did you have kids right away, after you were married?"

"No, we married quickly. I proposed to Lisa one month to the day after I met her, and we were married three months later, but then we waited almost two years to have Richard."

"So you *did* plan to have him?"

"Actually, if you would've talked to Lisa, from the moment she took one of those home birth control tests and found out she was pregnant she was convinced we were having a daughter. She even picked out her name, Moriah, and wrote a lullaby about her."

"Moriah … such a pretty name."

De Niro nodded, "And the lullaby was so beautiful." He started to laugh, "I'll never forget what she said the moment she saw Richard for the first time on the ultrasound. As soon as they touched that wand to her belly, Lisa's jaw hit the floor. She said, 'Cris, why does our daughter have testicles?'"

Both of them laughed.

De Niro watched as Michelle's laughter turned to tears. He reached across and put his hand on her knee, "Michelle, what's the matter?"

She wiped the tears from her eyes, "I don't know why this keeps happening to me lately. I go from laughter to tears and back again."

De Niro sat back, "You're pregnant."

She nodded, "I only found out the day Mugsy left."

De Niro hugged her, "That's wonderful."

She sniffled then giggled, "I know you're not supposed to say anything until you're 12 weeks along, but this mission Mugsy went on just turned me upside down. I don't want to tell my parents. In fact, I don't want anyone else to know except you for now. Is that okay?"

"Of course it's okay. And if there's anything I can do for you … anything you need …?"

"Right now, all I need is for Mugsy to come home safely … so I can give him a heart attack with the news."

They stared at each other a quiet moment before laughing.

CHAPTER 10

MEIKAKUKAI SEOUL DOJO
SEODAEMUNGU
SEOUL, SOUTH KOREA
2:00 PM (LOCAL), WEDNESDAY, MAY 22, 2013

Mugsy Ricci and Scipio stepped out of the back of a dark blue Mercedes-Benz W220 sedan driven by Soryeong Han of the Presidential Security Service. Cho told Han to use one of the W220s assigned to the presidential motorcade to pick them up, in order to minimize any government tie-in with the Americans. He also reminded the Soryeong not to wear his uniform, so Han was wearing a black suit, with a white buttoned shirt and black tie. Scipio's crack that he looked like a chauffeur somehow flattered Han, which amused the small man dressed in black.

The alternative would have been for them to be picked up in a Chevrolet Tahoe, Suburban, or Ford Excursion, also part of the presidential motorcade, but Cho thought those vehicles were more readily identified as official vehicles than was the Benz. Besides, for some reason Han didn't understand, it appeared that Daeryeong Cho wanted to impress the Americans.

The *dojang*, Korean for martial arts school was nondescript from the outside. A one-story red brick front wall was all that faced the street, with large black iron gates in the middle and a black garage door at one end. There was no signage anywhere. Over the top of the wall, the branches of trees protruded and hung down producing the effect of a green canopy.

Han kept the motor running as he stepped out of the car and opened the gate revealing cement stairs inside that led up to a small atrium.

"Please, the Daeryeong is waiting for you inside the dojang. Proceed up the stairs. The dojang is through the doors to the right. I will park the car in the garage."

Mugsy and Scipio stepped inside the gate, but Scipio stopped to watch the Han hurry back to the car and head down to the garage.

"Judging from our boy Han's nervousness, I'd say Cho definitely runs a tight ship … tight enough to bounce a dime off of."

Mugsy checked his watch, "Well, even though we kept him waiting, our boy Han got us here on time. Although I think he gave some pedestrians back there heart attacks with the way he was zooming up and down these narrow streets.

"And why again did we keep him waiting?"

Scipio shrugged, "Just to see how he'd react."

"So, what exactly did you get out of the man driving like a maniac to get us here on time? I mean, other than the fact we've confirmed Cho doesn't like to be kept waiting."

"Two things come to mind … that Cho is a control freak, and that he obviously wanted us here. Something tells me we're in for more than pre-mission bonding from a group workout."

Mugsy raised his brow, "I keep wondering how much of this you learned in Delta and how much comes from your twisted thought processes."

Scipio's eyes sparkled with amusement, "That's funny, so do I."

Mugsy led them slowly up the stairs, "So tell me, now that we know Cho was lying, either about his reason for being in Pyongyang, or for ever being there in the first place, how should we proceed?"

"Cautiously."

Mugsy stopped and turned, "Cautiously … that's your expert opinion, is it?"

Scipio smiled.

"I wish Karla would've been able to come up with more about the Colonel's background. According to the records she could find, it seems like he was born 10 years ago with the rank of *daewi*, a South Korean captain."

"That bothers me."

"One thing we know is he's been a decorated officer attached to the Presidential Security Service, now protecting his third president."

"That doesn't explain why he lied to us."

"It doesn't, but it gives him points, in my book."

"I think you just like him because he picked that restaurant."

Mugsy looked at his watch again, "Picked and paid. Well, let's not keep Cho waiting any longer or our boy Han might lose a finger."

They opened an ordinary wooden door and stood before a large, plainly painted room with a light blue mat that covered the entire floor. There was no furniture in sight and nothing was hanging on the walls.

Han was already in the room standing without shoes. Mugsy and Scipio mimicked him and removed theirs.

Cho appeared from an office. He was holding two white *gis* and wearing an identical one, the familiar uniform of a martial artist. His had a black belt tied at the waist.

"Welcome gentleman."

A small man followed him out of the office. He was older and wearing round spectacles, and he was also wearing a white gi with a black belt tied around his waist.

"It is my honor to introduce Grand Master, *Sa Boo Nim* Nobuo Maekawa. Sa Boo Nim Maekawa is the founder of Meikaku-kai and the owner of this dojang."

Master Maekawa bowed deeply with his hand covering his fist. Mugsy and Scipio reciprocated.

"Sa Boo Nim has graciously allowed us the exclusive use of his dojang for the afternoon."

Scipio bowed again and spoke in Japanese, "Your generosity is most appreciated, Teacher. Your noble name is well known in the martial arts circles of the United States, as it is throughout the world."

Master Maekawa bowed and answered in Japanese, "You are most welcome in my dojo." He switched to English, "Gentleman, please enjoy your workout."

Colonel Cho handed them the gis, "I believe these will fit you."

Mugsy took his but Scipio declined, "Most kind Colonel, but I took the liberty of bringing my own."

Cho squinted, "Very well. You may change in the next room."

Scipio preceded Mugsy into the small changing room. As soon as the door was closed Mugsy took the bag Scipio was carrying from his hand, "Do you mind?"

He pulled a black Kung Fu uniform out and gave a queer look, "This is yours?"

Scipio took the clothes from him and started changing into it, "Of course it's mine." He pulled a receipt from his pocket, "See, I just bought it this morning … *Bruce Lee's Famous Classic Kung Fu Uniform*. Cost me the equivalent of $90 American.

Mugsy shook his head and laughed.

"When I looked up the address for our workout, I saw it was a dojang and I remembered that the Cho was a martial arts expert."

"So you bought the gi just to piss him off."

Scipio winked.

"You know he's probably gonna kick both of our asses, but yours twice for your little taunt."

They finished dressing. Mugsy had trouble tying the white belt Cho gave him around his waist, so Scipio did it for him. Mugsy watched how he did it, "So, I see you do know about this chop suey stuff. The martial arts we were taught at SEAL school was more straight forward. It's called S.C.A.R.S. or *Special Combat Aggressive Reactionary Systems*. It's a mixed martial arts fighting system created by Jerry L. Peterson, based in part on his background in San Soo kung fu and from his personal experiences in the Vietnam War. How about you?"

Scipio winked, "I studied karate just long enough to know how to tie the belt."

Mugsy examined him, "Where's your belt?"

"Practitioners of Chinese Kung Fu don't use them for ranking and I'm personally from the Bruce Lee school of '... *belts are only good for holding your pants up.'* As you can see, my pants are staying up fine."

The two exited the changing room. They found Cho and Master Maekawa already sparring, exchanging punches and blocks with blurring speed. As soon as he saw Mugsy and Scipio, Cho stepped back and bowed to the Sa Boo Nim, covering his fist.

"Please gentlemen, join us on the mat for some stretching."

For the next 15 minutes the men stretched, with Mugsy following Cho's lead and Scipio off in a corner performing his own exercises.

Cho called them to attention with a loud clapping of his hands, "Captain, I know you were a member of that elite American fighting unit, the Navy SEALs. I would consider it an honor if you would exhibit some of their close quarters, hand-to-hand fighting skills."

Scipio whispered into his ear, "Remember, the only easy day was yesterday." It was one of the Navy SEALs mottos.

Mugsy shot him a look as he stepped into the middle of the mat. Cho faced him. The two men bowed before Master Maekawa sliced his hand between them and shouted, "Hajime!"

Mugsy assumed a traditional fighting stance while Cho remained still. Mugsy began moving to his right before suddenly charging at the smaller man.

Cho stepped back the moment Mugsy reached him, preventing him from being grabbed. Mugsy began throwing punches - first a left that Cho ducked under, then a right uppercut that he blocked, and then a roundhouse back-of-the-fist that he dodged by leaning back.

Mugsy attempted another punch that Cho blocked before bringing his knee up which Cho evaded, followed by a side kick that left a mark in the wall behind the Colonel.

"Sorry about that."

Mugsy backed up into the center of the mat. Cho glanced at the mark in the wall before calmly following him. He stared at Mugsy with cold eyes.

Mugsy moved his chin, cracking his neck, before throwing another jab. This time Cho caught his fist and stopped the blow before twisting it, causing Mugsy to twist with it and lose his balance.

Cho walked calmly to his right keeping Mugsy's twisted fist in his hand. He helplessly had to turn with him, stumbling repeatedly as he did.

Cho eventually stopped walking. He looked down at Mugsy and smiled in an almost compassionate way while Mugsy was snorting in pain.

Master Maekawa called out to Cho in Korean. Cho looked back down at Mugsy before twisting his fist in the opposite direction, forcing him to crouch in the opposite direction. He finished him off by grabbing the back of Mugsy's head and propelling him into a somersault using his twisted arm as the fulcrum.

Mugsy ended up flat on his back. He grabbed his shoulder.

"Yame!" cried Master Maekawa.

Cho looked down at him, "Have I hurt you?"

"Nothing a bottle of aspirin and bag of ice won't fix."

Cho offered his hand. Mugsy took it with his good arm and got to his feet.

"I did not realize the SEALs hand-to-hand fighting techniques are so … inferior. Forgive me."

Scipio looked on while standing next to Han who looked delighted with the outcome, so far.

"Han, can I ask you something? Has the Colonel ever lost when sparring?"

Han chuckled, "I have never seen Daeryeong Cho lose at anything."

"I see."

Cho walked over, "Perhaps the U.S. Army's special forces are more capable than the Navy's. What do you say, Scipio … shall we give it a go?"

Mugsy wandered over, still holding his arm, and whispered into Scipio's ear, "Remember to be all you can be."

"Hoo-ah," Scipio whispered back, before walking to the center of the room.

Cho and Scipio bowed to each other and once again, Master Maekawa dropped his arm between them and shouted, "Hajime!"

Neither man took a fighting stance. Instead, they stared and began circling one another.

This time it was Cho who engaged with a flurry of punches. Each one was either dodged or blocked by Scipio.

They traded punches and kicks, blocks and dodges, neither gaining the advantage of the other for almost 10 minutes until Cho finally caught one of Scipio's punches. He twisted Scipio's fist the same way he twisted Mugsy's.

Cho grinned at grimacing Scipio, "It seems your Army is as inferior as your Navy."

"Not quite," replied Scipio as he brought his leg up and kicked the back of Cho's knee sending him tumbling to the ground.

Scipio stood over him, "I always believed we're more resourceful in the Army." He held his hand out to help Cho up.

Cho took his hand, but as soon as he got to his feet, he didn't release it. Instead, he tugged on Scipio's arm pulling him off balance and then swung his other arm around until his forearm was pressing against Scipio's neck. Cho pressed until he felt Scipio losing his balance and stopped there.

"It seems I have the advantage."

"Not quite, Colonel." Scipio was squeezing Cho's testicles. Cho hadn't even noticed Scipio's hand was there until he felt the pressure.

"We're also known for fighting dirtier than our Navy counterparts."

Cho carefully removed his arm from under Scipio's chin. In turn, Scipio released his testicles.

Master Maekawa walked over with a big smile on his face. He spoke in very broken English, "I call that … tie!"

Cho's face reddened from either embarrassment or anger, Scipio couldn't tell which. Both men were covered in sweat.

"Let's continue, shall we?"

Scipio held up his hands, "Now, Colonel, I'd love to, but don't you think we should save some for the enemy?"

Cho stared back a moment with an intense gaze before softening.

He nodded, "We shall save the rest for the enemy."

Cho bowed to both men before following Master Maekawa into the office. Han nodded to Scipio before doing the same.

Mugsy was still rubbing his shoulder as he walked over, "The old ball grab … Bruce would've been proud."

"He should be proud. I learned it from him from *Fists of Fury*."

Mugsy laughed as they headed to the changing room, "And here I thought that was more elite Delta training you received. Come to think of it, I remember that fight scene. Why didn't I think of that when he was tearing my arm out of its socket? Just reach up and grab him by his balls."

Han waited for them to change and come back out into the main room, "The Daeryeong has already left. He sends his apologies for not saying goodbye, but he had a pressing matter to attend to. I have orders to take you back to your hotel, if that is where you wish to go."

Mugsy swung his arm around in a windmill motion, "That is where I wish to go. I need to soak my shoulder."

"Han, if you don't mind, do you know of any place where I can get a massage?"

"I do. I can drop you there first before taking Captain Ricci to the hotel, if you wish."

"I wish. Don't tell the Colonel, but I'm sore all over."

Han beamed a Cheshire cat smile as he led them out.

They all bowed goodbye to Master Maekawa before Scipio asked, "What's with the smile, Han?"

"I probably shouldn't share this with you. Do you know what the Daeryeong's pressing matter was? I heard him calling for a massage too."

CHAPTER 11

TERMINAL 2
SHENYANG TAOXIAN INTERNATIONAL AIRPORT
TAOXIAN TOWNSHIP, DONGLING DISTRICT
SHENYANG, LIAONING PROVINCE
CHINA
9:15 AM (LOCAL), FRIDAY, MAY 24, 2013

The customs officer took the passport from Scipio. He had already checked Colonel Cho's and Mugsy Ricci's.

The officer—wearing a light blue uniform shirt with a number tag over his left breast pocket—showed no emotion as he examined the Thai passport. He looked up at Scipio twice before finally allowing a soft smile and speaking in Chinese-accented Thai, "Welcome to Shenyang."

Scipio bowed his head and replied in Thai, "Thank you."

The small man dressed in black joined the others, "Well, that was easy."

"I was telling Cho exactly the same thing," replied Mugsy. "In fact, getting through LAX's customs is relatively barbarous compared to that experience. I almost felt like the customs officer rushed me through."

"That is probably because he does not speak very good Thai. Chinese customs officers are known for rushing Americans and other foreigners through customs just so they don't have to speak their languages too much."

"What about Koreans?" asked Mugsy.

"Depends on whether you are North or South Korean. If from the South they check your toothpaste. If from the North, they deport you back, where you are shot and your family spends the rest of their lives in a detention camp."

Cho let Mugsy's brow rise before winking at him.

Cho checked his watch and started walking, "Come. We need to get our bags and then take a taxi to the Shenyang North Railway Station."

"I thought you said on the plane that we're traveling to Ji'an by bus?" asked Scipio.

"We are. The square in front of the train station is the long distance express bus station. There are buses leaving there about every hour for Tonghua. From Tonghua, the bus schedules to Ji'an aren't quite as regular."

"How long will it take us to get to Tonghua?"

"About 4 hours."

"Why not just take the train to Tonghua," asked Mugsy. "I seem to remember when I checked the rail schedules that there's a train that travels from here to there."

"There is, but it takes seven to eight hours to get there by train."

"Crazy country," replied Mugsy, "you get places faster by bus than train."

"Then we should reach Ji'an later this afternoon or evening," replied Scipio.

"That will depend on which bus we can catch in Tonghua for Ji'an, but yes, the travel time between the two by bus is only about two hours."

The men retrieved their bags from the carousel. Cho led them out of the terminal and hailed a cab.

The 16-mile trip to the railway station took 34 minutes. No one spoke in the cab.

The taxi let them out on the curb in front of the massive building.

"Now that's what I call a train station," Mugsy announced to no one in particular. "In fact, that must be the mother of all train stations."

Cho pointed, "The bus station is over there." He began walking.

Scipio grabbed Mugsy's arm and spoke low, "Do you get the feeling our good colonel has been here before?"

"It certainly seems like he knows his way around," Mugsy mumbled back.

The three made their way to the bus station where Cho purchased the tickets for all of them. He handed one to each man.

"Were they expensive?" asked Mugsy.

"Seventy-eight Chinese Yuan."

Scipio spoke into his Big-Brutha™ cell phone, "How much is 78 Chinese yuan in dollars?"

A female voice sounding remarkably like the computer voice from *Star Trek*'s Starship Enterprise answered almost instantly, "Seventy-eight Chinese Yuan equals twelve dollars and sixty-nine cents."

Mugsy dug his wallet out of his pocket.

"Put your money away, Captain," replied Cho with a hint of annoyance. "I have been supplied with quite enough for all of our needs on this mission."

Cho checked his watch, "If the ticket agent is correct, the next bus for Tonghua will depart in about 15 minutes."

"Look, there's a Mickey-D's over there," said Mugsy.

"A what?" confused, Cho looked in the direction Scipio was pointing."

"A McDonald's."

Light rain started to fall from the grey sky.

Scipio motioned to Mugsy, "Come on, I can use a cup of coffee and an Egg McMuffin®. Can we get anything for you, Colonel?"

"Nothing, thank you, just please don't be late getting back here. They will not hold the bus if you're late."

"Not a problem. Maybe we can find a place that sells umbrellas."

Scipio and Mugsy started jogging in the direction of the double golden arches. Once inside and on the line, Scipio turned to Mugsy, "Curiouser and curiouser …."

"Now your quoting lines from *Alice in Wonderland*? I must say Scipio, your completely altering my perception of a Delta Force operator."

Scipio grinned, "And the fact you knew that was a line from *Alice in Wonderland* is completely altering my perception of a SEAL."

Mugsy shook his head, "Mind telling me what's curiouser and curiouser, other than the fact we're on a Mickey-D's line in northeastern China?"

Scipio looked around the packed restaurant, "They might consider us white devils but they sure like our Big Macs® and Chicken McNuggets®."

Mugsy remained silent waiting for an answer.

"Mugs, did you notice anything peculiar when Cho paid for our tickets? Or what we haven't done yet?"

"Other than the fact he paid for us and wouldn't accept any money, no, not really. Why? What should I have noticed?"

Scipio reached the counter. The young lady behind the counter said, "Welcome to McDonalds, May I help you?" in Mandarin.

Scipio ordered for both men then pulled his wallet out. He turned to Mugsy, "Now watch closely."

He handed the lady a Visa® card. The young lady looked at the card closely before finally swiping it and handing it back.

"Okay," replied Mugsy, "So now you paid for me. This mission isn't costing me very much."

"Did you notice how she looked at the card?"

"Yeah, like she never saw one before."

"That's because about 95% of all purchases are made with debit cards or cash in China. Only a chain like McDonalds or bigger stores would even accept a credit card."

"I see, but I don't see the tie-in with Cho paying for our tickets. I did notice enough to see that he paid in cash."

"Exactly, but in what currency?"

Mugsy thought about it then his expression turned serious, "Wait a minute, he paid in Chinese Yuan."

"Exact-a-mundo, and what haven't we done yet?"

"We haven't exchanged our currency. So, where did he get the Chinese money?"

"Give the man a prize," quipped Scipio.

The young lady handed Scipio a bag and a cup holder with two cups of coffee in it. He dug in the bag and handed Mugsy a wrapped sandwich before taking one himself. They walked near the door and found it had begun to pour outside.

Scipio headed over to a small table, "I didn't see any umbrella salesmen on the way in so we might as well eat here, then make a mad dash back."

Both men ate in silence, deep in thought. They ate quickly but had to sip the hot coffee.

Scipio finally drained his cup, "I have to say … no matter where on earth you go, McDonald's coffee is always the best."

Mugsy threw away his half-drunk cup, "Maybe he was issued Chinese currency."

Scipio zipped his jacket and lifted the collar, "By whom?"

"I don't know … his boss, maybe?"

"Mugs, there are only two people that outrank Cho, one is the head of the Presidential Security Service and the other is President Park. I can't be certain, but I don't think the head of the PSS even knows Cho is on this assignment.

"President Park was pretty explicit when she explained how she wanted no direct connection between this mission and the South Korean government. I wouldn't be surprised if she was the only person that knows he's here with us.

"That leaves only President Park herself. She wouldn't have dispatched anyone to procure any, and somehow I can't picture her handing him Chinese Yuan in an envelope."

"Maybe he went somewhere and exchanged currency in Seoul before we left?"

"Not possible. It's illegal to exchange Chinese money abroad."

"Really?" Mugsy's face flushed. "You'd think I'd know that."

"Not particularly. Like Hercule Poirot says, 'It's just one of those insignificant facts that take up space in my little grey cells.'"

"What about currency conversion here?"

"It's a whole lot easier here. Most major currencies can be exchanged at banks, top-end stores, and some of the larger department stores, and the rate is about the same everywhere. So, no need to shop."

Mugsy nodded, "Which leaves us where with Cho?"

"The most logical answer is that he's been to China before. And unless he dug that money out of a piggy bank, he must have been here recently and probably still had it in his wallet."

"So far, we know the Colonel is lying about being in Pyongyang, or the reason for being in Pyongyang, and now we find out he's most likely recently been to China."

Scipio typed something into his phone, "I just sent Karla a back channel to see if she can find out if there was any official reason for Cho to be in China in the last six months."

Scipio pushed the door open, "Come on, we better get back."

* * * * *

Cho stood as close as he could to the small glass ticket booth, but his back was still being pelted with rain. He pulled his cell phone out and hit a speed dial button.

He spoke in Korean, "It's Cho. We're at the bus station in Shenyang. We should reach Ji'an tonight."

The voice on the other end of the line was an older male's and it was stern, "When and where will you cross?"

"I won't know until I deal with the broker."

"You must tell me as soon as possible. It will take time for the snipers to get to the location and take up position."

"I will do my best."

"If I can't get the snipers to the border crossing location in time, we will have to come up with another place."

"Please make sure to assign your best men. They can't miss, or we will have two very deadly, angry Americans to deal with."

"Of course, I will assign my best men, Daeryeong. But, I still do not understand why you will not let me send a company of infantry instead of a couple of snipers."

"Because these men are the elite of the American special forces. They can spot a company of infantry as well as I could, especially in the rural terrain near the border."

"I think you are giving them too much credit, Cho. I have never been impressed with the American military. If you take away their technology, they are weak soldiers. In any case, I will send two of North Korea's best snipers. The Americans will be dead the moment they are in their crosshairs.

"Contact me as soon as possible."

"Yes, Taejang."

Cho slipped the phone back into his pocket as he watched Mugsy and Scipio running back with jackets pulled over their heads.

The bus pulled up and opened its doors just as they reached him. He held his arm out, "After you, gentlemen."

CHAPTER 12

YANGTZE RIVER HOTEL
JI'AN, TONGHUA
JILIN, CHINA
9:00 PM (LOCAL), FRIDAY, MAY 24, 2013

There was a knock on the door.

Mugsy and Scipio decided to share a room with twin queen sized beds while Cho took a room across the hall. After checking in 90 minutes before, the three agreed to rendezvous in their room.

That is, once everyone had the opportunity for, as Scipio put it, "the three s's." Mugsy had to explain what the three s's were to Cho. Cho's only reaction was to nod and head to his room. Scipio remarked, "He must have had to go as badly as we did."

Dressed in a buttoned shirt, jeans, and hiking boots, Mugsy answered the door. Cho was standing with his hands behind his back. He was wearing a black blazer over a black buttoned shirt, black slacks and black rubber-soled shoes.

Mugsy extended his arm, "Good evening, Colonel."

Cho made eye contact but did not reply as he entered. He scanned the room, "Where is Scipio?"

The small man, also dressed in all black appeared from the bathroom, "Just finished the last s … shaving."

There was another knock at the door. Cho knit his brows, but Scipio raised his hands with palms out, "Not to fear, Colonel. I was hungry and assumed you gentlemen would be too, so I took the liberty of ordering room service.

Scipio opened the door.

A waiter in white jacket and gloves rolled in a cart and set it in the sitting area nearest the floor-to-ceiling windows. He reached up to draw the drapes open.

Cho barked an order in what Scipio identified as the *Gao* dialect of Mandarin Chinese. The waiter nodded and immediately shut the drapes, before opening and setting the table. He left the room for a moment and returned carrying a large tray with covered plates and a carafe on it. He set it up on the table and Mugsy tipped him on the way out.

Cho waited for the door to close before approaching the table. There were three silver plate covers positioned around it. In the center were condiments, a glass carafe filled with dark red wine, and three large bottles of *Tsingtao* beer.

Cho lifted the plate cover closest to him.

"That, I believe is the Tasmanian beef and grilled mushrooms with rosemary oil," replied Scipio.

Mugsy lifted one.

"That looks like the Wagyu beef and potato puree with white truffles," he lifted the cover in front of him, "and this is the grilled salmon with mushy peas." He walked over to the other table and lifted each cover in order, "And this is dessert … chocolate orange cake with yogurt sorbet, a brownie with pecan praline, and exotic fruit salad with strawberry crème tuille. The carafe is coffee. Please Colonel, you choose first."

Cho returned an incredulous look, "The Tasmanian beef is fine."

"How about you, Captain?"

"I guess the Wagyu beef will do," replied Mugsy, a bit tongue-in-cheek.

The three took their seats.

Cho cut and tasted his beef. His expression softened.

"How is it, Colonel?" asked Scipio.

"It is very good." Cho pointed with his knife, "What is in the carafe?"

"A decent Cabernet Sauvignon, to go with your beef."

Mugsy lifted the carafe and passed it under his nose a few times before holding it up, "Colonel?"

"Please."

Mugsy poured two glasses and handed one to Cho, while Scipio opened a bottle of beer.

"Cheers …."

The three tapped their drinks together in unison.

"To surviving the bus trip," joked Scipio.

"Especially after leaving Tonghua," Mugsy chimed in. "Those dense forests and hairpin turns along the peaks of the Changbai range will be in my nightmares for awhile."

"Ji'an is a very special place to Koreans," replied Cho, somberly. "Remnants of the Koguryo kingdom, which ruled the area now known as North and South Korea, are located here. There is a nearby site that contains archaeological remains of three early Korean cities, Wunü Mountain City, Guonei City, and Wandu Mountain City, along with forty tombs of Koguryo imperial and noble families. Wunü Mountain City was the first capital of Koguryo Kingdom."

The Colonel looked between the men, "The Koguryo kingdom was once a leading power in this part of the world. My ancestors were able to defy the mighty Chinese Tang dynasty for a time. North and South Koreans alike consider themselves descendants of Koguryo.

Cho took a long sip of his wine, "One wonders how Korean history would have played out had the kingdom withstood advances of a deadly alliance in the 7th century. The Chinese Tang and Korean Silla kingdoms, a kingdom to Koguryo's south, conquered Goguryeo. That ultimately led to China seizing control and establishing itself as the dominant force of this entire area."

The men ate in silence for awhile. From only eye contact, Mugsy and Scipio both realized they took away the same thing from Cho's history lesson. Though his loyalties lied to the south, the Colonel considered himself, above all, Korean, and he was fiercely proud of his heritage.

"Speaking of the Chinese, Colonel," Mugsy changed the subject, "Scipio and I were wondering if the amount of Chinese troops we saw coming into town was normal."

"There were large groups of PLA soldiers on the streets," Scipio added, referring to the Chinese People's Liberation Army (PLA). "I also thought I saw tanks and APCs moving near the river."

"That would indicate a mechanized infantry … perhaps as large as brigade strength," said Mugsy.

"You are correct Captain, the 190th Mechanized Infantry Brigade, to be precise. You gentlemen do not miss much.

"To answer your question, it is not normal. China placed military forces on heightened alert throughout this entire area following the recent threats from Pyongyang. When North Korea declared a 'state of war' and threatened to conduct missile attacks against your country and mine, the PLA stepped up military mobilization across the entire border region. Along with the troop and mechanized movements on the ground, they also had warplane activity. It started in mid-March and was supposed to conclude at the end of April."

"From the looks of it out there, they haven't quite concluded yet," replied Scipio.

"Just what we needed," added Mugsy. "The whole town looks like a giant PLA camp.

"You are afraid of the Chinese, Captain? You should be, but that brigade is not the worry, nor is the whole Chinese Army. I am familiar with their tactics, which gives us the advantage. No. Our worry does not begin until we cross the Yalu River."

"But is it even possible for us to cross, with so many Chinese troops guarding the border?"

"The troops stationed here are really nothing more than a Chinese show of strength. Just look at their composition … mechanized infantry with no surface-to-air capabilities."

"That's true," replied Mugsy, "we didn't see any missile launchers out there."

Cho nodded closing his eyes, "The function of mechanized infantry is to repel a large mass of enemy forces that would try to cross into China over land. Does either of you gentlemen really believe an enemy force would try to cross into China from North Korea by land?"

Both shook their heads.

"I spoke with my contact in the Chinese National Police. He has a man staked out on the Thai smugglers. He gave me the location where they will be tonight."

"What about the North Korean broker?" Scipio asked between bites.

Cho took a sip from his glass, "They have not located the broker or the defectors, but we should have no trouble getting their location out of the smugglers."

Mugsy put his utensils down and lifted his glass of wine, "Colonel, I have a question. What happens to the defectors if we incapacitate the smugglers?"

Cho took time to cut another piece of beef bringing a forkful to his mouth to savor before replying, "What matter does that make?"

Mugsy looked over at Scipio who remained quiet, "What matter does it make? Colonel, the defectors are just innocent people trying to liberate themselves. I'm concerned that if we're too rough with the smugglers—"

"Captain Ricci," Cho placed his fork down, "After we extract the information we need from the smugglers, we are going to kill them."

"Kill them?"

Cho continued, as if not interrupted, "Their current location is not far from the river. It will be easy for us to dispose of their bodies."

"Colonel, you didn't mention anything about killing anyone."

Cho poured himself another glass, "Captain, there is no reason why we should risk leaving them alive."

"Colonel, you told us that all we had to do is, quote-unquote, 'render them harmless'. I took that to mean incapacitate them, not kill them."

Cho took a long sip of his wine, "Apparently, you misunderstood what I meant. Perhaps I should have spoken in Korean, and we should have used an interpreter. In any case let me be clear now, we will interrogate the smugglers, and then break their necks and toss their bodies in the river."

The two traded stares as tension filled the room.

"Then the Captain's original question is even more pertinent," Scipio broke in while taking a forkful of salmon into his mouth. "If we kill the smugglers, what happens to the defectors?"

Cho glared at him. Scipio acted as if he didn't notice and added while chewing, "Or were you intending on breaking their necks and tossing their bodies into the river too."

Cho shot to his feet. His nostrils flared, "What is this nonsense about? Once we kill the smugglers and take their place, we meet with the broker and convince him to sneak us across the border. The defectors will just have to make it on their own."

Mugsy held his arm out, "Colonel, please … sit."

Cho stood a moment more before slowly resuming his seat.

Mugsy poured himself more wine, "I brought this up because I had an idea. Instead of confronting the smugglers, why don't we just follow them? We could let them lead us to the broker then let them take charge of the defectors and go on their way. After all, we're only interested in the broker anyway."

Cho blinked his eyes trying to keep his impatience in check, "Captain, I had to call in … what do you call them … chips?"

Mugsy nodded.

"Lots of chips with my Chinese police contact just to have him locate the smugglers. As of 11 PM tonight, those chips will be totally spent and the stakeout will be pulled. We are supposed to make contact with the smugglers by then. It will be up to us to extract the whereabouts of the broker as quickly as possible.

"We won't have much time for that either in case the meeting with the broker is set for tonight, which I suspect it is."

"Why tonight?" asked Mugsy.

"Because the broker won't want to risk housing the defectors any longer than he has to," Scipio answered for Cho.

Cho nodded.

"Then my idea makes even more sense," replied Mugsy, leaning in with his elbows on the table. "Colonel, think of it, if for whatever reason the smugglers resist our interrogation, the meeting with the broker will be in jeopardy."

"The smugglers won't resist for long. That, I will guarantee."

"What are you gonna do Colonel, chop off a finger every time they don't answer one of your questions?" taunted Scipio.

Cho stared unblinkingly at Scipio before turning away and downing the rest of the wine in his glass, "Perhaps you gentlemen think we should offer them tea and ask them nicely to give us the broker's location."

"I don't think we should offer them anything at all, Colonel," replied Mugsy, "or cut off their fingers or break their necks. The smugglers may be working for a profit motive, but they're doing an honorable thing. They're not the enemy."

"Captain, what you are suggesting is to follow them. I told you, the Chinese police will break off their surveillance at 11 PM tonight. None of us is that familiar with Ji'an, and on top of that there is, as you saw, a large contingent of Chinese troops roving about town.

"If, for whatever reason, we lose the smugglers when we try to follow them, our entire mission will be blown."

"For the sake of the lives of the smugglers and the freedom of the defectors, I'm willing to take that chance."

"And I am not."

Mugsy glanced at Scipio, "And what do you say?"

"I say ... let's save our killing for the enemy."

Cho sat back in his chair staring at his empty wine glass. Mugsy filled it.

After a moment, he nodded.

Scipio lifted the covers off the dessert dishes, "Now that we've agreed on that, here's the toughest question ... which of us gets the chocolate orange cake?"

CHAPTER 13

LONGXIANG RESTAURANT
JI'AN, TONGHUA
JILIN, CHINA
11:00 PM (LOCAL), FRIDAY, MAY 24, 2013

Two men dressed in short-sleeve shirts, shorts, and flip flops, walked out of the chic restaurant.

Scipio walked out after them and stretched, facing a Christian church across the street.

Mugsy and Cho emerged from behind trees in front of the church, "That's the signal."

The two started walking briskly until they were parallel to the smugglers.

"Remember, if they have a car we take them," said Cho. They communicated via a two-way radio app on their Big-Brutha™ phones. The three were wearing earpieces and throat mics.

"Roger that," replied Scipio.

The two men walked past the small parking lot and started down the block.

"Looks like no car," replied Mugsy.

Cho glanced up and down the street, "Someone could be coming to pick them up."

Mugsy glanced himself and replied with a hint of sarcasm in his voice, "No vehicles in either direction."

Cho's nostrils flared, "I still think this is a reckless plan."

The two heard Scipio's voice in their earbuds. He was following behind the men on the other side of the street, "No sign of vehicles. The meeting location must not be far. They're wearing flip flops."

Cho squeezed his throat mic, "This road ends at the river. We cannot allow them near it in case they try to get on a boat."

The smugglers crossed the street and stepped onto the sidewalk several feet ahead of Mugsy and Cho.

Cho increased his pace. Mugsy walked aside him, "Easy, Colonel."

Cho continued to increase his pace. Mugsy grabbed his arm, "I said, easy, Colonel."

Cho pulled his arm from Mugsy's grasp and tried to speak in a low tone, "I told you, if they make it to the river there could be a boat waiting for them. They could disappear with no way for us to follow them."

Without warning, Cho rushed ahead.

Mugsy tackled him. Cho and Mugsy rolled around on the floor at the feet of the startled Thai men.

Someone shouted from the street in Mandarin. It was Scipio staggering, "We haven't even gotten to the party yet, and you two are already drunk!"

With the smugglers looking on with concern, Scipio grabbed Cho and Mugsy by their arms and lifted them to their feet.

Scipio continued in slurred Mandarin, "You must apologize to these men!"

Cho and Scipio glared at each other. They remained silent.

Scipio held up his hands with palms out. He bowed deeply, making it look like he was about to tumble over, "We are sorry. Kindly accept our apologies."

One of the smugglers dismissed him with a wave of his hand, before the two resumed walking.

Cho started after them again, but this time Scipio and Mugsy both grabbed his arms.

Cho stopped resisting, "So this is why you came … to obstruct me?"

"Colonel, you agreed to our plan," replied Mugsy.

With blurring speed, Cho reached up grabbing both men behind their necks and simultaneously kicked the back of their legs, knocking them to their knees.

"I agreed only for as long as we could follow them."

Cho attempted to walk. He stopped when he felt pressure on his testicles. He looked down to see, once again, Scipio gripping them.

"You seem to have a fixation for my manhood."

"Let's just say, I'm trying to keep hold of the situation."

Mugsy got to his feet, "Colonel, please, they're getting away. If they try to get on a boat, you have my word that we'll stop them, but if they don't, let's stick to the plan and just follow them … agreed?"

Cho looked down at Scipio's hand, and then up to his face. Scipio winked before releasing his grasp, allowing Cho to help him up.

Mugsy began to jog, "Come on. It looks like they're heading for that stretch of beach in front of the storm wall. We can tag along behind the wall and peer down on them."

The smugglers walked along a narrow patch of sand for about a hundred yards until they came upon a path. They stopped where the path met a dilapidated jetty.

Cho pointed to a nearby eight-foot section of the stone storm wall where it had crumbled. He waved for Mugsy and Scipio to follow.

The hole in the wall led to a very steep, rocky mound. They cautiously made their way to the end, leaving them only ten feet behind the gathering, standing below in the darkness.

They overheard the Thai smugglers speaking Korean, "Turn off your phones and put them away, okay?"

Five women and one man complied. Standing in front of them, a heavyset man, wearing a dark windbreaker and jeans, spoke on his cell phone.

Cho whispered, "He matches the description. That is *Dragon*. He is the broker."

After a minute, the man put his phone away. He took a paper bag out of an inside jacket pocket and handed it to the smugglers then turned to the defectors, "You will go with these men now. Do what they tell you, and you will survive. Disobey them, and you will die."

The three men watched as the smugglers began to lead the defectors away, retracing their tracks along the beach. Cho, Mugsy, and Scipio jumped down.

Dragon immediately raised his hands over his head.

Cho faced him and spoke in Korean, "You are Dragon?"

The scared man nodded.

"Put your hands down. We're not the police," replied Scipio, also in Korean.

"Any chance he speaks English?" asked Mugsy. "My Korean is rusty."

Cho whispered something to him. The man shook his head. He seemed to get more frightened.

Cho spoke again in Korean, "We want to hire you."

The man replied, whispering in Cho's ear.

Cho turned with a slight grin, "He said he wants to speak to me alone. Apparently, he doesn't trust you round eyes."

Mugsy nodded. Scipio and Mugsy watched as the two walked out of earshot.

"What do you make of that?" asked Mugsy.

"I don't know ... suddenly the North Korean trusts the South Korean, but not Americans?"

"He *is* a smuggler. Maybe it's just what the Colonel said."

Cho walked back over with Dragon behind him, "He said he will help us, but we cannot set out until dawn. He wants to take us to one his safe houses. It is not far from here. We can get some rest there."

Scipio stared at the man, but directed his remark to Cho, "Just like that?"

"Not exactly. He wants to get paid. We can either pay him, or persuade him to help us by other means. Either way, the safe house could be useful."

Scipio shot a skeptical glance at Mugsy, who shrugged. The small man dressed in black waved his arm in front of Cho and Dragon, "Lead the way."

CHAPTER 14

SAFE HOUSE
JI'AN, TONGHUA
JILIN, CHINA
6:30 AM (LOCAL), SATURDAY, MAY 25, 2013

Mugsy opened his eyes.

As soon as they arrived at the safe house of the North Korean broker known as Dragon, he, Scipio, and Cho found places on the floor of one of the barren rooms to sleep. He looked around. No one else was in the room.

The room opened to a small, square courtyard. He stepped outside and stretched. The only sound he heard came from the chirping of a nearby bird.

Something smells good … breakfast?

Mugsy sniffed the air trying to determine from which direction the savory aroma was coming. He started off to the left but stopped after only a few steps.

Voices echoed from a room across the courtyard. He turned and headed for them. A loud banging noise, as if something or someone thudded against a wall, disturbed the morning tranquility. Mugsy stopped just short of entering the room and began to back away.

Dragon emerged from within, with his arms folded across his chest. Feeling eyes from behind, Mugsy turned to see two men approaching from the direction of the aroma. Both were aiming AK-47's at him.

He turned back to Dragon, "Where are Scipio and Cho?"

A small, familiar figure stepped out from behind the heavyset man. He had his hands folded behind his back.

"I am right here, Captain," Cho motioned with his head, "and Scipio is inside."

The men with the rifles grabbed his arms.

"What exactly is going on here, Colonel? Is Scipio alright?"

Cho whispered to Dragon who barked out orders to his men. They pushed Mugsy forward. Cho turned, keeping his hands folded behind his back, "Come. You may see for yourself."

Cho led him through a few rooms before finally stopping. Mugsy saw Scipio lying on the floor. He knelt down next to him.

"Did you do this, Colonel?"

"I did not. Unfortunately, he is an early riser. He awoke and went walking through the house—"

"I was looking for the bathroom," replied Scipio, holding the back of his head.

"The bathroom was in the room next to the one in which we slept."

"I couldn't find any toilet paper in that one, so I was looking for another."

"There is only one bathroom in this house."

"As I discovered."

Cho came closer, "You were spying."

Scipio examined his fingers after touching a sensitive spot on the back of his head. They were bloody.

"And you were conspiring. I knew we shouldn't have allowed you to whisper. Whispering in company is very rude, you know."

"Spying on what?" asked Mugsy. "Colonel, what's going on here?"

Cho glanced at Scipio, who replied for him, "Apparently, the good

Colonel has gone over to the dark side."

"That is incorrect. I am still on the same side … Korea's side."

Cho barked orders in Korean at the two armed men. Instead of reacting, they looked at Dragon. The heavyset man nodded, and one left the room. The other kept his rifle trained on Mugsy.

"I apologize for your injury, my friend, but I had informed Dragon of your fighting skills. I think he may have scared his men into using excessive force."

"I'd feel flattered, if I didn't see two of you."

The man returned with a first aid kit, rope and two chairs. Cho barked more orders, prompting the man to set the chairs up in the center of the room with the backs touching.

"If you gentlemen would please take a seat …."

Neither moved.

Cho shot a quick look at Dragon who proceeded to point at the chairs. Instantly, both of his men used their rifles to force Mugsy and Scipio to take seats. One of them took their phones, while the other put his rifle down, and started to wrap the rope around both.

Cho opened the first aid kit and took a bottle of hydrogen peroxide from it. He poured some on Scipio's head wound.

Scipio kept his eyes locked on the Colonel's, "What's the game, Colonel?"

"The game …?"

"Yes, why not just kill us and be done with it?"

"Scipio, I'd appreciate it if you didn't give the Colonel any ideas," Mugsy interjected from behind him.

"Ah … for one reason, we are blocks away from the river here, so we could not easily dispose of your bodies. And for another, what sport would that be?"

"Sport …?"

"Yes. We have not finished our hand-to-hand combat competition." Cho looked at his watch, "I hope someday we get the opportunity to complete it. But I'm afraid that will have to wait."

The man tying them pulled tightly on each knot, before picking up his rifle.

"So, you're just gonna leave us here?" asked Mugsy. "Are you expecting anyone to find us, or are you condemning us to a slow agonizing death?"

Dragon whispered something into Cho's ear.

"Dragon thinks we should leave you with bullets in your brains." Cho bent down and looked closely into Scipio's eyes, "As I suspected, he understands more English than he leads on." He stood straight again, "This safe house is used by a number of brokers and smugglers. Dragon figures that once your bodies are discovered by one of them, your murders will be blamed on them."

Cho headed to the door. He motioned with a nod for Dragon and his men to precede him out the door, "Dragon believes this. I do not. I don't want to chance that your bodies will be discovered before we can cross the border."

Cho nodded to both men, "Farewell, gentlemen."

* * * * *

Mugsy struggled strenuously before stopping from exhaustion. He shook the sweat from his forehead, "I think the bastard that tied us must've worked in a rodeo. If we ever get out of this, I'm gonna kill that son-of-a-bitch Cho."

Scipio started chuckling.

"Scipio, maybe that head wound was more serious than it looked. Are you delirious?"

"I was just thinking about the old Batman TV show. Remember the one with Adam West?"

"You're a little older than I am. Why the heck would you be thinking of that now? Expecting the Caped Crusader to come rescue us?"

"No, but this reminds me of all those slow death predicaments Batman's enemies would subject him and Robin to. Even as a little kid I remember thinking, 'why not just shoot them?'"

"Nice to know you were a psychopath even as a child. And your point is …?"

"Mugs, the Colonel had a number of opportunities to kill us before this, including in our sleep last night. If he was gonna get rid of us all along, why didn't he? And leaving us alive here is just plain dumb … something the Colonel is definitely not."

"You heard what he said."

"Yeah, I heard, but I tend to side with Mr. Dragon. Leave us with bullets in our heads, and let the blame fall on the poor saps that find our bodies."

"Well then it's a good thing you weren't the one to jump to the other team."

"There were other things too …."

"Like what?"

"Like, he let us know Dragon understood English."

"So?"

"So, maybe he wanted to tell us more than he did, but he couldn't."

"What else?"

"He didn't search us for weapons."

"That could've just been an oversight. Besides, he doesn't know we have concealed weapons on us."

"Hence, the reason to search us. No. It might've been an oversight for the broker, but not for the Colonel."

Scipio could tell Mugsy was thinking about that.

"Anything else …?"

"Yeah … he let us know they were gonna cross the border, and that others will eventually come here.

"Scip, if he didn't jump ship, why are we sitting here tied so tightly I can't feel my hands? And your blood is dripping down the back of my neck."

Mugsy heard a faint sawing sound followed by the pop of a rope. The binds became slack. They slid out of them and stood. Mugsy turned to see Scipio holding one of his 8" ceramic blades in his hand. He nodded to the weapon as he rubbed his wrists, "How'd you reach it?"

"I didn't. I slipped it up my sleeve right before we were tied."

"You mean you let me struggle and the whole time you had it in your hand?"

Scipio smiled, "Frankly, I thought you did the same thing and were just being exuberant cutting through the rope. What's the matter, Captain, the SEALs don't teach being sneaky?"

"They do. I'm just not so good at sneaky before my morning coffee."

Mugsy took a look in the next room and out into the corridor before returning to see Scipio wiping blood from his neck.

"Are you okay?"

"I'll live. Actually, come to think of it, the good colonel saved my life. As soon as I stepped into this room, I felt the blow to my head. I was barely conscious, but I remember now … Cho prevented the guards from shooting me."

Mugsy took a look at Scipio's bandage, "Of course, he might've done that just so a gunshot wouldn't ring out."

"Oh ye of little faith," Scipio pushed his hand away. He walked over to a small desk in the corner, rifled through a pile of papers then checked the drawers.

"There's nothing here to tell us exactly where they were headed except for the fact the Colonel said they'll be crossing the border."

"That's only a fact if you're right about him, but I guess we'll have to move forward on that assumption. I'll bow to your Delta Force sneaky training … without our phones to track him, what do we do now?"

Scipio continued to rub the back of his neck, "I get the feeling the Colonel wanted us to meet whoever is coming here. Maybe we should do just that."

"You mean wait here for the next broker or smuggler to come along? Scipio, we have no idea when that'll be."

"I get the feeling it'll be sooner than later. Anyway, we'll need another broker to get us across the border."

"So, you don't think we should scrub the mission?"

"It's your call, Captain, but I think Cho still needs our help, and I think he's anticipating that we make it to General Kang on our own. I'm confident he'll find a way to hook up with us, once we do."

"You're sure putting a lot of faith in someone that kicked our asses."

"Correction, he kicked your ass. If I remember correctly, I had him by the balls … twice."

"Delta Force dirty pool. SEALs try to keep friendly competitions … friendly."

"You know what they say Captain … all's fair in love and hand-to-hand combat."

Mugsy sniffed the air, "Well, if we're gonna stick around here, why don't we find the source of that aroma … I don't know about you, but I'm starving."

* * * * *

Cho spoke softly, "Taejang, it's Cho. We have made contact with the broker and are preparing to cross the border." Cho took a peek out the bathroom door. He saw one of Dragon's men looking for him in the next room.

So this is how it is going to be – Dragon is watching me like a hawk. I guess I cannot blame him. I would do the same in his place.

The stern voice on the other side of the line belonged to Kang, "Who exactly is 'we', Colonel?"

Just as I thought, Kang had to be the one who gave the order for Dragon to kill the Americans. Why else would he ask that?

Neither Kang nor Dragon made any mention that they communicated. I see now why my contact in the Chinese police suggested Dragon so strongly. Kang had to be behind that too.

The Americans have complicated an already difficult situation for me. My objective is all that is important, yet, I have come to respect Captain Ricci and Scipio … even like them.

I had to tell Kang they were accompanying me, but once I did, I suspected he would try and take matters into his own hands. I told him I would take care of them, but I suspected he would not trust me.

I kept my eye on Dragon from the moment we met. I need to get some sleep soon, but I was right about remaining awake last night. If I did not, the Americans would be dead.

Dragon has not used his cell phone since we met. Kang probably told him not to for fear I would catch him. It is time for me to take advantage of that - and try to kill two birds with one stone. Then I will sleigh the dragon. But first, I must take a chance and see if Kang knows about the Americans. If he does, I may not even make it out of China …

"I'm here with the broker and the Americans."

There was a slight pause. Cho held his breath.

"Where and when will the crossing take place?"

Cho exhaled.

I still have no idea whether he believed me or not, so I will have to play this out without knowing.

"The broker said it will take one week to make the necessary arrangements. I intend to make the crossing next Saturday, June 01, at 3 AM."

"Where?"

Cho heard voices in the next room. It was Dragon and the man looking for him. Dragon started calling his name.

Cho spoke even more softly, "Please, listen carefully Taejang. There is a small islet south of and directly across from Minqiao Street, in Ji'an. Distance from the Chinese mainland to the islet is only 170 meters. The islet is technically inside Chinese territory, but the distance from the islet to the North Korean mainland is only about 30 meters.

"A fishing boat will take us to the islet. Once we are on it, it is just a barren strip of land … it will make for an easy killing ground for your snipers."

"I still don't understand why you insist on snipers, Cho. Our border guards could handle—"

Cho heard footsteps right outside the bathroom door. He lowered his voice to an intense whisper, "With respect Sir, we have already covered this. You are not the one crossing the border, I am, and I will not place my life in the hands of border guards."

Kang didn't reply.

Cho continued, "Have you given the snipers photos of me?"

"Yes, of course. Daeryeong, it sounds like you are having second thoughts. Remember, it was *your* idea to come here."

"It was not my idea, Sir. It was President Park's idea to send someone to get human intel on the Musudan missiles. If I did not volunteer, she would have sent someone else. Would you have preferred that?"

"Your insubordination is unacceptable, Daeryeong!"

Cho pulled the phone from his ear. He took a deep breath before continuing, "I apologize, Sir."

Cho heard a knock at the door.

"Daeryeong, are you in there?"

Cho flushed the toilet and started running water, "Yes, of course I am in here. Do you not see the door is closed?!"

Kang heard Cho's remarks, but continued with no sense of concern, "Your apology is noted, Daeryeong. I have noticed that you have been on edge since the Americans came into the picture."

Cho turned the faucet all the way up. Water began splashing out of the sink. After several seconds, he heard footsteps heading away from the door. He lowered the water flow but didn't shut it off.

"Cho, are you there?"

"Yes, sir, but I must go soon."

"I said that your erratic behavior seemed to start when the Americans showed up."

He is speaking as if he is completely unconcerned with Dragon discovering me. That would only be the case if Dragon is working for him. Kang may have placed Dragon and his men here to spy on me, but I am certain he could also order them to kill me, at any time.

I must continue to prevent Kang and Dragon from communicating. I can keep an eye on Dragon but how do I prevent Kang from trying to contact him?

"They have certainly complicated matters, Taejang. I implored President Park not to involve them, but she would not listen."

"That is exactly why she needs to be replaced. Our South Korean cousins rely too much on the United States."

"And our North Korean cousins rely too much on China."

"Perhaps, Daeryeong, we should hang Kim Jong-Un and President Park from branches of the same tree and televise it to the new, united Korea. What do you think?"

He repeatedly tests my loyalty.

"Then I think we should hang them both from an *Abies Koreana.*"

There was no immediate reply.

"I am afraid I do not share your familiarity with horticulture,

Cho," impatience was evident in Kang's tone.

Cho grinned, "Abies Koreana … also known as the Korean Fir tree. It is a tree indigenous only to the higher mountains of South Korea.

"What better way to make a statement to all Koreans than to hang the former leaders, who relied so much on outsiders, from a tree that only grows in our homeland."

Kang's tone improved just slightly, "That would, indeed, send a message to all Koreans, and the world. Your devotion to our cause is most … commendable."

That gives me an idea. I think I know how to prevent the General from contacting Dragon … and how to get rid of Dragon too.

"Thank you, General, and to further express my devotion, I will not allow any of these men out of my sight, even for a moment. Nor will I allow them to use their phones. And please remind the snipers to kill the three of them. I do not trust the broker anymore than I trust the Americans."

Cho detected a slight hesitation.

"A wise precaution, Daeryeong, though perhaps … a bit extreme."

"With the letter you supplied me, once I'm inside North Korean territory I won't need the broker anyway … he knows too much and will have seen too much, especially when the Americans fall."

Kang hesitated again, "You said you won't be making the crossing for a week. There might be something you can do for me once you get here. My adjutant has been acting very peculiar, giving me cause for concern."

He's onto Sojang Kim? Not another problem.

"I would deal with the problem with my own men, but my adjutant is very popular, even with my inner circle."

Cho didn't reply.

"Cho, did you hear me?"

"Yes, sir. Of course, I will … offer my assistance … in any way possible."

"You understand what will need to be done?"

"Yes, sir."

"Good, but Cho, I think you must get some rest."

"I will rest when my objectives are achieved."

Kang's tone became terse, "I believe you meant to say 'our' objectives, Daeryeong."

"Of course, Taejang."

"It is clear to me these Americans are vexing you. My snipers will take care of them. Perhaps then you can regain your composure."

The line went dead.

Cho squeezed the phone almost to the point of breaking it.

I will regain my composure, Taejang, when I am standing over your dead body.

CHAPTER 15

SAFE HOUSE
JI'AN, TONGHUA
JILIN, CHINA
4:00 AM (LOCAL), WEDNESDAY, MAY 29, 2013

The sound of a key being inserted in the front door lock reverberated throughout the dark residence. Six individuals soaked from rain stepped inside, a man and two women with their hands on their heads were being shoved ahead of three armed men.

The front door was closed and locked by one of the trailing men, while another, the leader, barked orders in Korean to the three in front, "Sit on the floor and remain perfectly still."

He turned to his men, "Check every room. Make sure we are the only ones here. He looked at the shivering women and smiled, "Oh, and check where the bedrooms are."

His men disappeared into the next room.

The leader bent down and caressed one of the women's faces. When she tried to pull away, he slapped her hard for her trouble.

The bespeckled man sitting next to the women moved to try to shield them. He too was backhanded hard across his face, knocking his glasses off and landing him flat on his back. The man attempted to get up, but the leader placed the barrel of a semi-automatic pistol against his head and worked the slide back, "You stay right there."

The man squinted but did not move.

The leader turned his attention back to the women, "I will personally enjoy you both, before we sell you. Then my friends will do the same."

The woman he slapped burst into tears, while the other moved over to console her.

* * * * *

The two armed men gained confidence as they walked through the many small rooms of the house. None of them were occupied. They entered the last room and smiled. There were two pillows and two blankets spread on the floor, one set on each side of the room.

Their smiles disappeared as they felt something cold and sharp pressed up against their throats just over their Adam's apples.

* * * * *

"There is no one else in the house and we found a bedroom!" The leader heard one of his men cry out from a distance.

He turned to the three sitting on the floor, "Get up."

The women got to their feet first, but the man stumbled until one of the women handed him his glasses.

The leader pointed out of the room with his gun, "That way."

The man put on his glasses and walked out first followed by one of the women. The leader grabbed the last woman, the one he slapped, around her waist. He pressed his gun against her head and whispered in her ear, "You and I will put on a nice show for your boyfriend."

As they entered the next room, the leader felt something sharp against his stomach. Someone was behind him. He gritted his teeth and spoke in Korean, "Whoever you are. I will kill this woman."

He received his answer in even-toned Korean, "Go ahead. It will be the last thing you do before you see your intestines spill out of your gut. I will enjoy gutting you like a pig."

The man trembled as he felt the tip of a sharp object beginning to pierce his skin.

"Wait, please!" Still holding the gun, he put his hands over his head but felt the object continue to pierce him. He tried to move away, but a strong hand around his throat kept him from moving.

"Wait, PLEASE! Don't!!"

The man wearing the glasses turned on the light and took the gun from the leader's hand. He looked down and spoke in Korean, "You wet your pants. I guess you are only tough when threatening defenseless women."

Scipio took the ceramic blade from the man's stomach and used it to poke him in the back. He continued to speak in Korean, "Get on your knees and place your hands on your head."

The man did as he was told.

The bespeckled man walked over to Scipio and handed him the gun. He switched to slightly-broken English, "My name is Father Kim Sung-eun. Who are you?"

"*Father* Kim?"

"Yes," Father Kim turned to the women, "This is Jee Sun and Sol-Bi."

Scipio nodded to them. The women looked terrified of him.

Father Kim turned nervously, "There are two more—"

"No there aren't," Mugsy cut him off as he pushed two men into the room in front of him. He held their guns in each of his hands.

"Father Kim, this is Captain Ricci," replied Scipio.

"*Captain* Ricci?"

"*Father* Kim?"

"Gentlemen, before we go any further …," Scipio stepped between them, "Captain, why don't we use that rope we have and tie these losers nice and tight. Then we can make the Father and these nice ladies something hot to eat. They look hungry. Maybe find them some dry clothes.

"That sounds like a plan."

* * * * *

Scipio walked back into the kitchen, "We found some dry clothes for the ladies in one of the dressers. They put them on and literally passed out on our blankets."

"I think they drank a gallon of broth each," added Mugsy as he walked to the stove.

"I apologize for that," said Father Kim, "but we have been traveling without rest for almost 24 hours now, with nothing to eat or drink. And the rain made it much worse."

Mugsy carried over a metal pot and refilled the Father's cup with hot, green tea, "You have nothing to be sorry for, Father. I wish we had more than blankets and broth to offer."

"For what it's worth, there are lots more blankets in the back rooms and the kitchen is stocked with food," added Scipio.

Father Kim took his time sipping the tea, "Thank you both for all that you have done. God has been merciful to us."

Mugsy refilled Scipio's cup and then his own, "So tell us Father, what exactly are you doing here with those women?"

Father Kim took more time sipping his tea. It looked to both men that he was contemplating whether to trust them.

He finally put his cup down and interlocked his fingers, "I am the Director of Caleb Mission, a Christian organization. For the last 10 years, I have been helping North Koreans find freedom from their repressive Communist nation. In that time, I have brought hundreds of people to South Korea, most of them hearing about my works by word of mouth or the Internet."

Scipio thumbed over his shoulder, "So those women are …?"

"Defectors, yes," Father Kim finished the sentence.

"Who are the men with the guns?" asked Mugsy.

"They work for a Chinese pimp. They followed us from another safe house. The pimps and their men know the locations of several of the safe houses that the brokers and smugglers use. They raid them and grab any women they can find to sell them into prostitution.

"The abominable Chinese two-child law has lead to families killing female babies at birth, as they consider males to be more valuable workers. That has led to a severe ratio of men over women.

"Many men in China will pay a month's salary for just one night with a prostitute but there are not enough volunteers. So, the pimps resort to kidnapping female defectors."

Mugsy glanced at Scipio with his brow raised.

"You are surprised, Captain, that I know about such things … such people?"

"Frankly, yes I am."

"More than a decade ago, I was a successful businessman. As a devoted churchgoer, I did my best to donate my time and money to help North Korean defectors in China.

"In 2000, I volunteered to visit the nearby Chinese-North Korean border. What I witnessed changed my life forever. I saw dozens of emaciated bodies of North Koreans in much worse condition than Jee Sun and Sol-Bi streaming down the Tumen River. It was too horrible to watch. Right then and there, I decided to dedicate my life to defectors.

"I saved money and vacation time to travel here. That same year, while working with the defectors in this area, I met my wife, Park Esther. She was a former North Korean soldier and daughter of a scientist. She had defected after her parents died of starvation."

Mugsy shook his head in disgust. Scipio remained stoic.

"She stood out by her passion for helping the defectors like herself. I saw her hands, coarse and torn all over and I was deeply moved by that. I felt that together we could carry on this mission."

Mugsy nodded, "Where are you based?"

"We work from the Caleb Mission headquarters in Cheonan, about an hour south of Seoul. It is really nothing more than a run-down commercial building, but it also serves as a church, as well as a home for my wife and daughter. Our congregation is made up of mostly defectors and a few South Koreans"

"How often do you come here?" asked Scipio.

"I'm afraid less and less often. Over the years, the Chinese authorities became aware of my efforts. They made my job here nearly impossible. So, I began sending others in my place, but the work is very dangerous. Whenever I think I can get away with it, I come myself.

"It breaks my heart to know that I won't be able to help all of the defectors who ask me for help. But I've also experienced miracles many times over. As long as I don't give up, I will be able to save at least one more precious life.

"These ladies wrote to me about the horrors they faced in North Korea. Many of their family members have starved to death while others have been imprisoned. I had to come."

Scipio leaned back in his chair, "What are your plans now, Father, and what would you like us to do with our tied-up guests?"

"Well, first I would like to get a few hours sleep, if you don't mind."

"Of course."

Father Kim nodded, "Thank you. Then I will go into town and purchase some things we will need to begin our trip to South Korea. As for those men, it is best to keep them tied for the present. I don't think they will be missed for at least another day or so."

Mugsy glanced at Scipio, who nodded, "Father, we would like to make you a proposition if you're interested."

"What kind of proposition?"

"We need a guide to smuggle us into North Korea."

"Smuggle you *in*?" Father Kim paused then leaned in, "Just exactly who are you gentlemen … American military?"

"American … yes, former military."

"Former military …?" Father Kim looked between them, "And just why would two American former military want to enter North Korea?"

Mugsy again glanced at Scipio, who shook his head slightly, "We can't tell you that."

Father Kim looked dubiously at them as he sipped his tea, "Are you intending to do harm to the people?"

"To the people … no. To one particular person … perhaps. But, rest assured it'll benefit both North and South Korea."

Scipio took over, "We came to this house, Father, to meet with a broker named Dragon."

Father Kim nodded, "I know of Dragon. He is someone who has smuggled people and goods in and out of North Korea. But he has also turned some of the defectors over to North Korean authorities, ones they really want returned."

"You're saying Dragon works with the North Korean authorities, at times?"

"Not exactly works with them, but he does have some sort of relationship with someone high up in the North Korean military."

Scipio glanced at Mugsy, "Are you sure about that?"

"I am certain of it. Two years ago, I saw with my own eyes the Chinese authorities arrest Dragon for smuggling. A week later he was released. I asked a Chinese police officer, an acquaintance of mine who is sympathetic towards North Korean defectors. He told me that a North Korean general personally called to have Dragon released."

Scipio smiled, "A North Korean general, huh."

Father Kim knit his brows, "What exactly is this all about?"

Scipio kept his eyes locked on Mugsy as he replied, "Dragon double-crossed us. He took our money then his men tied us up and left us here. He said he was heading back into North Korea. We would like you to help us track him, if possible."

"So, you want to catch up to Dragon, to kill him?"

"Hopefully, it won't come to that, but we'd like to get our money back from him."

"You are willing to risk your lives to get some money back?"

"There is more to it than that."

"I see," Father Kim sat back in his chair. "So, you want me to turn Jee Sun and Sol-Bi over to smugglers, whom I will have to pay—"

"We will gladly pay whatever—"

Father Kim held his hand up, "Then you want me to risk my life to smuggle you into North Korea without telling me the whole truth about why you want to go there. On top of that, you want to limit my flexibility as to how I would smuggle you in."

"Limit your flexibility?" asked Mugsy.

"Yes, you said you want me to try and track Dragon's trail across the border, did you not? That means I would not only have to discover his method of crossing the border, but also use the identical route. That can prove to be very dangerous. Those of us who sneak in and out of North Korea utilize a number of different routes - depending on date, weather, as well as North Korean guard movements.

"Even if Dragon was successful sneaking into North Korea from a specific route and method; that does not necessarily mean that we could utilize the same method without being captured and killed. Even the difference of one day … one hour, could alter the safety of any route. Besides, from what I know about Dragon, he normally utilizes land routes, while I have been exploiting water routes over the last couple of years."

"So you're saying you can't track him?" asked Scipio.

"I did not say that. Regardless of how he crosses the border, I'm confident I could pick up his trail once inside North Korea … but based on the little you have told me, and the fact that I believe some of what you have told me is not true … I am not sure I am willing to help you."

Father Kim stood, "If you don't mind, I would like to retire now."

Mugsy stood, "Of course, would you like me to show you—"

"That won't be necessary. I will sleep in the same room with the women."

Scipio looked amused.

"They would be very frightened if they wake up and not see me there," the Father added, with impatience in his voice.

He stopped and turned before leaving the kitchen, "I shall pray and meditate about it. I would suggest that you gentlemen do the same. And while you are praying, I also suggest that you reconsider trusting me with the truth."

After watching the Korean priest leave the room, they sat quietly facing each other. Scipio finally rose and headed for the door, "If you want to find me, I'll be on my knees somewhere, praying."

Mugsy chuckled and finished the tea in his cup. He stood up, turned off the light and added to no one, "Me too."

CHAPTER 16

SAFE HOUSE
JI'AN, TONGHUA
JILIN, CHINA
6:00 PM (LOCAL), WEDNESDAY, MAY 29, 2013

Father Kim stepped into the kitchen. Jee Sun and Sol-Bi, dressed in the now-dry clothes they were wearing when they arrived began to rise from their seats at the table.

Father Kim waved his hands down and spoke to them in Korean, "Please, remain in your seats and finish your meals."

The women nodded and smiled slightly.

Scipio walked next to them holding a sizzling iron wok and proceeded to place shredded pieces of marinated, lightly-fried chicken onto their plates. He already placed bamboo steamers filled with rice and vegetables on the table. He spoke to them in Korean, "Please ladies, help yourselves."

Neither woman moved, instead, they looked over at Father Kim. He approached the table, lifted one of their plates and began serving rice and vegetables onto it with chopsticks. He repeated the same for the other woman, before filling his own plate.

Scipio walked over and placed some chicken on Kim's plate.

Father Kim examined it and switched to English, "So you are a spy and a cook?"

Scipio filled Mugsy's plate and then his own, "I like to think of myself as a cook who also knows how to spy."

The small man in black sat down and lifted a piece of chicken with his chopsticks, "Buon appet—"

Father Kim coughed into his hand.

Scipio glanced at Mugsy, who was mouthing the word 'prayer.'

"Oh, sorry Father."

Father Kim bowed his head, followed by the women and then the men. The Father prayed in Korean, "Heavenly Father, we thank you for the food we are about to eat and for saving our lives with the help of these men. Please continue your blessings on Jee Sun and Sol-Bi. Continue to look after them and keep them safe on their journey to South Korea. We also ask, if the mission these men are on is a righteous one, stay with them, protect them, and help them succeed. We ask this through our Savior's name."

"Amen," Everyone said it in unison, with Scipio slightly trailing.

They ate in silence for a few moments before Father Kim spoke up, this time in English, "I slept much longer than I expected."

"That's understandable," replied Mugsy, "after all you've been through lately."

"The ladies only joined us a few minutes before you did. They really needed several hours of sleep," added Scipio.

"I want to thank you both, again, for all you have done for us."

"You've already thanked the right being," replied Mugsy pointing up.

Scipio winked, "Amen."

Father Kim nodded, "So, have you gentlemen given more thought to our last conversation."

Mugsy looked across the table at the women.

Father Kim followed his eyes, "Do not worry about them, Captain. They do not speak or understand a word of English. As opposed to South Koreans who are exposed to many different languages, most of our cousins to the North including, Jee Sun and Sol-Bi, have never even heard English spoken."

Mugsy nodded and poured himself some tea, "We have. Under the circumstances, you're leaving us with no alternative, but to trust you with the complete details of our mission."

"A wise decision."

"Perhaps for us, Father, but maybe not for you," replied Scipio.

Father Kim put his chopsticks down, "You mean you do not trust me."

"On the contrary, we do trust you, or we wouldn't contemplate sharing our mission details with you. No. I meant that if you help us cross into North Korea and we're captured, knowledge of our mission could mean a death sentence for you."

"I would never divulge—"

"Father, take it from me," Scipio interrupted, "there are ways to make anyone talk."

He took a sip of his tea and grinned softly, "Well, perhaps not me, but everyone else, and surely you."

"So, you should think hard about whether you want to know everything," added Mugsy.

"That is not an option. The only option is whether I decide to help you or not. If I do not, I do not need to know anything more. If I do choose to help, then I must know everything."

Mugsy raised a brow and nodded, "In that case, what will it take to convince you to help us?"

The middle-aged pastor joined his fingertips together, "I prayed about this before I went to sleep and then I awoke with an idea … a trade, if you will."

Mugsy grinned, "A trade? Shoot."

"Saving people is my number one priority. But collecting information on North Korea, revealing the harsh reality of life there is also important. I have been collecting such materials over several years from my sources inside North Korea."

"That's fascinating," replied Scipio, "how exactly have you accomplished that?"

Father Kim hesitated as he looked between the men, "I guess it is only fair for me to fully disclose my secrets since that is what I am asking you to do."

He exhaled, audibly.

"I send spy cameras to the border not far from here, and have them smuggled inside. My contacts use them to document North Korean life. The memory card with the video then travels back to South Korea via the same route.

"Because the work is highly dangerous for the contacts, they do the work in return for large sums of money, but these days, people from the North approach me first. For them, it's better to risk their life and make money than to sit there and starve to death."

Scipio folded his arms, "Truly fascinating. So what's the trade Father?"

"I will guide you with the help of my connections inside North Korea. They will be able to point us wherever you need to go within the country and guide us back out. In return, I want to accompany you. I will bring a camera along and shoot the documentation footage myself, along our travels."

Scipio looked to Mugsy who poured himself more tea, "This is where I'm supposed to say 'that's out of the question', but the truth is, I would trust your North Korean contacts a whole lot more if you were with us."

Father Kim smiled broadly.

Mugsy raised his hand palm facing out, "Hold it, Father. Let's get a few things straight. First, I'm in command of this mission. What I say goes, no matter what and without question."

"But of course. I have no problem with—"

He held his hand up again, "Let me finish. Our mission must be accomplished, no matter what. The lives of potentially thousands of people, North and South Koreans, as well as Americans and others could rest on its successful completion. And it is a time sensitive mission."

Mugsy leaned in, "That means that nothing can be allowed to stand in our way or slow us down … nothing and no one. Failure is simply not an option, but taking life is, if there's no other way."

Father Kim raised his chin, "I will not take life."

Mugsy arose and refilled the pastor's cup, "If you don't want to carry a weapon, that's up to you, but remember if the choice becomes whether to protect you or preserve the mission, we'll choose the latter. Is that clear?"

"Perfectly clear."

Father Kim rose and whispered between the women. They immediately jumped up and left the kitchen. He began clearing the table, "I sent the women to pack the things you will allow them to take, and I told them to wait for me in the bedroom. After we finish here, I will take them to a smuggler I know, who will make arrangements to take them on to South Korea.

"I will also begin to inquire about Dragon and the route he will use, but that could take some time. If he has not crossed into North Korea yet, we may have to wait until he does, in order to pick up his trail.

"Now, if there is nothing more to discuss about our agreement, please tell me everything about your mission."

Scipio pulled a map up on the screen on his phone. He placed the phone in front of Father Kim and leaned over his shoulder, "I thought you'd never ask. Welcome to the team, Father."

CHAPTER 17

ABOARD CHINESE FISHING VESSEL NO.92370
OFF COAST OF JI'AN
YALU RIVER
JILIN, CHINA
3:00 AM (LOCAL), SATURDAY, JUNE 01, 2013

An old Chinese fisherman, wearing a cap and faded orange life preserver pointed at an approaching vessel as he steered his rickety wooden boat from a rudder arm jutting up from the stern. Standing next to him, Cho looked through binoculars.

The North Korean defector-turned-broker known only as Dragon strained his eyes in the same direction. He asked with tension in his voice, "What is it?"

Less than a half-kilometer off their starboard bow, heading straight for them at top speed, Cho could barely make out the dark grey paint job of a North Korean patrol boat.

Cho handed Dragon the binoculars, "See for yourself."

It took the chubby man a few moments to focus, "It can't be. That's a North Korean patrol. They are not supposed to be anywhere near here!"

Cho took the binoculars back, "Apparently, your intelligence is flawed."

"That is impossible. I personally paid off the North Korean River Patrol officer in charge of this entire area of the river, and I double-checked with him before we embarked. He verified that he ordered all patrol vessels away from this area until daylight. I have done business with this officer before. He would not double-cross me. The crew on that boat must be here on their own."

Cho stared unblinkingly into Dragon's eyes. The stare intimidated him, "Daeryeong, I am telling you the truth."

"If that is so then we may have to kill every man aboard that boat," Cho pushed past him.

"Kill …," Dragon followed him, "Daeryeong, I counted six of them on deck and perhaps one or two more standing inside the small bridge enclosure. There are only four of us, and I am not skilled in killing people."

Cho looked at him a moment, "Then you will provide the distraction."

"Distraction, but how—"

Cho cut him off as he turned to the two armed men, "Keep your weapons near you, but do not shoot them unless you see they're ready to fire their weapons, understood?"

Both nodded their understanding without looking for permission from their boss.

Cho balled his hands into fists until his knuckles cracked, "If it comes to it, I will take care of them quietly."

Dragon's eyes went wide, "You will … all of them … alone?"

There was no time for him to question further. The patrol boat cut across the fishing boat's bow, forcing it to stop before pulling alongside. Three uniformed men armed with pistols stepped onto the smaller vessel and secured it while three more remained on the deck of the patrol boat pointing semi-automatic rifles. Cho noticed that Dragon was correct - two more men were visible through the windshield of the small bridge compartment.

The tallest of the three stepped aboard wearing the insignia of a

North Korean *Sowi*, or Ensign. He approached Dragon, "Who is in command?"

Dragon shot a quick glance at Colonel Cho, "I … I am. We are in Chinese waters, why have you boarded us?"

The Sowi looked around the small vessel, "What are you carrying aboard?"

"What do you mean? This is a fishing—"

The Sowi backhanded Dragon across the face hard enough to produce blood from his lip.

"Our Taewi ordered us away from this area, but I know he only does that when something of value is being smuggled into my country. So, I ask again … what are you carrying aboard that is so valuable?"

"There is nothing of any value aboard. You may check your—"

This time the Sowi struck Dragon across the face hard enough to knock him to the deck. His men leaned towards their rifles, but Cho shook his head ever so slightly.

The tall officer looked toward the bow and noticed Cho standing in the shadows.

"You, come here!"

Cho approached with his hands folded in front of him.

"I will ask you what I asked him. You will suffer as he did if you refuse to answer. What are you carrying aboard this boat that is of value?"

Cho looked at the other two uniformed men before turning his attention back to the Sowi, "Me."

The Sowi blinked. His delayed reaction gave Cho the opportunity to punch the tall officer squarely in the throat. The Sowi grabbed his neck and collapsed to his knees. Before anyone could react, Cho took the pistol out of the Sowi's hand and aimed it at the choking man's head. He twisted the Sowi's head, so all his men could see.

Cho shouted, "All of you, drop your weapons and place your hands on your heads … now, or this man dies!"

No one moved.

Cho twisted the Sowi's head to look up at him, "Tell them."

"Drop your weapons … do what he says!"

After looking among one another, one by one, the North Korean patrol officers complied. Dragon's men helped Dragon to his feet before picking up their rifles.

Cho ordered the North Korean crew back onto their patrol boat and motioned for Dragon's men to help the Sowi onto it. Then he handed the Sowi's pistol to Dragon, "Have your men tie them up on the bow. Then have them put the boat in gear and let it drift slowly down the river. When it eventually collides with something, it will cause a distraction that will work to our benefit."

Dragon barked the orders to his men then sheepishly faced Cho, "I am sorry for this unfortunate occurrence."

Cho stared back.

No need to admonish a man that will be dead within the hour.

"Look after your men. Make sure my orders are carried out without error."

CHAPTER 18

ABOARD *WARBIRD*
INCHEON INTERNATIONAL AIRPORT
JUNG-GU
INCHEON, SOUTH KOREA
5:00 AM (LOCAL), SATURDAY, JUNE 01, 2013

Chief Pilot of De Niro's fleet of personal aircraft, Colonel James "Duke" O'Rourke, USMC (Ret.) stepped from the cockpit and held his hands up, "Lady and gentlemen, as my co-pilot opens the door, let me be the first to welcome you to South Korea. I hope the flight was enjoyable—"

"As any flight you can walk away from should be," interjected a winking co-pilot, Captain Douglas "Charger" Miller, USAF (Ret.).

The towering O'Rourke chagrined with a glare, "and we look forward to your flying with us again."

De Niro approached both men with his hand outstretched, "Thank you gentlemen." He peeked out of the cabin door and saw a charcoal BMW-7 series pulling up in front of the jumbo jet's airstairs. Nearer the general aviation terminal, he also saw seven identically-clad women, dressed in black jacket and skirt combos, with white silk blouses, dark stockings and black leather pumps, hurrying out toward the plane.

Charger waved to them, "It looks like your welcoming committee, South Korean-style, is assembling down there."

O'Rourke squeezed Charger's shoulder, "You're with me. Let's get this beautiful bird plugged in and fed."

"Duke, do me a favor," De Niro stopped them at the top of the aluminum stairs, "tell our driver and welcoming committee that we'll be down in a few minutes. I have a few things I want to discuss with Michelle and Johnny-F while we're still aboard."

"Understood. I'll hand off your luggage in the meantime."

The Watchman Agency's Vice President of Intelligence Services, Michelle Wang, and Chief Information Officer, John "Johnny-F" Francis emerged from the back cabin. The cabin had been converted to the aircraft's sleeping quarters. One of the many remarkable features of the wide-bodied *Warbird* was the flexibility of its cabins.

At the touch of a button, walls could appear to create separate spaces or disappear to make one giant cabin. Tables, electronic equipment and even beds could appear or disappear within the cabin's functional layout.

De Niro held his hand up while glancing at his Big-Brutha™ iPhone, "I'm making a last check to see if Mugsy and Scipio uploaded any new info about Cho."

"I already checked," replied Michelle, "nothing new since he went rogue."

"I know we already discussed this Cris," added Francis, "but I still can't help thinking that we're gonna be wasting our time investigating Daejang Jeong. I mean … in light of Cho's actions and the fact that only he pointed a finger at Jeong. We could make better use of our time reporting to President Park what the Colonel did. At least that might calm her mind to know we uncovered the South Korean conspirator.

"Then we could focus all our energies into investigating Cho, and President Park could make that much easier by giving us access to his office and computer."

De Niro stared for a long moment, "I'm just not convinced that Cho *has* gone rogue, as Michelle puts it."

"Sorry Cris," replied Michelle, "just calling it the way I see it. It's been a week since the Colonel left Mugsy and Scipio tied up in that safe house. He's had more than enough time to get in contact with them … yet not a word from him."

"There's also been no word that he's crossed into North Korea either."

"There could be a number of reasons for that, including that he may've had second thoughts about leaving Mugsy and Scipio alive. For all anyone knows, Cho could be plotting with the broker to ambush Mugsy and Scipio now." She paused, "I'm almost afraid to say it, but I have to side with John on this."

Francis poked his head out of the cabin door and looked up.

"John, what are you doing?" asked De Niro.

"Looking for thunderheads. I'm afraid lightning's about to strike."

Michelle rolled her eyes, "Anyway … I think you should reconsider the situation, Cris, I really do. Poking our nose into the affairs of this country's Chairman of the Joint Chiefs of Staff and Chief Director of the Joint Defense Headquarters could get us into a world of trouble. It's not something we should do unless we have good reason, and after what Cho's done, we simply don't have good reason to anymore."

"And come to think of it, Cris," added Francis, "Cho couldn't have picked a better target for us to investigate if he wanted to divert our attention away from him. He knows we'll have to take our time and be very careful snooping into Jeong's affairs. And for all we know, the missiles could be launched by the time we even get near enough to the General to effectively investigate him. Cho could be counting on that."

De Niro scratched his chin, "So you guys want us to investigate Cho and totally forget about Jeong."

Michelle and Francis nodded in unison.

"You know, there probably won't be enough time left to investigate the General if we're wrong."

Michelle put her hand on De Niro's wrist, "But if we're right, we may be able to relay confirmation to Mugsy and Scipio before they catch up to the Colonel. That could save their lives."

"Maybe save the lives of a lot of other people too," added Francis.

"Maybe," De Niro remained skeptical. "Alright, I'll go along with investigating Cho, for now. But until we turn something substantial linking the Colonel to Kang, we don't bring this to President Park."

"But Cris—" Francis started.

"No buts, John. First, the President specifically said that she can't be part of our investigations. It would put her word in jeopardy with our President. And second … President Park trusts Cho, not only as an advisor, but with her life. I'm not about to cast aspersions on the man she relies on so implicitly without incontrovertible evidence against him. That's our job. That's what she's counting on us to do … and that's what we're going to do.

"By the way, did you get that mini-drone system installed?"

"Oh yeah, Richard and Louis had a ball with it—" Francis cut himself off when he saw the look on De Niro's face, "which is to say the system has been thoroughly tested. I'll explain some of the capabilities of the little buggers when we get a minute."

"Little buggers?"

Francis smiled, "My name for them."

"Those little buggers cost me a small mint."

"I know Cris, but trust me on this, for the jobs we can apply them to, they were worth every penny."

"I'll hold you to that. Now John, you said they can be controlled from your double-B phone?"

"Not just mine, once you download the control app I created, anyone can control them from their double-B phone."

"Okay, good, but how do they deploy? I mean, do Duke and Charger have to open the cargo door or something?"

"Nope," Francis shook his head with a big grin, "I had a 'bug door' installed in *Warbird*'s belly. The control app can also open and secure the door."

De Niro couldn't suppress his amusement, "A bug door … for the little buggers."

Francis nodded and looked at Michelle. She rolled her eyes.

De Niro held his arm out for Michelle and Francis to precede him out the door.

Standing alone, he bowed his head.

Please Father, guide us to the truth quickly … and protect Mugsy and Scipio.

CHAPTER 19

ISLET IN YALU RIVER
170 METERS OFF JI'AN COAST
JILIN, CHINA
4:00 AM (LOCAL), SATURDAY, JUNE 01, 2013

Colonel Cho, Dragon, and his two men armed with Chinese AK-47s, jumped feet first from the fishing boat into the dark, murky waters. Though, less than three meters from the shore of the small swatch of land, their objective, they each sank under the surface. Cho was the first to walk out of the surf, followed by the armed men who had to help Dragon get his footing.

Colonel Cho looked through a small pair of binoculars he took from a plastic bag he kept in his breast pocket. He pointed into the pre-dawn darkness, "There. That is the narrowest point between this islet and the North Korean coast. We cross there."

Dragon slicked his wet hair back, "We will need to look for a shelter as soon as we cross. It is too dangerous to walk around like this and we will need a vehicle. There is an uninhabited shack about a half-kilometer north, on the closest road to the coast. I arranged for a car to be left there for us. There is also a metal barrel next to the shack for us to make a fire to dry our clothes. That is, if it doesn't start raining."

Dragon took his phone out of an identical plastic bag, "Do you mind if I try my phone? I hope it hasn't gotten wet."

"No. There will be time to try your phone at the shack. We need to get off this lily pad of an islet as quickly as possible."

Dragon nodded with some tension. He put his phone away.

Cho turned around and faced in the direction of China, "Have your men spread out a bit and take the point. You follow and I will watch our backs. We must move."

Dragon nodded to his men.

* * * * *

Two soldiers dressed in camouflage, a North Korean *Sangsa*, equivalent to a U.S. Army Master Sergeant, and a *Hasa*, equivalent to Sergeant lay on their stomachs next to each other. Both were armed with Yugoslavian Zastava M76 semi-automatic sniper rifles. Set between them on the ground were photos of Cho and Dragon.

The Sangsa made a minor adjustment to his night vision scope, "I have them at 40 meters." He shined a small pen light over the photos, "Remember, the Taejang said these two are not targets. It looks like we put down the ones with the rifles."

The Hasa nodded and took aim, "I will take the one on the left."

* * * * *

Cho kept his back to the men, but looked over his shoulder as he slowly walked backwards. Two meters behind him, Dragon walked just as slowly, while beyond him his men advanced quickly in a zigzag pattern.

Breaking the quiet, the report of rifles erupting somewhere in the distance. Before their echo faded, both of Dragon's men fell to the ground.

Dragon and Colonel Cho froze in their places.

Seconds went by without another shot being fired. Dragon finally overcame his fear enough to approach his fallen men. He examined both then turned to Cho, "They are dead!"

Cho looked through his binoculars.

Dragon's eyes were wild with fear, "What do you see?!"

"I see … nothing." Cho scanned the North Korean coast before putting the binoculars away, "We must—"

He looked down to see that Dragon had picked up one his men's rifles and was now pointing it at him.

"No one else could have known that we were crossing here tonight except for you!"

Cho glanced over at the other rifle lying in the dark sand, three meters away. Dragon noticed and pulled the trigger. Four shots rang out in quick succession and pierced the space where Cho had been standing. After firing, Dragon saw he was no longer there.

Before the chubby man could locate him, Cho sprung up from a forward roll and landed a front kick directly to Dragon's solar plexus. The blow propelled him backwards onto his back with rifle still in hand.

Dragon struggled to get to his feet. He looked around sweeping the barrel of his weapon from side to side, but once again, there was no sign of Cho.

A disturbance coming from the North Korean coast behind him diverted his attention. As he turned, he felt his head being twisted. The sound of a bone snapping in his neck was the last thing he would ever hear.

Cho brought the portly broker's body down to the ground as gently as he could.

Then he collapsed.

He knew one of the bullets Dragon fired hit him, but the sensation was not what he thought they would be.

Taking a round from an AK should have stopped me cold, but instead, I am alive and conscious and was able to take Dragon down. Maybe it was adrenaline, but the sensation of being shot does not seem right either. Instead of piercing pain, I feel a dull ache like I was hit with a sledgehammer and I cannot catch my breath.

Slowly, his breathing became easier. He reached a hand into his shirt and felt around for the bullet hole, but found none. Instead, his fingers came out with only a little blood on them.

The bullet didn't enter my body, but why?

Rising to his feet, Cho felt something rattling in his breast pocket. He reached in and withdrew the remnant of the Big-Brutha™ phone he was given. The screen was shattered almost directly in the center.

That's why. Now I have no way to contact the Americans, but it is better to be alive without a means of communication than dead with one.

Lights were illuminating from the North Korean shore. He rushed to each body and removed the plastic bags containing their phones and identification.

Their identification is false, but it is still possible to trace it back to who created it.

The North Korean coast watchers had heard the gunfire, and were now converging on the beach, exactly where he had planned to cross. They were beginning to shine large spot lights onto the islet.

Cho ran as fast as he could, He reached the southern tip of the small land mass just as a dozen North Korean soldiers came upon the bodies. They released dogs. As he backed into the water, Cho watched as the dogs ran in his direction. He watched with only his head above water as they sniffed at the shore. Half of the dozen North Korean shoulders followed after them with large flash lights bouncing in the darkness, but Cho didn't wait for them to get any closer.

He started wading in the direction of the North Korean coast, now some 50 meters away, instead of 30 meters at the northern tip of the islet. He was careful not to make splashing sounds, as he heard the sounds of the soldiers grow fainter.

Reaching the shore, he crawled out of the water and gazed back at the ruckus still taking place on the islet.

It is impossible for the snipers to have misunderstood Kang's orders, which means the Taejang ordered them to leave Dragon alive. That confirms my suspicions. Kang placed him with me. Probably to keep an eye on me, which means he does not trust me.

I cannot know if the snipers witnessed what I did to Dragon. If so, they will most certainly report it to Kang. If that is the case, it is possible Kang gave them new orders ... to kill me. I will have to be even more careful.

He felt raindrops on his head and looked up.

At least I won't be too conspicuous walking around in these wet clothes.

Deciding they could also be traced if used, Cho took the batteries out of each cell phone then buried all of the men's possessions under the sand. He had considered taking one of the rifles, but had no way to conceal it, so he left them where they lie.

He reached the road and crossed it, heading further inland, until he reached a dirt path that cut north along a hill. There, he stopped a moment to look back at the islet. Cho could see the lights from the North Korean soldiers fanning out to look for him.

This hill is most likely where the snipers took position. I need to think this through. If they saw what happened they would have already reported it, and Kang would be confused. As far as he knows, two Americans were killed at my request. If the snipers got a good look at what happened, they would tell Kang that Dragon shot at me first before I killed him. Kang would wonder why he shot at me in the first place, certainly not because two Americans were slain.

That means Kang will have to verify whether the men killed were, in fact, Americans. When he finds out they were not, he will give the snipers sanction to kill me. But first he still has to contact the morgue, which is what he is probably doing right now. That still buys me a little time.

Cho glanced all the way around him.

It also means that the snipers are probably still in the vicinity, but have to conceal themselves from the border soldiers. I will need to stay near enough to the shore where the border soldiers are, in order to keep the snipers at bay, at least until I reach the shack.

Once I am on the road in the car there will be plenty of opportunities for them to snipe me, and just as many for me to ambush them. Until then, I will have to be very cautious.

The sounds of dogs barking emanated from the direction where Cho came ashore. He began to walk quickly, but cautiously.

* * * * *

General Kang had his cell phone in one hand and the receiver of his desk phone against his ear, "You say they are not Americans? Are you certain?"

He placed the receiver back in its cradle and thought a moment. The more he thought, the angrier he became.

Finally, he opened his laptop and put the cell phone to his ear, "I have just established that the lone survivor is an enemy spy. Your orders are to kill him, but do so under cloak. There is a tracking device attached to the car he driving. I am sending you a link via email that will show you his real-time GPS coordinates on the map.

"I do not want our military or the local police to know of your actions. He most likely is heading for my headquarters here, but if he remains on the main road north, it will be difficult for you to catch up to him. The road winds through the mountains in several places between Manpo and here, so you better make haste. Under no circumstance is he to reach this facility. Is that clear? Contact me as soon as you have carried out your orders, but verify that the target is dead before you do."

Kang tossed the cell phone onto his desk and gritted his teeth. He banged the desk with his fist.

I should have known better. Our cousins to the south are dishonorable and untrustworthy. I know now that only fear will bring them in line. Fear flows from power, but I will not have that power until after our nations are at war.

He touched his fingertips together sitting back in his seat.

Our intelligence confirmed Colonel Cho's animosity towards President Park. I detected no sign of deceit when we met in Pyongyang, a meeting he came to at some risk to himself. And my spies in Busan have detected no undue troop or civilian movements, but that could be a ploy. Still, I cannot understand why he attempted to deceive me.

Then another thought crossed his mind, *if those men were not the Americans, where are the Americans and who were those men? Dragon's men perhaps ... but why have them killed?*

Perhaps I am wrong and there is an explanation, but the time is too close for me to take any chances. Losing the Colonel leaves me without a South Korean collaborator, but there were other potential candidates. After I begin this war, my spies can inform me of which to pursue. For now, it would be prudent to initiate my contingency plans.

He pulled up a map on his monitor.

I can only fire the Musudan missiles from here if I have any chance of hitting Busan, but I … can move one of the short range missiles without anyone, including Kim, suspecting anything.

We just completed test-firing one two weeks ago. I can explain the need to test-fire another to Pyongyang without raising an eye. Now I just need to find an isolated location. Ah, the site of our third nuclear test would be ideal. It is reachable from here and secluded.

He picked up the phone, "This is Kang. I am scheduling another test firing. This time we will test the No-Dong 2 with the GPS guidance systems. Have a battery of seven missiles moved to the following coordinates … 41.3060000, 129.065000. Begin immediately and inform me when it is in place."

He placed the receiver down and sat back again.

It appears that keeping the secondary target confidential from Colonel Cho was a wise precaution, after all.

His cell phone vibrated. He looked at the caller I.D.

It is Bok, my man in Seoul. The South Koreans are on high alert and he contacts me? I gave everyone I sent to South Korea specific orders not to contact me unless it was of vital importance!

"This better be urgent."

"Taejang, my informant at Incheon Airport notified me that a private jet registered to a Mr. Cris De Niro has just landed. I only contact you because my informant tells me that their landing clearance came directly from Daeryeong Cho."

Cris De Niro … that is who Cho told me President Park met with in Washington. The Americans work for him.

"I want them followed and I want their activities monitored."

"Yes, sir."

"Contact me only if you discover suspicious activity … anything connected with Daeryeong Cho or President Park."

"Understood, sir."

"And Bok, you did well. Remain vigilant."

He placed his cell phone down, took a cigarette from an ornate desk box and lit it.

Cho tells me to have snipers kill the Americans. Then I find they were not the

Americans. Cho kills Dragon and now the Americans' boss lands in Seoul less than a week before the attack is planned.

He took a long slow drag and held it before blowing the smoke from his lips and nose.

When I was just a boy, I remember my grandfather teaching me old Korean proverbs. He told me once, 'Even if you know the way, ask one more time'. When I asked him what it meant he said, "Do not be overconfident and assume that you know anything perfectly well. There are always unknown or unexpected details." My grandfather was wise indeed.

CHAPTER 20

DIANCHANG STREET & YANJIANG ROAD
ALONG JI'AN COAST
JILIN, CHINA
5:00 AM (LOCAL), SATURDAY, JUNE 01, 2013

Mugsy Ricci, Scipio, and Father Kim Sung-eun huddled under the priest's umbrella. Dawn had broken over the horizon less than an hour before and with it came rain.

At about the same time dawn broke, Father Kim had received a phone call from one of his contacts in the North Korean town of Manpo just across the river from Ji'an. He had alerted all of his North Korean contacts in the area to be on the lookout for anything suspicious near the border. This particular contact was a low ranking soldier assigned to coast watch duty.

The soldier told Father Kim of two very suspicious happenings – a North Korean patrol vessel had apparently run aground on the coast just south of Dianchang Street in Ji'an. Its crew had been tied up and left on the bow. Additionally, approximately a kilometer north, three men were found dead on a small islet in the middle of the Yalu

River.

Even more suspicious, two of the men were apparently shot dead, while the third, identified as a known human broker, appeared to have had his neck broken. Father Kim thanked the man and assured him that he would be recompensed for his information before waking Mugsy and Scipio and filled them in.

Mugsy spoke over his shoulder as they put on their boots, "Still trust the good colonel, Scip?"

Scipio ignored the question, "Our problem now is going to be how to cross into North Korea. I have a feeling Father Kim is gonna tell us that it'll be impossible crossing anywhere near Ji'an with all that activity this morning along the coast."

"That's quite possible," replied Father Kim, "but I won't know until we go to the coast ourselves and I talk again with my contact in Manpo."

Mugsy nodded, "Then let's saddle up."

Father Kim dialed a number on his cell phone, "I will call for a taxi. Where do you want to go, Captain?"

"Let's go to the location directly across from the beached boat first. It's worth taking a look."

* * * * *

In pouring rain, Mugsy and Scipio were using binoculars to look south across the Yalu River, while Father Kim spoke on his phone. The two focused on a gathering of North Korean soldiers, some standing in shallow water on a sand bar that jutted out over 200 meters from the North Korean coast while the others were aboard the patrol boat attempting to pilot it. The ones in the water appeared to be trying to help push the grounded patrol boat off the bar.

Mugsy spoke first while still peering through the binoculars, "What do you make of that?"

Scipio took some time to reply, "I'm not sure, it's hard to say without knowing more."

Mugsy turned his sights north in the direction of the islet, "Do you think the two events were connected?"

"It's possible. That patrol boat ran aground facing south. That means it came from the direction of the islet. And I think the timing of the two events is more than coincidental."

"I think so too."

Father Kim ended his call, "I just spoke again with my North Korean soldier contact in Manpo. He is so frightened, he asked me not to make contact with him again even to pay him. Apparently, there are many strange aspects to what happened earlier this morning. First, that patrol boat wasn't supposed to be patrolling these waters."

"That's curious," replied Mugsy, "did he say why?"

"He didn't want to explain further, but I quietly threatened to expose him."

"Father, that was downright evil of you," said Scipio.

"Scipio, leave the Father alone," Mugsy replied. "Go on, Father."

"He said that many of the soldiers aboard the patrol vessels shake down the local fisherman, both Chinese and North Korean, and also extort the brokers. He thinks the crew aboard that patrol boat might have been aware of an illegal crossing taking place and was attempting to do just that."

"But why would the patrol boat be ordered not to patrol these waters in the first place?" asked Scipio.

"That he did not know, but he said that it was highly unusual and I agree. The Yalu, between Ji'an and Manpo is very narrow. It is a location that is usually highly patrolled by the North Koreans."

"What about the crew?" asked Mugsy. "Did he mention their conditions? Was anyone killed?"

"He said only the Sowi … I don't know what you call that in the American Navy—"

"Sowi is equivalent to ensign," replied Mugsy, "which would most likely make him the commander of a boat that size. Go on Father."

Father Kim nodded, "He said the Sowi was the only person injured. He was punched in the throat."

Mugsy and Scipio glanced at one another.

"Punched in the throat, huh?" replied Scipio.

Father Kim nodded again, "No one was killed."

"Did the Sowi or any of the crew give statements?"

"Yes, but their descriptions were vague. Other than the crew of the vessel, they said there were four men. One was heavy set, two were larger and had hidden rifles and the one that punched the Sowi was a small man." The priest smiled.

"What's so funny?"

"I'm sorry, but my contact said that many of the crew have been using a nickname to call the small man that punched the Sowi. They said between his stature and the speed of his punch, he reminded them of the Chinese actor, Jet Li."

Scipio winked at Mugsy, "I'd say that's a good description of Cho."

"The crew also was in agreement that he was the one in charge. He was shouting orders to the others."

"What about the dead men on the islet, did he mention anymore about them?" asked Mugsy.

"Yes," replied Father Kim scratching his head, "and I will quote him word for word because I do not fully understand what he meant.

"He said that they believe that the gunshots came from high-powered rifles. He said they came to that conclusion for two reasons … apparently both were head shots?"

The men nodded motioning for him to continue.

"And the fact that the bullets passed completely through each man's head … is that significant?"

Mugsy looked at Scipio to explain.

"Head shots are difficult to pull off, especially from a distance. That indicates that the shooters were expert marksmen. And the fact that the bullets passed completely through each man's head indicates that the rounds were high-powered. Our guess would be snipers."

Father Kim looked at Mugsy, who neither nodded nor replied.

"I don't understand. Why would snipers kill those men?"

"Snipers only kill who they are ordered to kill," replied Scipio. "They don't choose their own targets. No. The question isn't why they killed those men. The question is who ordered them to."

"And the other question is why were the snipers only ordered to kill those two and not the others," added Mugsy.

"And while we're tagging on questions, why was the third man killed by a neck snap?" added Scipio. "At least we can be fairly sure of who did that … our friend Jet Li."

Father Kim wore an expression that was a combination of confusion and fear, "He also told me that they found footprints leading to the end of the islet and their tracking dogs had picked up the scent of a person, but they found no one."

"That's because the dogs lost the scent the moment he entered the water," replied Scipio.

"So he swam his way to North Korea right under the noses of their soldiers," Mugsy thought out loud. He turned again to Father Kim, "Father, did your contact mention whether they were tracking anyone inland?"

"He said that an entire company of soldiers are now patrolling the whole coastline from Manpo to points directly across from Ji'an. But, he did not mention anything about tracking anyone inland."

Mugsy nodded.

"That causes us a problem though. There is no way that we can cross anywhere near here. I'm afraid we will not be able to trace the steps of this man Cho after all."

"We won't need to Father," replied Scipio. "We know where he's heading. We showed you on the map back at the safe house. Our question to you is - can you help us cross into North Korea somewhere near the destination?"

Father Kim thought a moment, "Can you pull up a map on your phone's screen again, please?"

Scipio did so and handed him the phone.

Father Kim used his finger to move the map around until he zoomed in on one location, "I used to have a contact in Hyesan. The industrial town you told me about lies about 15 kilometers to the east of the city. The town itself is only about 60 kilometers from your destination."

"If the Colonel's plans haven't changed, he'll be heading to that town to make contact with the dissidents. He needs them to lead him to Kim. That's where we need to go," replied Scipio.

"How do we go from here to there Father?" asked Mugsy.

"We can travel by bus to the Chinese city of Changbai. It is in the district of Baishan, in Jilin province. Changbai is directly across from Hyesan. If we catch the next bus, we can probably get there today, but then it may take a day to cross over the border, perhaps longer. I will call to verify my contact is still in Hyesan. If he is there, I will have him arrange for a car to be waiting for us there."

"Then we better get started," replied Scipio. "If we assume Cho has access to a car, it looks like it's a curvy, circuitous route to Hyesan from Manpo. That should still put him in there sometime this afternoon, so we'll be trailing him by at least a day."

Mugsy took his phone, "Come on, let's get back to the safe house so we can pack our things and hit the road. I'll send a message to Cris now and let him know our plans."

CHAPTER 21

PRESIDENTIAL SUITE
FOSTER LAFAYETTE HOTEL, SEOUL
SEOUL, SOUTH KOREA
6:30 AM (LOCAL), SATURDAY, JUNE 01, 2013

Michelle Wang walked out of the oversized master bedroom and into the parlor of the magnificent suite, "Okay, that is the biggest bedroom I've ever seen. It's actually bigger than my first apartment."

John Francis put an arm around De Niro's shoulder and kissed his cheek, "Yeah, well you probably don't know this Michelle, but our billionaire boss here grew up in a railroad apartment that could fit in the bathroom."

Michelle dropped onto the sofa. She grabbed a banana from a large fruit bowl and started peeling it, "Actually, Mugsy told me that. He's been telling me a lot of things about you guys."

De Niro wiped his face where Francis kissed it, "He has, has he? Remind me to have a talk with him, John. Have to remind him about the vault."

Michelle tried to reply with banana in her mouth, "What's the …," she chewed and swallowed, "what's the vault?"

Francis took an apple from the bowl and shined it on his sleeve before taking a large bite. He didn't bother chewing before replying, "The vault … is code … for keeping your mouth shut about the past. It's a guy thing."

"Guy thing huh," replied Michelle, "who do ya think invented it. I just asked 'cause I didn't think guys knew about it."

De Niro smiled and winked at Michelle as his cell phone rang. He looked at the screen, "Mugsy?"

Michelle jumped up.

"Hey Cris. I'm here with Scipio and Father Kim."

"I'm putting you on speaker. I'm here with Michelle and Johnny-F."

"Hi baby."

Michelle blushed but smiled, "Hi. How are you? Where are you?"

"Hello to you too, Mugs," added Francis.

De Niro glanced at his childhood friend with a grin, "Mugsy, Do you have time to talk?"

"I do. We're on our way back to the safe house to pack our things. Then we have to board a bus that'll take us farther north. Cris, a couple of hours ago Cho crossed into North Korea. Apparently, he was with the broker, Dragon, and Dragon's men, but they're all dead."

De Niro looked at Michelle, a sign for her to take over. His grin disappeared.

"Dead … how?"

"Dragon's men were downed by sniper rounds—"

"Sniper rounds …?" Francis interjected.

"And someone broke Dragon's neck."

Michelle and De Niro's eyes remained locked as she continued, "And the Colonel?"

"They found no trace of him, but we suspect he made it into North Korea."

"Mugsy, it's Cris, any idea who ordered those men killed?"

"Negative, but whoever it was, had to have known the exact time and place where they were gonna cross. I'll bet dollars-to-donuts the good colonel snapped Dragon's neck."

"Understood."

"Where are you going to cross?" asked Michelle.

"I won't say here. We're in a taxi. The driver doesn't speak a word of English, at least he acts like he doesn't, but he'd certainly understand names of cities and towns. I'll send it to you guys now."

A moment later, an encrypted text messaging app opened on everyone's phone with the message, 'Changbai in a day or two' written.

Michelle replied with 'Got it.'

"Mugs, it's Cris again, what's your plan?"

"Our plan is basically the same, Cris. We intend to cross with the help of Father Kim and then make it to the town with the dissidents. Perhaps there, we'll be able to rendezvous with Cho."

Michelle's face became tense, "Mugs, we've changed our plans. We're no longer going to investigate Daejang Jeong. We believe … we believe Cho is Kang's contact in South Korea. He might even be a co-conspirator with him. There's not enough time left to investigate both and we … I … think Cho's our man."

"I had similar suspicions Michelle, but Scipio maintains that Cho is on our side. I'm starting to believe it too."

"Mugs, it's Cris, if you're wrong about Cho, you, Scipio, and the Father could be heading right into a trap."

"And it's going to take us time to investigate him," added Michelle. "I'm not sure we can find anything conclusive before you may run into him, and maybe not ever. Cho might be too sharp to leave a trail."

There was a slight pause before Mugsy replied, "Understood. Then we'll have to proceed on our hunch. In the meantime, you still have a couple of days. Make 'em count. I gotta go. I'll be in touch."

"Take care of yourself, Mugs," replied De Niro.

"I love you. Be careful," added Michelle. De Niro noticed her eyes reddened.

"I love you too, babe. Take care of her, Cris."

The line went dead.

"Don't worry about me, I'll just take care of myself," replied

Francis aloud.

De Niro ignored him and sat next to Michelle. He took her hand in his, "They'll both remain in our prayers until we see them again."

Michelle nodded without speaking.

"Cris, I'm confused," said Francis. "First Mugsy didn't trust Cho, but Scipio did. And Cho doesn't trust General Kim, or not? And now it sounds like both Mugsy and Scipio kind of trust Cho, but now we don't … or do we?"

De Niro took a long time to reply, "I don't know. I don't know what to think of the Colonel at this point. The best course of action for us is to investigate him as thoroughly and quickly as we can. If we can turn anything conclusive linking Cho with Kang, we may save Mugsy and Scipio's lives as well as the priest's."

He stood and walked to the phone, "Let's get to work. I'll order breakfast with tea for you Michelle and coffee for us. My dad used to call coffee 'thinking fluid.'"

Francis opened his laptop, "I'll start seeing if I can hack into the South Korean Secret Service servers. I doubt he kept anything incriminating on their network, but we still may learn things from his emails and files."

"Where would he keep anything incriminating," asked De Niro, "local on his own computer?"

"Maybe, or on a zip drive or memory stick … or maybe he just deletes the most secret files. There's no way to know, and if he doesn't keep it powered there's no way for me to access his local drive without plugging into it."

Michelle already opened her laptop, "Then that's what I'll work on … getting access to his home and office, if possible. And I'll see if I can trace his whereabouts from credit card receipts."

"We can do that?" asked De Niro, startled. "That sounds very NSA."

"Thanks to Johnny-F, we can."

"A round of applause for Mr. John Francis," cried Francis, in a mock voice.

De Niro placed his hand on Michelle's shoulder to comfort her as he called room service. She covered his hand with hers.

CHAPTER 22

OFFICE OF THE COMMANDER
MANPO AIRBASE
CHAGANGDO PROVINCE
NORTH KOREA
10:00 AM (LOCAL), SATURDAY, JUNE 01, 2013

Sojang Kim walked past a burly chungwi (lieutenant) who had opened the door for him and stood at attention. He entered the office of Sojang Hyon Yong-chol, Commander of Manpo Airbase, and stood before his desk. Both men saluted, though Sojang Hyon did not rise from his chair.

Kim ignored the slight, "Good morning, Sojang. I hope I have not taken you away from anything."

"In fact, you have," Sojang Hyon's tone was terse. "First, you send me instructions that sounded like orders, without explanation. Then I receive further instructions to remain here in my office until you arrive, again, without any explanation. I had to cancel a breakfast engagement. May I remind you, Sojang, we are of the same rank. On whose authority—"

Kim cut him off turning to the chungwi, "Leave us, and close the door behind you."

Hyon rose from his chair. His cheeks reddened, "Sojang Kim, this is outrageous! How dare you order my staff without asking my—"

"Sit down, Hyon."

"I will do no such thing. Who do you think you are giving me orders in my own office?!"

"Sit down or I will call security and have you placed under arrest for dereliction of duty and perhaps even treason."

"Treason … what are you talking about?!"

"I said sit down. I will not tell you again."

Hyon rubbed his chin with anxiety before lowering himself into the chair.

Kim placed his fingers on the edge of Hyon's desk and leaned in towards him, "Now listen carefully, for I will not repeat myself, nor will I verbally spar with you.

"I am here by orders and authority of Taejang Kang to investigate into the circumstances that took place this morning. I am speaking of the illegal incursion of an unknown individual across a stretch of border that is directly under your authority."

"But, you are Taejang Kang's adjutant. Taejang Kang is in charge of our missiles—"

"Hyon, before we go further, do you accept the authority given to me, or would you like to speak to Taejang Kang personally? I should warn you, the Taejang is hosting a reception for visiting Cabinet members this morning."

Hyon hesitated. His tone softened, "Perhaps you would show me your orders?"

Kim leaned in further. *If he calls my bluff, Kang will have me shot. He specifically told me not to investigate this, which is exactly why I have to. It makes no sense for Kang not to want a border crossing incident investigated, especially one that left three dead and one on the loose in our country close to Punggye-Ri.*

"Hyon, Taejang Kang sent me here without written orders to preserve your military career. The Taejang fully understands how even the perception of impropriety can be misread by those in Pyongyang.

"My orders are merely to investigate what happened here this morning. There is no reason to even include your name in my report, unless of course, you want to start the paper trail with written orders. In that case, I will contact Taejang Kang immediately and have him cut them. The choice is yours."

Hyon's face became tight, "This is all very unusual."

Kim began punching numbers on his cell phone.

"What are you doing? Who are you calling?"

Kim put the phone to his ear, "I told you I do not have the time or the inclination to spar with you."

"Wait … there's no need to call. Please."

Kim waited until he heard his own voice mail then disconnected the call, "Then you accept the authority that has been vested in me by the Taejang?"

Hyon nodded sharply.

"Very well. Understand though, the details of this investigation are classified top secret, including anything discussed in this office. Is that clear?"

Hyon nodded again.

"To satisfy your curiosity, the reason Taejang Kang sent me here is because he is concerned. We received credible intelligence that a foreign operative, perhaps South Korean, is planning to sabotage the Punggye-Ri Test Site."

Though that is a lie, it is also my hope. I need to find out who this infiltrator is. Either the South Koreans sent someone to stop Kang or Kang's South Korean accomplice has come instead.

If the former, I will have to find a way to contact him and perhaps even help him. If the latter, I must know if he is aware of me, from my note. If he is, does Kang also know about me? I doubt it. I would be dead already, but I have to be sure.

Sojang Hyon's brows lifted, "That is insanity. It could provoke a war! But why …?"

"Apparently after the Americans sent their B-2 bombers to participate in war games with the South, our country's threats to launch missiles provoked this desperate action.

"Now you understand why I am here, and why this investigation must remain covert? If Pyongyang discovers that a South Korean has infiltrated our country, they may escalate their rhetoric. That could lead to war. In any case, they will most certainly look for someone to blame. That would be you, Hyon."

Hyon rubbed his chin again, "How can I be of service to your investigation?"

"Did you carry out my instructions?"

"Yes, we had the crew of the patrol boat look at the photos you sent. I viewed them too. They were all high-ranking South Korean officers. Kim, you cannot believe that the one who escaped is a high-ranking South Korean officer."

"That is a question you should not ask if you value your freedom, Hyon. Now ... were any recognized?"

"Unfortunately, they did not recognize any of them as the man that took them captive."

"I brought more photos. Please have the head of the crew report here at once."

Hyon made a phone call then smiled immodestly, "The sowi who was in command of the patrol boat is here. He was injured in the attack, but I anticipated you may have wanted to speak with him. I took the liberty of having the hospital release him, and had him report here. They are fetching him from the barracks."

Kim made no gesture, "While we wait I would like to take a look at the incident report and the autopsy reports on the three that were killed."

Hyon handed Kim four manila folders from atop his desk. Kim opened each and scanned them as Hyon explained, "As you see, two were shot with high-powered rifles and the third had his neck broken."

Kim studied the reports, "What do you make of that, Sojang?"

Hyon rested back in his chair, "With respect, Sojang, these things happen on the border. One of the men was a known broker, and the other two were most likely his bodyguards. Smugglers and brokers are notoriously unscrupulous individuals. Undoubtedly, these men died as a result of some underhanded deal gone bad."

Kim looked up, "So you believe what, Sojang? All these men died at the hands of the man that escaped into our country? What about the two shot with high-powered rifles?"

"The one that escaped most likely had accomplices."

"Accomplices where …? I have already read the incident report. It made no mention of other accomplices on North Korean soil."

"Ah, but the bodyguards were shot with high-powered rifles, Sojang. You may not be aware, but the distance is not far, between the Chinese mainland, and that islet. The accomplices must have been positioned on the Chinese coast."

I'm fully aware of the distance, you condescending fool. If this idiot would have examined the reports instead of jumping to baseless conclusions, he would have noticed that the bodyguards were shot in the front of their heads.

Their bodies came to rest on their backs, with their legs facing our country, which means — they - were facing our country.

How could anyone on the Chinese coast shoot them in the front of their heads, if they were facing North Korea when they were shot? Idiot!

If this man is any indication of the level of competence of our border commanders, it is a wonder that we have not yet been invaded. I will keep my deductions to myself, though. The less this fool knows the better.

Kim looked up from the files, "And what can you deduce from the other man … the broker's death?"

Hyon grinned, "Apparently, his personal combat skills were inferior to the fourth man's. As a result, his neck was snapped."

Once again, this fool deduced nothing. He has not asked himself why the snipers did not kill the broker also. And the photos of the scene clearly show that the broker had one of his bodyguard's rifles in his hands when he met his fate.

At least the men on the scene did their jobs taking photos and measurements, as well as counting the rounds in each magazine. The rifle the broker was holding was the only weapon fired. A reasonable assumption can be made that he did indeed, fire at the fourth man.

Additionally, the broker's body was lying with his legs facing China, which makes me think that: a.) He turned to face the fourth man to fire at him; b.) the fourth man must be extremely agile to both evade the shots and get to the broker; and c.) the fourth man is proficient in the martial arts. It's not as easy as one may think to snap a man's neck.

Only the most disturbing conclusion can be made of this.

Taejang Kang is the highest ranking officer in this part of the country. There is no way snipers could receive kill orders without at least his knowing about it. Combine that with Kang explicitly ordering me not to investigate this incident and it can only mean that Kang sanctioned the snipers actions.

That also means Kang wanted the broker and the forth man left alive. I am unsure why and I am also unsure why the broker attempted to kill the forth man.

There was a knock at the door.

"That would be the sowi." Hyon raised his voice, "Enter."

The same chungwi opened the door for the sowi to enter. The junior grade officer, a tall, bony figure, stepped into the office, saluted, and came to attention, "You wanted to see me, Sojang Hyon?"

"Sowi, this is Sojang Kim. He is the one that wants to see you."

"Yes, sir?"

Kim took a binder from his attaché, set it down on Hyon's desk and opened it, "I want you to take a look at more photos."

The Sowi nodded and began turning pages.

"I understand from your report that you had a good look at the men. Is that so?"

"Yes Sojang, I was face-to-face with them."

"I also understand that you were not supposed to be patrolling those waters at that time. Who gave you those orders?"

The Sowi looked up with anxiety, "As I stated in the report, Sojang, the Sangwi issued the order for us to patrol farther north on the river. He is the River Patrol officer in charge."

Kim turned to Hyon, "Have the Sangwi report here now."

Hyon nodded and made another phone call.

Kim noticed that Hyon was obeying his orders without question now.

"Why did you disobey your orders, Sowi?"

The Sowi fidgeted, "I also stated that in my report, Sojang. We followed the fishing vessel from our patrol area—"

"You are lying."

"Sojang, I—"

Kim held up his hand, "Sowi, stop before you get yourself into even more trouble. Let me be clear, I will ask the question again, and you will answer that question and every question thereafter honestly, or I will have you shot. Is that understood?"

The Sowi's face lost color, "Yes Sojang."

"Why did you disobey your orders?"

The Sowi glanced at Sojang Hyon, "I had a feeling that the Sangwi ordered us away from that area because … he knew those men would be crossing there at that time."

Sojang Hyon jumped to his feet, "You lied in your report! I will have you thrown in prison!"

"Hyon, please, let me finish my questioning then you may do what you want with him."

Hyon nodded, never taking his eyes off the cowering sowi.

"What gave you that feeling, Sowi? Why would you think the Sangwi would do such a thing?"

The Sowi took a moment before replying, "Because he has done it before. It is common knowledge in the River Patrol."

There was a knock at the door. This time Hyon hollered, "Enter!"

Once again, the chungwi opened the door. The Sangwi, a rough-looking, pockmarked man entered, saluted, and came to attention, "You wanted to—"

"Sit down, Sangwi," the order came from Kim. "Chungwi, remain here."

The Sangwi gazed at the gaunt Sowi, as he took a seat.

"I am Sojang Kim. You are here to answer my questions. While you are here, your family is being rounded up."

Kim nodded to Hyon, who understood and lifted the phone.

"If you refuse to answer any of my questions, if you lie, or omit any pertinent fact, one by one, I will have your family members shot starting with your wife and children. And if we run out of your family members I will have your fingers cut off and fed to dogs, one digit at a time. Do you understand me?"

The Sangwi's expression of terror was enough to answer the question, but he added in a cracked voice, "Yes Sojang."

"Understand something else … I am not interested in what you have done. If you have done something wrong, Sojang Hyon will deal with it."

"And I will, Sangwi, trust me, I will," added Hyon.

"I am only interested in the truth. First, did you know those men were going to try and cross into our country at that location this morning?"

The Sangwi's eyes filled with tears. He nodded.

"Sangwi, I know you are frightened, but I will not repeat my questions again. You will answer in full voice. Did you know those men were going to try and cross into our country, at that location, this morning … yes or no?"

"Yes Sojang."

"How did you know?"

"The broker … he and I have done business before."

"Done business? Explain."

"Yes Sojang, from time to time Dragon … that is his name—"

"Correction … that was his name."

The Sangwi nodded, "He would pay me to allow him to smuggle certain goods into the country. Just things like food and cigarettes, I swear—"

Kim backhanded him across the face, knocking him from the chair. Kim motioned to the Chungwi to lift him back into it.

"You lie. For that, Sojang Hyon, please have this man's wife shot right outside this window so he can watch."

"No, Sir, please! I misspoke. I meant to say, it used to be only things like food and cigarettes."

"And progressed to what?"

The Sangwi wiped blood from the corner of his mouth, "It progressed to … smuggling defectors out of the country."

Sojang Hyon rushed from around his desk and punched the Sangwi in his face knocking him backwards off the chair. Again, the Chungwi helped him back into it.

Kim pushed Hyon back. Hyon pointed at the Sangwi, "You did this right under my nose?! If you were caught, I would have been shot along with you!"

Kim led Hyon back into his chair, "Please Hyon, do what you want after I question him."

Hyon nodded glaring down at his desk.

Kim pulled tissues from a box and handed them to the Sangwi, whose nose was now bleeding along with his lip.

"Sangwi, you said smuggled defectors out of the country, but this Dragon was attempting to sneak into our country, was he not?"

The Sangwi nodded before remembering to answer, "Yes Sojang. Dragon originally said that he needed to smuggle three men into the country along with himself and his two bodyguards."

"Three men …?"

"Yes Sojang, but then he contacted me again to say it would only be one man with him and his men."

"That is interesting. Go on."

"That is it, Sojang. Dragon told me the time and place and I just had to make sure no patrols would be in the vicinity."

"He did not tell you the names of these men, or their identities?"

"No, Sojang."

"And you didn't ask?"

"No, Sojang."

"So you could be letting our enemies in and not even care?" said Hyon.

"No. Dragon would never do that, Sojang. He knows … he knew I would kill him if he ever did something like that. Besides, we both made a lot of money. He would never have risked it."

Kim paced a moment before stopping in front of the Sangwi, "Did Dragon mention where the men were heading?"

"No, Sojang, he did not." He thought a moment, "He did say he would call on me again, anytime from a few days to a week or so later, in order to arrange for them to cross back into China."

"He said a few days to a week or so?"

"Yes, sir."

"Sojang Kim," the Sowi cried out from the side of the desk. He was pointing down to a page in the binder. "This is the man! I am sure of it!"

Sojang Hyon got up from his desk.

"Sojang," barked Kim. "You will leave this office at once and take the rest of these men."

Hyon checked his temper, but only with effort, "I only wanted to see—"

"If you see, I must report. Do you understand?"

Once again, Hyon nodded his head crisply.

Kim waited for everyone else to leave the office and for the door to be closed before walking next to the Sowi. He looked down at the photo, "Are you absolutely certain that is the man?"

"Yes Sojang. He is the man that punched me in the throat."

So, this is Kang's South Korean accomplice. I must get word somehow to President Park.

"Very well," Kim turned to the door and shouted for the Chungwi, "Take this man out of my sight."

When the room was empty, Kim took the photo of Daeryeong Cho Jung-woo of the Presidential Security Service of the Republic of Korea from the binder and placed it in his breast pocket. He sat on the edge of the desk thinking until Sojang Hyon returned.

Hyon took a seat in the chair behind his desk, "I want to thank you for bringing this to my attention. I assure you I will put a stop to all of the illicit activities going on in the River Patrol. Have you completed your investigation?"

"No, I have not."

Hyon watched him, confused, as Kim walked over to a copier and made a copy of Cho's photo. He wrote a message on it and signed it.

"May I have an envelope please?"

Hyon pointed to a small file cabinet, "There are supplies in there."

Kim took an envelope from the cabinet, folded and placed the copied sheet inside and sealed it.

He wrote, 'For eyes of President Park only' then dropped the envelope into a larger manila one.

He turned to Hyon, "Do you have any captured defectors here?"

"Defectors, why yes. In this weather, we capture some practically every week trying to cross the river."

"May I see their dossiers?"

"Of course, but you should know that we do not hold them for very long. They are transported regularly to nearby detention camps. We only have the files on ones that are currently here. The files are in the cabinet next to the one with the supplies."

Kim opened the cabinet and started reading the dossiers.

Hyon walked over to him, "Are you looking for anyone in particular?"

I'm looking for the brightest one I can find, hopefully brighter than you, you fool … and one with family.

He pulled the file of a young woman, "Bring this woman to me right now, and then I would impose on you again, Hyon, to please allow me to speak to her privately."

Hyon took the file and made another phone call. It took less than five minutes for the woman to enter the office, and for Hyon to leave. She looked terrified.

Kim held his arm out, "Please sit down."

The woman did as she was told. She looked like she was on the verge of crying.

"Your name is Kim Hyun Hee?"

The small woman, with short black hair and wire-framed glasses nodded affirmatively.

"You wish to leave our country, Hyun Hee?"

Kim used her familiar name to try and ease her nerves. It had little effect. She remained silent.

Kim knelt down and looked up at her, "Hyun Hee, I need you to do something for me. In return, I will not only allow you to escape, I will facilitate it. I do not have time to wait and see if you believe me. Tell me now whether you do or else I will get another."

The frightened woman tilted her head in confusion, but finally replied, "I … believe you."

"Good. I do not have much time. It is very simple what I want you to do."

He handed her the manila envelope, "I will make arrangements for you to cross the river and enter Ji'an. From there, you will have to make your way to Beijing. I will have you given enough money, not only to make it to Beijing, but also to buy your way to South Korea.

"But first, I need you to go to the FedEx location in Beijing. It is a store where you will mail this envelope, to an address I will give you. I will also supply you with the address of the FedEx location. Do you understand what to do?"

She nodded, "I believe so."

"It says in your dossier that you were a teacher."

"Yes."

"I chose you because I believe you have the aptitude to carry out this assignment and are smart enough to not ask any questions, to me or anyone else. I also chose you because you have a large family living nearby. I am not a vicious man, Hyun Hee, but this assignment is crucial so I will tell you, I am expecting a reply from the recipient within 72 hours. If I do not receive that reply, I will assume that you betrayed me. I will have your entire family killed, if you betray me. Do you understand?"

She nodded, holding back tears.

Unlike my peers, I am unable to do something that horrific, but she would not know that. And I will not receive a response, but I needed some way to compel her to send the message.

"Very well," Kim stood up. "You are to send the package by the fastest method possible. From the time you cross into Ji'an it will take you approximately 48 hours to get to Beijing. That includes the stops in between. I will allow another 24 hours for the package to reach the recipient. The recipient will be able to communicate directly with me instantly. Are you clear on all of this?"

"Yes, sir."

"Good, come with me. I will take you somewhere to eat. Meanwhile, I will make the necessary arrangements."

And then I will try my best to track down and kill this Daeryeong Cho before he makes contact with Kang. That might not stop Kang, but it may at least derail part of his plans.

Kim walked past a confused Sojang Hyon on the way out, "You may have your office back."

CHAPTER 23

WAREHOUSE
OUTSKIRTS OF INDUSTRIAL TOWN
15 KILOMETERS EAST OF HYESAN
NORTHERN RYANGGANG PROVINCE
NORTH KOREA
10:00 AM (LOCAL), SATURDAY, JUNE 01, 2013

Without the Big-Brutha™ phone he was given, Cho had to recall from memory the exact location of the abandoned warehouse the dissidents were using as their headquarters. Though his memory was nearly photographic, the fact that he only saw it from overhead satellite imagery made finding it difficult.

From the ground, the building was nondescript and set back 100 meters from the main road with only one dirt path that led to it. And that path only broke off from the main road for west-bound traffic while he was traveling east. Upon arriving in the vicinity, Cho ended up passing it and having to turn around, but that was no problem. There was virtually no traffic in sight – not on the main road or in the industrial town he just traversed.

The town itself had no name. On the Big-Brutha™ map it was marked with the generic name "small industrial town." The town stretched less than a kilometer in any direction, with its only distinguishing feature being that it was wrapped on three sides – west, north, and east, by the same irrigation canal that the main road roughly followed.

Cho remembered that the warehouse was situated at the eastern tip of a small industrial complex that jutted out from the town on its southeastern border. After passing the last building on his left and seeing nothing but vacant expanse, he made a u-turn.

What he saw as he drove up the dirt path was not what he expected to see. Instead of a rugged industrial cement structure, he was approaching a drab, long, rectangular, one-story wooden building with a blue angled roof. The only features demarking its front were two windows and a door.

He stopped in front of the door. There were no other vehicles parked outside.

Cho stepped out of the car and looked around. He glanced up at the overcast sky. It was a humid morning but the temperature was comfortable, which made his sore ribs ache a bit less.

He took only a few steps towards the door when it opened. One by one, men stepped out, seven in all, two wielding AK-47 rifles. Cho could also see women staring out of the windows inside.

The two seem uncomfortable ... inexperienced with toting weapons, or perhaps both.

A thin man sporting thick, black glasses and black suit stepped from their midst with hands folded behind his back. He bowed his head slightly and spoke softly, "This is a secure area. You are not permitted to be here."

"Nor are you, I suspect," replied Cho, folding his hands in front of him.

The bespeckled man tilted his head slightly, "Are you with the government?"

"And if I am?"

The man hesitated before replying, "Perhaps I should introduce myself. I am Song Keun-woo. I am a propagandist for the state."

Cho looked past him, "And who are they?"

"They are my staff. I am in charge, as well as being the head artist. My staff and I operate a printing facility inside."

Cho grinned, "And do your art staff always carry automatic weapons?"

"Only when confronted by strangers, which brings us to you …."

"I am Cho Jung-woo. I am here to see Kim Gil-su."

Song blinked unthinkingly while the men behind him were even more unable to conceal their shock.

Song remained soft-spoken, "That name is unfamiliar to me, as is yours."

Cho unfolded his arms. The action caused the men with the rifles to point them at him.

"Perhaps you should ask your art staff to lower their weapons, before someone gets hurt."

Song nodded to one of the unarmed men. He stepped up to Cho cautiously. The man made a frightened and sloppy attempt to frisk him. Cho obliged by raising his arms away from his body.

I could be concealing a rocket-propelled grenade launcher and I think this one would miss it.

The scared man shook his head before returning to his place. Song nodded to the rest who returned single file back into the building.

"As I have said, I do not know the person you—"

"Mr. Song, I believe you know exactly who Sojang Kim is. You are the leader of the dissident cell in this area, are you not?"

"Who are you?"

"I told you my name, Cho Jung-woo of the Presidential Security Service of the Republic of Korea. I'm in charge of her Excellency President Park's security detail."

The slender man's only visual *tell* revealing his anxiety was the flutter of his eyelids. His voice remained calm and only a fraction over a whisper, "You must forgive my skepticism, but you come here alone, and I assume without any identification?"

"One does not infiltrate behind enemy lines with identification,

Mr. Song."

"And why exactly would a member of President Park's security detail infiltrate enemy lines?"

"You may address me as Daeryeong Cho, Mr. Song, and I have told you why. I am here to speak with Sojang Kim. The Sojang handed a note to the leader of the dissident cell here to give to a certain soldier whose family lives in the town to the west. He gave the note to you, did he not?"

Song looked down at the ground and rolled his foot over a stone, "Even if you are who you say you are, I still cannot understand your purpose for being here."

"Mr. Song, the soldier to whom you gave the note defected with it. It was addressed for eyes only of my President, but of course it needed to be verified for authenticity. Once President Park was certain that Sojang Kim was in fact the author of the note, she dispatched me to make contact with him."

I do not need to tell him the real reason President Park sent me. To investigate what Kim asserted, that a South Korean was collaborating with Kang making the President unsure who she could trust.

I also do not need to mention that I was that official.

Song finally revealed some shock.

I am unsure how much of that he already knew, but it makes no difference. Now he knows that I know.

Song's brows lifted, "But why come here … to me?"

"For reasons unknown, Sojang Kim neglected to tell us how to get in contact with him. Our only avenue was to interrogate the soldier—"

"You tortured Sae-hoon?!"

Cho furrowed his brow but let his grin remain, "Mr. Song, I said we interrogated him. In contrast to your North Korean methods of interrogation, our methods allow the interrogated party to survive the experience with all his body parts.

"In fact, you said his name was Sae-hoon … Sae-hoon practically volunteered your location when he realized we only intended to offer assistance to Sojang Kim."

Song breathed a sigh of relief before regaining is composure,

"Sae-hoon and I were friends from childhood. I am pleased to know that he is unharmed, but is he imprisoned?"

"No, after the interrogation, he was released and put in touch with a group of fellow defectors. I believe they found lodgings and a job for him in Seoul. If you would like, I can carry a message from you to him."

Song shook his head in fear, "No, I could never …." He cut himself off.

Cho stepped closer, "Take your time and think about it. Just let me know before I depart."

Song nodded and added with sincerity, "Thank you, Daeryeong."

Cho replied with one nod, eyes closed.

Song began to pace, "I am grateful for what you told me about Sae-hoon and appreciate you kind offer, but I cannot take you to Sojang Kim. For one thing, I do not know where he is. He does not tell me. And for another, from what you told me, I am not sure he wants you to contact him. If he did, he would certainly have instructed you on how to find him."

"Mr. Song, that may be true, the Sojang may very well have thought he could merely inform us of impending disaster and then expect us to intervene without his help."

Cho noticed fear on Song's face. *So, he did not know the details of the letter.*

"Yes, Mr. Song, I said impending disaster, for both of our countries and perhaps for the rest of the world too, if we do not do something now."

"But, I told you, I do not know where the Sojang is."

"You must have some way of contacting him?"

Song looked down at the ground again, "He gave me his cell phone number, but admonished me only to use it that one time when I was to retrieve the note from him. He told me never to use it again."

"You will contact him now. Tell him that a representative from President Park is here and wants to see him immediately."

Song hesitated.

"Mr. Song, you and your followers are obviously brave men

and women. In the face of tyranny and with the constant threat of exposure and risk of capture, you press on. Why do you do this?"

Song straightened up, "We do this for our people. Our people starve. Our men are beaten, and our women raped by the immoral animals that are in power. They keep us cut off from the rest of the world … cut off from our cousins to the south."

"That is true, but what if I told you that one man is intending to ignite a confrontation between north and south that will lead to our mutual destruction? This confrontation will lead to suffering on a scale that even your countrymen have not experienced. That was what Sojang Kim explained in the note and that is why I must speak with him now. Time is very short."

Song took another minute before pulling a cell phone from his pocket.

"Mr. Song, do not tell Sojang Kim my name. Only say that I am a representative of my President."

Song's expression changed to one of suspicion, "But why?"

"Because we must make sure that the Sojang comes. The less he knows about my identity, the more he will need to come to find out who I am."

"Perhaps you are worried that he will know who you are?"

"On the contrary, I'm almost certain he knows who I am, in the vaguest terms. However, curiosity is a much more powerful motivator than remote familiarity. Is that not so?"

Song looked confused, but nodded quickly as he heard Sojang's voice on the other end of the line. As he spoke, Cho noticed a vehicle passing slowly on the main road. He used binoculars but could not see the occupants of the car.

There were two of them, just like there were two snipers … Dragon's bodyguards dropped almost simultaneously. If the road had more vehicular traffic, I would not even have noticed.

Song put his phone away and stepped next to Cho, "The Sojang was not happy that I called him or that I could not supply him with your identity. I told him that you would not give it to me."

Cho kept his eyes facing in the direction of the car with the two men in it, "Is he coming?"

Song tried to follow his eyes, "Yes. He said he will arrive here tomorrow morning. Did you see something?"

Cho ignored the question, "What else did the Sojang say?"

"He … told me to place you under armed guard until he arrives, but I explained to him that you are not armed and pose no threat."

Cho grinned in a way that made Song feel unsure of what he just said.

Song continued to look out to the road, "What do you see?"

Better not to complicate matters by having to explain that snipers are probably here trying to kill me.

"Mr. Song, might I impose on you to allow me to lodge here tonight?"

"Here? I see no reason why you could not come home with me. I live in town."

Cho let his eyes follow the car with the two men in it, "I think it might be safer if I remained here."

Following Cho's eyes, Song's understanding grew, "In that case, we will all remain here with you tonight. Come."

* * * * *

The car with the Sangsa sitting in the passenger seat and the Hasa driving, pulled over to the side of the road a half-kilometer after passing the GPS coordinates of Cho's car. Both stepped out and used the scopes from their rifles to look back towards the warehouse.

The Sangsa scanned the area adjacent to the road. He pointed to it, "That path leads behind the structure in the distance. The GPS signal must be emanating from the car parked in front of it. I do not see any windows on the side of the structure."

"There are none," said the Hasa still looking through his scope."

"Do you see the oil tanks about 100 meters beyond it?"

The Hasa redirected his scope, "Yes."

"We will park the car in the row of buildings behind that structure, cross the rest of the terrain on foot, and take positions on top of those tanks."

"An ideal perch," replied the Hasa."

The Sangsa took the photo of Cho out of his breast pocket, "The way he moved and snapped that man's neck, we will have to be very careful with this one."

CHAPTER 24

WAREHOUSE
OUTSKIRTS OF INDUSTRIAL TOWN
15 KILOMETERS EAST OF HYESAN
NORTHERN RYANGGANG PROVINCE
NORTH KOREA
6:00 AM (LOCAL), SUNDAY, JUNE 02, 2013

The Hasa sat with his legs crossed. The barrel of his sniper rifle leaned on the edge of a guard rail that ringed the top of the oil tank. He glanced back at the Sangsa who was lying down with his head resting on his nylon drag bag, the bag in which snipers carry their weapon and equipment. He had his legs crossed and his eyes closed.

The Hasa was going to let him sleep when he spotted the familiar shape of a BTR-80 armored personnel carrier (APC) motoring down the main road. He watched as the APC made a sharp turn onto the dirt path a half klick down the road and started heading in the direction of the warehouse.

"Sangsa, wake up, we have company."

The Sangsa joined his subordinate at the railing. They put eyes to their scopes and watched the APC lumber down the path, kicking up dust behind it with its eight wheels. It came to a stop directly in front of the warehouse's entrance right next to Cho's car. One of the lids in front of the vehicle popped open. A man's torso emerged.

"Sangsa, do you see ... he wears insignia of a Sojang!"

"I see."

"What do we do?"

"We watch."

* * * * *

The angle of the warehouse and lack of windows prevented Cho from spotting the APC until it had literally come to a stop in front of the door. Song looked over his shoulder and the rest of the men crowded around the only other window.

Song spoke softly into Cho's ear, "What is it?"

"It's a personnel carrier."

Everyone watched as one of the lids on top popped open and a man appeared. Cho and Song recognized him immediately.

"It is Sojang Kim," said Song.

Cho noticed the same two men had the AK-47's in their hands. They watched as Sojang Kim put a microphone to his mouth and then heard the momentary feedback from the APC's public address speaker.

"Daeryeong Cho Jung-woo, you have 10 seconds to come out with your hands on your head before I give the order to open fire. Song, if you are in there, you are to send Daeryeong Cho out, unarmed, and with hands on his head immediately. The countdown begins now!"

* * * * *

Mugsy and Scipio sat behind Father Kim, who was taking pictures out the front passenger window and a driver in a dirty, old white van. Stenciled on the doors of the van—including across the back doors—and written in Chosongul translated *Rang Delivery Companies.*

The driver was Rang. He was Father Kim's contact in Hyesan and he was also a smuggler.

Just before sunrise, Rang drove across a short bridge connecting the North Korean city of Hyesan with Changbai County, part of Jilin province, China. He crossed under the guise of making a pickup of supplies from a warehouse operated by a friend, destined for the Hyesan Airfield.

The supplies were supposedly packed in one large container strapped to a palette. Rang signed for the pickup then proceeded to reenter North Korea. He pulled over in a deserted spot where he opened the container and allowed Mugsy, Scipio, and Father Kim to step out of the cramped surroundings.

Mugsy kept his eyes focused on his Big-Brutha™ phone, tracking their GPS location as they approached the coordinates of the dissidents' warehouse while Scipio had his eyes closed.

Mugsy tapped the side of the driver's seat, "It should be coming up on the left."

Father Kim translated that to Rang and added, "We will leave you, then. Thank you, Rang."

The gaunt old man smiled, "No need to thank me, Father. You have paid me well. Contact me again when you need to leave my country."

"I will do that, if God spares us."

After passing four large oil tanks, the warehouse came into view, in the distance. Mugsy looked through binoculars and saw both Cho's car and the APC.

"What the …?" He nudged Scipio, who opened one eye in reply.

Mugsy motioned out the rear driver's window with a nod of his head, "We got trouble."

He handed the binoculars to the small man dressed in black, who immediately tapped the driver's seat and spoke in Korean, "Slow down, but don't stop."

Old man Rang complied.

"What do you make of it?" asked Mugsy.

Scipio didn't reply. He was watching as the figure of a man appeared from the top of the APC.

Scipio glanced out the windshield, "No traffic in front of us. Do you see any behind us?"

Rang and Father Kim replied, "No," in unison.

Scipio slid open the side door. He continued to speak in Korean then repeated just the first sentence in English for Mugsy, "We have to jump. Don't stop. Once we jump, drive on and don't turn around. Take another route back to Hyesan. You ready Father?"

Father Kim said a silent prayer before opening his door, "Ready as I will ever be …."

Scipio warned, "Try to hit the ground on your feet. If you don't, get up as quickly as possible and run off the road towards the building. As soon as you're off the road, flop to your belly. Got it?"

Father Kim swallowed hard and nodded.

Scipio returned the nod and jumped, followed closely by Mugsy and Father Kim. Scipio and Mugsy landed on their feet and within seconds were lying on their bellies in the dirt.

Father Kim didn't fare as well. He lost his footing and tumbled to the ground, scraping his arms, legs, and head in the process. After tumbling, he dragged himself to his feet and collapsed next to them.

Mugsy patted his shoulder, "You okay, Father?"

The priest wiped blood from his forehead, "I'm okay … just clumsy."

"You did fine."

Scipio was already kneeling and looking through binoculars, "This ain't good. If Cho's in that building, he's done. And with that BTR-80 parked out front, there's nothing we can do to help him."

Mugsy peered through binoculars then handed them to Father Kim. He refocused the lens before taking a look and handing them back, "Perhaps the men inside that thing will get out."

"Even if they did, there could be up to 11 men inside – the operating crew … the driver, commander and gunner, and up to eight combat ready soldiers in the fighting compartment. As long as they're there, there's nothing we can do."

Father Kim stared a moment, before bowing his head and putting his hands together, "There may be nothing we can do, but there is always something He can do if it is His will."

Scipio looked over to Mugsy, who shrugged and winked.

Gunfire erupted from the APC. 7.62mm PKT machine gun rounds began to rip through the front of the wooden structure. Reflexively, Mugsy and Scipio both pushed Father Kim flat on his stomach.

The terrified priest gazed up at Scipio.

"His will be done, Father."

* * * * *

Song backed away from Cho. The rest of the men crowded around him including the two armed with the AK-47s. They now were pointing them at him.

Everyone heard Sojang Kim counting down the 10 seconds through the PA speaker, "... 9 ... 8 ... 7"

Song motioned to the door, "You must go out now!"

"Mr. Song, Sojang Kim is mistaken about me ...."

"... 6 ... 5"

"It does not matter, you must go out there or he will give the order to open fire! We will all be killed! Go now or I will order my men to shoot—"

The voice of Sojang Kim yelling, "Open fire!" was followed immediately by a hail of bullets ripping through the wall, door, and windows.

Everyone inside fell flat on the floor, just in time, as the barrage continued. They became covered in sawdust and glass. Finally, the gunfire ceased.

Sojang Kim's voice was heard through the PA speaker again, "If you heeded the countdown and my warning, you are all still alive. I ordered my men to shoot high, but I will not give that order again. This is your last chance. Either Daeryeong Cho comes out now, or we will turn the whole building into dust."

Within seconds, the bullet-ridden door creaked open. Cho stepped into the threshold with hands on his head.

Sojang Kim handed the mic down into the turret deciding to raise his voice instead, "Step out, Daeryeong."

Keeping his hands raised, Cho scanned from left to right with his eyes, "Sojang, I cannot step out there. There are snipers somewhere nearby with their sights set on me. Taejang Kang sent them to kill me."

Cho watched as Kim looked around from atop the APC, "I see no one …."

"Sojang, yesterday morning I crossed the border near Ji'an, China with three other men, a broker named Dragon and his bodyguards. The bodyguards were gunned down by snipers. The same snipers that I believe are lurking out there somewhere waiting for me to step out of this building. I assume that is how you knew my identity, so you know I am telling the truth."

Kim didn't reply, so Cho continued, "Sojang, I am here to speak with you. Please, allow me to do so. If you are not satisfied with what I have to say then you may do what you want with me, but please hear me out first."

Cho watched as Kim barked orders down into the hatch. A moment later another larger hatch opened in the middle of the APC. Eight soldiers exited through split doors on the side of the hull. They took up positions forming two lines stretching from the front of the APC to Cho's position. Sojang Kim climbed out of the top hatch and approached between the two lines.

Cho lowered his hands and offered one to Kim. The Sojang didn't take it. Unaffected, Cho motioned into the warehouse, "Please come in, Sojang."

"I prefer to speak here for the moment."

"That might not be safe for you."

Kim cocked his head, "If Taejang Kang did send snipers to kill you, why would they target me?"

Cho didn't reply.

"Perhaps, you should explain why you have snuck into my country, and why I should believe anything you say."

* * * * *

The Sangsa took a cell phone from his pocket and made a call. He heard three rings before the line connected, "Taejang, I am sorry to bother you."

The voice was Kang's, "You have carried out your orders?"

"No sir, well … I am in need of your guidance."

"My guidance … Sangsa, I gave you explicit instructions not to contact me until your orders were carried out, and the kill was confirmed. What further guidance do you require?"

"Taejang, we were about to carry out our orders when a personnel carrier arrived, with a sojang commanding it."

"What sojang …? Explain!"

"Taejang, there is a sojang speaking on a loudspeaker, I believe to our target. Wait, now there are soldiers exiting the APC."

"Are you sure it is a sojang?"

"Yes Taejang, we have verified his insignia. Now he is stepping out of the APC and approaching our target."

"Shoot the target! What are you waiting for?"

"Taejang, the target is obstructed from our view."

"Then you have chosen a poor location! Move immediately."

"Taejang, I fear we cannot move from this location without the risk of being spotted, but I assure you it is an ideal location. We just need the soldiers to retreat, and the target to step a foot outside."

"Are you saying the soldiers are sheltering your target?"

"Yes Taejang, at least they will be if the target steps from the building. So is the sojang."

"What are they doing now?"

The Sangsa looked through his scope, "It appears the sojang is speaking with our target. They are standing at the threshold of the door."

There was silence on the line.

"Taejang, are you there?"

"Of course, I am here. Shoot the soldiers and the sojang. Then shoot your target!"

"Taejang, if we open fire on the soldiers, the crew of the APC will certainly open fire on us. We cannot shoot them while they are inside."

There was silence again. This time the Sangsa waited for Kang's reply, "Sangsa, This is what you and the Hasa will do …."

* * * * *

"I cannot say much more with these men around, Sojang, but I assure you I am here at your request."

"But I did not request a face-to-face meeting."

"I understand, but there are decisions that have been made of which you are unaware. Again, I cannot say more until we are alone."

Kim glared at Cho before replying, "You are asking a lot of me, Daeryeong."

"I could say the same thing, Sojang. Please, let your men frisk me. I will even agree to have my hands bound, just allow me to speak with you private—"

The sound of high-powered rifles was heard in the distance, followed closely by two soldiers collapsing to the ground just behind Kim and Cho. Realizing the fallen soldier behind Kim had protected the sojang from being shot, Cho grabbed Kim and attempted to pull him inside. Kim froze, causing Cho to lose his grip on him.

One by one, the other six soldiers were gunned down, as everyone inside the warehouse looked on helplessly. Some tried running back to the APC, while others looked for their attackers. None of them were left standing.

The APC's 14.55mm KPVT anti-aircraft heavy machine gun turret spun in the direction of the oil tanks, as Kim's cell phone rang. Still in shock from what happened, he gazed at Cho as he answered it. The color drained from his face when he heard Taejang Kang's voice on the other side of the line.

"Sojang, this is Kang. Order the men inside the APC to surrender immediately. Tell them to step out of it. Now, or I will order a missile launch that will destroy the APC and everyone inside that building."

Kim stepped back outside, his anxiety growing. The APCs turret stopped rotating when it was aiming directly at the nearest oil tank.

Kim shouted, "This is Sojang Kim to the crew inside the APC. Exit the vehicle!"

No shots were fired, but no one stepped out.

Kim heard Kang's voice again, "Sojang, order those men out of that vehicle now or I will give the launch order. Perhaps you think you can rely on how inaccurate our missiles are, but I assure you, I will fire more than one. This will be a better test than shooting them into the Sea of Japan. Order them now!"

Kim lowered the phone. He hollered with intent, "I said EXIT NOW!"

A hatch opened. The driver appeared first, followed by the gunner. They made it within five feet of the door when simultaneous shots, once again, rang out. Their bodies joined the others on the ground, with blood pouring from their heads.

Kim shouted into the phone, visibly shaken, "Kang, have you lost your mind?!"

"It is not I who has lost my mind, Kim. Now let us end this. I want you to tell Daeryeong Cho to step outside. It will be over quickly and painlessly for your friend."

"Taejang, please, this is insanity!"

"I give you one minute to comply."

Kim turned to Cho, "It is Kang. He wants you to step out. He said he will launch a missile strike that will obliterate this entire area if you do not comply. He is giving you one minute."

Their eyes remained locked as Cho stood motionless just inside the door.

Kang's voice could be heard on the phone's speaker, "You have 30 seconds."

"… 20 seconds."

"… 10 seconds."

Catching both Kim and the snipers by surprise, Cho stepped out, but kept moving until he was standing virtually on top of Kim. He turned and faced the oil tanks with his middle finger raised before kicking the back of Kim's knees and shoving him in the direction of the door. They tumbled inside as sniper bullets ripped up the door jamb.

Cho winked at a startled Kim, "Ever since the incident with the U.S.S. Pueblo your people know what *the finger* means. That is probably the only cultural advances your country has made since then."

Kim ignored Cho and grabbed his shoulder. His tunic was ripped and blood was soaking the tear, "What have you done? I assure you, at this moment Kang is giving the order to fire the missiles! We will all be killed!"

Cho examined Kim's wound.

"It is nothing. A bullet grazed me."

Cho nodded and looked out the now glassless window, "I would take my chances with the accuracy of your missiles over the accuracy of your snipers any day, Sojang."

"Daeryeong, by now, the snipers have communicated the exact coordinates of this building. Our NoDong missiles are accurate within 50 meters. They have a payload of 985 kilograms of high explosive, which produces a blast radius of 160 meters to 250 meters. Just one missile would kill us all … two would leave nothing of our bodies."

Cho continued to stare out the window, "We will have a better chance if we can make it to the APC."

Kim walked next to him, "If we even take one step outside that door the snipers will gun us down. Our fates are sealed."

With caution, Cho peered out in the direction of the oil tank. Something caught his eye, "Sojang do you have binoculars?"

Kim struggled to open a leather case on his belt and handed Cho a small pair. He left blood stains on them from his fingers.

Cho only looked for a moment. Kim noticed a grin grow on his face.

"What do you see?"

"It appears our fate is taking a serendipitous turn."

* * * * *

Scipio lowered the binoculars and pointed at the oil tank, "Snipers, up there. Two."

Father Kim kept Mugsy's pair. He looked on in horror, "They are murdering all of those soldiers!"

Scipio handed Mugsy his. The former Navy SEAL Captain

focused on the APC, "The turret is turning. Those are AA guns. They'll chop the snipers to bits."

The three looked on and waited, but nothing happened. Mugsy turned his sights back on the APC, "Why don't they fire?"

Within a minute, he got his answer, "The crew is surrendering? What the heck?"

Scipio got to his feet, but remained crouched, "I'm gonna make a dash for the tanks. Stay here with the Father." He took off before Mugsy could answer.

Hearing the sound of rifles firing, Scipio ran 40 meters to a fence and scaled it in one lunge. He did his best to conceal himself at the fence's perimeter.

From here to the base of the tank is about 70 meters, with no cover. If I'm spotted I'll be cut down.

He looked for a better route, but found none.

Well, I can't stay here forever.

Glancing up to heaven, Scipio said a prayer before taking off. Midway to the tank, he heard the sound of rifles being fired again. Realizing they were not firing at him, he kept running until reaching the base of the nearest tank. He circled around to the ladder leading up the side and climbed it as quickly and quietly as he could, until he was able to peek over the top.

He saw two men on the far side sitting with their backs to him, looking through the scopes on their rifles.

Scipio hopped onto the roof and pulled two knives from their sheaves sewn into the sides of his undershirt. Crouched, he snuck up to them without either man noticing him.

He slit the throat of the Hasa and before the Sangsa could react, tossed the other knife at him. The blade pierced the startled man's neck with enough force to exit out the back. For a ghoulish moment, the Sangsa gawked with anguish before falling on his face.

Scipio knew there was no way for anyone inside the building, or for Mugsy and Father Kim for that matter to see he had completed his task. A thought came to him.

* * * * *

Cho pulled the binoculars from his eyes and motioned for Kim to step outside. Song and the others came out from their hiding places and followed them out. Cho pointed up to the top of the nearest oil tank, "Look!"

Everyone peered up just in time to see someone tossing two bodies over the top rail.

Cho wasted no time. He swung his arm and cried out, "Quickly, everyone, follow me! We must get inside the APC!"

* * * * *

"Well, I'll be dam—" Mugsy cut himself off when he saw the disapproving look Father Kim was giving him. He stood up, "Come on, it should be safe now."

They took off running toward the APC.

* * * * *

"Shut the hatches!" cried Cho as he took a seat at the controls. It took him a moment to find the right ones. Before everyone was seated, the armored vehicle lurched forward and turned sharply.

Kim fell into the commander's chair, next to him, "Where are you going?"

"Away from the building." He turned to everyone behind them, "Brace yourselves!"

* * * * *

Scipio was pleased as he saw that his message was received by everyone on the ground. He reached for one of the rifles when he saw two small streaks in the distant sky, streaks with white smoke tails.

He knew at once what they were, "Oh shit!"

* * * * *

Mugsy reached the moving APC before Father Kim did. He waved his arms until it stopped. A hatch popped open and from it appeared Cho, "Quickly jump in!"

Mugsy waited for a breathless Father Kim to precede him, before diving inside, head-first. Cho reached up and secured the hatch, "Hold on to something!"

Before Cho's last word was uttered, everyone felt the force of the explosion behind them. The heavy APC was shoved forward with enough force to knock the breath out of many of the passengers. The first blast was followed closely by a second that shoved them just as violently backwards.

Cho's body slammed into the steering wheel, knocking him senseless for a moment. He fought to regain his composure as he floored the accelerator.

* * * * *

Scipio slung the rifle over his shoulder and took off running to the stairs. Reaching them, he swung himself over the side and began to step down. Soon deciding that was too slow, he placed his feet against the railings and began to slide down, burning the palms of his hands in the process. He only fled a few feet from the tank when the first explosion shook the ground. He fell hard and covered his head.

The first explosion was followed closely by a second more powerful one. He realized that because it hit the ground much closer.

Scipio didn't look up until he felt the ground vibrating behind him in a different way - not from an explosion, but from a heavy vehicle. It was accompanied by a metallic squeaking and the roar of a single V-form 8-cylinder KamAZ-7403 series diesel engine, delivering 260 horsepower at 2,600rpm.

Scipio got to his feet as the BTR-80 stopped just inches short of him. Cho popped out of the hatch.

Scipio fanned a faux-salute, "You cut that a little close, Colonel, don't you think? You almost ran me over."

"Not to worry, my friend. I can let nothing happen to you until our next sparring session."

Everyone stepped out of the APC. They stood staring at the scorched earth behind them. Just as Kim predicted, the first missile demolished the warehouse, along with Cho's car, while the second left a crater that could have swallowed the APC whole.

Cho spoke first in Korean and then English, "Is everyone okay?"

Song answered, "My men and I have some cuts and bruises from the machine gun fire, but we are okay."

Cho looked between Mugsy, Scipio, and Father Kim. They nodded.

Father Kim noticed Sojang Kim's wound. He walked over to him, "May I take a look?"

Kim hesitated.

"I am a priest, but I have some medical training. You are losing a lot of blood."

"A priest …?"

Father Kim nodded, "Please, allow me to look."

Kim pulled his arm away, "It is just a flesh wound."

Father Kim gently maneuvered his arm to examine it, "It is more than a flesh wound, Sojang. The bullet passed through your triceps muscle. The wound looks clean enough, but you need to have that stitched as soon as possible. Take off your tunic."

Kim didn't move.

Father Kim took off his shirt and tore a long strip from the bottom, "I need to apply a tourniquet to your arm or you will pass out from blood loss."

Kim still didn't move.

"For His sake, Sojang, please!"

Father Kim helped Sojang Kim remove his tunic, causing the latter some pain. He wrapped the strip around the top of the Sojang's arm and tied the ends then turned to Cho, pointing to a wooden stick on the ground, "Daeryeong, would you please hand me that?"

Cho complied and Father Kim inserted the stick into the looped strip. He twisted it until it became very tight around Kim's arm. The blood reduced to a trickle. Father Kim secured the stick in place.

Sojang Kim bowed his head, "Thank you."

Cho looked around and spoke in Korean, "We have to get out of this area as quickly as possible."

Song started jogging ahead of them, "Come, my men and I live in town. It is just a kilometer from here."

Sojang Kim called to him, "It is too risky to take us to your home. Taejang Kang will be able to trace you and your men from the warehouse."

"How long do you think it'll take Kang to discover their identities?" asked Mugsy.

Cho began to translate.

"There is no need, Daeryeong," replied Sojang Kim. "Before I became Taejang Kang's adjutant, I was a member of the Ministry of State Security. One of my jobs early in my career was analyzing American communications. I was sent to school for a year to learn English. I retained my lessons even after leaving the ministry."

He turned to Mugsy, "As we speak, the Taejang is probably having the warehouse investigated. He will also dispatch troops from Hyesan. I expect soldiers will enter the town in less than 30 minutes."

"There is an abandoned depot across the canal, just outside the northern end of town," offered Song. "But in order to get to it, we will have to cross the western bridge and then follow a dirt path that passes very near an anti-aircraft site. The path will only take us part way. Then we will have to travel about a kilometer, over rugged terrain, in order to reach the depot."

"I wish my Korean was better," replied Mugsy tight-lipped. "I could only understand some of what he said, and my ability to speak Korean is even worse … something about a place for us to go?"

Scipio nodded, "Yeah, he said there's an abandoned depot." Scipio looked at his watch. "Time is short. What do you think, Colonel?"

Cho looked at his watch, "I think we better get going."

"The shortest route from here to the western bridge would be along the main road," said Song.

"It's too risky to travel along the main road," replied Cho.

"Why don't we use that tank?" asked Father Kim.

"Because it'll act as a neon sign when the soldiers get here," replied Scipio.

"I can take us to the bridge on paths only my men and I know about," said Song, "but it will add a kilometer to the distance. We have to cross the bridge before the soldiers come."

Cho replied for the rest, "Let's get going."

Song started jogging. His men did the same, leaving Mugsy, Scipio, Father Kim, Cho, and Sojang Kim standing there. All together, without a word spoken, they began to follow.

CHAPTER **25**

ABANDONED TRAIN DEPOT
OUTSKIRTS OF INDUSTRIAL TOWN
15 KILOMETERS EAST OF HYESAN
NORTHERN RYANGGANG PROVINCE
NORTH KOREA
8:00 AM (LOCAL), SUNDAY, JUNE 02, 2013

Mugsy, Cho, and Scipio used binoculars to look across the irrigation canal into the town. They focused on an armored personnel carrier that rolled to a stop on one of the residential streets. Soldiers exited and appeared to be going door-to-door.

"They're looking for us, no doubt," replied Mugsy.

"They probably found Song's home and the homes of his people deserted," said Scipio. Turning to Song, he switched to Korean. "They could be looking for your family."

"That is why as soon as we arrived here, I sent my people back to town to evacuate our families to the east."

"That was foolish of you. It would have been better to bring them here," replied Sojang Kim. "If they are captured, they will lead the soldiers right to us."

Song banged the table, "Bringing them here would have placed them in even more danger. My people would never betray us, Sojang!"

The men glared at each other.

Scipio broke the silence, "I just hope they got out in time."

"I will pray they did," added Father Kim, as he stitched Sojang Kim's bullet wound.

Song glared a moment longer before turning to the priest, "Thank you, Father. Our families accept the risks we must take in order to bring an end to the Kim regime. We have lost many at the hands of his father, Jong-il. We know we will lose more to the son, but we will never give up."

"You think the same as Taejang Kang," replied Sojang Kim with anger, "and look what it has gotten us!"

"They may think the same," said Father Kim, pulling the thread tight until the Sojang grimaced, "but their methods of overthrowing the regime are vastly different. They are not trying to start a war."

"At least not with missiles," replied Song. "Our weapons are information and knowledge of the outside world. Once enough of our countrymen know what lies outside our nation's borders … how food and opportunities are plentiful … how our cousins to the south and their American allies are not devils that will eat our babies … change will come."

"Their motives are vastly different," added Father Kim. "Song and others like him want freedom for their people … your people, Sojang. But from what the Americans explained, the Taejang wants only to replace Kim's regime with his own. His purpose is not freedom but ambition."

"He also wants to unify the north and south into one Korea," Cho replied as he took a sip of tea from a dirty metal cup. "That is not a dishonorable motive."

"But at what cost, Colonel?" asked Father Kim. "Surely you realize the devastation that will occur if war erupts."

"Taejang Kang considers that devastation collateral damage," replied Sojang Kim, "a price worth paying for unification." He waved his hand dismissively, "Unification … nothing more than a pipe dream."

"Perhaps only a pipe dream today, Sojang," replied Cho, "but someday I believe our countries will be united again."

"As do I and my men, and those like us," added Song. "But there can be no unity until disharmony is removed. The author of our disharmony is the Kim regime."

"Unity … north and south?" Sojang Kim chuckled. "We have generations of our citizens brainwashed to believe Kim is a god and the south and their allies are devils on earth … and you speak of unity?"

"Sojang, you speak as though our cause is futile," said Song, "yet you sent that note to the south. Colonel Cho told me what you wrote."

"And what did I write, Song? Only that Taejang Kang needs to be stopped before he starts a war that we cannot win. Do not mistake my actions as sympathy for your pathetic cause."

"But you reached out to us."

Kim chuckled again until he winced in pain, "I only reached out to you because I knew you could get the note into the hands of that soldier."

Song crossed his arms with confusion, "I don't understand. If you are not sympathetic to our cause, and you already knew about us, why did you not have us arrested even before you sent that note?"

Kim shook his head slowly. He paused before replying in a sarcastic tone, "Of course I knew about you. It is part of my job to know of any troublemakers near Punggye-Ri. That is all you and your band are, nothing more than troublemakers … like undisciplined children."

Song's face reddened, "So then why did you not have us arrested or shot?"

Kim leaned back and waved his hand as if shooing a fly, "If children become too disruptive you spank them. You don't send them to concentration camps or have them shot. That is where I differ from my superiors, including Taejang Kang.

"Besides, I had an idea that you and your group might come in handy one day. I was correct."

Song didn't reply.

Kim sat back straight, "Freedom is just another word for chaos. As for unity … it is nothing more than a typical desire of foolish souls."

The room went quiet.

"I beg to disagree, Sojang," Scipio walked from the window.

"Do you?"

"One of our greatest American presidents, Abraham Lincoln spent much time contemplating the ideal of freedom. He once said, *Freedom is not the right to do what we want, but what we ought. Let us have faith that right makes might and in that faith let us; to the end, dare to do our duty as we understand it.'* Freedom doesn't give license for disorder; it allows us to fulfill our moral obligation to our God, to our families, and to our country."

Kim didn't reply.

Scipio poured himself some tea and took a sip, "Not bad. Surprisingly fresh." He continued, "As for unity, Sojang, you are dead wrong. In fact, unity is anything except typical, as you put it.

"For fear of sounding like my old college history professor, I'm reminded of something the great Roman orator, Cicero wrote in 45 B.C., in his *De finibus*. It begins *There is nothing so glorious nor more wide-spread than the unity of mankind ….'* Unity is glorious, Sojang, not typical."

Scipio swept his arms open, "Look at us here. North Koreans, South Koreans, and Americans working together … all gloriously united for a righteous cause. I would say that is definitely not typical."

Kim shrugged. He hesitated before nodding in concession.

Mugsy whispered to Scipio, "You never cease to amaze me with what you keep stored in your deviant little grey cells. I'm beginning to agree with Cris … there may be hope for you yet."

Father Kim used scissors to cut the needle from the black thread before tying the end. He took a gauze pad and medical tape from a rusty metal first aid kit and covered the stitched wound.

"I think I did a good job, but please be careful moving your arm, Sojang."

Sojang Kim was cautious putting his tunic back on, "I did not know that first aid kits contained needle and suture."

"They do not. It is a blessing for you that I always carry a needle and thread with me wherever I go … something my mother taught me to do from childhood."

The Sojang looked down at his arm and then back up at the priest before bowing, "Well then, I thank both you and your mother."

Cho handed a clipboard to Sojang Kim, "I think I found a way into Punggye-Ri. This is a train schedule showing the last month's arrivals and departures of this depot."

Kim scanned it, "The dates end in November, 2009. What good is it?"

"If memory serves, the second nuclear test conducted at Punggye-Ri was on the 25th of May, in 2009. Those arrivals and departures ended six months later. The last nuclear test was on the 12th of February of this year."

"Just four months ago," added Mugsy.

"Exactly," said Cho.

Sojang Kim reexamined the schedule, "But this depot has been abandoned. I don't see how any of this is helpful."

"It has not been abandoned completely," replied Cho. He took a long sip of his tea, "You see, I agree with Scipio, this tea tastes fresh."

"Meaning someone must have brought it here fairly recently," added Scipio.

"Perhaps just prior to the last nuclear test," added Cho.

"Wait," cried Song, "I remember, my people *did* report seeing activity here, starting last November. We investigated several times, but no one was ever found."

There was silence as everyone took a moment to think.

"Song, back in 2009, why would the train stop here? What did your town produce that might've been shipped to Punggye-Ri?" asked Mugsy.

"I am not aware of anything produced in town that was shipped from here. We are an industrial town. We produce many things, but I know of nothing."

He walked to the window, "With the canal between us, as you saw, there are no roads linking the town to this depot. I cannot imagine how anything would be delivered to this place."

Mugsy joined Song at the window.

"Then this depot makes no sense," said Scipio taking his Big-Brutha™ phone out to access the map app. Cho took a seat next to him. Together, they began zooming in from overhead, and examining the map closely.

Father Kim poured two cups of tea and offered one to Sojang Kim.

"Perhaps there was something to what the American said," the Sojang said softly. "I spent my whole career doing all I could to protect and defend my country from the devils outside our borders."

"And I spent most of mine rescuing people from the devils within," replied Father Kim.

Sojang Kim glowered for a moment. His expression softened into a tired grin, "And look at us now, sipping tea together, while an American and one of your colonels, who I am still not convinced can be trusted, plot our fate."

Father Kim took a seat next to him, "While at college, I was able to study the great literary works of the great English playwright William Shakespeare. I do not expect that you heard of him Sojang … or Abraham Lincoln, or Cicero, for that matter."

Sojang Kim shook his head, "English … American … Roman … all considered inferior races. Yet, there was wisdom in the words the American recited."

Father Kim slightly shook his head in dismay, "I am not sure if the deprivations of art and culture are not the most devastating. As meat and rice are food for the body, art and culture are food for the soul. Starve the body and the person dies; starve the soul and the spirit dies.

"In any case, I will add the wisdom of an English playwright. My favorite play by Shakespeare was the last one he wrote alone, completed in 1611, titled, *The Tempest*. It is about a lord who plots to restore his daughter's rightful place as heir to a throne. Our glorious unity, as the American put it, reminds me of a line from the play, '… *misery acquaints a man with strange bed-fellows*.'"

Sojang Kim thought a moment then smiled, "I think I would like to read this Shakespeare's writings."

Father Kim returned a smile, "Perhaps you will get the opportunity someday."

"I think I found it," exclaimed Scipio, waving everyone over. He placed his phone flat on the table and used a pen to point, "Look, do you see the line starting from this building here at the edge of town and running north to the canal? It's barely noticeable."

"That's an underground pipeline. Now, let's follow it, from the side of the building to the canal … and assume it shoots straight across … then nothing until here, where we see the profile of the pipeline again. It bends to this structure here, right next to the rail line."

"So a pipeline from that building to the rail line … carrying what?" asked Cho.

He turned to Song, "What is that building, Song?"

"That is the Hyesan Mineral Water Factory."

"Mineral water …?" Scipio glanced over at Sojang Kim. The realization left him staring back, realizing. Father Kim leaned in and put a hand on his knee, "Sojang … now is the time for our glorious unity."

Sojang Kim switched his glance to the priest and took a long moment before closing his eyes and nodding. He stood up, walked next to Scipio and looked at the map.

"It is a heavy water production facility. Fifteen kilometers west of Punggye-Ri, on the same line, is a nuclear enrichment plant. Water is shipped from the facility here to that plant."

"There have not been any shipments since 2009?" asked Cho.

Sojang Kim tilted his head at the clipboard, "There is no more paperwork after 2009 because we digitized the entire process including the train schedules."

"Then why was that left here?"

Sojang Kim shrugged and resumed his seat, "I cannot say. Perhaps it was an oversight, or perhaps it was left here to make those who happened onto this depot believe it was abandoned."

Cho shook his head with doubt.

"It fooled you, Colonel, which means it most certainly would fool simple townsfolk."

Cho, Mugsy and Scipio studied the map intently. The latter two looked up at virtually the same time.

"You thinking what I'm thinking?" asked Mugsy.

"It all depends," replied Scipio.

"On what?"

"On when the next shipment is scheduled," replied Cho, the last to look up. "Sojang, can you find that out?"

Sojang Kim thought about it, "By now, Taejang Kang has arrested my staff. I know of no other way to access the system except from my office. Any attempt to gain access, other than from authorized computers, will be discovered and traced."

"Johnny-F could help with that," said Scipio.

"I'm sure John could hack their system, given time," replied Mugsy, "but we don't have time. It won't be long before the soldiers in town decide to look for us here."

"Song, do you know the name of the person who runs that water factory?" Colonel Cho asked with his back to the room. He was standing at the window with binoculars.

"Yes, his name is Ri Ji-hun. I do not know him very well. He does not live in town."

Cho returned to the table and studied the map, "That will not matter. Sojang, does this Ri Ji-hun know who you are?"

"He does not know me personally, but he knows of me, I am sure."

"Good, you will call Ri Ji-hun and ask when the next shipment is to be made."

"I'll get the number," said Mugsy.

Sojang Kim rubbed his chin, "What if it is not scheduled for some time?"

"Then you will tell him the following: a partial shipment will suffice; that the shipment is a top priority and must be set up immediately; and that he is not to inform anyone, including the consignee, nor enter the shipment into the schedule on your system. You will tell him that your staff will handle the arrangements with the nuclear enrichment plant."

The Sojang thought about that, "If the shipment is not entered into the schedule on the system, it will be rejected at the destination."

"That will not matter. We will be getting off before the shipment gets here."

Cho pointed to a place on the map. Everyone took a look at what appeared to be a large depot.

Sojang Kim confirmed what Mugsy, Scipio, and Cho thought, "That is the main depot for Punggye-Ri from that rail line. It lies seven kilometers due west and accesses the site via underground tunnels."

"I've never seen a country with so many tunnels," said Mugsy. "North Korea even puts Mexico to shame."

Mugsy handed Sojang Kim his phone, "The number is there, Sojang, just hit the 'call' button."

Scipio walked over to Cho, "Think they left any food here with the tea?"

"I found bags of dry noodles, and a small stove and pot. We can boil them."

Father Kim and Song walked over with Mugsy, "I just told the good Father that he should make his way back to Hyesan. Song said he would take him there via back roads."

"And I told the Captain that it would be better if I remained with you," protested Father Kim. "The Sojang's wound needs looking after and it would be good to keep me around in case anyone else gets injured."

"It's too dangerous," replied Mugsy.

"The Captain is right, Father," said Scipio. "We've already put your life at risk and from here on out there's a good chance none of us will survive what needs to be done."

"We would be much obliged if you waited for us in Hyesan, in case any of us do make it back," added Mugsy.

"But I can help—"

"Father," Scipio cut him off, "if something happens to you we'll all be trapped here, even if we survive. You'll be helping by waiting for us in Hyesan. Besides, Song can't come with us, nor remain here or in town."

The priest looked hurt but didn't reply.

"We shouldn't leave until nightfall, Father," said Song. "I will keep watch outside until then."

"Then I will make good use of the time praying," replied the Father.

Sojang Kim handed Mugsy back his phone, "That is good, Father, though I doubt your God can help us achieve victory."

He turned to the others, "Ri was not there, but I was connected to his home. As soon as he realized who I was his obedience was no longer in question.

"He told me the next shipment is not scheduled yet, that it will take another month before a full shipment is ready. I told him I wanted whatever he has on hand ready to ship immediately, but he said the factory is closed today. It will take all day tomorrow to have what he has on hand made ready for shipment.

"After assuring me Tuesday morning is the earliest possible, I had him schedule a train with tanker and appropriate crew to arrive here at 8 AM. He said that the 63 km trip to the enrichment facility takes approximately 90 minutes."

"Which means we arrive at that depot sometime after 9 AM," said Mugsy.

"There is a company of men stationed at that depot," replied Sojang Kim. "And by now, Kang has issued arrest or shoot on sight orders for me, so I cannot help to get past them.

"And if we somehow survive the guards at the depot, there are even more guards in the tunnels leading to the facility, not counting the Punggye-Ri security and Kang's own personal guards. There will be another contingent of guards, at least a squad, posted around the mobile launchers."

He looked between the men, "We are unarmed and vastly outnumbered. And your plan is?"

Scipio walked over to the pot and stove. He began filling the pot with water. He reached up and took a bag of noodles from the cupboard above.

"I don't know about the rest of you, but my immediate plans are to make some noodles. Anyone else hungry?"

"Make enough for everyone," replied Mugsy. "I think I'll join Father Kim and get on my knees while they boil."

Cho walked over to the table, "I found a deck of cards. Do you know how to play poker, Sojang?"

"Did you hear what I said?" replied Sojang Kim.

"We heard you, Sojang, but first things first. We have to eat," replied Scipio.

"And pray," added Father Kim.

"And relax," added Cho.

Sojang Kim looked around the room and shook his head. Waving his hands in frustration, he walked over to a tin full of wooden matches and brought them over to the table. Then he took a seat across from Cho, "I prefer draw poker. These will be our chips."

Song walked back in and approached Scipio. He spoke in a low tone, "I heard what Sojang Kim said … about all the guards at Punggye-Ri. I don't know if this is any help, but there is an old man in our village that has security clearance to enter the facility."

Scipio stopped stirring the noodles and gave Song the 'hold-that-thought' indication with the raising of his finger, "Mugsy, do me a favor and spot me. I want to go over our friend Song's route to Hyesan."

With a curious look Mugsy picked up the wooden spoon and began stirring the noodles. Scipio held out his hand in the direction of the door, "Let's talk outside."

Song preceded him out. They walked to the clearing near the bank of the canal.

Scipio started, "I assume you didn't want to speak in front of the Sojang?"

Song looked back at the depot, "I do not trust that man and I do not think you should either."

"For the record, I don't trust anyone, but in this case we have to."

Song locked eyes with Scipio. Finally, he nodded in futility, "The old man is a cook. He is also my grandfather."

"I see. And you say he has a security clearance into Punggye-Ri?"

Song nodded, "The Taejang likes a certain soup … chueotang."

It has to be prepared in a specific way. Ever since he had it at my grandfather's restaurant, the Taejang has demanded that he come to the test site once a week to prepare it."

"What day does your grandfather go?"

"That is another problem. The Taejang usually has him come on Saturdays, though there have been times when the Taejang has called him in on other days if he has guests."

Scipio paused, "You didn't want Sojang Kim to know this because you're afraid he'd endanger your grandfather."

"Yes."

"But telling me means you're asking me to decide. You trust me, Song?"

"Yes."

"Why?"

"Because you and the Captain … and Colonel Cho for that matter were willing to risk your lives, without knowing about my grandfather's access.

"I am not sure if his access can be helpful. It is only a pass that he must wear around his neck, and he still has to go through all the security stations."

Scipio looked down at the ground, "Let me ask you the most important question, would your grandfather be willing to risk his life to help us?"

"You … no … but his favorite grandson …. He would do anything for me.

"Besides, my grandfather has grown to hate Taejang Kang. Too many times the Taejang has forced him to travel the 60 kilometers—at all hours of the day and night—in rain or snow, just so he could snack on chueotang." Song chuckled to himself.

"What's funny?"

"I just recalled our conversation about how we each show defiance in our own ways. Well, my grandfather's way has been to spit into the Taejang's soup."

Scipio smiled, "That could get him killed as much as bringing in knowledge of the outside world. Courage must run in your blood."

"Or foolhardiness."

Father Kim approached them, "Is everything okay?"

Scipio winked at Song, "You might've prayed for a boat Father. Instead God sent us a paddle."

Father Kim looked confused.

Scipio handed Song his phone, "Call your grandfather. Ask him to sneak away and meet you at the depot. Make sure he tells no one."

Song ran off.

Thunder roared in the distance, as Father Kim waited for an explanation. Scipio told him about Song's grandfather.

It began to drizzle.

Father Kim let out a long breath, "Have you already figured out how the old man's access will help you infiltrate the facility?"

Scipio replied through tight lips, "No."

Song rushed over and handed Scipio's phone back to him, "There is a problem! My grandfather said that soldiers are heading this way. He saw a squad cross the bridge and turn on the path."

Scipio pulled his daggers, "How long ago?"

"He said 10 minutes, maybe a little longer."

"If they head right for the depot they could be here in 10 minutes. Okay, let's get—"

"Wait! I need your help. My grandfather said he wants to beat them here. He intends to cross the canal!"

"Can he do that?" asked Father Kim.

"When he was younger he could. He is still a very strong man for his age, but I'm afraid the currents will be too strong for him."

The drizzle turned to rain as a louder thunder clap grumbled. Scipio gritted his teeth, "Damn ... alright, Father run back to the depot. Ask Captain Ricci to look for some rope. If he finds any, tell him to run it down to us. And tell Colonel Cho to lead you and Sojang Kim across the railroad tracks. You can hide there. Try to take up positions in the overgrowth."

Lightning bolted across the sky, followed a few seconds later by thunder. The rain poured down heavier.

"The rain may work to our advantage. Go!"

Father Kim took off in the direction of the depot.

Song pointed across the canal, "There he is!"

Through the heavy downpour they saw Song's grandfather stepping gingerly onto the rocky surf.

Scipio put binoculars to his eyes and scanned the town, "It's a miracle he wasn't spotted."

"My grandfather is a wily old man."

"Wily or crazy?"

Scipio walked over to the water line and put his foot down in a few places, "Both sides of the canal are lined with smooth, slippery rocks. If he falls, he could be washed downstream before we could reach him."

Scipio looked behind them, "Come on Mugsy, hurry with the rope!"

He scanned in the direction of the path, "Song, the soldiers are only about a klick away. Go hide with the rest. I'll stay here with your grandfather."

"I am not leaving."

The sky lit up from a giant bolt just behind Song's grandfather, followed almost immediately by a ground-shaking thunder burst. Song and Scipio watched helplessly as the old man waded waist-deep in the powerful current. They could see him battling to move forward.

Both turned from a peculiar sound, a jingling. It was Mugsy running while carrying something heavy.

"I couldn't find rope but I found this." He dropped a ball of rusted chain into the mud.

Scipio examined it, "One-inch links. This could do the trick." He quickly tied one end into a loop and began spinning it over his head, "Mugs, make sure I have slack."

"On it."

"Song, yell to your grandfather, tell him to grab the end."

Song cupped hands around his mouth and shouted.

"Here goes nothing ... hi ho Silver!" Scipio tossed the looped chain as far as he could. It dropped into the water just in front of the old man.

Song gasped when he saw his grandfather dive for it.

Mugsy came up next to him, "Did he fall?"

Song became frantic, "I don't see him!"

"But I feel him," shouted Scipio. He began yanking the chain ashore. "Help me!"

The three men pulled the chain with all their might. It felt like an eternity to Song, but within a minute they saw his grandfather emerge from the white-caps.

Scipio pointed to him, "Quickly, you two get him across the rail lines! I'll stow the chain and follow."

The rain poured down in diagonal sheets and whipped sideways by the increasing wind. Mugsy and Song practically carried the old man up the rough path to the depot before stopping at the door.

Mugsy looked in, "Shit … we forgot the bucket of noodles on the stove! The soldiers won't miss it for sure. Song, take your grandfather across the rail—"

The old man spoke up in a stern tone, in Korean.

Song answered him.

Before Mugsy could stop him, Song's grandfather walked into the depot and slammed the door behind him.

"What the hell!" Mugsy started for the door but Song grabbed his arm and pointed. The soldiers had reached the foot of the path.

Song pointed across the tracks. Mugsy cursed to himself and nodded. Both men took off running.

Scipio made his way around the back of the depot. The torrential downpour allowed him to follow and then slip around the North Korean squad. He hoisted himself onto the wooden roof, timing it with the next roar of thunder, and crawled his way to the center. There were no holes or openings to look through, so he took out his Big-Brutha™ iPhone and tapped an app. Raindrops began pelting it.

Johnny-F really thought of everything, including waterproofing our phones to scuba depth.

He laid the back of the phone on the roof and activated his earpiece.

OUCH! He almost screamed out loud from the sound of raindrops amplified to point-blank shotgun blasts. He tapped a control on the app that automatically activated a tonal dampening, squelch, compressor, and limiter – all advanced sound manipulation processes. The result allowed him to clearly hear the conversation and movement of everyone inside the depot.

* * * * *

A dozen North Korean shoulders fanned out around the depot's perimeter, while a young officer approached the door with pistol in hand. He waited for one of his men to open the door before marching inside. He aimed his pistol at the only occupant – an elderly man. His men surrounded the old man with their rifles.

The officer approached with his weapon still pointed, "You there, who are you and what are you doing here?"

Song's grandfather didn't turn around. He continued to stir whatever was steaming in the large pot.

"I said—"

"I heard what you said, young man. I am Song Hyun Su," he turned around, produced the security pass from his pocket, and held it up, "Chief Cook for Taejang Kang Kum-Sok."

The officer hesitated not knowing what to do. He finally decided to holster his pistol and examine the pass.

"This pass does not say anything about being Chief Cook for Taejang—

Once again the old man cut him off with a condescending tone, "Of course it does not. It is the highest security pass into our most secret missile facility where the Taejang is headquartered."

The officer's face flushed from embarrassment. He glanced at his men. None of them made eye contact with him, though he noticed a few of the older soldiers fighting back smiles.

The officer attempted to regain his authority by raising his voice, "What are you doing here?!"

The old man rolled his eyes. He turned his back to the officer and resuming stirring, "Is it not evident what I am doing? I am cooking noodles."

"For whom …?"

"For the train crew that will be stopping here, of course."

"What train crew? I am not aware of any—"

"Young man, I have no interest in what you are or are not aware of. I receive my orders directly from Taejang Kang. He informed me to prepare a meal for the train crew that will be stopping here."

The old man turned around with a grin on his face, "Come to think of it … the Taejang did mention that no one was to know about the train that will be stopping. I am to report to him anyone that learns about it."

The officer and his men became visibly nervous.

Song's grandfather chuckled, "Ah, so you are all aware of Taejang Kang's reputation, I see. I can tell you the last person I informed the Taejang about was a nosy captain who took it upon himself to investigate this depot. He too came upon me pointing a weapon."

The young officer's eyes widened, "Honorable Sir, I meant no offense. I was merely following my superior's orders. In fact, I believe my superior received his orders from Taejang Kang."

"I am sure he did, young man, so did that captain." Song's grandfather took the officer by his arm and began walking him towards the door.

He spoke under his breath, "I can tell you from personal experience the Taejang often forgets one set of orders he gives while enforcing contradicting ones. Why, more than once he has even ordered me to prepare fish for dinner, only to throw it in my face when I served it to him. He reminded me that years before, he had told me he never wants to be served fish on Thursdays. Well, I thought I was doing right by following his most recent orders … but."

The old man stopped in front of the door and opened it, "I came very close to having my throat slit and being fed to his dogs. You do know about his dogs, do you not? They were raised on human flesh."

The officer was speechless. He rubbed the back of his neck and shot a blank stare at his men.

Song's grandfather chuckled again to break the tension. He patted the officer's back, "Young man, I see no reason why if you and your men leave at once and do not return, I need to inform the Taejang of your presence or of your knowledge of the train.

"By the way, why did you come here?"

The officer's expression was mixed with fear and relief, "We ... were looking for criminals ... members of a resistance cell and—"

The old man belly laughed, "Why how foolish of you to come out in this pouring rain looking for criminals and almost becoming criminals yourselves. Now, I would advise you to hurry back and tell your superior you checked here and found it abandoned ... in case he sends others to look for you."

The officer nodded sheepishly, before shouting to his men, "Out immediately!"

* * * * *

Scipio waited until the soldiers were completely out of sight before jumping down and entering the depot. He found Song's grandfather sprinkling spices into the pot of noodles. Before he spoke, the old man turned, taking a sip from the pot with a wooden spoon. He didn't seem surprised by Scipio's Caucasian features, "Do you speak Korean?"

"I do."

"Are you a friend of my grandson?"

"I am."

"Do you know who made these noodles?"

"I did."

The old man smiled, "They are not bad, though I can show you how to make them tastier."

CHAPTER 26

ABANDONED TRAIN DEPOT
OUTSKIRTS OF INDUSTRIAL TOWN
15 KILOMETERS EAST OF HYESAN
NORTHERN RYANGGANG PROVINCE
NORTH KOREA
10:30 AM (LOCAL), SUNDAY, JUNE 02, 2013

"There is a tunnel entrance here at this rail station that leads east," Sojang Kim pointed to a spot on the map. While Colonel Cho and Mugsy Ricci stood on each side of him. Scipio stood across from them while Father Kim, Song, and his grandfather remained in the kitchen area.

Colonel Cho examined where Sojang Kim pointed, "That station is approximately 16 kilometers due west from Punggye-Ri."

"16 kilometers away from the test site," Scipio corrected him, "not Kang's headquarters. It's another 15 klicks south from the test site to his HQ."

"How contaminated is the area immediately around the site?" asked Mugsy.

"It is difficult to say," replied Sojang Kim. "For the most part, those tunnels have been off limits since the nuclear tests. The tunnels themselves were built to withstand a nuclear blast. However, the ground shock from the explosion severely loosened the ten feet of sand into which most of the tunnels sections were buried. As a result, some sections are reported to be contaminated with fallout."

"So then, what is difficult to say?" asked Colonel Cho.

Sojang Kim's face flushed just enough to show embarrassment, "After a number of our inspectors became ill and died from reconnaissance in those tunnels, the Taejang decided to call off their survey."

"Call off the survey?" repeated Father Kim approaching the table. Song and his grandfather followed. "I couldn't help eavesdropping. You said, Sojang, 'for the most part' they were off limits. Are you still allowing your people to pass through them?"

Sojang Kim nodded tiredly, "Taejang Kang utilizes those tunnels at times … for expediency."

"Expediency …?" Father Kim raised his voice, "So you risk the lives of your faithful staff to save time?"

"Time and money, Father," replied the Sojang in an unrepentant tone. "Neither of which we have in abundance in North Korea."

"Are your staff aware of the risks?" asked Colonel Cho.

Sojang Kim shook his head, "Not entirely. They are only aware that some of the staff who traversed those tunnels have become sick."

"Some?" asked Father Kim, with doubt in his eyes.

"Many," the Sojang conceded.

"Can we get our hands on radiation suits?" asked Scipio.

"The only radiation suits I know about are located inside the compound," replied Sojang Kim.

"I don't like it," uttered Mugsy as he hovered over the map. "We may need a miracle just surviving our objective. If we use those tunnels, we could end up dying, even if we're blessed enough to get home."

"Asking God for one miracle is an act of faith," said Father Kim. "Asking Him for two is an act of lunacy."

Scipio folded his arms and addressed Sojang Kim, "There must be another way."

"I know of no other way. We cannot simply enter through the main gate. Other than those tunnels, there are no other entrances into the headquarters bunker that I know of."

"I know of a way," replied Song's grandfather catching everyone by surprise.

The old man looked up from the map. He spoke in Korean, "I am allowed to bring a few men to help prepare and serve when the Taejang is entertaining."

Sojang Kim waved dismissively, "But he will not be entertaining anyone this close to the launch."

The old man was unmoved, "I believe I can convince the guards otherwise." He turned to the others, "I have been serving the Taejang chueotang for a long time. It is his favorite dish. He will allow no one else to prepare it. The Taejang has made my importance known to all of the guards. As a result, they have never given me a problem."

"Yes, that may have been true before, old man" replied Sojang Kim, "but as I have said, it is too close to the launch. I know for a fact that the Taejang has already instituted the highest level security protocols throughout the entire compound. And even if you somehow were allowed entry, there is no way they would allow other men to enter without security badges."

Again, Song's grandfather turned to the others, ignoring the Sojang, "I am telling you. I have done it before and I can do it again. Even with heightened security, the Taejang's mistake is that he has implanted too much fear into his men. They will not dare risk angering him."

Father Kim translated for Mugsy.

Mugsy rubbed his chin, "I don't think we have an alternative. Time is running out, and I won't risk exposing anyone to radiation poisoning. Besides, it sounds like the old man's plan is perfect cover. That is, if we're not shot dead at the entrance."

Song's grandfather waited for Father Kim to translate before shaking his head vigorously and pointing at Mugsy and Scipio. He followed that up by pointing at Colonel Cho and Sojang Kim and nodding.

"The old man has a point," said Scipio. "We're not equipped to impersonate Koreans, Captain."

Mugsy put hands on his hips and exhaled, "Well I'm not prepared to ask anyone else to accompany the old man. It could be a death sentence, even for him."

"With respect, Captain," replied Colonel Cho, "you need not ask me. Consider that I ... and the Sojang volunteer."

"Wait a moment," replied Sojang Kim holding his hand up with palm out, "I told you, I would be shot on sight, I am sure of it."

"Perhaps you would be if you were wearing your uniform, but no one looks twice at a *nodongja* ... a laborer."

The Sojang's anxiety was apparent, "But I don't know how—"

"I will take care of your disguise," replied Cho, cutting him off.

"Then it's settled," replied Mugsy. "Song, tell your grandfather we welcome his help."

The old man bowed with a grin.

Scipio took a seat, "Okay gentlemen, we have a lot more to plan. Getting in is only the first hurdle. The Sojang says he knows where the Musudan missiles are located. If we work from the premise that Kang hasn't relocated them, we still need to devise a method to prevent their launch or render them harmless."

"I know of a way to do that if I can gain access to the missiles' control room," said Sojang Kim.

"Then, what to do with the Taejang himself," added Mugsy.

"We must kill him," replied Sojang Kim, with emphasis.

That provoked stares from the rest.

"And what about how you intend to escape the compound once you cause all this havoc?" asked Father Kim.

"The Father's right," replied Mugsy. "We can't anticipate that they'll be allowed to leave the same way they came."

"That leaves only the tunnels," replied Scipio. "Sojang, do you know where they keep those radiation suits?"

"Yes, near the compound-side entrance to the tunnel, in a row of lockers, but there are guards on both ends."

"We can take care of the guards inside the compound," replied

Cho.

"Then the Captain and I'll need to take care of the ones on the depot side," said Scipio.

"Impossible," said Sojang Kim. "There is at least a company of men stationed at that depot. It is too much for only two men."

"Three men," replied Father Kim. "I volunteer."

"Negative," replied Mugsy, "you have to accompany Song—"

"I am going too," interjected Song. "I will do all I can to free my grandfather. And I'm sure I can count on my cell to help too."

Scipio folded his arms and started counting with his fingers, "Let's see … we have a North Korean general, a South Korean colonel, two foolish Americans, a priest, an old cook, his grandson, and their hippy resistance cell versus at least a company of North Korean soldiers and a North Korean nut with his finger on the launch buttons of a bunch of missiles. I'd say our chance of success is at least 50/50, wouldn't you?"

Sojang Kim looked puzzled, "What is … hippy?"

Colonel Cho put his hand under Mugsy's elbow and urged him outside.

"Captain, we are still not sure the Sojang isn't the one who has planned all this."

"You still have your doubts about him, Colonel?"

"I do. He could be allowing us to launch this raid only to betray us once he gets to the compound."

"What about the missile strike Kang ordered. The Sojang could easily have been killed."

"Perhaps, but it is difficult to predict the motivations of North Koreans. The Sojang could have considered that an acceptable risk. Or perhaps the Taejang did. In any case, we will be at the Sojang's mercy once we reach the headquarters compound."

"I think that's a risk we'll have to take, Colonel. Don't you?"

Cho thought about it before nodding his head once, "Know this. Once we arrive there, if I see the Sojang doing anything suspicious, I will kill him myself and proceed alone."

Mugsy smiled, "Fair enough."

Cho walked back inside as Scipio stepped out.

Mugsy thumbed back in the Colonel's direction, "That Cho is a hard nut to crack. I still can't figure him out."

"I think the time for worrying about that is over, don't you Captain?"

Mugsy patted Scipio's shoulder, "Come on ... let's plot the raid of the Keystone Kops."

CHAPTER 27

OFFICE OF THE DEPUTY MINISTER
INTERNATIONAL ECONOMIC AFFAIRS
MINISTRY OF STRATEGY AND FINANCE
GOVERNMENT COMPLEX-SEJONG, GALMAE-RO
SEJONG SPECIAL SELF-GOVERNING CITY
SEOUL, SOUTH KOREA
4:00 PM (LOCAL), MONDAY, JUNE 03, 2013

De Niro and Michelle Wang sat across from Korean Deputy Finance Minister Jong-Ku Choi. Behind the minister stood a young intern who under normal circumstances also acted as translator. Though Minister Choi understood and spoke adequate English, he only felt comfortable communicating complex financial matters in his native tongue.

For simplicity, the Deputy Minister and De Niro agreed that Michelle could translate for them both. The tall, bespeckled official radiated a quiet, distinguished demeanor that De Niro liked.

Michelle translated with a hint of anxiety in her tone, "… The

Minister wants you to understand his reasoning. His view is that forex transactions and/or bond transactions must be taxed. The Minister says that a form of Tobin tax, introducing a foreign exchange tax, is necessary to curb the won's rapid appreciation, and to control the volatile foreign exchange market. The Minister adds that the forex tax would be tailored to domestic market conditions, as well as a new tax added on bond sales."

De Niro sipped the last of a glass of water, "I understand. However, the Deputy Minister must also realize that by taxing forex and bonds, he may disenfranchise a critical mass of foreign investment. The same foreign investment causing the volatility he is intending to control with the tax in the first place."

Wang translated. The Minister nodded.

De Niro leaned in and spoke directly to the Minister, "It's like a wake of air caused by the rush of a fire engine. The wake extinguishes the fire even before the firemen attach hoses to the pump."

Michelle saw by the grin on the Ministers face that she did not need to translate.

Minister Jong-Ku leaned in and took time to carefully consider his words, in English, "So, there would be no fire to extinguish … in other words, no tax to be collected."

"My illustration exaggerates the outcome, Minister, but yes. I believe there will be much less tax revenue generated than your analyses might be predicting."

"Because the analyses were conducted when the fire was raging, before the gust from the fire engine extinguished it." The Minister maintained his grin as he spoke.

De Niro smiled and sat back, "Minister, I am aware of your description of recent quantitative easing programs by major economies—like the United States—as 'unprecedented'. And that you also stated that the massive influx of foreign capital into the local financial market is making it increasingly vulnerable to a mass exodus of foreign capital."

Choi nodded and continued in English, "Movement in the foreign exchange market has remained worrisome since the fourth quarter of last year. The three traditional measures we use to control it are limited in what they can do vis-à-vis global market conditions, which is why there is a need to tax forex transactions and bond sales."

De Niro glanced at his watch trying hard not to make it obvious to the Deputy Minister.

I promised Michelle we wouldn't spend more than an hour here and we're already going on two.

De Niro stood prompting Michelle first, and then the Deputy Minister, to rise from their seats.

De Niro offered his hand, "Deputy Minister, I see your mind is made up, and we have taken far too much of your time. All I suggest is to take care that your measures to protect against an exodus don't cause one."

"Thank you, Mr. De Niro. I will consider your advice carefully. It was a pleasure. My assistant will escort you to the lobby."

"No need Sir, we can find our way."

Michelle waited to make sure they were the only ones on the elevator before speaking, "I got the feeling the Deputy Minister enjoyed your company."

"I know … I said only an hour. I could see the tension on your face."

Michelle put a hand on her stomach, "That wasn't tension, it was indigestion."

"But you hardly ate any lunch."

"At lunch I felt like I was going to puke. In the Deputy Minister's office, I just felt indigestion … now I'm getting hungry. It's weird, I feel hungry for … cookies."

"Cookies …?"

She nodded, "Italian cookies … you know the ones with that candied fruit in the center."

"You mean Italian macaroon cookies?"

"I guess. I only tasted one once at your house on New Year's Day."

"Oh no … not cravings," said De Niro, "I lived through Lisa's cravings. I remember she had this uncontrollable desire for ice cream from this one ice cream parlor. I'll never forget … one scoop coffee and one scoop cheesecake."

"That doesn't seem so odd. Mugsy said his sister loved ice cream."

"She did, but not from that ice cream parlor. In fact, as soon as she gave birth to Richard, she never wanted ice cream from there again. She said she hated their ice cream and couldn't stand the smell of the place."

"The smell of the place …?"

"Uh-huh."

"You know, come to think of it, I noticed the smell of coffee is starting to make me sick."

"Oh no," De Niro started typing into his Big-Brutha™ phone.

"What are you doing?"

He held the door for her. They exited the Ministry and De Niro hailed a taxi.

"I'm making dinner reservations at *Tuscany*. It's the best Italian restaurant in Seoul, and it also happens to be located in our hotel. I'll text John and tell him to meet us there in 30 minutes."

* * * * *

Chef Maurizio Ceccato, the owner and chief chef of *Tuscany* walked over to the table and greeted De Niro with a hug.

The Chef spoke Italian into De Niro's ear, "But what is this … one eats like it's his last meal and the other …," he nodded at Michelle and switched to broken English, "… I don't even want to say. Hot, stuffed peppers with macaroon cookies … somebody is pregnant."

John "Johnny-F" Francis dropped his fork full of spaghetti, "Pregnant?! You're pregnant, Michelle?"

Michelle's face turned crimson. She stared at De Niro silently.

"It's not something she wants advertised John."

Adding to her embarrassment, Francis leaned over and kissed her cheek, "That's friggin' awesome! Congratulations … wow! Man, Mugsy must be stoked!"

Michelle continued to stare at De Niro. Francis noticed.

"Wait a minute … you mean, Mugsy doesn't know?"

"Which is why Michelle doesn't want it advertised, Mugsy has a right to know before the rest of the world."

"Of course, but now that I think about it. This explains a lot."

Michelle's blush turned to a glare, "What does that mean?"

"Well for one, it explains your odd dietary habits lately. Stuffed peppers with macaroon cookies … and what was that … chocolate-covered pretzels with a pickle you snuck before we left for South Korea."

De Niro raised his brow and smiled, prompting Michelle to blush even more.

"Oh yeah," Francis continued, "I caught her in your kitchen munching on that disgusting combination and washing it down with a Starbucks … what was that drink?"

She shrugged, "A grande, vanilla soy latte."

De Niro folded his arms, "I didn't know you like soy?"

"I don't. Heck, I don't even like Starbucks."

Francis called the waiter over, "How about a plate of cannolis and some more macaroon cookies, Cris?"

"With two espressos, please. Michelle?"

"Nothing for me, thanks."

"Sure you don't want any more stuffed peppers to go with those cookies?" Francis teased.

"Uh … no … thanks, but I did scope a Starbucks down the street. I think I'll take a walk there after we leave."

De Niro stretched, "Michelle, are we done with all the meetings?"

"Except for the gathering on South Korea's Memorial Day … yes."

"When is that?" asked Francis.

"Thursday – we have to attend a memorial ceremony at the National Cemetery followed by a VIP-only get-together afterwards. That's where you'll get to meet Daejang Jeong, Cris."

De Niro looked over her shoulder at a small group of men in uniform—four in all—that entered the restaurant. They headed directly over to the table. The first three took positions standing around the table, while the fourth, an older, stocky man with a soft grin, wearing the stars of a four-star general, bowed slightly.

After a second of scanning the table, he directed his broken-English comments to De Niro, "Mr. De Niro, I presume."

De Niro stood, "I'm Cris De Niro. Daejang Jeong, I presume."

The man acknowledged with the blinking of his eyes.

"I'm honored Sir, please, would you and your men like to join us?"

Before Francis could grab one, one of the Daejang's men fetched a chair and held it for him.

"You are too kind. My men have already eaten."

The waiter approached the table with the desserts. Jeong examined them with curiosity.

"It's called a cannoli, General," said Francis.

"A … cannoli," Jeong repeated.

"Yes, sir," replied De Niro, "it is an Italian dessert originally from the island of Sicily. The word is slang for 'little tube'. It's a fried pastry filled with a sweet, creamy cheese filling. Please, try one."

The waiter rushed to set a place setting with dessert plate, in front of the Daejang, while Francis used a fork and spoon to place a cannoli on it.

Jeong looked momentarily confused as to how to eat it.

Francis lifted one to his mouth, "It is customary to eat cannolis with your hands, Daejang."

Jeong nodded and mimicked Francis. He took a bite and smiled approvingly, "It is very good. I confess, I have never eaten Italian food before."

"That's dessert, Daejang," replied De Niro as he waved over the waiter. "This restaurant is actually a great place to sample fine Italian cuisine. I'm friends with the owner. He's a master chef, born and raised in Italy."

The waiter handed Jeong a menu. He scanned it for a moment before lowering it to his lap, "Mr. De Niro, I only came here to speak with you, but you have convinced me. I would appreciate it if you would do the honors for me."

"I would be happy to … what do you like?"

"Perhaps pasta … something tangy?"

"I know just the thing," De Niro addressed the waiter, "Please, bring Daejang Jeong a bowl of *penne arrabiata* and a bottle of your best Barolo wine."

He turned back to Jeong, "You do drink wine, Daejang?"

"I do."

De Niro paused for the waiter to leave, "You said you came here to speak with me?"

Jeong paused, "I understand you have been meeting with a number of our ministers."

"I have. In fact, we just came from a meeting with Minister Choi of your Ministry of Strategy and Finance."

"I know. I just left him. He was very impressed with you."

"I'm flattered. I didn't think the Minister and I saw eye to eye on most issues."

"He said the same, but in his words, your 'provocative ideas have caused him to reexamine some of his own.

"Mr. De Niro, may I ask your purpose in visiting Seoul at this time?"

"My purpose … is to accompany the chief information officer of my agency to investigate the possibility of opening a manufacturing facility here in Seoul."

Jeong smiled softly, "Is that so … I thought perhaps you might be investigating something else."

"Something else, Daejang …?"

"Yes, something like the South Korean official that is allegedly collaborating with that nut in the north, Taejang Kang."

De Niro didn't reply.

The waiter returned with a bottle of Giacosa Barolo Falletto 2007 and a carafe. The table remained silent as the bottle was opened and decanted.

De Niro was handed the cork and poured the traditional taste. He nodded approval to the waiter.

"Have you ever had Barolo wine before, Daejang?"

"No, I have not."

"It's a robust red wine that needs to breathe for its complete flavor to come to bear."

"I am a patient man, Mr. De Niro."

"I like to think that I am too, Daejang. My dad was the most patient human being I have ever known. He used to say, 'All good things come to those who wait'."

"We have a similar saying. My grandfather was a fisherman. He taught me that fishing is less a sport of technique as it is of patience. With the right hook, bait, and patience, he said any fish can be caught.

"Tell me, am I correct about your reason for being here?"

"I can't answer that."

"You can't, or won't, because of giving your word to President Park?"

De Niro didn't flinch. Jeong looked around the table. Michelle kept her eyes pointed downward, while Francis reached for another pastry.

"Don't worry, Daejang, I'll leave you one."

"You see, I know about President Park's meeting with you in Washington."

I get the feeling he doesn't know anything more though. Like his grandfather, he's a fisherman.

De Niro finished his espresso. Immediately, a waiter appeared and refilled his cup.

"President Park and I happened to be staying at the same hotel."

"And you offered her your suite."

"Actually, I merely made the suite in which I normally stay available to the hotel. They offered it to the President."

"That was a kind gesture."

De Niro ignored the compliment, "President Park found out about my kind gesture and decided to come knocking to thank me."

"And to tell you about the defector and Sojang Kim's note."

"I have a high security clearance, Daejang. President Park knew that, if that's where you're going with this."

"Not at all, Mr. De Niro … not at all. I am not accusing President Park of divulging national secrets. I am aware of your security clearance. What I am more interested in knowing is … exactly who are you investigating here?"

The waiter walked over and set Jeong's plate before him. He tasted the pasta.

"This is very good … very tangy. What did you call this?"

"Penne Arrabiata, Daejang. Penne is the type of pasta and arrabiata literally translates … angry, named for the spiciness. Please, enjoy it while it's hot."

Jeong nodded and forked some into his mouth. De Niro winked at Francis when he washed it down with a gulp of wine.

"The heat sneaks up on you."

Jeong wiped his mouth, "Mr. De Niro, I want to thank you for this excellent meal. I will return here again, soon with my wife."

"Then before you leave, I'll introduce you to my friend, the chef."

"I appreciate that. Let me return the kindness with frankness. I am aware, as are others, of your true reason for being here. My primary interest is in protecting my country. If you know the identity of the collaborator, the individual is an enemy of the state. What do you intend to do with this person?"

De Niro hesitated.

Jeong seems to be one of the good guys, but I need to be careful. I can't divulge everything for fear of putting Mugsy, Scipio, and Colonel Cho at risk.

"Surely, you can tell me that?"

"If we uncover the collaborator, rest assured Daejang, we will be handing the person over to the proper authorities."

"Which is who, exactly, Mr. De Niro … Daeryeong Cho perhaps?"

Francis coughed. He quickly reached for the wine, "Apologies … cannoli went down the wrong pipe."

Jeong continued, "Come to think of it, Daeryeong Cho has been out of contact for awhile. No one seems to know where he is. Do you know where the Daeryeong is, Mr. De Niro?"

"I'll answer that question if, first, you answer one of mine, Daejang. Tell me … are you a supporter of President Park?"

"And if I lie with my answer?"

"Then I will lie with mine."

"Very good, Mr. De Niro. Tell me, do you play chess, by chance?"

"Does Cris play chess," replied Francis, "he beats me and I'm rated a master."

"I can believe that, Mr. Francis. As for your question … I think you know the answer."

"And I think you know mine, Daejang."

The two men's eyes met. Jeong blinked first, "Very well, your interrogation is over, Mr. De Niro. Perhaps the three of you will remain, while I enjoy the rest of this excellent meal?"

Michelle stood, prompting the men rise with her, "If you gentlemen would excuse me, I have an appointment down the street."

De Niro kissed her cheek, "John, accompany her please."

"Yes, sir. Would you like us to bring you back something?"

Jeong looked at De Niro.

"I'll explain later, Daejang. No John, that won't be necessary. Just see that you return to the room with Michelle."

"You mean no clubbing tonight?" Francis offered his hand to the General before De Niro could reply.

Jeong waited for them to leave the restaurant, "I read their dossiers. You have an impressive team working for you, Mr. De Niro."

"Cris, Daejang, call me Cris, my friends do."

"And my friends call me Seung-jo. Cris, without asking anymore questions, I would like you to know, if you need my help, I will make my men and myself available to you."

"I appreciate that Seung-jo."

"One more thing ... looking for a collaborator with the North can get you and your people killed."

"You mean spies?"

Jeong nodded, "The North infiltrated many, and they are not only spies, but assassins. If I know about your true reason for being here, they know too."

"If that's true, why haven't they struck yet?"

"That, I do not know. Perhaps they have not been able to get to you yet, or perhaps they are monitoring your progress and will only strike if you get too close."

"I'll admit ... we haven't ... come close, that is. I appreciate the warning."

"I wanted to make contact with you before, but my schedule has been so hectic."

"I'm aware. I was planning to introduce myself at the Memorial Day ceremonies."

"Ah, that explains why I wasn't on your list of officials to meet."

"We really are looking into a manufacturing facility here, Daejang."

Jeong savored another forkful of pasta, "And I really am enjoying this angry pasta."

The two chuckled.

CHAPTER 28

PULLING INTO STATION
ABOARD TRAIN NKSR H-HYEKIL9-4
PAEKTUSAN CH'ŎNGNYŎN LINE
PAEGAM-NODONGJAGU (PAEGAM WORKERS' DISTRICT)
PAEGAM-GUN, RYANGGANG PROVINCE
NORTH KOREA
9:30 AM (LOCAL), TUESDAY, JUNE 04, 2013

"We're pulling into the station," Mugsy retracted his head into the boxcar and slid the door closed.

The dissidents, now being referred to as *Song's people*, had loaded a number of heavy water-filled drums along with two empty ones before boarding the train. They were joined by Mugsy, Scipio, Cho, Father Kim, Song, Song's grandfather, and Sojang Kim. The trip from the depot north of the industrial town to the Paegam-Nodongjagu station took 90 minutes.

Mugsy and Scipio climbed into the empty drums. Song's people placed lids fitted with rubber gaskets over them and sealed them with bolts. The night before, air holes were drilled into one side of the drums, which were then loaded onto the boxcar with the drilled sides facing away from the door.

Cho bent and tapped on the drum containing Scipio, "I hope you are not afraid of small, dark places, my friend."

Scipio's voice resonated baritone by the metal container, "Now I know what a sardine feels like."

Father Kim kneeled next to Mugsy's, "Are you okay, Captain?"

His voice was almost indistinguishable from Scipio's, "Have you ever heard the term, 'fish in a barrel', Father?"

"No, but I think I know what it means. Don't worry Captain, trust in God."

"Always, Father, especially when inside a metal drum, in North Korea."

Cho added additional flour to Sojang Kim's hair. Their eyes met, "What happens if I am recognized?"

Cho scanned his handiwork and wiped the remnants of the flour from Kim's shoulders, "If we are not all shot on the spot, we will be taken into custody."

Kim stared back silently.

"Don't worry, Sojang, just do what I told you – stay close to the old man and keep your face pointed to the ground."

"And what are you doing, while I bring shame upon myself?"

"I will be doing the same as you. The old man will do the talking."

Kim glanced over at Song's grandfather who was in earshot. The old man smiled broadly, enraging the Sojang, "We are putting our lives in the hands of a cook."

Cho winked at the old man, "With respect Sojang, I trust him more than I trust you."

"The feeling is mutual, Daeryeong."

It took just under a minute for the 12-car freight train to screech to a stop. Cho slid the door open and jumped down. He was followed by Sojang Kim. Cho motioned to Kim to help him assist Song's grandfather down.

The old man found his footing and began patting his clothes. Cho placed his hands on the old man's shoulders, "Are you ready?"

Song's grandfather took a deep breath then took off in the direction of the front of the train, "Follow me, gentlemen."

Kim glanced at Cho before following. Cho couldn't suppress a grin.

* * * * *

One of Song's people slid the door closed, leaving it open just enough to look out. Father Kim knelt between the drums containing Mugsy and Scipio so both could hear, "They are off."

Mugsy's voiced bellowed, "Good. You know what to do."

Song appeared behind Father Kim, "Soldiers are approaching."

Father Kim walked to the door then turned to address Song and his people, "Again ... they knock and we open the door. I show them the paper Sojang Kim drew up listing us as employees of the water plant. That gives us authorization to travel with the heavy water. We let them board to inspect and we stay out of their way.

"Remember what the Americans taught us - no one looks in the direction of the drums containing them, and no one panics.

"One last thing ...," Father Kim bowed his head. The others did the same, some not knowing exactly why.

"Father in Heaven, bless us and protect us ... and let us be successful, through Messiah's name ... Amen."

Mugsy and Scipio's voice echoed the last word.

The sound of a rifle butt being rapped against the door rang out. Father Kim slid the door open.

A tall, thin *Chungwi*, equivalent to an American lieutenant, stood in the center of a half dozen soldiers. The soldiers were armed with Chinese-produced AK-47 assault rifles. A few pointed them while the others held theirs casually, across their waists.

Father Kim jumped down and handed the Chungwi the authorization Sojang Kim forged. The young officer took time to examine it before looking up, "Who are you?"

"I am Kim Sung-eun. I am in charge of this work crew."

The Chungwi waved his hand. His men slung their rifles and boarded the boxcar.

As Mugsy and Scipio instructed them, everyone stood aside and showed no interest in the inspection.

The Chungwi was last to board. He scanned the drums then turned to Father Kim, "Open them."

Father Kim's eyes met Song's for an instant. He could see the fear in them.

"They are sealed."

"You can reseal them after they are inspected."

"Chungwi, you have the paperwork in your hands … may I ask why you are putting us to all this extra work?"

The tall officer stepped close. He towered over the priest, "I said, open them."

Father Kim hesitated.

"Open them, or I will place you all under arrest and my men will open them."

Father Kim smirked, "If you do that, Chungwi, you will have a lot to explain to Taejang Kang … but we will open one for you."

The priest faced the drums and bellowed, "Open one of the drums for these soldiers to inspect."

Song and two others pried the top off of the nearest drum.

The Chungwi bent over and started to put his hand into it.

"I would be careful, Chungwi, that is special water. It cannot be contaminated, which is why it was sealed with care."

The Chungwi glowered, but decided not to dip his hand in, "Open another."

Father Kim exhaled audibly with annoyance. He pointed to another drum in the front. Song and his men walked over.

"No," said the Chungwi. He pointed, "Open the ones in the back."

Song and his men waited for Father Kim's order. He gave it with a terse nod. They made their way to a drum next to the one Mugsy was in and began prying the top up.

Father Kim walked over with the Chungwi. He looked in then pointed at the next drum, "Now this one."

Father Kim stepped next to Song and began shaking his head vigorously, "You cannot make us open all of these drums! Every time we open one there is a risk of contamination."

"You will open them or my men will!"

Father Kim continued shaking his head. Song saw the priest taking the screwdriver they were using to pry the tops off into his hand. After a moment, Father Kim leaned over the opened drum, "Look! What is that?!"

The Chungwi looked into the opened drum and saw red droplets spreading out on the surface of the water.

Father Kim kicked the side of it, "Just what I said … your stupid inspection has led to contaminating this drum! Do you realize how expensive a drum of this water is, Chungwi?!"

The Chungwi straightened up, "That was not there when I first looked in!"

"Well, it is there now!" Father Kim pressed his bloody hand into Song's and passed him the screwdriver.

"It looks like blood. Obviously one of the men cut his hand opening the drum … obeying your command!"

"Everyone, hold up your hands," ordered the Chungwi.

Everyone complied except for Father Kim. The Chungwi began examining them with impatience."

"It does not matter whose hand is bleeding. You were the one that gave the order … an order you still have not even explained to us! I tell you this, Chungwi, the blame will be laid on your head when the report is submitted to the Taejang and he will not be happy. This was a special, expedited shipment for a top secret project."

The Chungwi blinked nervously.

Father Kim grabbed his chin and began pacing, "The Taejang will probably have you shot, but he could imprison me and my men too. I must think."

The priest ignored the glance with just a touch of amusement from Song, as he continued to pace.

The Chungwi stared at the blood speckles, "Wait, can we not just spoon them out?"

"No, we cannot just spoon them out, Chungwi. The contents of that drum are now contaminated at a molecular level. Obviously, you know nothing about heavy water."

The Chungwi's face flushed.

Father Kim stopped pacing, "This is what we will do ....." He pointed to Song, "Seal that drum."

"But, the other drums must be inspected!" said the Chungwi.

Father Kim waved for the young officer to follow him to the door, "Chungwi, I may be able to make that drum disappear, but only that drum. We cannot take the chance of contaminating another one."

Father Kim could see the confusion on the Chungwi's face. He led him to an empty corner, "Chungwi, what exactly are you looking for?"

The Chungwi wiped a hand across his mouth, "We were ordered not to say."

Father Kim lowered his voice, "I can help you if you tell me what you were looking for."

"Men."

"Men?"

"Yes, enemies of the state."

Father Kim rubbed his forehead, "You have put all of our lives in peril to look for men inside sealed heavy water drums?"

The Chungwi's nostrils flared, "We were told to search everywhere! The orders came from Taejang Kang, himself."

"Well, I'm sure the Taejang would not have authorized you to contaminate this heavy water and jeopardize his top secret experiments."

The Chungwi's shoulders slouched.

"Listen to me. I personally watched the drums being filled and sealed from the water plant and my men and I have been with them ever since. There is no way that enemies of the state could have pried any open, emptied their contents, climbed in and resealed them. Do you understand?"

The Chungwi squinted and nodded.

"Besides, even if they did, they would be dead within minutes. The containers are air tight."

Father Kim led the Chungwi back to the door, "Take your men and leave. The drums have been checked. I will attest to that."

The Chungwi hesitated for only a moment before waving to his men. They began jumping down. The tall, junior officer was the last.

"Chungwi," Father Kim called to him, "I need the paper back."

The Chungwi held it out. Father Kim took it back with the hand that was not dripping blood.

The priest smiled as he slid the door closed, "Thank you and do not worry, I will handle this."

Song patted Father Kim's back, while the others helped Mugsy and Scipio out of the drums, "Father, you used the screwdriver to cut your hand?"

Father Kim held his hand up. There was a two-inch gash in his palm, "I'm afraid I did a good job."

Song motioned to his men. They brought over a first aid kit, "We will patch that up in no time."

Mugsy and Scipio joined them. Mugsy examined the wound, "I'll shake your hand, Father, after it's bandaged."

Scipio folded his arms, grinning, "Father, I thought it was a sin to lie. Contaminated heavy water?"

Father Kim smiled, "What do I know about heavy water."

"Apparently, a lot. Let's see, if I heard you correctly, the heavy water was 'contaminated at the molecular level'. We didn't know you had such expertise."

Father Kim blushed, "Neither did I."

Everyone laughed.

Mugsy slid the door open a crack and peered out, "What a performance. I gotta hand it to you Father … that was some act. There's not a soldier in sight out there."

"What now?" asked Song.

"Now, we wait," said Scipio. "According to the map, the track that needs to take us the rest of the way branches off behind us. That means the engine has to be moved from one side to the other, and the switch has to be thrown. That could take a couple of hours. I'll introduce myself to the engineer when we're close to the Sandone Station."

Song wrapped a small piece of gauze with medical tape around Father Kim's hand, "That should do it."

"Thank you."

Scipio patted the priest on his shoulder, "You know Father, if we live through this our boss might want to hire you. You're turning out to be quite the spy."

Father Kim pointed up, "That is very kind, but I already have a boss."

* * * * *

Song's grandfather marched over to the Station Manager's office with Cho and Sojang Kim in tow. There were soldiers standing at attention near the door. He knocked and heard someone holler "enter" from inside.

The old man turned to Cho and Kim and ordered with authority for the sake of the soldiers, "You will wait out here!"

Sojang Kim fumed. Cho winked at him.

Kim whispered, "That old fool is going to get us killed." He started for the door, but Cho stepped in front of him.

"Step aside, Daeryeong."

The guards looked their way.

Kim tried to pass, but Cho grabbed his arm.

"I said step aside. That fool could get us killed."

Cho grabbed Kim's wrist and twisted it, "Lower your voice Sojang or you will get us killed. And let me remind you that the old man told us to wait outside. He is in charge until we get inside the compound."

One of the guards stepped over to them. Cho released the Sojang's wrist and lowered his head. Realizing why, Kim did the same. The guard stood a moment longer before resuming his post.

* * * * *

Song's grandfather entered the Station Manager's office with an air of authority and stopped in front of the portly, middle-aged bureaucrat's desk.

The Station Manager looked up with a tired expression, "What can I do for you?"

"First, you will address me as Chef Song. I am the head chef for Taejang Kang," Song produced his security pass. The Station Manager examined it.

"I apologize, Chef Song, what can I do for you?"

"You can dispatch a train to take me and my helpers to Taejang Kang's headquarters immediately. The car the Taejang sent for me broke down outside of town. I must arrive at the Taejang's headquarters as soon as possible to prepare a meal for his party."

"His party …? I was not informed of any party for the Taejang?"

The old man shook his head, "I did not say 'party for the Taejang', I said 'for the Taejang's party'. And of course you would not have been informed. As I have told you, my helpers and I were to be transported by the Taejang's own car, but the car broke down."

The Station Manager picked the phone up on his desk, "Then I will contact his headquarters for orders."

The old man leaned in and disconnected the call with his finger, "You will do nothing of the kind … unless you want to be executed and probably have me and my helpers executed with you!"

The Station Manager placed the phone back in the cradle, "Executed, I do not understand."

The old man shrugged his shoulders, "Without forcing me to divulge more top-secret information, I will tell you that the party whom the Taejang is entertaining is from Pyongyang and does not want his presence here known."

The Station Manager rubbed his chin, "But this is highly unusual. I cannot simply dispatch a train without diverting one from its scheduled route without authorization. I will need a viable explanation."

Song's grandfather smiled, "I have given you an explanation and I am giving you authorization."

It was the Station Manager's turn to smile, "Pardon me Sir, but a cook—"

"Chef," the old man corrected.

"Chef … does not have the ability to authorize something of this nature, not even the Taejang's chef."

The old man stared back then reached for the phone and handed the Station Manager the receiver, "Then by all means, go ahead and contact the Taejang's headquarters. Tell them that his chef is here in your office waiting for a train to take me there. They will ask what the importance is and you can tell them about how the Taejang is entertaining the Supreme Leader and his … female friends."

The Station Manager froze with the phone in his hand, "The Supreme Leader …?"

The old man motioned with a nod, "Go ahead, as I said, time is of the essence here." He belly laughed, "I would wager that you will be taken into custody, interrogated, and shot before the Supreme Leader and his female companions even have the *Ho Dduk* I am making for dessert."

The paunchy man slammed the phone down and wiped sweat from his brow, before lifting the phone again, "This is the Station Manager, where is the 4:15 out of Hyesan now? Namjung … why is it running so late?! I will take that up with you later. For now, tell the engineer to skip his stops in Ryŏngnam and Ryŏngha. Have it head directly here. Yes, here! I know this is not one of his stops. Tell him to embark immediately and make best time."

The Station Manager slammed the phone down again. He sat slowly and composed himself before speaking in an official tone, "Chef Song, I have dispatched a train to take you to Taejang Kang's headquarters. The train is departing Namjung now and should arrive here in about 15 to 20 minutes. Is that satisfactory?"

Song's grandfather bowed, "That is satisfactory Station Manager. I appreciate your assistance."

As if jolted by a thought, the Station Manager jumped to his feet and raced to open the door for old man Song. He spoke barely above a whisper, "Chef Song, will it be necessary for you to report what you told me?"

"What I have told you?"

The Station Manager appeared visibly pained.

"Ah yes, what I have told you about … you know who."

The Station Manager looked past the old man at Sojang Kim and Cho. To them, he appeared to be more frightened than annoyed at their presence.

He nodded his reply.

Song's grandfather put an index finger to his lips, "I do not recall telling you anything. You were simply kind enough to offer me transportation to the Taejang's headquarters."

The Station Manager bowed his head, "Thank you. I will have one of my men escort you and your helpers aboard when the train arrives." He nodded to Kim and Cho as he closed the door.

Song's grandfather stood with a smug expression. Sojang Kim eyed the guards and spoke out of the side of his mouth, "What was that all about? What happened in there?"

The old man winked at Cho. He pushed between them, "In the valley where there are no tigers the hare is king."

Sojang Kim stared at Cho with confusion.

"Come," said Song's grandfather, "we have a train to catch."

Cho held his arm out for Kim to precede him with a twinkle in his eye.

CHAPTER 29

PRESIDENTIAL SUITE
FOSTER LAFAYETTE HOTEL, SEOUL
SEOUL, SOUTH KOREA
11:00 AM (LOCAL), TUESDAY, JUNE 04, 2013

"Are you sure you don't want to come, John?" De Niro asked Francis as he slipped on his jacket, the last article of his Brooks Brothers, navy, Fitzgerald Fit Golden Fleece® suit.

The balding, pudgy tech-genius didn't reply or look up from the row of monitors before him. He dug a handful of chips from a bag of Doritos® and crunched nosily.

Michelle Wang emerged from the bathroom in a dark green pant suit and heels, "How do I look?" She directed to De Niro.

"Beautiful."

A dimpled smile appeared, "You know, you're the only boss that would go there."

"Go where?"

"Describing a female employee as beautiful, that's not politically-correct, you know. In fact, some women could consider that a form of harassment. Fortunately, for you, I'm not one of them."

"Well, for the record I was describing my soon-to-be sister-in-law, not my employee … and it's the truth."

"I have to get used to that … my employer becoming my brother-in-law."

"How about your boss becoming your husband?" said Francis, crunching on a mouthful of chips.

"That too."

"So John, last call," said De Niro, "you sure you don't want to join us? You haven't been out of this suite in days."

"Michelle just gave me the Colonel's laptop this morning. The rest of the time I was just spinning my wheels, digging for info inside the South Korean Secret Service hub. He used some sophisticated encryption but I can penetrate it. I should have it cracked by the time you get back."

Michelle looked in a mirror, "It took me that long to locate and get by the security measures. I never saw a home with more alarms and motion detectors. Just to get to the house I had to recon the private security and police patrolling the gated community to gain entry."

"One thing's for sure, the Cho is security-minded," De Niro turned for the door. "Catch you later, John."

Francis waved with one hand, while the other dug into the Doritos® bag. It came out empty. He rushed to the door, "Wait up guys, I'll tag along to the lobby … I need to make a snack stop."

"Why not just call room service," asked Michelle.

"Because they don't have Doritos® on the menu and I've become hooked on the Jacked Enchilada Supremes."

"You found Enchilada Supreme Doritos® in Seoul?"

"Not exactly … I called over to our embassy and got someone to fly them in."

Michelle's nostrils flared as they stepped onto the elevator, "John, tell me you didn't!"

"Easy Michelle … it's not like I had them flown in on Air Force One. I just asked the woman in charge of stocking the embassy kitchen if she flew food in from the States."

"And …?"

"And … well it turns out she loves Doritos® as much as I do …

but she never had the Jacked, so I told her about them ..."

"And?!"

The elevator doors closed.

* * * * *

Reading the last page of *The Pyongyang Times*, Taejang Kang slurped his favorite breakfast loudly from his spoon — seaweed soup with turnip and sardines. As the top military official in charge of North Korea's nuclear and ballistic missile programs, all six of the country's newspapers were delivered to Kang each morning, including the unofficial *Rimjingang*, which remained unread outside the secure area. Published by the Asia Press, initially in a co-joint venture between a North Korean defector and a Japanese journalist, Kang was convinced they delivered the controversial newspaper to him as a test of his national loyalty.

He knew there were Pyongyang spies among his headquarters staff that kept an eye on him - where he traveled; with whom he met; what he read, listened to, and watched. That was why he rarely ventured outside of Punggye-Ri. It was also why he had his office placed inside the most secure area of the compound—the fortified bunker--for the purpose of keeping his meetings, TV and radio preferences confidential.

As for the Rimjingang, Kang decided to continue to allow it to be delivered, so that whoever was watching would report that he had no interest in the dissident movement. Of course, he also had one of his more-trusted staff members keeping an eye on the paper to see if anyone else would read it. No one did.

Kang did nothing more than scan the other newspapers. Each had a different focus, and each was equally dull. The *Rodong Sunmun* (The Workers' Newspaper) was the official newspaper of the Central Committee of the Workers' Party of Korea. It was six-pages long and focused on editorializing the Party's view on different issues; The *Minju Choson* handled more administrative matters, such as decisions and orders of the Cabinet, laws, regulations and policy issues; and the *Pyongyang Sinmun*, started by the former leader Kim Il-sung, was the mouthpiece of the Municipal Committee of the Workers' Party of Korea Pyongyang, and focused mostly on the administrative functions of its city.

Though its print edition was only published in English, *The Pyongyang Times* was Kang's favorite. The eight-page tabloid was only published once a week and was broken up into sections. The front cover was devoted to praising anything and everything about Kim Jong-un. The next few pages detailed various technological and ideological exploits of the nation. Propaganda against North Korea's enemies followed. The last pages were what Kang read most. They contained "foreign news."

Though the paper usually focused on like-minded or socialist nations, Kang was obsessed with knowing what was going on in the rest of the world. Convinced his once-feared nation was woefully falling behind their hated cousins to the south, he had little interest in domestic issues. He recalled telling Sojang Kim that North Korea had become, *"... a nation of starving idiots run by well-fed fools."*

Kang put the spoon down and picked up steel chopsticks next to a bowl of *kimchi*. Like many, he was addicted to the spicy-sour flavor of the fermented vegetable concoction – Korea's national dish.

The phone rang with his mouth full. He recognized the number, so he let it ring until he swallowed. It was Bok.

"What have you to report?"

"Sir, I can finally gain access to the Americans' hotel suite."

"Why has it taken so long?"

"Taejang, someone has always remained in the room."

"The suite is empty now?"

"Yes. I have a camera set up in the corridor monitoring the door. I just saw all of them get on the elevator. I checked – a limo is waiting for them at the entrance."

"Then go. I must know what Cho has told them and if he is in contact with them. I need to know now."

"Understood, Sir."

"It will be your life if you fail, Bok. The time is too close and the stakes too high."

* * * * *

The line went dead. The North Korean spy thoughtlessly stroked the three-inch scar on his cheek. He put gloves on, then checked the clip of his Type 68 pistol and tucked it into his belt. Next, he picked up a leather case containing a keycard microcontroller and opened the camera surveillance app on his cell phone before leaving the room.

Though his room was on the opposite end of the hotel, Bok thought it fortunate to be given a room on the same floor as the Americans. It just made his job that much easier.

He stepped in front of the door to the American's suite. Without looking around, he plugged the microcontroller into the socket used to charge the battery inside the door lock. The socket was also used to program the lock with the hotel's own sitecode, a 32-bit key that identifies the specific hotel.

Bok switched the power on to the microcontroller. It took only 200 milliseconds for the device to unlock the door.

He closed the door behind him and used the app to allow him to monitor the corridor outside the room. Then he turned on the lights.

Bok approached Francis's computer setup. He sat down, took a FireWire cable from his pocket, plugged the ends into his cell phone, and then into the laptop. The action triggered the laptop to shut down. He immediately heard a chime emanating from a cell phone resting next to it.

Bok examined the cell phone. The only thing now appearing on the screen was a logo that read "*Big-Brutha*™." The phone appeared to be locked. He put it down.

Turning back to the laptop, he hit the power button. In less than a second, the machine booted to an identical Big-Brutha logo. That caused a decryption program on his cell to begin running in the background while still being able to monitor the camera in the corridor on the phone's screen.

A minute passed … then two … then five.

Bok mindlessly stroked the scar on his cheek.

It never takes this long. Our best techs created this decryption program. It has never failed me before. This American must be a genius."

Bok rose from the seat and examined the other laptop in the room. The image on the screen was the same, so he turned his attention to the rest of the suite. All he found was scribbling on a few note pads.

He returned to Francis's laptop. The encryption program was still running.

I didn't want to have to take the laptops, but I may have no choice. This is taking too long.

He checked his watch and then the monitor of the corridor. He saw no one.

I'll wait a little longer.

* * * * *

Outside the hotel, Francis watched as De Niro and Michelle were whisked away in an armored Mercedes limousine before jumping into the first cab in the line.

He leaned forward to talk to the driver, "Do you speak English."

"Yes, sir."

"Excellent. Do you know where the American Embassy is?"

"Yes, sir."

He sat back, "Awesome … okay, the American Embassy please." The taxi left the curb.

Francis stared out the window for a block before digging into his pockets.

"Damn!"

The driver looked in his rearview mirror, "Something wrong, Sir?"

"No … I mean yeah," he patted all his pockets, "I left my phone in my hotel room. Can I use yours?"

"I'm sorry Sir, I don't carry a phone."

"You don't carry a phone? Who doesn't carry a phone nowadays."

The taxi driver stopped at the light and turned his head. Francis could now see his age – he looked to be in his late 60's or early 70's, and he looked annoyed.

"My wife died and we had no children. I do not have relatives, and the few friends I have do not need to call me while I am working."

"I see," Francis rolled his eyes. He mumbled to himself, "In a city of over 10 million people, I get the one person who doesn't carry a cell phone."

"Sir …?"

"Nothing … nothing. Okay, we need to turn around, so I can get my phone. Okay?"

"They have a front desk at the embassy. Maybe you can ask them to help you."

"Trust me, they won't help me. The person I need to see there doesn't want me to be seen with her. Showing up and asking the front desk to fetch her is out of the question."

"I understand, Sir," The driver turned the taxi around and smiled in the mirror.

"You do? I mean, you do. Wait, what do you understand?"

The driver just grinned in reply.

"No-no-no … you don't understand. This isn't some weird love tryst. I mean, I never even met the woman, I just talked to her on the phone."

The driver grinned wider.

"No … no! It's not what you think. You see, I love hot spicy chips."

The driver began to nod his head vigorously, "Hot spicy chicks … yes. I like this too, but at my age …" he chuckled.

"What? Nooo, not chicks … chips … Doritos® … hot spicy Doritos®. You know … chips?"

"Chips?"

Francis sunk in his seat, "Let's just be quiet now."

* * * * *

Bok wiped sweat from his forehead. He stared between Francis' laptop monitor and his cell phone screen with the image of the corridor on it.

I cannot wait here any longer. I have to take the laptops.

He raised a finger to tap the decryption app's *stop* button when an image of a man exiting the elevator appeared on the screen. He had noticed a few others come and go, so he didn't panic. Instead, he waited to see if the man was heading in the direction of the suite.

Bok slipped into the bathroom as the door opened.

Francis hurried in and headed directly for his laptop. He saw his cell phone lying on the table and reached for it when he noticed the Big-Brutha™ logo on his screen.

Then he saw the FireWire cable.

He had just enough time to tap out *SOS* onto his phone's screen, the Morse code distress signal. That activated a "panic" application he designed that simultaneously turned on the mic and cam, and turned off the lights on the phone, making it appear powered down.

Then his lights went out.

* * * * *

Francis came to with his arms and legs tied to a chair and his mouth gagged. He could see that sections of the drape were torn away to use as binds. He felt a sharp pain in the back of his head and a dull ache inside it. He also felt something wet and warm running down his neck and knew it was blood. His double vision slowly began to recede. He realized someone was standing behind him.

"Turn around and I will slit your throat. Now, I am going to remove the gag. If you try to scream, I will cut the fingers of your left hand off. Do you understand?"

Francis nodded. The gag was removed.

"What is this about? Are you robbing me? Go ahead, take whatever you want and just leave."

"I intend to, but first you will tell me the password to access your laptop."

The hairs on Francis's neck bristled.

"My ... my laptop?"

Francis felt the cold steel of a blade being pressed against his neck, just over his Adam's apple.

"Yes, your laptop. Tell me the password and I will take it and leave ... and you will live."

"The password … right," he thought frantically. "Well, that's not my laptop."

"Whose laptop is it, Mr. Francis?"

"You know my name? How … how do you know that?"

"Because you are not Cris De Niro and you are not Michelle Wang. I know their names too, and I know that you are the Chief Information Officer for The Watchman Agency."

"You do? You do. Well, then you should know that … that … I would never … ever be caught dead using a laptop like that one." He strained to turn his head, but felt the blade dig in, "What … what I mean to say is … I'm a Mac guy."

"Then whose laptop is it?"

"It's Cris's … I mean Mr. De Niro's, and I don't know his password."

Francis heard noises behind him – the sound of something being unplugged and a wire being cut, followed by the sound of something being plugged back in. A silent moment passed before he saw what he had heard.

Two hands—one protruding from each side of his head, with arms resting on his shoulders—held the exposed power cable wires to one of the suite's lamps. The hands touched the wires together a few times just inches from his nose, producing loud sparks.

"Hey … there's no need for that. I'm telling you, I honestly don't know the password to Cris's laptop."

Francis saw the arms withdraw. It was another tense minute before a pillowcase was placed over his head. Then he felt his shirt, jeans, and underwear cut from his body.

"What … what are you doing? Hey … I told you … I don't know his password. What are you gonna do?!"

There was no reply. The gag was replaced. Francis's heart pounded. He felt sweat pour down from his scalp. Then, he felt his body spasm even before the pain kicked in. Every one of his muscles contracted at the same time. The fear that had been building materialized. The nightmare, realized. He was being electrocuted.

He felt the wires being placed in different places all over his body – applied and removed – applied and removed. Francis heard the loudest screams he ever heard in his life. Until the screams were muffled by the gag and pillowcase, he did not realize they were his own.

The agony lasted for over two minutes – minutes that felt like hours. When the wires were withdrawn the last time, his body went limp. He was covered in sweat.

The next thing he felt was a punch to his face and then another and another. The pillowcase became so saturated in blood that it stuck to his cheeks.

"I ask again, what is the password?"

CHAPTER 30

TO SOK CHON RESTAURANT
JONGNO-GU
SEOUL, SOUTH KOREA
11:30 AM (LOCAL), TUESDAY, JUNE 04, 2013

As soon as the sleek black Mercedes came to a stop, the back door was opened. De Niro and Michelle were greeted with a simple nod in the direction of the restaurant's door, by a dark-suited man wearing sunglasses and an earpiece. There was a line outside the ornate restaurant that extended from the entrance and wrapped around the building. Two lines of dark-suited men, all wearing sunglasses and earpieces, marked their path through the crowd.

Inside, they were greeted by an identically-clad Secret Service agent who, after waving over a half-dozen other agents, walked ahead and led them into a private room in the rear. Upon entry, the doors closed behind them. Agents positioned themselves on each side. They saw President Park seated at the head of a large table talking on a cell phone.

De Niro waited for the President to end the call before extending his hand. The well-dressed head-of-state placed her phone down and stood to greet both of them.

"It is good to see you both, again."

"It's an honor, Ms. President," replied De Niro.

"I hope you don't mind this impromptu meeting. In order to keep our association covert, Daeryeong Cho's second-in-command thought it best to schedule it immediately before the luncheon being held here.

"It is a meeting of the board of the Federation of Korean Industries. The FKI is considered South Korea's most powerful business organization, so it would not seem out of place for you to be invited. The luncheon will not start for another hour. I usually dine alone before I speak, so this is also not unusual."

She swept her arm, "Please take a seat. I hope you don't mind, but I am a little pressed for time, so I took the liberty to order for all of us. Have either of you ever eaten here?"

They answered, "No," in unison.

"Really, I'm surprised. To Sok Chon is probably Seoul's most popular restaurant with visitors to my country."

"That could be the reason," replied De Niro, "I've never considered myself much of a tourist. I prefer the local flavor."

The President touched his arm and smiled, leaning in, "I am the same way. Unfortunately, as President, I am usually confined to state dinners, so I no longer get to … eat with locals. However, in the case of To Sok Chon, you may want to make an exception."

An army of waiters were allowed into the room. Among many other smaller bowls of various items set on the table, larger, steaming stone bowls were placed in front of them.

"This looks so good," said Michelle.

"It is called *samgyetang*. It is a young, spring chicken stuffed with chestnuts, garlic, dried jujubes, and ginseng. It is then slow-cooked for many hours. Are you familiar with *The Sambok*?"

"Doesn't that have to do with the hottest days of summer?"

"Very good, yes it does. It is also known as *boknal* … the dog days of summer. The Sambok covers the month-long peak of growing season, traditionally the hottest days, and a holiday for farmers. This year, it begins on July 13, and runs through August 12.

"The farmers get away to a mountain valley or the coast to cool off and visit family before the rice harvest. Nowadays, most people don't follow the tradition, except to eat rejuvenating and stamina restoring food."

"It seems like the Jews and Koreans have something in common, after all," said De Niro, "chicken soup to restore good health."

The President smiled, "Actually, it is based on Eastern medicine – the belief that blood concentrates near the skin in hot weather to cool the body, which can lead to bad circulation in the stomach and muscles, causing loss of appetite and fatigue. To offset this, Koreans believe in the need to warm the body. Bosintang, jangeo, and samgyetang are eaten. I chose samgyetang because it is my favorite, and I am aware of your dietary limitations."

"My dietary limitations?" said De Niro.

"I understand that your faith prohibits you from eating shellfish and pork, among other things. Jangeo is eel."

"And bosintang?"

"Bosintang is dog meat stew. Honestly, I have never liked it. Only the older generation eats it nowadays."

De Niro saw the horror on Michelle's face, "Well, Michelle and I both thank you for taking the time to know our dietary preferences."

Everyone spooned their soup.

"This is really delicious," said Michelle. "The chicken almost melts in your mouth."

President Park motioned to the aide standing behind her. He handed her a manila envelope. The President placed it on the table next to De Niro's bowl.

De Niro saw what was written on it, 'For eyes of President Park only'. He glanced at the President.

"Please …."

He opened it and read from the single page that was inside. When he was done, he looked up, "May I show this to Michelle?"

"Please do."

Michelle read it mumbling quietly to herself, "Has this been verified, Ms. President?"

"It has. It was written by Sojang Kim and dispatched from a FedEx location in Beijing. My agents have already pulled the surveillance footage from that store." She motioned again to her aide. He handed her a photo which she passed to De Niro. "This is the woman who mailed it yesterday, and specified for next day delivery. Unfortunately, we have no further information on her."

"Let me see that again, Michelle," said De Niro. He took a moment to re-read it.

"What do you make of it?" asked the President.

"According to this, Sojang Kim is accusing Daeryeong Cho of being Kang's co-conspirator, and he's basing that on Cho's manner of infiltration at the Chinese border. But we've been in regular contact with our people, as recently as early this morning. Cho is with them and so is Kim. In fact, their plan of infiltration into the Punggye-Ri facility pairs the Cho with the Sojang. Obviously, this letter was written before they met up."

"As you know, I have not been aware of any of Daeryeong Cho's activities since he left for China. Nevertheless, I would never consider him a traitor, no matter what this North Korean general believes. I also felt confident that you would have somehow gotten word to me if you or your team suspected Cho.

"Still, if Sojang Kim did subsequently make contact with the him, and they are now working together … did Cho dispatch another letter with instructions to disregard this one?"

No one replied.

"I guess we cannot know the answer to that until tomorrow at the soonest."

"By tomorrow, it will be a moot point," replied De Niro. He looked at his watch, "They've already left for Kang's headquarters."

The President's aide bent down and whispered something in her ear.

"The members of the association have begun to arrive. We will have to end our meeting now. I continue to leave this in your capable hands, Cris."

"I'm honored by your trust, your Excellency."

They all rose. The President offered her hand to both, "If you have the time, you should remain. Many of our most powerful business leaders will be here today. I promise not to bore with a long speech."

De Niro and Michelle's phone vibrated as President Park left the room. Their screens read, "Panic-Francis, J."

Both opened their Big-Brutha™ apps. All they saw was the ceiling, but what they heard sent shivers down their spines - a sinister rustling, as if listening to a robbery in progress.

"John, are you there?!" De Niro shouted, catching the attention of the Secret Service agents still in the room.

"It's no use, Cris. John activated his panic app. Only John's retinal scan can override the lock."

De Niro's face flushed. He rushed out the door with Michelle on his heels, "That's right, he schooled me on it. So he's in trouble. We've gotta get back to the hotel."

They hurried out of the restaurant, passing a number of Korean business magnates who recognized De Niro. He moved swiftly, navigating around them and into the limo with Michelle in tow.

He leaned forward to speak to the driver, "Please take us back to our hotel as quickly as possible."

With a nod, the driver immediately pulled away from the curb.

Michelle turned the volume up on her Big-Brutha™ phone. Both listened with tension. They heard banging and shuffling noises followed by silence and the sound of fabric tearing in the distance.

The limo raced a few blocks before coming to a stop. De Niro rolled down the window and cursed, "We're stuck in a traffic jam. How far are we from the hotel?"

The driver turned his head and replied with a shrug, "Miles."

De Niro focused his attention on the sounds coming from Michelle's phone. The banging was replaced with noises that neither could identify.

"What do you think is happening?"

Michelle held her index finger up and turned her ear closer to the phone.

De Niro stared at her, "You hear something?"

"I thought I heard … a moan."

De Niro closed his eyes. For a moment, Michelle thought he was in physical pain when she noticed his lips moving – he was praying.

She tapped on her screen several times, "I'm calling the police. Then I'll call the hotel and have them send their detective up to the suite. I just wish we knew what was going on there."

De Niro opened his eyes and began tapping his phone, "Maybe there is."

Instructions started flashing on the screen:

Calibrating … GPS coordinates fixed … Black Hornet One ready for launch. The pre-launch process took less than 20 seconds.

A *LAUNCH* button appeared. De Niro tapped it. Instantly, the screen changed to a camera-view from one of the *Warbird*'s mini-drones, but this one wasn't inside the giant aircraft. The camera showed its location – inside Johnny-F's bedroom.

Good thing I paid attention when John explained how to fly one of these things and thank God he's a child at heart. He couldn't resist playing with the mini-drone, even inside the suite. He especially loved driving Michelle crazy, buzzing it by her head.

Below the camera-view information began appearing: grid coordinates, battery life, the height of the drone off the ground, and the current wind strength.

Below that was a line for target input. Francis designed the application so targeting could be input by coordinates or by simply typing a location like an address or landmark. De Niro left it blank and began piloting the drone manually.

Good thing he left the door open.

He looked over at Michelle. She returned a quizzical glance, as she spoke in Korean to the police.

De Niro flew the toy chopper around the bedroom to get the feel of it before steering it out the door. Immediately, he saw the images of two men on the other side of the large main room, one sitting with his head slung down, the other standing over him. He could see at once that the man standing wasn't Francis.

De Niro maneuvered the drone close to the windows spanning the room before advancing it nearer the men. He got within 12-feet before dropping it almost to the floor. There, he pointed the camera directly at the men and gasped.

The Asian man standing was cutting the clothes off the man

seated who he could now see clearly was Francis.

De Niro considered flying the mini drone directly at them. *And what happens if the attacker sees the drone and destroys it ... would he kill John?*

Another idea came to him. He turned the chopper around and flew it back into the bedroom. There, he saw his target – two ornate boxes, for decoration—the smaller one sitting atop the larger one—adorning a table in front of the foot of the bed.

He flew the drone over, careful not to let the blades come in contact and positioned the front of the tiny aircraft against the top box.

This can work. If I can aim it just right, I can save the drone too.

I wish I could hear what was going on. I hope John is okay.

De Niro said a quick prayer as he flew the drone in reverse a few feet. He steadied it in the air then before flying Black Hornet One directly at the top box.

The camera flickered the moment the drone came in contact with the box. When the image reappeared, De Niro wasn't sure what he was looking at. It took him a moment to realize it was sideways.

Damn! The prop must have come in contact with the box. That's exactly what I was trying not to do.

He examined the image closely.

It's pointing outside ... wait ... that looks like the bedspread. It must have come to rest on the bed.

De Niro tried the controls but nothing happened. An error message flashed on his screen: *FAULT: PROPELLER.*

Michelle got off her call, "I had to tell them someone had a gun in the room and a fight was going on to get the police and hotel security to respond. They're on their way now." She leaned over to see De Niro's screen, "What are you doing?"

"Remember the mini-drone John kept dive bombing at your head ... I took control of it."

"Did you see anything?"

De Niro nodded, "It wasn't good. Someone—an Asian male—was giving John a hard time. I tried to knock something over with the drone to distract him. I don't know if it worked."

They kept their eyes on the screen.

"It's lying on its side on the bed. I knocked over one of those decorative boxes, but I'm not sure if—"

Reflexively, they both backed their heads away as the image became garbled before changing to the attacker's face. He looked to be examining the drone.

Michelle glanced at De Niro wide-eyed, "I guess you were successful."

The image became garbled again. This time it stabilized in an upright position.

"He must have tossed it back on the couch."

Michelle squeezed his arm, "Let's hope you freaked him out enough that he'll leave."

De Niro tapped the controls and grinned. The drone had responded by leaping into the air.

"There's only one way to find out. Let's go take a look."

He flew Black Hornet One into the main room, just in time to see a man rushing out of the suite.

Then he turned the small craft back towards Francis.

Tears came from both their eyes.

Johnny's F's body sat motionless with a bloody pillowcase over his head.

CHAPTER 31

PRESIDENTIAL SUITE
FOSTER LAFAYETTE HOTEL, SEOUL
SEOUL, SOUTH KOREA
11:45 AM (LOCAL), TUESDAY, JUNE 04, 2013

"I ask again, what is the password?"

Bok reached for the pillowcase when he heard something – a noise coming from one of the bedrooms.

He pulled his pistol and scanned the main room before approaching the bedroom with caution.

Bok spun himself into the room, aiming his weapon wherever he looked. He took time to check every closet and the bathroom before ending up in front of the bed. He noticed a box on the floor.

Looking around again, he checked the balcony before returning to the room. Nothing seemed out of place except the box and …

What is that?

Bok spotted what looked like a small toy helicopter, lying on its side on the bed. He picked it up and examined it.

This is no toy.

Bok looked from the small chopper to the box on the floor. An idea came to him that made him uneasy.

Time to leave.

He tossed the toy chopper onto the bed and hurried out of the room.

Bok pulled the pillowcase off of Francis's head and cut his right arm free. He held the laptop near him, "Type in your password or I will leave you with the wires attached."

Francis strained to reach his hand over the keyboard. It was difficult for him to steady his hand. He was shaking uncontrollably.

He felt a slap to the back of his head, "Hurry!"

Francis took care to enter his password, *W-1-l-e-E-C-0-y-o-t-e.*

Bok saw the Big-Brutha™ logo disappear on the screen and a menu appear. He slammed the laptop closed then faced Francis and placed the pillowcase over his head.

Bok delivered a kick to Francis's face before racing from the suite. The blow sent the tech genius's body tumbling backwards.

The North Korean spy closed the door behind him. He only made it a few feet before he saw police and a man who acted like the hotel detective stepping off of the elevator at the other end of the corridor.

Bok walked casually in their direction, until he came upon a housekeeping cart parked outside an open door. He entered the suite and saw two uniformed women, one in the bathroom and one making the bed. The woman turned to look at him.

He nodded to them, "Have either of you seen a wallet? I think I may have left it here?"

The lady making the bed walked over, "Wallet, no Sir. We saw no wallet here."

Bok feigned searching for it while keeping an eye on the corridor. The police and the man finally passed. They looked in but didn't stop.

Bok opened the closet and reached in, as if picking something up from the floor. He held his wallet up to the women, "I found it … must have fallen out of my trousers. Thank you."

He entered the corridor and headed in the direction of the elevators, fighting the temptation to turn around.

* * * * *

De Niro blinked the tears from his eyes. He spun the mini-drone around and headed it in the direction of the door. It was closed.

Father, please let him be alive. The rage ... I feel it welling inside me. The same rage I felt on 9/11 ... it exists in me. This bastard has no idea what he's unleashed!

He spun it around and scanned the room, "No way out."

The limo driver turned his head, "The traffic is beginning to move. Once we get to the corner, I can turn and get you to your hotel in a few minutes."

De Niro nodded.

"Go back to him, Cris," said Michelle, "see if he's moving."

De Niro flew near Francis's body. He and Michelle looked for any signs of movement.

She exhaled audibly, "It's so hard to tell. Come on John, move!"

He flew the drone near the door to suite, keeping as close as he could to the wall, "The police and hotel detective have to come sometime."

As if on cue, the door to the suite opened, coming within an inch of crushing the small drone. Two uniformed police officers entered followed by a man in a suit. They paused in front of the door before one of the officers and the man in the suit rushed over in the direction of Francis. The other officer headed to the bedrooms.

"Now!" Michelle ordered needlessly.

With care, De Niro flew the drone around the door and out into the corridor. He pointed it to the elevator and used the zoom function. There was a housekeeping cart outside one of the other suites. Beyond it, a man approached the bank of elevators.

De Niro tapped the throttle to full, "That's him!"

The sleek mini-drone sped down the corridor. De Niro tried to keep it as close as he could to the ceiling.

"Come on little Black Hornet, fly baby!" Michelle cheered.

They saw the man push the elevator button then stand there.

"Think fast, Cris," said De Niro.

Within seconds, the elevator doors opened.

"Damn ... he's getting on. What now, Cris?"

De Niro bit his lip. He moved his finger across the cell phone screen, "We're getting on too."

The mini-drone raced behind the Korean thug and entered the elevator behind him. De Niro continued to keep the small aircraft close to the ceiling.

Michelle shook her head, "I can't believe he hasn't spotted it yet."

"It operates quietly but Muzak would've helped."

The elevator doors closed and the screen began to flutter.

"Hold on little bird!"

De Niro and Michelle watched as Black Hornet One fell from the air. The camera was still working, so De Niro tilted it up as far as it would go. They saw the Asian man reaching down.

"Damn … He saw it!"

Please Father!

As quickly as it closed, the elevator door opened again. A woman and young boy entered.

The monitor became garbled. It cleared again for just a moment before going black. It revealed the face of the boy.

Michelle glanced up. De Niro noticed she had her phone to her ear, "I have the police on the line. They have me on hold. They're communicating with the police in the room now." She motioned to the camera feed on De Niro's phone, "It looked like the boy picked it up before that bastard could."

"Let's see what happens when the elevator opens."

* * * * *

Bok heard something fall to the floor. He looked down and couldn't believe his eyes. The same toy chopper was lying at his feet. He bent to pick it up when a hand appeared between the doors. The doors reopened and a woman and a boy entered. The boy immediately spotted it.

"Mommy, look!" The boy swiped the mini-drone from the floor. His eyes went wide as he held it in front of him, "It's a helicopter! I always wanted a helicopter."

Bok reached for it, "That is mine."

The boy pulled it away, "It was on the floor."

"It fell out of my hand. Give it to me."

The boy stepped behind his mother. The woman looked frustrated, "Give the man back his toy."

"It's not his toy. It was on the floor."

The woman looked at Bok with tired eyes.

Bok's nostrils flared, "He must give it back to me."

The woman rolled her eyes and turned to her son, "I said to give the toy back to the man. Give it back this instant."

The elevator opened to the lobby. The boy rushed out, followed by Bok and his mother.

Bok scanned the lobby with tension. He chased the boy and finally cornered him, "Give that to me now."

The boy's mother raced after and got between them. She reached for the mini-drone but the boy put it behind his back. He began to cry, "I want to keep it! I found it on the floor!"

Bok pushed her aside. He grabbed the boy's arms from behind him. The small chopper's propellers started to spin.

Everyone froze.

They stopped after a second.

The boy took off running in the direction of the main entrance, with Bok in pursuit. The North Korean spy cornered him again before he could reach the doors.

"Now, you will give it to me or I will take it from you."

The propellers began spinning again. This time they didn't stop. A smile appeared on the boy's face as he glanced up at Bok.

"No!"

The boy opened his hand. The small chopper took off and headed straight up.

The boy began laughing, "You can have it … if you can catch it."

Bok almost forgot where he was as he drew his hand back. A scream from the boy's mother reminded him.

The North Korean spy cursed. He looked up to try to find the mini-drone. It was gone.

He cursed again and headed out the door.

* * * * *

De Niro and Michelle stared at the dark screen while they felt the speed of the limousine increase.

De Niro leaned forward and tapped the driver's shoulder, "How far are we?"

"Maybe two miles … five minutes?"

"Can you step on it?"

"Step on it … yes, but I cannot run lights."

De Niro dug in his pocket and produced a wad of Korean currency. He held it up for the driver to see in the rearview mirror, "Run lights."

The black on the monitor was replaced by garble, followed by crooked images of the lobby.

Michelle turned the monitor to face her more, "Where is he?"

De Niro pointed, "There … there he is. I gotta get this kid to let go."

He revved the small motor, "At least I regained control. Here goes nothing." He slid the throttle control to full again. They were both surprised to see Black Hornet One lift off.

"Way to go, kid!"

De Niro flew it high and began scanning the lobby below. They saw the boy, and the man standing near him. They also saw the boy's mother running towards the two.

"I wish we could hear," said Michelle. "We have to ask John if …." She caught herself. De Niro saw tears form in her eyes.

He touched her shoulder, "We'll ask him to get ones with microphones, as soon as he's able."

De Niro knew the last time they looked, Johnny-F, his friend since childhood, might have been dead. Neither he nor Michelle could be sure.

I pray Father, please let him be alive.

They watched the man rush out of the hotel's main entrance. De Niro looked up to talk to the driver, "How much farther?"

"We are only five blocks away."

De Niro brought the mini-drone down and let it hover about six feet off the ground. He scanned the doors and saw his chance.

"Here goes nothing … again."

He began counting to himself. Michelle was confused until she saw what he was doing. The camera was focused on the revolving doors – and they were revolving with people entering and leaving.

De Niro increased the altitude to just below the door's ceiling and nudged the screen-throttle forward. He pulled up at the last second, when it was apparent he wasn't going to make it into the slot he aimed for.

"So much for counting."

He took a deep breath and nudged the throttle forward again. This time he entered one of the rotating booths. He slowed it and angled the camera down just a touch to see a woman below hadn't even noticed.

Once outside, De Niro increased Black Hornet One's altitude to twenty feet and began rotating it to scan for the man. They caught a glimpse of him taking keys from the valet and hustling to a sports car parked in front. The car took off and De Niro steered the mini-drone in pursuit.

The limousine turned into the circular entrance of the hotel just as Bok's car was leaving from the other side.

The driver pulled up in front. He turned around with a smile, "We are here. I told you I could get you—"

"Listen to me," De Niro interrupted, concentrating on his cell's screen, "I need you to follow directions I'll shout out to you. Can you do that?"

"Why don't you just tell me where you want to—?"

"There's a thousand dollars American in it, if you just do as I say."

The driver's eyes widened. He pulled away from the curb as the doorman grabbed hold of the door handle, almost ripping the startled man's arm off.

"Now, turn right out of the entrance and go straight … and step on it."

"Yes, sir."

De Niro kept Black Hornet One on the dark sedan's tail for the first couple of blocks. Then, as prey does when discovering its being hunted, the sedan suddenly accelerated, leaving the mini-drone behind.

Michelle squeezed his arm, "Can't it go any faster, Cris?"

"I have the throttle floored."

He rolled his finger over the altitude control, "I'll take it higher. Help me keep an eye on the car."

Michelle pointed at the screen, "He's turning."

The limo slowed. The driver spoke over his shoulder, "Traffic up ahead."

"What's the range of that thing?"

De Niro kept his eyes focused on the screen, "I think John said something like 6.8 miles. He's already over a mile ahead now, and pulling away fast."

Michelle's cell rang. She listened for a moment then her body crumbled. De Niro couldn't tell if it was good news or bad until he heard her ask, "Can I speak to him?"

She lowered the phone, "It's the hotel detective. He said he travelled with John to the hospital and that the doctor told him John is in critical condition." She had to hold back tears, "They're not sure he'll survive." She paused. De Niro noticed.

He wiped his own tears away, "What else, Michelle?"

"The doctor said John has blunt force trauma injuries. And injuries that indicate ...."

"Indicate what?"

Her voice broke down, "He was electrocuted, Cris. He was tortured."

She put her arms around him. De Niro's muscles tightened as if he felt his friend's pain.

Then his faced hardened.

He focused back on the cell screen, "It looks like he's driving through a residential area now. No high buildings, but we're starting to lose sight of him."

The limo picked up speed.

"I got him. He's turning onto a main thoroughfare. He's starting to book again."

They watched as the car became smaller and smaller.

De Niro punched the seat, "Damn it … lost him."

He leaned forward and turned the cell's screen towards the driver, "He turned into this area. Do you know it?"

The driver looked between the road and the screen a few times, "Yes. That is Gajwa Business Park. Lots of small technology companies there. Many times, I drive visiting business people there."

It took five more minutes for the limo to turn into the business park. The driver stopped and turned around, "Where to now?"

De Niro and Michelle studied the cell phone screen. As the mini-drone hovered more or less in its center, he slowly rotated the camera.

"The battery is almost dead. Our little bird is about to fall from the sky."

Michelle lowered her head closer to the screen, "Come on, where are you … there … there's the car!"

She pointed to a spot on the screen then looked out the window to find a blue canopied building located almost directly in the business park's center.

"I think the car is behind that building."

The driver pulled in front.

De Niro tapped the screen, "Let's see if we can find our man."

The mini-drone's slow decent became erratic. Then the screen went black.

"Damn." He tapped the driver's shoulder, "We're gonna get out. Stay put, okay?"

The driver nodded, "Sir, you should call the police."

"I already informed the police of our location," replied Michelle. "Just sit tight."

CHAPTER 32

GAJWA BUSINESS PARK
NAMGAJWA-DONG
SEOUL, SOUTH KOREA
12:30 PM (LOCAL), TUESDAY, JUNE 04, 2013

Michelle had to run to catch up, "Cris, what's the plan?"

De Niro rushed over to a kiosk with a map of the building's layout.

"There's a security desk right inside the front office. There may be security floating around the entire building. We'll just have to be careful."

Michelle turned him to face her, "Cris, what's our plan? We can't go inside. We're unarmed and we have no idea what we're walking into. For all we know, it's a building filled with bad guys."

Their eyes locked.

He took off walking. She caught up with him again.

"Where are we going now?"

"You said the car's in the back, right? Let's take a look." He picked up the pace. Michelle followed.

She tugged his sleeve, "And what do we do if he is still in the car and he's armed?"

De Niro pointed at the dark sedan parked in the middle of the crowded lot, "We duck."

They crouched and slowly approached. There was no one inside. De Niro shielded his eyes from the sun's glare and looked around.

Michelle blocked his view, "Cris, the police should get here soon. I think we should wait for them."

He started walking, continuing to look in all directions, "No you don't."

She caught up to him, "What do you mean no I don't?"

"You don't want to wait for them. In fact, you're probably raring to bust inside. It's me you're worried about." He stepped around her.

She caught up to him again, "That's part of my job, but it's not the only reason. I told you – we're unarmed and have no idea what we're walking into. Heck, we don't even know if he entered that building."

De Niro ignored her and pointed his phone at the ground then looked at the screen, "Yes, we do. Hold on a sec." He tapped more commands into his cell phone then spun around and started walking.

She chased after him, "What now?"

De Niro bent down and picked up the mini-drone, "This little bugger cost me a bundle. I wasn't about to leave it behind."

He folded the propellers and slipped Black Hornet One into his pocket, then took off in the direction of the dark sedan.

Michelle exhaled in frustration, "You were saying …?"

"Saying what?"

"You said we know he went into that building … how?"

De Niro pointed at the empty parking spot next to the sedan. There were words written in Korean painted on the floor. He held his phone up to her, "John told me this translation app he created was cool. One of the things it can do is …," he positioned the phone over the words, "you can just point the camera at anything written, and it'll translate it from over 500 languages.

"That says, 'Employee Parking Only' … and you knew that. Like I said, you're trying to protect me."

She stepped in front of him again, "Okay, I'm trying to protect you and I'm also trying not to get myself killed. You're not a field agent, Cris."

De Niro looked over her shoulder. A man was heading for a rear door of the building.

"I'm a pissed-off Italian from Brooklyn." He started after the men. This time she didn't follow.

He turned at a distance, "You coming?"

They saw the man swipe a plastic card through a reader next to the door, attached to the wall. A red light atop the reader turned green, followed by a loud buzz, and a click.

"Hold the door, please!" Michelle called out as the man opened the door.

Hurrying over, she beamed her prettiest smile, "Thank you so much." The man returned a smile and held the door open for her. He didn't notice De Niro, who nodded and followed her in.

De Niro waited for the man to disappear out of sight before furrowing his brow, "And what was that?"

She winked and started down the carpeted hall, "Field craft."

There were doors on both sides of the hall running its length. A few were opened or ajar, but most were closed. They watched the man walk to one of the doors, swipe his card again and disappear inside.

Michelle whispered to De Niro with sarcasm, "What now, start knocking?"

De Niro passed her and approached the door closest to them, "Not a bad idea."

He knocked. No one answered.

She shook her head, "Now what?"

He pointed to the door across from them. This time, she knocked. An old man opened the door.

He glanced at De Niro then scanned Michelle from head to toe and smiled. He spoke in English for De Niro's benefit, "And what can I do for you, young lady?"

She bowed her head slightly trying to see inside and held her hand up, "We are looking for a man, about this tall, wearing a dark jacket. He just arrived."

The old man waved and stepped back, "Please, come in."

They entered and looked around the small, sparse office, noticing only one wall covered in picture frames and mementos. Across from the wall was a neatly-kept desk with a laptop on it.

"Now, why are you looking for this man?"

"He dropped this toy," De Niro replied, taking Black Hornet One from his pocket. "Probably something for his son, but it looks expensive."

"We wanted to return it to him," added Michelle.

The man examined the mini-drone with ohis eyes, but returned a quizzical look.

De Niro wandered over to the covered wall, "May I?"

The old man nodded, with a smile.

He took a baseball bat down from a rack, "Signed by … is that Mickey Mantle's signature? Are You a Yankees fan?"

The old man's smile widened, "Since *The Mick* was the center fielder, though I only got to see him play center field once. In '67 the Yanks moved him to first base. Joe Pepitone took over in center." He looked between De Niro and Michelle and saw the curiosity on their faces.

"My parents migrated to the United States at the onset of the Korean War. I was 12-years-old."

"It must not have been easy to get a visa back then," said Michelle.

"It wasn't, but my father was a scientist, as am I, or at least I was. I'm 75 years old now and mostly retired."

"What kind of scientist?" asked De Niro.

"My PhD is in electronics, from M.I.T."

De Niro glanced at the mini-drone still in his hand.

"Yes, I could tell that is not a child's toy. May I see it, please?"

De Niro handed it to him.

The old man turned his desk lamp on. He took a moment to look at it, lifting his glasses several times.

De Niro cleared his throat.

The man handed it back to him, "I noticed you are in a rush or I would have asked to see it fly. It is a sophisticated little aircraft with a very high-resolution camera affixed. Are you two with the CIA?"

De Niro slipped the mini-drone back into his pocket and glanced at Michelle. She shrugged her shoulders.

"No, we're not. What's your name, by the way? I'm Cris."

The man extended his hand, "I am Philip Kim. Nice to meet you Cris …?"

"De Niro, Cris De Niro."

"I thought I recognized you." He turned to Michelle, "And who is this lovely, young lady?"

She offered her hand, "Michelle Wang, Professor Kim."

"Please, please, call me Phil. I haven't been called Professor Kim in a long time."

De Niro held the bat as if standing at home plate, "Phil, is this really the Mick's bat?"

The old man nodded with a wide smile.

"May I ask you something?"

"Go right ahead."

"Are you still a Yankees fan?"

"Sadly, I can no longer go to the games, but I sometimes catch them on cable or satellite TV. After returning to Seoul when I retired, I have never returned to America, but I will always be a Yankees fan."

De Niro winked, "We are too. You said you recognized me?"

"You were on many magazine covers and all over the media when your agency prevented that terrorist bomb."

"So then you know about my firm, The Watchman Agency. You know what we are?"

Kim nodded, "A counter-terrorism firm. Is that why you're here … I mean why you are paying me this visit? Something to do with the man you look for?"

De Niro nodded, "We suspect him to be a North Korean spy. He just seriously injured one of my best friends."

Kim waved them back into the hall. He pointed, "If I had to guess which office contained North Korean spies, it would be that office, at the end of the hall, on this side.

"The company that employs me provides this office for me to work from, but I'm afraid they are no longer interested in my research. Once upon a time, I made them a lot of money. I think they feel sorry for me now.

The old man sat down, "I have become, what's the word …

obsolete. So, I just sit here now, mostly reading and occasionally waiting for pretty young ladies to knock on my door.

"The one advantage of being old is that I am no longer noticed by most people, including the men that enter and leave that office at the end. They looked suspicious to me, so I humor myself by keeping an eye on them."

"That's a dangerous thing to do, Phil," said De Niro.

The old man grinned, "At my age, going to the bathroom is a dangerous thing to do. Besides, I don't try to be James Bond. I just pass their door and eavesdrop when I can." He chuckled, "The last time a man inside saw me and slammed the door."

"Did you hear anything?"

He shook his head, "No, my hearing has really gotten bad, but I did see inside for a moment. It is a room filled with sophisticated hardware, including what I thought to be a satellite communication base station of some sort. If I could have gone inside for just a few seconds, I could have told you their whole setup.

"One more thing, I think I heard footsteps in the corridor a few minutes before you knocked on my door. Most of the people on this floor go to lunch at noon and do not return for an hour. I never go to lunch. The restaurants near here are terrible and overpriced. In any case, that is why I noticed the footsteps. At the time, I thought it was just someone returning from lunch early. I wish I would have checked."

"You did fine. It was probably him. Just two more questions and we have to go. Is there any way to get past the door locks?"

"There is and I still have the ability to do it, if we had the equipment. I'm afraid I don't though."

De Niro nodded. He held the bat up again, "Second question … May I borrow this bat? I promise to bring it back."

"In one piece …?"

"In one piece … more or less."

The old man frowned, "This better be worth it."

They turned to see Michelle. She was staring at the desk with her finger tip in her mouth, "Could we also borrow your laptop. I have an idea on how we can get him to open the door, if he's in there."

The old man unplugged the machine then handed it to her, "For a lovely, young lady like you, of course. Besides, nowadays, I mostly only use it to play Solitaire."

De Niro winked and headed for the door.

"Mr. De Niro …."

De Niro turned.

"Take care of that lovely lady … and wipe the blood off the bat before you return it."

* * * * *

With John Francis's laptop tucked under his arm, Bok had used his key card to open the door to the suite. The door had a sign on it that read *Kim Electronics*.

Two years before, the North Korean spy signed a lease under the generic name. He quickly established the business in the local area as an inexpensive computer and electronics repair shop.

From time to time when he had to travel, Bok employed repair techs, never more than two or three, to keep the small business running. He carefully managed the company to produce just enough income to meet the payroll, keep the rent paid, and the lights on.

Bok walked over to a work bench and swept the parts of another computer away before setting Francis's laptop down and booting it. The machine booted to the Big-Brutha™ logo, with a box to enter the password. He entered it and instantly, the menu appeared.

Bok attempted to exit the menu screen to bring up a command prompt but the system wasn't complying. He took a deep breath before taking out his cell and tapping a speed dial button.

"Taejang, it is Bok. I have the American's laptop. It was necessary to take it. The American returned to the room unexpectedly. No sir, I incapacitated him but I did not kill him. I needed to interrogate him to get his password. There was no time, but there is no need for concern. He never saw my face. I am positive that he cannot identify me, Taejang, but another situation arose.

"Yes, sir, another situation …," he cleared his throat, "a remote-controlled, miniature helicopter was somehow activated and it …

began to pursue me. I have no idea, sir, who was controlling it, but I strongly suspect it was the other Americans."

Taejang Kang's voice bellowed from the small speaker.

"No sir, I have no idea how they could have known I was there. In any case, I was able to escape with the American's laptop and password. There are other security measures to overcome, but I should be able to transmit intelligence from it to you soon. Yes, sir, I will not fail."

Bok slipped his phone away and took another deep breath. He plugged one end of a cable into Francis's laptop and the other end into a desktop unit next to the work bench. He typed some commands on the desktop's keyboard and watched as a program opened on the desktop's large monitor.

Command status began appearing:

Connection ...... established.

Analyzing hardware ...... complete.

Analyzing hard drive ...... complete.

Copy remote drive ready ...... Transmit when complete?

Bok typed, "y."

Copying remote drive ......

He sat back and wiped his eyes.

After about 30 seconds, the readout changed to:

Copying remote drive ...... 5% complete.

Bok looked at his watch then glanced out the window. He scanned the parking lot before taking an ice-cold bottle of beer from the refrigerator. He pressed it against the back of his neck before opening it then downed half its contents in one gulp.

Bok resumed his seat at the work bench and closed his eyes.

* * * * *

Bok was riled from his nap by a knock at the door. He blinked his focus back and looked at the monitor, just in time to see the readout update:

Copying remote drive ...... 95% complete.

Bok took the gun from his belt and pulled the slide back.

There was another knock.

He approached the door and checked the small black-n-white monitor built into the intercom system. It provided a view of the area immediately outside the door. He saw a woman standing there with a laptop in her hand.

He waited to see if she would walk away, but she knocked again. He pressed the intercom button, "We are closed."

"Please, I need help. I am Chinese. My Korean is not that good. I am applying for a job down the hall." She flipped the laptop over and pointed, "There. I think it is the battery. They said you repair computers. Please, can you help me?"

He pressed the intercom button again, "I said we are closed. Go away."

Bok slid the pistol back into his belt and turned to walk away.

She knocked again … and again.

He slapped the intercom button, "I said to go away, before I call the police."

He watched as the pretty lady pouted. She lingered a moment before walking away. He made it almost all the way back to the work bench when he heard more knocking. It was louder this time.

He pulled his gun and rushed to the door, "I'll teach this bitch."

He swung the door open and pointed the pistol, "I said to—"

No one was there.

Bok leaned his head out to see around the door.

He never saw what hit him.

As soon as he saw the pistol emerge, De Niro swung the bat down in a diagonally direction. He intended to knock the gun from the man's hand. Instead, he bashed Bok almost directly over the head.

The North Korean spy dropped to the floor. The pistol bounced from his hand.

"Hell Cris, I think you killed him," Michelle knelt and checked for a pulse.

"He's alive."

De Niro leaned the bat against the wall, "Help me drag him inside."

Stepping over him, De Niro noticed Bok moved. He was reaching his hand out for the gun.

De Niro stomped his hand with the heel of his shoe. Bok cried out in agony.

"His head must be made out of iron, but his hand isn't. Now help me drag this bastard inside."

They sat him in the chair in front of the work bench. Bok's head was bleeding and his eyes were groggy. He cradled his hand and didn't look up.

De Niro tilted Bok's chin up using the end of the bat, "Do you speak English?"

Bok didn't reply.

De Niro drew the bat back, "The first time, I was aiming for the gun and hit your head. I guess I'm not much of a baseball player. This time I'll aim for your knee. Who knows what I'll hit."

Bok jerked his leg away, "Yes, I speak English."

"De Niro returned the end of the bat under Bok's chin, "I thought so. You know, the guy you tortured in our hotel room is one of my oldest and dearest friends. He's like a brother to me."

His senses slowly returning, Bok stared back with a combination of anger and pain. The blood from his head mixed with sweat and drizzled down his cheek.

"You messed him up badly. They said he's critical. A guy that couldn't defend himself if you gave him a loaded gun … and you tortured him, perhaps to death. I don't know if that means anything to you, but where we're from … family is everything."

Michelle looked up. She was gazing over the equipment, "Cris, that's John's laptop. There's a wire running from it to that desktop."

De Niro yanked the cable out of both computers.

They noticed the desktop's monitor at the same time. Bok turned too. The screen read:

Transfer complete.

Transmission complete.

Bok forced a smile through his wincing, "You are too late."

Michelle typed awhile on the desktop's keyboard. She looked over to De Niro, "As far as I can tell he copied John's hard drive and uploaded it."

"Uploaded it to whom?"

"That, I can't tell. The recipient only appears as a number sequence. Why don't you ask him?"

De Niro turned back to Bok. The scar-faced man returned an amused smirk, "You hit my head … really hard with a baseball bat. I cannot even remember my name."

De Niro lifted the bat to his shoulder.

Bok's smirk widened, "You're really not very experienced at this, are you?"

De Niro flashed a curious grin, "What makes you say so?"

Bok pointed, "Your choice of weapon, for one. A baseball bat is a very inefficient tool for interrogating someone. Sure, it is intimidating, but it is also clumsy and inaccurate. It is noisy to use and as you admitted, it takes some expertise to wield … expertise you do not possess."

De Niro spun the bat, "Oh, I don't know about that. For instance, I grew up in Brooklyn, New York. You heard of it? Brooklyn is a tough place … lots of gangster-types. Baseball bats were used by enforcers. If you borrowed money from loan sharks and didn't pay on time, you'd get a broken kneecap from a Louisville Slugger like this one. I bet the mafia bought as many bats as the little league did."

De Niro looked down at Bok's knee.

Bok sneered, "I won't tell you what you want to know, no matter what you do to me with that bat."

De Niro put his face close to Bok's, "That, I believe."

He turned to Michelle, "Take John's laptop and wait for me in the car."

"Cris, what are you—"

De Niro cut her off, "Michelle … go."

Bok watched with curiosity as De Niro waited for Michelle to leave the room before walking over to the door and flicking the light switches. He found the one that controlled the fluorescent fixtures built into the ceiling. He grabbed a roll of electric tape and taped the switch in the 'off' position.

Then he tried the other. It controlled the power that ran to an outlet behind the work desk at which Bok was sitting. A tall lamp stand was all that was plugged into it. De Niro turned the light off.

Bok wiped sweat from under his lip as he watched De Niro close all the blinds.

"What are you doing?"

De Niro didn't reply as he searched the work desk. He held up wire cutters, "This is what I was looking for."

He grabbed a couple rolls of black electric tape and walked back over to Bok, "If you try to move, I'll show you my homerun swing."

He taped Bok's arms and legs to the chair then used more tape to secure the chair's base to the heavy work desk.

There was tension in Bok's tone, "You will have to kill me. Tell me Mr. De Niro, have you ever killed someone before?"

De Niro ignored him while he located an extension cord. He plugged one end into the same outlet as the lamp and cut the other end off with the cutters. Then he pulled the cord apart and used his teeth to strip the insulation from the wires.

Bok blinked anxiously. Sweat appeared on his forehead.

De Niro found scissors and used them to cut Bok's shirt from him. He placed the ends of the cord under each of Bok's armpits and wrapped electric tape to keep them there.

"Am I doing this right? You're quite a sweater, aren't you … what's your name?"

Bok didn't reply. For the first time De Niro saw fear in the man's eyes.

De Niro cut a strip from Bok's shirt and used it to gag him. When he was done he stood before him.

"You asked if I ever killed anyone, as if you knew the answer.

"I have read your file, Mr. De Niro."

"My file, huh … North Korea has a file on me … interesting."

De Niro crouched and spoke softly into Bok's ear, "People kill for a lot of reasons, some for their god … some for their country … some for money.

"Like I said, for me it's all about family. After my wife and son were murdered on 9/11, my family actually grew. Instead of getting smaller by two, it's grown to include everyone that hates evil. Most people think I only want to protect Americans, but here I am trying to protect Koreans, both North and South.

"John, the man you tortured has always been like a brother to me. That's his name. Did you know his name when you beat him and electrocuted him? John came here to protect your countrymen too … and what did you do?"

Tears filled De Niro's eyes. He began pacing, "You tortured him. Like every bully, you picked on the little defenseless guy, and for what? What you did had nothing to do with interrogating. It was torture and I think you enjoyed it."

He swung the bat and began smashing the high-tech equipment. "His laptop …?"

He smashed some more, "His password?"

He swung the bat again and again, smashing everything in the room. Then he made a call while Bok looked on.

After speaking to someone, he put his phone away, picked up the desktop computer and walked to the door. He looked back at Bok, "Don't worry. I called the North Korean embassy. I gave them this address and told them one of their spies is all tied up here. I figure they should be here in about … 10, 15 minutes, with traffic."

De Niro stepped into the hall, "I'll leave the door cracked open a bit, so they'll have no problem getting in.

Bok began screaming into his gag.

"I bet a tough guy like you isn't afraid of the dark. Let's see how you are with the light."

* * * * *

With their guns drawn, building security led the way and pointed to the door. Two North Korean embassy officials charged past them. One pushed the door open.

Now covered in sweat from struggling, Bok screamed with every ounce of his energy. His words were incomprehensible from the gag.

All the men rushed into the room. One of the men found the light switch.

* * * * *

De Niro, Michelle, and the driver sat with their eyes on the suite. Moments before, they watched as a dark sedan pulled up in front of the building. Two men got out and headed in.

"You're not going to tell me what you did, are you?" asked Michelle.

Light suddenly radiated from the suite, flickering like a strobe before darkness returned.

Michelle glanced at De Niro with a confused look.

De Niro tapped the driver's shoulder, "Take us back to the hotel."

CHAPTER 33

HEADQUARTERS OF TAEJANG KANG KUM-SOK
PUNGGYE-RI NUCLEAR TEST SITE
KILJU COUNTY, NORTH HAMGYONG PROVINCE
NORTH KOREA
12:30 PM (LOCAL), TUESDAY, JUNE 04, 2013

Colonel Cho, Sojang Kim, and Song's grandfather disembarked the chartered train in a small village, a mile and a half south of Taejang Kang's headquarters. Usually, explained the old man, he would be met by one of the Taejang's low-ranking officers and driven the rest of the way by staff car. He suggested they walk the rest of the way this time and stopping at a local fish monger to purchase several pounds of loach.

They arrived at the main gate to Kang's headquarters at 11:30 AM, but based on the old man's suggestions, they waited until 12:30 PM to request entry. According to Chef Song, that's when most of the headquarters staff and many of the guards went to lunch at the base's mess hall.

Cho checked his watch, "12:30, on the dot."

Three guards walked out of the guard shack and headed in the direction of the main building.

Cho tapped Sojang Kim's shoulder, "The old man was right, only one guard to get past."

"It only takes one guard to sound the alarm and shoot us," replied Kim lowering his head.

"Silence, remember I alone speak." The old man took the bundle of fish from Cho, "The priest's God must be with us. I know this guard. His mind is controlled by his stomach."

Old man Song approached the guard shack holding the bundle in front of him. The guard stepped out with his eyes locked on it.

"A challenge for you Hasa, use your nose to guess what is inside this bundle and you will get a serving of it upon my departure."

The Hasa, equivalent to sergeant of the guard duty, raised his hand palm out, "Hold it …." He picked up a clip board and used his index finger to scan it.

"Your name does not appear on the visitor's list for today."

"That is because I am not here."

"Say again?"

Chef Song stepped close and whispered, "Taejang Kang is entertaining some very important dignitaries from Pyongyang this evening." He lifted the bundle, "He sent for me to prepare this for him and his guests."

The Hasa shot a skeptical glance.

"The challenge still stands, though I gave you too many hints. Go on, use your nose and take a guess."

For a tense moment, the Hasa didn't move before finally lowering his rifle. He put his nose above the bundle and took a deep breath.

"It is fish … if it is for the Taejang you must be preparing chueotang … so that must be loach."

The old man dropped the bundle on a table, "Go ahead and see for yourself."

The Hasa slung his rifle then used his knife to cut the twine.

"I am correct!"

Song's grandfather patted him on the back, "You are correct, my friend, and I am a man of my word. Will you be on duty here tonight, around 8 PM, when I depart?"

"My duty shift ends at 5 PM, but you may leave it with the guards on duty. I will leave word for one of them to bring it to my home."

The old man rewrapped the fish then patted the Hasa's back again. He motioned to Cho and Sojang to follow him, "I will do that."

The three passed through the gate and walked about 10 feet, when they heard the Hasa's voice ring out.

"Wait!"

"I knew this wouldn't work," Sojang Kim cried under his breath."

"Quiet!" Song's grandfather shouted his whisper, before turning.

The Hasa jogged up to him, "Make sure you place the chueotang in a plastic container. And use something to wrap the container before you give it to the guards. If they discover what is in it … they will likely only deliver half."

A tired smile crept slowly onto the old man's face, "I will remember."

He turned and resumed the lead speaking loud enough for the Hasa to hear him, "Come, we have much to prepare."

* * * * *

After knocking and being ordered in, an officer entered Taejang Kang's office and marched up to his desk holding a typed-written paper. The Taejang didn't look up, "What is it, Taewi?"

The North Korean equivalent of a captain extended his arm straight out, "I have just downloaded and decrypted the data sent by Agent Bok, Taejang."

Kang looked up and took the single sheet with a curious look, "This could not have been the entire contents of the American's laptop."

"It is not, Taejang. Per your orders, I have isolated and transposed all information that referenced either Sojang Kim or Colonel Cho. That led to a folder named *November-Kilo 051013* that contained a number of files uploaded by various individuals. I took the liberty of extrapolating the intelligence on the Sojang and the Colonel for you."

Kang dropped his eyes and began reading. After a moment he slowly looked up, "Who else is aware of the contents of this message, Taewi?"

"Per your orders sir, no one, I downloaded and decrypted it myself."

He looked down again, "Well done, Taewi." Kang rose from his seat and walked over to a wall full of photos, many of him with Sojang Kim. He didn't turn when he spoke again, "I want you to inform the captain of the guard. Let him know that there is a high probability that … Sojang Kim, along with two others, the Daeryeong and … my cook, Song … have or are in the process of infiltrating this facility. Have him quietly place the base on lockdown without audible alarms, and double the guard around the missiles."

"Yes, sir!" The Taewi turned for the door.

"And Taewi …,"

The small officer stopped on a dime, "Yes Taejang?"

"I want Sojang Kim and Daeryeong Cho taken alive. Come to think of it, bring the cook to me too … alive. He will prepare a last meal for me."

"Understood!"

Kang took one of the photos from the wall and threw it to the floor, "That will be all, Taewi."

"Yes, sir."

* * * * *

Old man Song led Cho and Sojang Kim across a large courtyard, to the entrance of the headquarters building. Once again, they had to pass through a checkpoint to enter, but this time all Song had to do was show his access pass. The guard merely nodded.

The building was large and to Cho, looked more like an office space than a military installation. The center was filled with cubicles, surrounded by large individual offices around the perimeter. Cho stopped to look around. He noticed only a dozen staff scattered about.

The old man waved him over, "Come and don't stop walking. There are cameras everywhere. I am not sure if they can hear us, but it would be better to keep your voices low."

They caught up to Sojang Kim. Kim spoke, keeping his face

pointed down, "Kang's office is underground. The only access is from an elevator located up ahead."

"But we must go to the kitchen first," said Song. "It is located in the mess hall in a small building behind this one. Please say no more until we get there."

Chef Song led them past the guard-protected elevator and out the back door directly into the mess. It was a spacious, but otherwise bland dining room, laid out like a cafeteria at one end with long narrow tables. There were smaller tables and booths at the other for officers of field grade rank or higher. About a dozen people were sitting around a few of the longer tables. On the other side, only one officer was sitting in a booth.

Song led them past the smaller tables and booths and into the equally spacious and spotless kitchen. The officer didn't even look up when they passed. Inside the kitchen, a dozen kitchen staff were busy at work. A few nodded to the Song as he walked by.

The old man dropped the bundle on one of the stainless steel counters and grabbed a chef's knife to cut the twine.

He raised his voice so others could hear and pointed with the knife, "You two should stay near, but remain out of my way. Once I am done, you can take the Chueotang to the Taejang in his main dining room. You must change into the waiter jackets though. They hang on a hook against that wall."

Cho and Kim walked over and, after checking the sizes, donned the white waiter jackets.

One of the kitchen staff approached, "I could use you two. An entire platoon of infantry is on maneuvers nearby and will be dining here this evening."

Cho glanced at Kim, who looked up before turning his back to the man, but Kim knew Cho wanted him to reply, "I am sorry. We are only here to deliver Taejang Kang's food."

The man stretched to see Kim's face, "I was not aware the Taejang requested any food?"

Kim pointed at Song, "That is because he called the old man to prepare it for him."

"Ah … you mean Chef Mudfish," the man chuckled. "Say, you're voice sounds familiar. Have we met?"

Kim knelt down and pretended to tie his shoe, "No, we have not."

The man stepped around and leaned down, "Are you sure? There is something very familiar—"

Old man Song's voice rang out from behind them, "You … leave those men alone and get back to work or I will report you."

"Chef Mudfish …," The man sneered as he walked away.

Sojang Kim nodded to the old man. He returned a smile. Kim turned to Cho, "Listen to me, Daeryeong. We have to split up. As you witnessed, it is too dangerous for me to wait around.

"We have two objectives, but only I am necessary to neutralize the missile threat. I need to make my way to the missiles' command and control room now, while you wait for the Taejang's food. You can use the tray and your jacket to gain entrance into his office. Then you can do what needs to be done with him. Once we complete our missions, we can rendezvous back at the tunnel entrance."

Cho grabbed Kim's arm. He kept his voice soft, "Hold on Sojang. You are not going anywhere without me. Perhaps you have forgotten. I do not trust you."

"I have not forgotten, nor do I trust you, Daeryeong, but circumstances dictate we overcome our mutual mistrust. The longer we remain inside this compound, the more likely it is we are captured."

Kim tried to tug his arm free.

"Daeryeong, you trusted me until now."

"Perhaps, you are having a change of heart."

"I assure you, I have not. I want to alleviate the threat and stop Kang as much as you do. Or perhaps it is you who are having a change of heart?"

Their eyes remained glued until Cho released his grip.

Kim straightened his jacket, "The missile's command and control room is located in a building behind this one, closer to where the missiles are stationed. It's a remote area of the compound. There should only be one guard."

"Will you be able to get past him on your own?"

"I believe I can, Daeryeong," Kim replied with a hint of

annoyance. "There is a staircase nearby that leads down to the tunnel entrance. I will be waiting for you at the entrance."

Cho nodded.

"One more thing," said Kim, "our phones will not work inside this compound. Whoever arrives at the tunnel first should not wait very long there. We can still rendezvous on the other side."

Cho nodded again.

Kim extended his hand, "Good luck, Cho."

"I think I will put my faith in the priest's God instead."

Old man Song approached with a large ceramic tureen, "Cho, bring that cart here, if you please."

Cho wheeled over a stainless steel push cart.

"Now spread that linen table cloth over it."

Cho did as he was told.

The old man placed the tureen down gently in the center of the table top. He added bowls, napkins, soup spoons, and a bottle of Pouilly-Fumé, along with wine glasses.

"This is how the Taejang likes to be served. Now, when we approach him, it would be best for you to walk behind me as I push the cart, but—"

"I will be the one pushing the cart to approach him, old man."

"But he will be expecting me."

"By the time he notices it isn't you, it will be too late for him."

"But … how will you get past the guards at the elevator. Even with me, they will check with the Taejang. At least I can plead mindlessness of age as reason for my unexpected appearance. He enjoys my chueotang so much, I do not believe he will turn it away."

"That is what we are counting on. As for the guards at the elevator, I would ask you to push the cart to that point and speak to them.

"You will tell them you have prepared the Taejang's favorite and he is waiting for it. Let them check with him. If the Taejang approves, you will tell them you forgot the rest of the soup was left cooking in the kitchen. You will then order me to bring the cart down to the Taejang."

The old man's disappointment was apparent, "I wanted to be there when that bastard gets what he deserves."

"After the bastard gets what he deserves, we will have to make a quick getaway."

"In other words, I would slow you down."

Cho put a hand on the old man's shoulder, "In other words I need you to get to the tunnel entrance, and if possible, get to the radiation suits. Sojang Kim should be there by then, but then again, he may not. Slip into a suit if you can … anything to speed things up.

"There is no telling what will happen once the Taejang meets his fate and the Sojang sabotages the missiles. We cannot count on being able to linger here."

"What if the Taejang does not approve?"

"Then you will still proceed to the tunnel entrance and do as I said."

"And you?"

"I will have to find another way to get down to the Taejang."

The old man shook his head. He started pushing the cart, "We should go."

* * * * *

Sojang Kim exited the mess hall carrying a tray of pastries, a pot of coffee, and two mugs, and proceeded outside past a row of barracks. He was tempted to check if the barracks were occupied but reasoned it would not matter very much either way, with what would soon transpire.

He walked down a small set of cement steps to a narrow bunker. To the right was an earthen wall, and to the left, a long narrow building not occupied since the nuclear detonation tests back in April.

At the end of the bunker he saw a guard sitting in front of a door built into the earthen wall. Kim knew the door was made of lead-lined iron and had no lock.

The guard raised a lazy eye.

"With the Taejang's compliments," Kim bellowed with enthusiasm. "Apparently the Taejang is having a good day."

The guard rose from the chair and surveyed the tray, "They look good. I like the chocolate donuts."

Kim nodded towards the iron door, "Let us go inside so I can set the tray down."

The guard shook his head, "We are not allowed in there."

Kim looked around and chuckled, "And who is going to see us? You are the only guard on duty in this whole area."

The guard hesitated.

"Come on friend, I have to get back soon."

The guard looked in both directions before pulling the heavy door open. He let Kim enter first.

Kim waited as the guard drew the door closed and turned around. He tossed the pot of coffee in his face.

The guard roared in agony as Kim slammed his head into the door, crumbling him to the ground. Kim pulled the pistol from the guard's holster and shot him twice in the head.

No one could have heard the shots through that door.

Kim tucked the pistol into his belt and took a seat at the controls. He booted the missile launch sequence and examined it one line at a time, stopping at the 'unlock' command.

He highlighted the entire line of code and deleted it before closing the program down.

Kim thought about dragging the body back out and sitting it in the chair, but decided it would smear too much blood on him. Instead, he closed the door with the body inside and headed for the stairs.

CHAPTER 34

COORDINATES: 41°18'19"N 128°55'19"E
ABOARD TRAIN NKSR H-HYEKIL9-4
PAEKTUSAN CH'ŎNGNYŎN LINE
10 KILOMETERS SOUTH OF SANDONE STATION
NORTH KOREA
1:30 PM (LOCAL), TUESDAY, JUNE 04, 2013

Scipio turned his phone screen towards Mugsy, "We're 10 clicks out of Sandone Station … time for me to say hello to the conductor."

He slid the boxcar's door open.

"Scipio …," Mugsy called to him. "I don't know how to pilot one of these things, so unless you do, make sure nothing happens to him."

"It's on a track, Captain, how hard could it be?"

Mugsy watched as Scipio climbed the ladder attached to the side then slid the door closed.

On the boxcar's roof, Scipio felt the 50 mph wind push him as he steadied himself and looked forward.

Three cars from the engine …

He hopped from one boxcar to the next with relative ease until he reached the rounded roof of the engine.

This could be tricky.

He looked left and right and saw nothing but the patchwork markings of brown and grey tundra.

Miles of nothing.

The clanking of the wheels changed pitch. He looked up ahead and saw a sharp turn drawing near.

"Shit!"

Scipio jumped just as the engine bore around the turn, but the suddenness made him overshoot the landing. Centrifugal force and momentum propelled him off the engine's side and directly over a rear ladder. He grabbed hold of it and hung on until he felt the engine heading straight again.

Scipio peered up. He mouthed the word, "thanks," before returning to the engine's roof and looking down the line.

That's gotta be a stretch of straight track ahead. Better to make my move now, so I don't go through that again.

He stepped carefully towards the front of the engine and climbed down the forward side ladder. The door to the cab was just ahead of it. The small man dressed in black leaned sideways and looked in. He saw the conductor seated directly inside the door, alone.

Scipio pulled one of his ceramic blades and tried the door. It was locked.

Damn ... nothing's easy.

Taking a moment to think, he leaned sideways again. This time he used the knife to tap on the door's window. A moment passed before a clicking sound rang out.

He saw the door open.

With all the grace of a circus clown, Scipio reached over and pulled himself inside the cab.

Ending up lying across the startled conductor's lap, he lifted the blade to the man's throat and spoke in Korean, "Do as I say and you live."

The conductor put his hands up.

Scipio struggled to get off him while keeping his blade's point pressing against the terrified man's neck. He righted himself and took a seat in the chair next to the conductor.

Scipio saw now the conductor was a small, frail man that looked to be in his 60's.

"Put your hands down."

The conductor complied.

"Do you speak English?"

He shook his head.

"Okay, then I will tell you what to do, and you tell me if you do not understand. Understood?"

The conductor nodded.

"We will be stopping at the Sandone Station."

The conductor shook his head, "I am not scheduled to stop there."

"You will call ahead now and have the switch thrown, so that we can stop at the station off the main line."

"But, they will ask why?"

"Repairs."

Confusion replaced some of the fear on the conductor's face, "Repairs … of what? Nothing is in need of repair."

"Your fuel line is clogged. You will have to check the lines and might need to replace the fuel filter."

The conductor shook his head more vigorously, "They will be suspicious if we stop there under full power, saying our fuel line is clogged."

"Tell them that the problem is …," Scipio paused and switched to English, "intermittent. How the hell do you say intermittent in Korean?"

The conductor stared with uncertainty, waiting for a reply.

"Stop and go, stop and go, stop and go."

The conductor's eyebrows came together in bewilderment.

Scipio pointed to the controls, "The throttle, which one?"

The conductor pointed to a metal shift lever.

Scipio reached for it. The conductor tried to prevent him until he felt the blade at his throat again.

Scipio took hold of the throttle and pulled it back to idle. The engine lurched. Scipio lost his balance. He pulled the knife away just before slitting the old man's throat.

Let me show him another way.

He took the conductor's hand and placed it on the throttle then made back and forth motions with his own.

Still confused the conductor pushed the throttle forward.

"Now back," Scipio demonstrated with his hand.

The conductor mimicked him.

Scipio rotated his hands, "Again and again, until we reach Sandone Station."

The old man nodded.

"I want our speed to go up and down for others to see."

Another nod.

Scipio handed him the mic, "Call and tell them to throw the switch."

The conductor did as he was told. To the frail man's relief, Scipio put the knife away as soon as he heard the station's confirmation.

The train undulated for a few jarring minutes before Scipio felt a slight change in direction, as they came to a stop off the main line.

"Shut the engine."

The conductor complied.

Scipio pointed to the door.

"Out."

He followed the conductor out of the cab and walked to the front of the engine to scan the area. Only a smattering of soldiers was standing guard, with a few others patrolling the vicinity. None seemed to be paying any attention to the train.

"Where is the office?"

The conductor pointed to a large building in the station's center, across the tracks about 100 feet away. Scipio saw a man exit and head for them. He walked the conductor to the side of the engine and pointed to the cowl, "Open it."

The old man struggled with the large hood. Scipio pulled a blade and put it to the conductor's throat, "Tell him you called for help already. Say nothing more … and remember I understand Korean."

Scipio climbed back into the cab and lowered the window.

The Station Manager, a larger and slightly younger man than the conductor, walked over, "What is the matter?"

The conductor reached into the engine compartment with a dirty oil rag and jiggled the fuel lines.

"There is a clog somewhere, maybe in the filter or one of the lines."

The Station Manager picked up a rag and reached in, "They feel secure."

The conductor looked past the manager at the open window in the door of the cab. He raised his voice, "What do you know. You sit behind a desk. I am telling you there is a clog in the fuel line. Did you not notice our fluctuation in speed?"

The manager waved with annoyance, "Take it easy. As a matter of fact I did notice." He wiped his hand and started away, "I will call for—"

"I have already radioed for assistance."

The manager looked back quizzically, "Very well. Would you like to wait in the office? We have tea and some food."

"No!" The conductor replied with too much enthusiasm. He quickly recovered, "Thank you, but no. I prefer to remain here. There are a few other things I can fix while I wait."

The manager let his look of suspicion fade into a shrug, "Suit yourself."

Scipio waited for the man to disappear into the building before stepping out of the cab. The conductor wasn't there. He spotted him yards away jumping into a shallow, dry gully.

Scipio walked over and looked down with his arms crossed.

The terrified man held his hand up, "Please, I am just frightened. I will come up."

Scipio lifted him up and patted dirt off of him, before making eye contact, "I will not harm you if you do exactly as I say. Do you understand?"

The conductor bowed his head, "I understand."

"Return to the cab and do not try to leave." He flashed the ceramic blade, "I can throw this. You would not make it 10 meters.

Do you understand?"

The conductor nodded and headed for the cab. Scipio waited for the old man to enter before jogging back to the boxcars. He knocked on one of the doors.

Mugsy slid it open and jumped down, "Any problems?"

"My Korean needs improvement."

"What's our status?"

"The conductor has been compliant for the most part. He's just a scared old man."

Mugsy exhaled, "Seems like this whole mission relies on old men."

Scipio nodded, "The Station Manager already visited. I had the conductor tell him there's a clog in the fuel line. He's already called for help. Barring the manager checks on that, we should have bought several hours … maybe a day."

"And if we have to sit here longer?"

"Then I could lock the manager in a closet. Obviously, the longer we sit here, the more eyes we attract."

Mugsy nodded, "Do we need to turn the locomotive?"

"No, but at some point, I'm going to have the conductor move it to the other side of the boxcars. Proceeding in the direction that took us here, the track leads directly north. It ends at a large power facility that I'm sure has a battalion stationed there. Our only chance of escaping this God-forsaken country is to go back the way we came."

"What about here … have you seen any soldiers?"

"Only a small number in the immediate vicinity, so far. Based on satellite imagery, I'd say the buildings on the far side of the station's office are barracks. They look big enough to house a company of infantry. I'm not sure why we haven't attracted the attention of the patrolling guards."

"They're probably used to seeing trains come and go. This station is so remote I imagine only the young or undesirables are assigned here … certainly not the cream of the North Korean army crop. Advantage us."

Scipio studied the map on his phone, "Well, I'd like to add to that advantage if possible. I'm gonna take a little walk. A few buildings look like they could be weapons lockers."

Mugsy brought the map up on his phone, "I'll help."

"Count us in," added Father Kim as he and Song jumped down.

"Negative," replied Mugsy, "too dangerous."

"With respect Captain, what is more dangerous … two Korean civilians that look like common laborers or two Americans?"

"With respect Father, Scipio and I aren't just two Americans."

"We certainly aren't," added Scipio, "we're two extremely foolish Americans."

Mugsy shook his head, "Okay … why not. Operation Keystone Kops is officially underway. Song, tell the rest of your men to sit tight. Father, you and Song check the buildings on the other side of the tracks while Scipio and I check this side. Remember to keep your heads down and don't take unnecessary chances. If you spot weapons or even suspect a building of containing them, return here. Scipio and I will figure a way to get to them. Is that clear?"

"Crystal, Captain," replied Father Kim. "Did I say that correctly?"

Scipio chuckled.

CHAPTER 35

HEADQUARTERS OF TAEJANG KANG KUM-SOK
PUNGGYE-RI NUCLEAR TEST SITE
KILJU COUNTY, NORTH HAMGYONG PROVINCE
NORTH KOREA
1:30 PM (LOCAL), TUESDAY, JUNE 04, 2013

Colonel Cho followed Chef Song as he pushed the metal cart up to the elevator. A guard walked around the security desk and began his inspection. He lifted the cover of the tureen and hovered over it.

Chef Song pushed his head away and returned the cover in a huff, "You know who I am, you know what it is, and you know for whom it is for, so why do you play this game?"

The guard ignored him and lifted the wine bottle. He rotated it to examine the label and wrapping, "Because it is my job, old man. Now, why are you here?" He looked past Song, "And who is he?"

"He is my new sous-chef. It should be obvious why we are here. You have seen me serve chueotang to the Taejang countless times."

The guard set the bottle down and returned behind the security desk. He lifted a clipboard and examined it for a full minute then replied, "You are not scheduled to serve chueotang to the Taejang today."

"There must be some mistake. The Taejang contacted me personally and arranged my transportation here. Perhaps he did not make you aware."

The guard placed the clipboard down with impatience, "The Taejang makes his adjutant aware of every potential visitor. His adjutant makes the captain of the guard aware and the captain of the guard makes me aware. So, I repeat, you are not scheduled to serve chueotang to the Taejang today."

Old man Song pushed the cart closer to the elevator. The guard stepped in his path with an outstretched hand.

Song crossed his arms, "Young man, unless you want to encounter the wrath of Taejang Kang, you will step aside and allow me to bring him his favorite dish."

"Remain there. I will contact the Taejang's adjutant."

The guard returned to the desk and picked up the phone. He spoke a moment then placed the phone down, "The Taewi is not in his office. Apparently, he has gone to speak to the captain of the guard."

Song glanced at Cho. The Daeryeong kept his head down.

"Young man, how is it that you did not see the Taejang's adjutant pass you? Is not the office of the captain of the guard down this hall?"

The guard paused before replying, "I just came on duty. We have implemented rotating shifts. The Taewi must have passed before I arrived. Hold on, I will find him."

Cho leaned in and whispered into Chef Song's ear, "I don't like this. Time for you to check on the pot you left over the fire."

Song nodded and spoke up, "Never mind … uh … my sous-chef just reminded me that I left the rest of the chueotang simmering. I must check on it."

"Hold on," the guard spoke into his radio, "Taewi, the old man that makes chueotang for Taejang Kang is here at the elevator. He says that the Taejang—"

The guard stopped midsentence and raised his eyes. He looked from Chef Song to Cho.

Cho whispered to Song again, "Go directly to the tunnel. Try to reach the Americans. Tell them what happened."

Old man Song froze. Cho pushed him, "Go!"

The guard reached for his pistol, but the holster strap was buttoned. By the time he drew, Colonel Cho was standing in front of him behind the desk.

His hand trembling, the guard pressed the pistol to Cho's head, "Do not move."

Cho folded his hands.

The guard glanced back at his radio with caution.

Cho looked too, "It is pretty far away. No way for you to call for help. What will you do?"

The guard's expression changed from fear to anger, "I am the one with the gun to your head. We will wait until someone comes."

Cho glanced at his watch, "That will not do."

He lifted his eyes and simultaneously smacked the guard's wrist with his right hand while snatching the pistol with his left. The Daeryeong performed the maneuver with such speed the guard felt the gun pressing against his own head before realizing what happened.

Neither had time to utter a word as guards began appearing from the hall leading to the captain of the guard's office and the corridor to the kitchen.

The guards drew their weapons and surrounded Cho. He looked beyond them and could make out Chef Song's form stepping from a doorway.

I have to buy the old man time to escape, before worrying about escaping myself.

With blurring speed, Cho withdrew the pistol from the guard's head, spun around him, and placed a forearm across his throat. He returned the barrel to the guard's temple for all to see, including old man Song.

"Everyone … place your weapons on the floor … now!"

The guards froze. Old man Song put his head down and scurried quietly away behind them.

Cho waited until he saw the old man disappear from sight as the guards began advancing on him. He fired a shot into the air bringing

them all to a halt, "I said everyone put your weapons on the floor …
now, or this man dies!"

None of them complied.

Cho dragged the guard towards the elevator. As he reached for the
button, the doors opened.

He found himself standing in front of two more guards inside the
elevator, both frozen from surprise.

In one move, he shoved the guard in his grasp at the throng of
guards in front of him, while propelling himself backwards into the
guards on the elevator.

The doors closed before anyone else could board.

The guards inside drew their pistols. Cho grabbed one by the arm
and guided the barrel of his pistol to press the bottom button. The
elevator began descending.

He knocked the guns from both guards' hands as the three
grappled. They were able to grab hold of his arms, but Cho used
his feet to walk up the side of the doors. He propelled himself
backwards with enough force to slam both guards hard against the
back wall. They lost grasp of his arms in the process.

Cho spun around and delivered synchronized punches to their
throats. Both guards crumbled to the ground gasping for air.

* * * * *

The doors opened on the basement floor.

A half dozen guards and an officer were standing with weapons
drawn. The officer stepped onto the elevator. He looked down at the
injured men first, before gazing up at the open hatch in the elevator's
ceiling.

* * * * *

Cho climbed a slim ladder along the side of the shaft to the top,
and entered a crawlspace leading to a small, dark repair room. He
stepped with care until he found the light switch. The room was
empty except littered with elevator parts.

Without delay, he opened the only door and entered a narrow, concrete corridor leading to a stairway. With speed, he descended two sets of stairs and landings until he found himself in front of a door with the number "1" painted on it.

Cho opened the door a crack and listened. He heard voices from somewhere down the hall. Looking back up the stairs first, he pushed the door open and jutted his head out.

I'm virtually back where I started, down the hall from the elevator. It's only a matter of time before they trace me here. I have to get out of this stairwell.

He took a deep breath before stepping out. At the other end of the corridor, a growing crowd of guards gathering in front of the elevator came into view.

That's my only way out.

I can't go back. By now, they must have reached the repair room and could already be descending the stairs.

He saw only one door in the corridor. Quietly, he approached with haste and read the name on it. It was the captain of the guard's office.

Cho swung the door open and burst in. He found the light on but no one was there. He quickly, but gently closed the door.

The only furniture in the office was a single wooden desk with chairs on each end. The desk had two flat screen monitors and a keyboard atop it.

No windows ... no back door ... no way out except back into the corridor ... and nowhere to hide except behind the door. My only advantage is the fact this is probably the last place they would look for me. I hope the captain of the guard remains an active participant in my search.

He ran his hands along the walls.

They're lead-lined ... and why not ... these maniacs conduct nuclear bomb tests just a few kilometers away.

He checked the desk. There was an open bottle of *soju* in the bottom drawer. The Korean liquor, distilled from rice and combined with other ingredients like sweet potatoes, wheat, or barley, was one of his favorite drinks.

Taking a seat behind the desk, Cho poured two fingers worth and downed it. After replacing the bottle into the drawer, he noticed what appeared on the monitor screens – camera feeds from all around the compound.

Cho watched as guards deployed in all directions.

I hope they don't capture the old man.

Deciding against pouring another glass, he lifted his feet onto the edge of the desk.

At least I'll have fair warning of the captain's return.

* * * * *

Chef Song rushed into the access room to the tunnels and caught his breath. There were no guards posted at the entrance. Instead, the room was plastered with the familiar yellow-and-black radiation hazard warning symbols. The room was nothing more than a bare, reinforced concrete box, except for a row of metal lockers running the length of the wall to the left with a large, imposing opening near its center.

Song walked over and peered inside the upside-down U-shaped tunnel and shivered. With an eight-foot height and width and lined with one-foot by three-foot cement blocks of various hues, the overhead lamps, spaced at 20-foot increments, cast ominous shadows. The main passageway led off ruler-straight and seemed to disappear into a black abyss.

Eight-feet in, sitting idle on rail tracks running down its center, Song was relieved to see a powered railcar. The orange vehicle could seat four and was adorned with a single lamp affixed to a handrail running across the front.

Remembering the instructions he was given, Song walked over to the lockers and opened one. He found a single yellow radiation suit hanging inside, complete with black rubberized gloves and a bulky head and neck covering. A radio was attached to the front of the suit and a small oxygen tank sat inside an attached bag. A white tube emanated from the bag and disappeared up the right sleeve.

Song took that suit and two more. He placed them into the railcar before donning one. Wearing it made him feel like a folklore monster. He didn't understand much about radiation, but from the looks of the suit, he realized it had to be deadly.

Song found it difficult to see and move with the suit on, and worse, he had no idea how to operate the oxygen tank. He started walking around the room trying to acclimate himself. In less than a minute, he started to feel faint from lack of air. Struggling unsuccessfully to remove the head canopy, he collapsed.

* * * * *

Chef Song came to staring up at a blurry image of an angry man in uniform. When his focused returned, he saw it was a guard. He was confused that he could see so well, when it occurred to him that the guard had simply opened a rectangular portal built into the clear plastic mask – something he hadn't noticed.

The guard was speaking to him, but all Song heard was a muffled garble. The cowl made it difficult to hear. The guard was getting angrier as he raised his voice and repeated himself.

What ... am I doing here ... what do I tell him?

Old man Song didn't have to reply as he watched the butt of a pistol slam against the back of the guard's head. The guard's body fell on the old man, but someone lifted it off.

Song recognized his rescuer, "Sojang Kim! You saved my life."

Kim dragged the guard's body over to one of the lockers and placed it inside, before helping the old man to his feet.

He asked with annoyance, "What happened to you?"

"I ... seemed to have passed out. I could not breathe in this suit."

Kim opened the bag containing the small oxygen tank, "You did not turn on the oxygen flow you old fool."

Song waved his hand dismissively, "Yes, well, I would like to see you try to prepare *bulgogi* without the recipe. I am sure you will look as foolish overcooking beef."

"Where is the Daeryeong?"

The old man began walking to the tunnel, "Come, I will tell you as we walk. Then you can tell me how to drive a railcar."

Kim remained where he was.

Song noticed. He waved to him, "I said come. We have no time to waste.

Shaking his head, Kim joined him.

"Daeryeong Cho was discovered in front of the elevator. He instructed me to go for help. I am to ride through this tunnel to Sandone Station and make contact with the Americans."

"The Americans … what can they do?"

Kim had to help Song into the railcar. Song thumbed at the radiation suits in the back, "I am to take those to them so they can return through the tunnel."

"That is a ridiculous plan! The Americans would be spotted and arrested on sight. And then we will lose any chance of escape."

The old man ignored him, "Show me how to operate this thing."

"I will do better than that, I will operate it," Kim reached for a suit.

Song grabbed his arm. The two struggled before Kim finally released the suit.

"Sojang, I can see the despair in your face, but all is not lost. I will go to the Americans for help, but you must remain here and try and find the Daeryeong."

"You said he was arrested?"

"I did not say arrested. I said discovered. The last I saw of him, he had a gun to the head of one guard, while surrounded by others."

"So then he must have been arrested … or killed."

"Sojang … I am but an old cook, but it occurs to me that the guard you placed in the locker was in this room for a reason. I have heard the guards talk about this room and the tunnels. None of them would come near here if they were not ordered to."

"What are you driving at old man … that the guard was looking for Daeryeong Cho? Did it ever occur to you that the guards already captured or killed him and they were looking for you?"

The old man shrugged, "Perhaps, but I tell you this, Daeryeong Cho is a formidable man … and so are the Americans."

Kim reached for a suit again, Song prevented him.

Kim raised his voice, "Even if you are correct, old man, my objective is complete here. I have sabotaged the missiles' controls. I can do nothing for the Daeryeong."

He reached again. This time, Song grabbed his wrist, "You will try, Sojang. You will try!"

Sojang Kim glared back and pulled his wrist free. He let his temper cool before replying, "I will try … for what good it is worth. Now, tell me exactly how the Daeryeong was discovered."

Song allowed a slight grin, "We approached the elevator. The guard at the security desk radioed the captain of the guard to authorize our access. The next thing we knew the guard reached for his gun, but the Daeryeong moves like a tiger … lightning fast and so powerful. He made it possible for me to escape. I feel certain he also found a way for himself."

"The guard became suspicious after speaking to the captain of the guard?" Kim paced a few steps. "That could only mean he made the guard aware of your identities. And there would be no way for the captain of the guard to know unless … Kang must be aware of our presence!"

Chef Song moved the solitary lever forward and depressed the accelerator. The railcar lurched forward, "I guess I do not need your help after all … but Daeryeong Cho does. Find him and help him, Sojang."

Song closed the portal in his mask and twisted the oxygen valve then floored the pedal. The railcar raced away.

Kim watched the railcar disappear into darkness. He headed for the locker containing the guard. He heard rumbling and knew the guard had come to.

He took a few deep breaths and opened the locker. Their eyes met. He placed a cowl over the guard's head and brushed his arms away, as he placed his hands around the guard's throat.

Kim squeezed as hard as he could until the guard stopped moving. Unsure whether the man was dead, he squeezed for several more minutes.

Eerily quiet minutes.

Kim became aware that he was covered in sweat. He wiped some from his brow before lifting the headpiece off the guard and checking for a pulse. Feeling none, he closed the locker and straightened himself then left the room.

Kim hadn't noticed that blood from the guard's head wound had pooled on the bottom of the locker.

That blood slowly started dripping from the locker to the floor.

CHAPTER 36

SANDONE STATION
COORDINATES: 41°18'19"N 128°55'19"E
NORTH KOREA
4:00 PM (LOCAL), TUESDAY, JUNE 04, 2013

Someone banged on the boxcar's door.

Mugsy picked up a rifle then nodded to Song. The young man rolled the door open. It was Father Kim. He had two assault rifles in his hands.

"Here, take these."

Song grabbed them. Scipio lowered his hand and hoisted the priest up.

Scipio examined the rifles, "Not bad. You're pretty good at this, Father. Are you sure you weren't a thief before you received your calling?"

Father Kim winked and pulled a small tub of rice from his jacket. "This is more valuable than those."

The men crowded around.

"Where did that come from?" asked Mugsy.

"It was strange ... I spotted crates inside this small building, so I was about to investigate when a soldier spotted me. He was taking this to his commanding officer."

Song's eyes opened wide, "You were spotted?!"

"I was."

"What did you do?"

"The soldier called to me, so I had to go to him. I can tell you that my heart was racing. He did not even bother to ask who I was or what I was doing there. He just ordered me to take this tub of rice to his commander." Father Kim chuckled, "With that paltry amount, he likely did not want to face his commander's wrath."

"He probably helped himself and was setting you up for the fall." said Scipio.

"I think so too, replied Kim. "Anyway, I tucked it into my jacket and continued to the small building. I found the rifles in the top crate. It is sad, there were at least a dozen more crates, but it took me forever to pry one open. So I had to settle for only those two rifles."

"That's fine," said Mugsy. "Scipio and I brought back two each, and Mr. Song here brought back four."

"I found two crates like the ones you described on a push cart," replied Song. "It was so easy."

Scipio stretched, "I have to say, the security around here is pathetic."

Father Kim handed the tub to Song, "Give this to whoever needs it most." He turned to Scipio, "What is more pathetic is that these soldiers have an over abundance of assault weapons, but have to steal their commanding officer's rice."

Scipio grabbed a rifle and jumped down, "Now that we're armed, it's time to find the station's tunnel access. There's no way for us to know when they'll arrive, so we'll need to keep a man posted there from now on. I'll take first watch."

Song jumped down and looked up at Mugsy, "Would it not be safer to send me or one of the other Koreans?"

Mugsy leaned against the boxcar door and shook his head, "You may blend in better, but we don't know the exact location of the tunnel entrance. Sojang Kim was sure there's one at this station, but he's never seen it. So, as far as snooping around goes, Scipio is most qualified."

Song slung a rifle, "But he shouldn't go alone."

"Scipio is used to working alone. In fact, he prefers it."

"Still, I will go with—" Song looked around. There was no sign of Scipio.

Mugsy motioned for the conductor to jump down with him, "Like I said, he prefers to work alone. I'm gonna keep an eye on our friendly conductor while he makes believe he's fixing something. Get back in and remember to slide the door closed all the way. Keep it that way unless you hear our knock."

* * * * *

Chef Song strained his eyes to look ahead of him. Along the way, he had passed through several areas of the main tunnel where the lights dangling from the ceiling were inoperable. This was another one of those areas. Total darkness enveloped him.

Please let this be it!

He stopped the railcar and got out to look around. Behind him, a solid wall of pitch black swallowed up the two red brake lights like an all-consuming monster. It made him shiver.

He turned and looked ahead. In the distance, there was just enough light spilling from somewhere for him to see that the tracks ended.

Fighting the urge to take off his radiation suit and scratch himself, Song began walking ahead. He realized the itchiness was a result of being drenched in sweat, due to the combination of the cumbersome suit and abstract fear.

Chef Song was less afraid of radiation poisoning than he was of North Korean soldiers. He simply did not understand what radiation poisoning was. At his age, he decided to limit his anxiety to known causes of fear.

His steps were cautiously slow and fatigued. The journey on the railcar was a perilous one. He ran into trouble just northwest of the Punggye-Ri test site. It was the sight of the second North Korean nuclear test in May 2009. The track became disjointed and unstable. There were places when Song thought the railcar was going to fly off the tracks and smash into the solid-rock walls.

Then, two kilometers before reaching his present position the track branched off in two directions. The switch was set to a spur that headed directly north. Making matters worse, the track in that direction dove dramatically and the lights on the spur were not working.

Song found himself propelled at increasing velocity into utter darkness. He thought the South Korean priest's God might have had a hand in saving him from destruction when—just after the track flattened out—he realized he was heading for a solid wall of stone. He was able to slow the railcar down just enough so that the front merely banged the wall, the only damage, a dent in the front fender and the fraying of his nerves.

He had to pilot the railcar in reverse until he reached the main track again. There, he got out and manually threw the switch before proceeding to his current location. He continued to look around.

Wherever this is.

Song reached the end of the tracks. He finally decided to remove the head cowl and allowed himself a number of deep breaths before investigating further.

To the right of the tracks was a small cement platform. Positioned in the center was a machine that looked like a combination crane and forklift. Song noticed light poles along the perimeter, as well as a bank of overhead lights. None of them illuminated. He decided against looking for the switch. Instead, he thought it was as good a place as any to remove the rest of the radiation suit.

Though the suit wasn't particularly heavy, it made him feel clumsy and obese. His already impaired vision was also obstructed.

With the cowl off, he could see his surroundings with slightly more clarity. He realized he was standing in what appeared to be an immense cave, one that linked the main rail tunnel behind him with a much smaller tunnel beyond the cement platform. He headed for what turned out to be nothing more than a short passageway that led to a broad cement incline. The incline rose about 30 meters at an angle that he judged to be about one meter up for every three meters distance.

The old man sighed before starting the climb. Fatigue was setting in. He felt his age.

Reaching the top, he saw the light of the sun. He entered what appeared to be some sort of freight terminal building. Sunshine pierced through dirty windows.

His suspicions were confirmed upon reaching the main entrance. He opened one of the doors and peered out. Ten meters away were railroad tracks with a smaller cement incline leading from them to the front of the building.

Song looked out in both directions. To the right were three more buildings with no sign of people, but to the left was the center of Sandone Station. The Station stretched over 200 meters.

Next to the building were a number of other structures set off the tracks at various distances. Across the main rail there appeared to be a shorter set of tracks lying parallel. In the distance, Song could make out a locomotive with a number of boxcars sitting idle on them.

That must be the train ... but how to get to it?

Chef Song saw soldiers scattered everywhere between him and the train. Some were standing guard in front of the various buildings while others were patrolling along the tracks.

He suddenly became aware of the soldiers standing guard in front of the building. They noticed him at the same time. One turned pointing his rifle, "You ... old man, what are you doing there?!"

* * * * *

Scipio spotted Chef Song's head sticking out from the freight terminal building's main entrance, but was too far away to warn him of the soldiers on each side of the doors. The situation presented an advantage though. As the soldiers turned their attention to the old man, it allowed him to cross the tracks and take up a position just around the corner of the building.

Scipio couldn't risk using his rifle. He carried it in case of a full blown battle. He was also out of knife throwing distance. All he could do was watch as the soldiers pointed their rifles and started barking orders at the old man.

Scipio looked up to Heaven.

I don't know how you feel about aiding a heathen, but that old man could use your help right about now.

* * * * *

As he was ordered, Chef Song stepped out of the building. He stood defiantly in front of the two soldiers pointing their rifles at his head.

One barked, "What are you doing in there?!"

Song responded with impatience brewing, "I was about to catch the train for my daughter's house … and I tell you this, if you have made me miss the train, I will report you to Taejang Kang!"

With their rifles still pointed, the soldiers glanced at each other in confusion.

The soldier scolded him again, "This is not a passenger train station! No one is allowed inside that building. You must come with us!"

Chef Song stepped back shaking his fist, "I will not go with you! I told you, I am waiting for the train to take me to my daughter's house in Hyesan. It will be coming any moment. Now leave me alone or I will report you to Taejang Kang and he will have you shot!" He reached into his pocket and pulled out his pass, "I am Taejang Kang's personal chef!"

The soldiers lowered their rifles and examined the pass. Again, they looked at each other, unsure of what to do.

The soldier spoke in a calmer tone, "That is a pass into Taejang Kang's headquarters."

"I know what it is, young man. As I told you, I am Taejang Kang's personal chef. Taejang Kang will be livid when he finds out you have detained me. He will probably have you shot for making me miss the train to my daughter's house. Taejang Kang is my daughter's godfather."

The soldier asking the questions stared back. When he spoke again, his tone was soft, "Sir, we are only doing our jobs. This is a restricted area." He pointed behind him, "The train for Hyesan stops there."

Chef Song looked where the soldier pointed, then struck his forehead with the palm of his hand and chuckled, "I am becoming a foolish old man. Of course the train for Hyesan stops there. I knew this building was unfamiliar to me." He started out but the soldiers stopped him.

"Sir, I am afraid we will still have to take you to our superiors. You were inside a restricted area."

"Do not be silly. I was merely trying to get my bearings. I told you, I am becoming a foolish old man. I became confused by the buildings. That is all."

"I understand that sir, but you still must—"

"Young man ... who is being foolish now?"

"Sir ...?"

"If you bring me to your superiors they will ask me how I was able to enter this restricted building. I will have to tell them that I walked right past both of you."

Song suppressed a smile as he watched the soldiers contemplate the consequences.

"Perhaps it would be better if you allowed me to go my way. After all, the train for Hyesan has not yet arrived. So, there is no harm done."

The soldiers came to a silent agreement. The one doing the talking stepped aside, "Have a good day, Sir."

Song passed them and replied over his shoulder, "Thank you, young man."

When he reached the end of the building, he heard Korean spoken by a non-Korean.

"That was a great performance."

Chef Song glanced back as he continued walking. He saw the soldiers resuming their posts.

Scipio joined him.

"I am still being watched."

"You mean by Abbott and Costello?"

The old man raised his brow.

"Forget it and forget them. Security around here is not a concern."

Song let his eyes fall on the rifle Scipio was carrying, "Apparently not when an American can walk in broad daylight carrying one of those."

Scipio nudged him in the direction of the tracks, "We have to cross here." He waited for them to cross both sets of tracks before inquiring, "You are alone? Something went wrong?"

Old man Song stopped walking, "We were discovered. Daeryeong Cho has gone missing. He might have been taken into custody. He was the one to tell me to fetch you."

Scipio showed no emotion, "What about Sojang Kim?"

"I last saw the Sojang at the compound's tunnel entrance. He was more disturbed by the news than you appear to be. He wanted to accompany me here, but I told him to remain and try to locate the Daeryeong."

"Good."

"How is my grandson?"

"He is fine. Let's go."

* * * * *

Song slid the door open and saw his grandfather. He jumped down and the two men hugged.

"Grandpa, why are you here? Where are the others?"

Scipio stepped between them, "Help your grandfather up."

As soon as the door was closed, Scipio waved Mugsy and Father Kim over, "Chef Song just returned with disturbing news. He and Cho were discovered and Cho has gone missing. Chef Song isn't sure whether Cho was taken into custody … or killed. It was Cho that told him to make contact with us. He also ran into Sojang Kim. The Sojang remained at the compound to try and locate Cho."

Mugsy asked Song to translate, "Was Cho able to complete his mission?"

Song translated his grandfather's reply, "No. he said they were discovered at the security desk outside the elevator bank, leading down to the Taejang's office. They never even made it onto the elevator."

Song switched to Korean, "How did you escape, Grandpa?"

"The Daeryeong is a very able and brave man. He charged at the guard that discovered us and took his gun away from him. Then he used it to keep the other guards at bay while I snuck away. The last I saw of him he was holding the guard's pistol against the man's head. There were a dozen other guards waiting to pounce on him like hungry lions."

"What about the Sojang?" asked Scipio. "Was he able to complete his mission?"

The old man's face reddened, "I am embarrassed to admit that I did not even ask him. I have no idea."

"I caught that. The Sojang should be the one embarrassed," replied Mugsy. "He knew you were returning to us. That would have been an important thing for us to know."

Scipio tapped his chin, "Maybe the Sojang didn't want us to know. This way we couldn't be sure … extra incentive for us to make our way there."

Mugsy looked back confused.

"According to Chef Song, the Sojang wasn't too excited at the prospect of remaining there and looking for Cho. He wanted to return here with the Chef. Only the Chef's power of persuasion changed his mind."

Mugsy looked from Scipio to the old man, "Well, if possible, we have to go look for them."

Scipio turned to old man Song, "Can we return the way you came?"

The old man smiled, "Yes. Inside the tunnel is the railcar I used to get here. I placed extra radiation suits in the back seat. Come, I will—"

"Hold on a moment," replied Scipio. "This is what you are going to do." He turned to young Song, "Get your grandfather some paper and a pen. I want him to draw us a map of the compound." He turned back to the old man, "Chef, draw the route. The Captain and I will take it from there."

"But, it would be better if I showed you."

"And you two could use some help?" added Father Kim.

"Negative," replied Mugsy. "Chef, you need to stay with your grandson. You've risked your life enough. And Father, we need you, Song, and his men to maintain control of this train until we return. It's our only method of escape.

"If we're not back in 24 hours, I want all of you to abandon the train and make your way back to the industrial town, staying off the main routes. From there, Father, you should be able to make contact with your people and arrange to get yourself back into China."

Scipio looked at his watch, "We still have some time before the watch changes. We should make our way to the tunnel by then."

Old man Song took the pencil from his grandson and began drawing.

CHAPTER 37

HEADQUARTERS OF TAEJANG KANG KUM-SOK
PUNGGYE-RI NUCLEAR TEST SITE
KILJU COUNTY, NORTH HAMGYONG PROVINCE
NORTH KOREA
5:00 PM (LOCAL), TUESDAY, JUNE 04, 2013

Two soldiers walked past and disappeared down the hall. Sojang Kim emerged from the stairwell. He walked to his office door and punched in a code. The LED changed from red to green and he heard a click.

They did not change the code. I thought as much. Kang never was one for details. That is why he made me his adjutant.

He entered but kept the light off.

Kim walked to his desk and took a seat in the dark. He recalled how his military career had started – top in his class – quickly climbing the ranks until he caught the eye of Kang, only a Sojang at the time – and then upon Kang's promotion to Taejang, himself being promoted to Sojang.

He remembered with clarity the day when Taejang Kang appointed him his adjutant. Kang told him the time would come when the fate of their beloved North Korea would rest in their hands.

Kim opened the bottom drawer of his desk. He withdrew a bottle of Baekdusan blueberry whiskey and a highball glass, a bottle given to him by Kang, on his first day as his adjutant. He remembered Kang telling him with pride that the whiskey's name was taken from the mountain region at the tip of North Korea, the ancestral home of all Koreans.

Kim unscrewed the top, filled the glass halfway and raised it.

It seems you were correct, after all, Taejang.

He downed the glass in one gulp. He considered the aroma as strong as its Western counterparts, yet Kim thought the blueberry taste that the whiskey imbued took the sharp edge off the strong liquor. He considered pouring another, but fought the urge. Instead he walked over to a closet and opened the door. Two identical uniforms were the only things hanging from the rod. He began undressing.

Kim examined himself in the full-length mirror inside the door.

This is something I must do. There are no more options. I cannot continue to sneak around. It is only a matter of time before I am caught anyway.

He straightened his collar and shot his cuffs from underneath the tunic.

If Cho is still alive, I need to buy him more time. If he has not been caught and is paying attention, perhaps he can save me while carrying out his objective.

His mind turned to another scenario, one that filled him with anxiety.

If he was already caught or killed … then I will be too.

Kim placed the cap on his head and took care to tilt it, just so.

My objective is complete. This is the only thing left that I can do for my country.

He pulled his tunic down to flatten it and left the office, walking with authority down the hall to the security desk next to the elevator. The guard on duty recognized him immediately. Even with the Taejang's 'arrest on sight' orders, the guard felt compelled to snap to attention and salute.

Kim's eyes met the guard's, "Call downstairs. Have them tell the Taejang that Sojang Kim wishes to speak with him."

"Yes, sir," the guard picked up the phone and spoke softly for only a moment before turning back to Kim, "Taejang Kang has authorized access."

Kim nodded and walked in front of the elevator. Within a minute the doors opened to two soldiers with AK-47s slung over their shoulders. Both saluted crisply. Kim returned their salutes and stood between them.

The elevator descended in silence. Kim took a deep breath as the doors opened to two more soldiers, both pointing rifles at him. He held his hands with palms out as he stepped off, "I am unarmed."

"Of course you are, my old friend," Taejang Kang appeared from behind the soldiers.

Kim saluted, and then bowed, "Taejang, I wish to speak with you."

Kang nodded to the soldiers still on the elevator. One smacked the back of Kim's head with the butt of his rifle. Kim crumbled to the floor.

Kang looked down, "And I you, Sojang."

The soldiers waited for Taejang Kang to walk away before lifting Kim and dragging him behind.

* * * * *

Cho watched as Sojang Kim was dragged away. He first noticed Kim on the security monitors when Kim entered his own office. He continued to watch as Kim emerged dressed in his uniform, approached the guard desk, and rode the elevator down. Finally, changing camera feeds, he was able to witness Kim's reception by Kang.

What does he think he is doing? Buying time for me perhaps ... or turning coward and attempting to beg for mercy from his old boss? Why is he wearing his uniform?

Cho heard noises coming from outside the door. He switched the camera view and saw three uniformed men approaching from down the corridor.

One of them has to be the Captain of the Guard.

* * * * *

The familiar tones of a code being entered on a keypad were immediately followed by the clicking sound of a door being unlocked.

The Captain of the Guard entered his office and tried the light switch several times. The room remained dark. He gave up and walked behind his desk while the two soldiers accompanying him took positions in front of it.

At once, the Captain of the Guard noticed the monitors on his desk were not on. The only light in the room was coming from the corridor. That light was suddenly extinguished when the three heard the door close.

Before they could turn, Cho broke the necks of the soldiers simultaneously, twisting their heads under each of his arms with force. The snapping sound froze the Captain of the Guard in fear.

"Who is there?"

Letting their bodies drop, Cho reached down and pulled the soldier's knives out of their scabbards. He threw them underhanded in the direction of the Captain of the Guard's voice. The knives flew across the desk in synchronistic flight line stabbing into the Captain of the Guard's chest with a single thud.

Cho then moved quickly, first circling the desk and removing the knives, before slipping the Captain of the Guard's tunic off. The blood from the wounds had already begun to soak through his shirt, so he left it alone and untied the dead man's shoes before removing his trousers.

Cho turned the monitors back on and viewed the camera feeds from the corridor. No one was approaching. He screwed the lights back into their fixtures and turned them on then began piling the bodies in the closet.

CHAPTER 38

TUNNEL ENTRANCE
HEADQUARTERS OF TAEJANG KANG KUM-SOK
PUNGGYE-RI NUCLEAR TEST SITE
KILJU COUNTY, NORTH HAMGYONG PROVINCE
NORTH KOREA
9:00 PM (LOCAL), TUESDAY, JUNE 04, 2013

The crackling of radiation suits reverberated off the tunnel walls as two figures climbed onto the platform. Mugsy and Scipio exited the tunnel and removed their head gear. Immediately, Mugsy pulled the map old man Song drew from one of his pockets while Scipio looked over his shoulder.

Mugsy pointed to doors on the side of the room with the large vaulted-ceiling, "The elevator is that way and down the corridor to the left."

Scipio swept the locker-laced room, "All clear for now, but something tells me it won't stay this way."

Faint voices could be heard from the corridor.

Scipio tossed Mugsy's head gear to him before picking up his own, "Quick, put 'em on."

Two soldiers—one tall, one short—entered and immediately raised their weapons.

The smaller one, a chunggŭp, equivalent to an American corporal, did the talking. (In Korean) "This is a restricted area. What are you doing in here?"

Mugsy looked away. Scipio was also careful not to allow the soldiers to look into his face shield, "Stay where you are! Keep away. Taejang Kang ordered us to search inside the tunnels. We just returned."

"The Captain of the Guard's orders were specific, no one in or out of the tunnels. This area is restricted—"

"Taejang Kang ordered us directly, Chunggŭp."

The chunggŭp looked them over from where he was and pointed to their chests, "Where are your badges? You cannot access this area without badges."

"Our badges are on our uniforms under the suits."

The chunggŭp's face showed suspicion, "Show me."

Mugsy tapped Scipio's shoulder and pointed at a sign over a door to an adjoining room. The sign read "Showers."

The chunggŭp and the soldier behind him raised their rifles. "Show us your badges now!"

Scipio pointed to the room, "We must shower first."

The soldier behind whispered into the chunggŭp's ear.

The chunggŭp lowered his rifle, "Very well, we will wait here."

Scipio motioned for Mugsy to follow him. They walked around the wall to a row of shower heads. Scipio turned the water on and started stripping out of the radiation suit. Mugsy did the same.

Mugsy nodded toward the door, "My Korean was good enough to understand … badges. Any ideas?"

Scipio stuck his head under the water then grabbed a towel and threw it over his head, "I think it's time we showed them our pens instead."

Mugsy wet his head, grabbed a towel and followed.

The chunggŭp and the soldier kept their rifles lowered as they watched Scipio and Mugsy approach with towels over their heads.

"Where are your badges?"

They twisted the pens in their hands.

Scipio held out his hand, "Do you have paper. I must document this."

The chunggŭp patted his pockets confused, "Document what?"

Mugsy stepped next to the soldier.

The chunggŭp pulled out a notepad and ripped a sheet from it. He held it out to Scipio but it slipped from his hand. When he bent to pick it up, something caught his eye. There was a thin stream of blood leading to a small puddle in front of one of the lockers. Everyone else saw it too.

Scipio pressed the needle tip of the pen into the chunggŭp's neck, as Mugsy did the same to the soldier. Both men struggled to raise their rifles. Mugsy and Scipio disarmed them.

Within a minute, the chunggŭp and soldier grabbed their chests and collapsed. Their hearts had stopped.

Scipio nodded towards the lockers, "Let's strip 'em and stow 'em."

After donning their uniforms and placing the bodies inside two of the lockers, Mugsy opened the locker with the blood in front of it.

"This must be the one Kim took care of."

Scipio showed no interest. He peaked into the corridor, "No one's out there."

"Let's load the radiation suits onto the railcar first then shove off." Mugsy put a finger in his collar, "I can hardly breathe in this uniform."

Scipio winked as he passed, "You won't breathe at all without it."

* * * * *

Cho watched as Mugsy and Scipio placed the bodies of the soldiers into the lockers. He took a mirror out from the top drawer and checked the knife wounds in the Captain of the Guard's tunic he was wearing. There were traces of blood still visible but there was nothing he could do about them. If he scrubbed anymore the marks it would leave would be noticeable.

He altered the nametag by just a few letters then placed the

Captain of the Guard's cap on his head before leaving the office. Just outside the door a soldier saluted him as he passed in the hall. Cho returned the salute and grinned as he headed off.

* * * * *

"More heading this way," Mugsy pulled his head back from around the corner and pointed in the opposite direction. Scipio walked ahead of him. Behind them three soldiers turned the corner.

Scipio and Mugsy turned left at the end of the corridor. The soldiers turned right.

Mugsy exhaled audibly, "This is getting ridiculous. At this rate we'll never make it to the elevator, never mind ride it down to Kang."

Scipio peaked around the corner, "It didn't look so far on the old man's map ... of course he didn't include the soldiers we keep running into at every turn."

He waved, "Let's go Captain ... the coast is clear ... for now."

They made it halfway down the corridor when a chungwi and two soldiers carrying rifles appeared at the end.

Mugsy and Scipio turned on a dime, but not quickly enough.

"You two ... halt!"

Mugsy and Scipio made eye contact but didn't turn around.

"What are you doing in this area?"

Scipio raised his brow. Mugsy gently shook his head.

"You face a chungwi when he speaks to you, now turn around!"

They let their ceramic blades slide from their sleeves into their hands.

"I said turn around!"

"There you are," the voice came from behind the chungwi. It was Cho's voice. "These men are reporting to me, Chungwi. They were exposed to radiation in the tunnels."

The chungwi turned to him and saluted, "Taewi ... these men do not belong in this area. A level-four security protocol is in effect."

"I was the one to institute the level-four protocol, Chungwi. You and your men may go."

The chungwi's brows furled. He looked back at Mugsy and Scipio before turning to Cho again.

"Sir. You are not familiar to me. Where is Taewi—?"

Cho approached with hands folded behind his back, "Apparently not, Chungwi, or else you would know never to hesitate when I give you an order."

Cho stared up into the young officers eyes, "You and your men are dismissed."

"Yes Taewi," The Chungwi waved to his men to follow him.

Mugsy and Scipio retracted their blades up their sleeves. They were careful to avert their faces as the soldiers passed them.

"Hello Cho, the cavalry's arrived and we're here to rescue you," said Scipio.

Cho grinned, "It appears the cavalry needed rescuing of its own."

"You mean the chungwi and his men ... oh ... we were never in any immediate danger."

"I see ... were you two going to stab them with your pens? I watched with interest on the Captain of the Guard's security monitor."

Mugsy let his ceramic blade spring back out, "Actually, this time we were gonna use these."

"Ah, ceramic ... very nice. That would explain how you smuggled them on the flight to China, but you should have informed me. You could have had us all arrested."

Scipio patted his back, "Our motto is 'better to ask for forgiveness than permission.'"

Cho shook his head but kept his grin as he headed back in the same direction, "Come, we need to move."

Scipio and Mugsy followed.

"Where to?" asked Scipio.

"First, the infirmary. We need to bandage your faces. Radiation burns are hard on the eyes."

"Cunning ... then?" asked Mugsy.

"Then ... I need to carry out my mission."

"Kang ...?"

Cho nodded as he entered the infirmary. Mugsy and Scipio followed with blades in hand.

"Don't worry. I had this entire area placed on—"

"Level-four security protocol," said Scipio, "we heard."

Cho took bandages from the cabinet, "We will be able to stay here until the next shift arrives. Now, both of you please … sit. I have more to tell you while I turn you into proper mummies."

"The old man told us you were unable to get to the Taejang," said Mugsy, as Cho began wrapping Scipio's face.

"I sent the old man back for you because I need your help, but there is a complication. Earlier this afternoon Sojang Kim surrendered to Kang."

"Surrendered … why?" Scipio mumbled.

"Please, you must not move your mouth while I do this. We can't have you unravel in front of soldiers.

"Yes, I was able to see the whole thing on the security monitor."

"Why would he surrender?" asked Mugsy.

"Your turn to sit quietly, Captain," Cho began wrapping his head. "I think the Sojang's intention was to buy me time. He could not know whether I was captured, dead, or alive, but I think the priest might have given him faith."

Scipio looked at himself in the mirror as he returned the cap to his head, "That I doubt, but let's say you're right. How does surrendering to Kang buy you time?"

Cho clipped the end of the bandage, "There you are, Captain.

"I think the Sojang surmised that Kang knows why we are all here. He knows the Taejang will have to interrogate him to find out if we were successful or not."

"Were we successful?" asked Scipio.

"I don't know. The last I saw of the Sojang before he surrendered, he was heading to the missile control room. He said he knew how to prevent their launch."

"But you don't know if he was successful," said Mugsy.

"I don't."

"Where is the Sojang now?" asked Scipio.

"They are holding him in a secure area downstairs."

"Kang didn't question him yet?"

"No. I have continued to monitor the camera feeds."

"That's good then."

"I wouldn't particularly say ... good, though it could be worse. At least he is still alive, and Kang has not interrogated him yet, but there is also no way for us to free the Sojang based on where they are holding him."

Cho turned to Mugsy, "Captain, though I intend to complete my mission, I still consider you in charge. What is your assessment?"

Mugsy checked his bandages then returned the cap to his head as Scipio had done.

"My assessment ... depends on whether you think there's a way for us to sabotage the missiles or at least determine whether the Sojang was successful."

Cho shook his head, "It is impossible for us to get anywhere near the control room, let alone the missiles."

"Then we need to focus our energies on your objective ... taking out Kang. Say you, Scipio?"

Scipio winked at Cho, "Thanks for asking, Captain. I agree, but we're running out of time. The longer we remain here, the more we risk discovery ... wrapped like mummies or not. The Taejang's timeline is also coming to an end. He could launch those missiles anytime."

"What now?" Mugsy asked Cho.

Cho checked his watch, "Now, we wait. We have to get to Kang's office. The only way down is the elevator."

He walked over and sprawled out on a couch to rest, "The guards' shift will end in two hours. That will be the best time for us to make our move."

Mugsy glanced at Scipio, who shrugged his shoulders before hopping onto an examination table to take a nap.

Mugsy took a seat near Cho, "And how exactly do we 'make our move'? That's taking for granted we're not arrested at the guard station and we're actually able to ride the elevator down."

Scipio lifted his head to hear Cho's reply.

Cho opened his eyes, "I took the liberty of placing an early morning meeting on the Taejang's busy calendar tomorrow. Apparently, you two have gone beyond the normal call of duty in looking for the infiltrators. As a result, you have received radiation burns to your faces that will leave you disfigured for life."

Mugsy paused, "You mean the Taejang is gonna pin medals on us?"

"Let's make sure we don't kill him until we get our medals," added Scipio.

"To the contrary, from what I know of the Taejang, he does not embrace failure."

Mugsy tapped Cho's shoulder, "What failure?"

"Kang will consider your inability to find us, failure. We will hope he considers the burns to your faces proper punishment."

"Or else what …?" Scipio called over.

"Or else he may order you both shot."

Mugsy tapped his shoulder again, "You're kidding us, right?"

Cho closed his eyes again, "Do not worry. We will make our move before he has you shot … if that is what he intends."

Mugsy looked over to Scipio, who shrugged again before closing his eyes.

CHAPTER 39

SECURITY DESK – SECURE ELEVATOR
HEADQUARTERS OF TAEJANG KANG KUM-SOK
PUNGGYE-RI NUCLEAR TEST SITE
KILJU COUNTY, NORTH HAMGYONG PROVINCE
NORTH KOREA
12:00 AM (LOCAL), WEDNESDAY, JUNE 05, 2013

Cho, Mugsy, and Scipio watched as the guard from the graveyard shift saluted and took the place of his predecessor. They waited until he was alone before Cho approached ahead of the others. The guard saluted.

"These men have a meeting with Taejang Kang."

The guard lifted a clipboard, "Taewi, their meeting with the Taejang is not until 08:00 hours."

"That is correct. However, they were just released from the infirmary, and cannot return to active duty for another 24 hours." Cho answered his unasked question, "They do not want their families or others on the base seeing them with the bandages. The bandages will be removed later this evening. They cannot wait in the infirmary and they cannot wait anywhere else on this floor with the security protocol in effect."

The guard looked Mugsy and Scipio over then walked over to the elevator and inserted a key attached to a chain tethered to his belt. The elevator door opened.

Cho stepped onto the elevator first followed by Mugsy and Scipio. Cho looked up at a dark mirror in the corner of the ceiling and directed everyone's eyes to it. They remained quiet for the ride down.

The door opened to another security desk. The guard behind it merely nodded without looking up.

Cho led them into the reception area for Kang's office – a large room with couches lining the walls. He pointed to one of the couches, glancing up at another dark mirror, "You will sit there and wait. Do not move from the couch."

Mugsy and Scipio saluted and sat. Cho left the room.

Scipio whispered, "Cameras in all four corners."

Mugsy nodded to the door, "Where's he going?"

"Probably to try and pay a call on the Sojang." He rested his head back, "Better make yourself comfortable. We're gonna be here awhile."

* * * * *

Cho entered the detention area and approached the guard sitting in front of the steel-reinforced door.

The guard looked up, "May I help you, Taewi?"

Cho thumbed towards the door, "Sojang Kim?"

The guard stood stiffly.

Cho showed his hands, "Easy, It is common knowledge. I used to be on the Sojang's staff. It sickens me that I served under a traitor."

The guard relaxed, "He is in there, but the Taejang gave orders that no one can speak to him."

"I understand," Cho took a pack of gum from his pocket. He offered a stick to the guard, who took it with a nod and sat back down.

Cho brought a stick to his mouth, "Would it be okay for me to just look in? I want my last memory of him to be sitting in that cell."

The guard thought a moment before heading to the door and opening a small viewing portal. Cho stepped next to him and nodded. He looked in and saw Sojang Kim lying on a cot with his arm over his face.

Cho kicked the door.

Kim sat up. He looked over at the door then got up and walked over. He recognized Cho.

Cho sneered then spit.

The guard slammed the portal shut and pushed Cho away, "Taewi!"

Cho bowed, "I apologize. I lost my head seeing him standing there so defiantly. I expected to see him hanging from his ankles. Was he not interrogated yet?"

"Taejang Kang has ordered that there will be no interrogation."

"Why not …?"

"The Taejang said that the Sojang surrendered voluntarily and has agreed to cooperate fully, so he ordered that no interrogation take place. He said that he will personally question the Sojang later this morning when he returns."

Cho glanced back at the door, "I guess he had a change of heart." He bowed to the guard and left.

The guard looked back at the steel door. He shook his head before returning to his seat.

* * * * *

Kim wiped the spit from his face and cursed.

So, Cho was not captured after all. I wonder if the old man made it to the Americans. Cho obviously wanted me to see him, but why? Perhaps there is still hope.

Kim noticed a small aluminum ball on the floor and picked it up. He sat back down and stared at the gum wrapper. Looking up at the door, it came to him. He unraveled the ball.

The message read, *8 AM Rec. Rm.*

CHAPTER 40

RECEPTION AREA – OFFICE OF THE TAEJANG
HEADQUARTERS OF TAEJANG KANG KUM-SOK
PUNGGYE-RI NUCLEAR TEST SITE
KILJU COUNTY, NORTH HAMGYONG PROVINCE
NORTH KOREA
7:55 AM (LOCAL), WEDNESDAY, JUNE 05, 2013

Cho nodded to Mugsy who tapped Scipio's leg. The three rose to their feet, stood at attention and saluted.

Cho decided not to share Kim's betrayal with them.

I told them before he was not to be trusted. Now this entire operation is in peril, our lives are at stake, and my country is at great risk.

I will deal with the Sojang. He will not betray us.

Taejang Kang entered the reception area surrounded by four of his elite guards – two preceded him, two followed. Kang's adjutant appeared from his office and approached him. He also came to attention and saluted.

Kang didn't return the salute, "Who are those men?"

"Sir, the two bandaged soldiers received burns to their faces inside the tunnels."

"And ...?"

Cho approached with Mugsy and Scipio behind him and saluted again. He made no eye contact and raised his voice, "Taejang, I apologize for disturbing you, Sir. These men were ordered to look inside the tunnels for the trespassers. In so doing they received severe radiation burns to their faces."

Kang turned to his adjutant, "Why am I being bothered with this?"

Cho glanced at the entrance to the reception room then spoke again, "Taejang, I thought you should see them before I am forced to return them to active duty."

"You thought ...?" Kang turned back and finally looked at Cho then looked beyond him at Mugsy and Scipio, "Taewi ... why were these men not wearing radiation protection in the tunnels?"

Cho glanced again at the entrance, "They were unaware of the danger ... Sir."

"Unaware of the danger ...? Taewi, your name is not familiar to me, but your face is. Why is that?"

"I do not know, sir."

"I know all of the men under my command, but I do not know you ... or do I?"

Behind them, two guards escorted Sojang Kim into the reception area. His hands were cuffed. Everyone turned when they entered.

Kang noticed the way Kim eyed Cho – a few blinks of surprise. He looked carefully at Cho and noticed something, "Taewi, are those holes in your tunic from a knife?" Kang ran his finger on them and looked closely, "They are stained with blood. How did you get them?"

Cho placed his hands behind him and balled them into fists. Mugsy and Scipio noticed and brought their ceramic blades down from their sleeves.

Kang moved even closer until they were toe to toe and studied Cho's face. After a moment, he looked back at Sojang Kim and grinned, "Daeryeong Cho ...."

Cho exploded into action. He spun Kang around, sliding a

forearm across his throat. Behind him, Mugsy and Scipio let their weapons fly. The guards behind the Taejang were the first to fall while the guards in front hesitated. Mugsy and Scipio pulled their second blades and were on them. Mirror images of one another, they stabbed the guards in their chests then slit their throats in identical fashion.

Sojang Kim reacted an instant later, slamming the back of his head into one of the guards behind him. That left him too far from the other guard, who raised his rifle and pulled the trigger.

Kim fell to his knees.

Cho squeezed his forearm, "Tell your men to stand down now, Taejang, or I will snap your neck."

The guard head-butted by Kim returned to his feet and pointed his rifle.

Cho squeezed harder. Kang gasped for air.

"Tell them to stand down now!"

He released pressure.

"Stand down … put your weapons down!"

The guards looked among one another.

"I said put your weapons down!"

They dropped their rifles.

Cho dragged Kang towards his office while Mugsy helped Kim to his feet.

"You okay?"

"I am shot! No, I am not okay."

Scipio picked two of the rifles up and slung them over his shoulders, then picked up another and pointed it at the guards, "Move."

Cho kicked Kang's legs from under him, dropping him to his knees, "Stay." He waited for the others to enter the office before closing and locking the door.

Mugsy gently lowered Sojang Kim onto a chair and examined his wound, "It looks like the bullet passed through your triceps without hitting the bone, but we have to stop the bleeding."

Scipio ordered the guards to join Kang on their knees with hands on their heads and fingers interlaced. He let the rifles slip off his shoulders and offered the one in his hand to Cho then reached into his breast pocket and tossed a silver package to Mugsy, "It's QuikClot for his wound. I took some from the infirmary ... thought we might have use for it."

Two shots rang out.

The bodies of the guards fell to the floor.

Cho held a hand up, indicating to Mugsy and Scipio not to move. Then he turned the rifle on Kang, but spoke over his shoulder to Kim, "Were you successful in achieving your objective, Sojang?"

Kim nodded and winced as Mugsy wrapped the kaolin-soaked gauze around his upper arm, "Yes. The Musudan missiles will not reach their target."

Kang chuckled, "So now you intend to kill me, Daeryeong? You think the threat has been neutralized?"

Cho pressed the barrel of the rifle against Kang's temple. Kang grinned, "It has not. You can kill me, but it will not stop the missiles from launching."

Cho looked back at Kim, who rose to his feet and walked over. He bent down to be eye level with Kang, "The Musudan missiles have been neutralized, Taejang."

"I believe you, Sojang."

Kim stared back with confusion.

Kang let his eyes fall to the floor, "I long suspected your disloyalty ... your treason and capacity for treachery. So, I put in place ... a contingency."

Cho banged the barrel against the side of Kang's head, "What contingency?"

Kang looked up at him and smiled.

Cho spun the rifle around slamming the butt into Kang's face. He crashed to the floor.

"I said what contingency, Taejang?"

With blood flowing from his mouth, Kang pushed himself onto his knees.

Cho held the rifle over him.

"If you hit me again, Daeryeong, I will never tell you. Either shoot me or put the rifle down."

"You are in no position to make demands, Taejang," Cho raised the butt of the rifle again.

Mugsy grabbed it, "Let's hear what he has to say."

Cho looked fiercely at him.

"I'm in command, remember?"

Cho hesitated before letting Mugsy take the rifle.

Kang rose to his feet holding his mouth. He turned to Scipio, "Give me one of those bandages."

Scipio looked over at Mugsy who nodded.

Scipio tossed the package onto the floor at Kang's feet. He shrugged, "My aim is bad."

Kang shook his head bending over to pick it up, "Americans … barbarians."

Mugsy stepped in front of him, "What contingency?"

Kang opened the package and started dabbing the gauze on the side of his mouth.

Cho squatted, "Taejang, you will need many more bandages if you do not start talking." Kang's eyes met Cho's and remained locked.

Kang was first to blink. His grin returned, "The Sojang may have neutralized the Musudan missiles … but there is another missile battery. I had it positioned in a secluded location, one which the Sojang is totally unaware, and it is activated for launch."

Cho's demeanor remained calm, "You will tell us where this missile battery is and you will deactivate it."

Kang ignored him, "The target is also different than the one for the Musudan missiles. Sojang Kim is completely unaware of the secondary target."

Mugsy looked back at Kim.

"Captain, the only *true* medium-range missiles currently under Taejang Kang's control are the Musudan missiles. However, the Taejang has control over several batteries of shorter medium-range missiles."

Kang nodded, "Very good, Sojang. Now inform your American and South Korean friends of the capabilities of our NoDong 2 missiles … the ones with GPS guidance."

Kim blinked from shock, "Those missiles have not even been

tested."

"They will be … soon."

"I am aware of the capabilities of NoDong 2 missiles," said Cho, "but I was not aware the North equipped any with GPS guidance."

"Exactly what are the capabilities, Sojang?" asked Mugsy.

"The NoDong 2 has a shorter range than the Musudan, and a smaller payload. However, it does have a range of 1,500 kilometers and it can be armed with a high explosive, chemical, biological, or nuclear warhead."

Mugsy brought a map up on his phone. He adjusted the scale and turned the screen so Scipio and Cho could see.

Scipio pointed, "Busan is still in play."

"Wait … no, it is not," replied Kim. "I remember now, the Taejang is talking about a special battery of NoDong 2 missiles … ones with GPS guidance. In order to improve their accuracy to levels that would allow the targeting of hard military installations, their range was reduced to less than 500 kilometers. Busan is almost 700 kilometers from Punggye-Ri."

Mugsy adjusted the scale again, "That still leaves a long list of military installations in play, including all of the bases in and around Seoul, Incheon, and Suwon."

Scipio took a closer look, "How improved is the accuracy, Sojang?"

"Without GPS guidance, the circular error probability (CEP) of a NoDong 2 missile is two kilometers. That means there is a 50% probability that it will strike within a two kilometer radius. With it, the CEP drops to less than 50 meters."

Cho took Mugsy's phone from him and held it in front of Kang, "You will show us the target and the location of the missile battery, then you will disarm the missiles."

Kang looked up at him with scorn, "The launch sequence for the missiles is programmed and fully automated. I have given the launch order. The countdown has already begun, Daeryeong."

Kim put his hand on Cho's shoulder, "Cho, if the Taejang is telling the truth, normal countdown procedure begins 72 hours before launch."

"And I will tell you, Daeryeong," added Kang, "there is much less than 72 hours left."

Mugsy raised his voice, "What exactly do you want, Taejang?"

Kang looked from Cho to Mugsy and back to Cho. His eyes sparkled as he stood. He held the bandage up, "May I throw this away?"

Cho took the bandage from him and tossed it to the floor, "You were asked a question, Taejang, what do you want?"

"I will start with what I do not want. I have no desire to die, Daeryeong."

"Tell us what we want to know and you may survive this."

"Forgive me if I do not take you at your word, Daeryeong, but I prefer to insure my survival."

Scipio put his ear to the door, "There's a party forming out there."

Mugsy grabbed Cho's arm and whispered into his ear, "We're running out of time if we ever expect to survive this ourselves."

Cho nodded. He locked hands behind his back and faced Kang, "Taejang, if you want to survive this, you will give us what we want now."

"And what about the party outside … how do you propose to get by them? Or is this a suicide mission for you and your friends?"

"Taejang, my patience is running thin. Tell us what we want to know and you live. That is the only deal I am offering."

"That may be the only deal you are offering, Daeryeong, but what about your American friends? I think they might entertain another."

"Tell us your deal, Taejang," said Scipio.

Kang grinned at Cho then turned serious, "I have two demands before I give you what you want, but know this … I have no desire to die, but I am prepared to. You may believe you can torture the information out of me. I assure you, in the time left you will fail. I believe Sojang Kim can confirm this."

Kim turned his back to Kang and spoke into Cho's ear, "The Taejang is telling the truth."

"Do not worry Daeryeong, I only have two demands. They are simple and one is beneficial to you. The first is, once I stand down the launch, I will provide safe passage for you out of my country."

Cho had no reaction, "We have our own plan of escape."

"I am sure you do, but can it *guarantee* that you will not be captured?"

No one replied.

"If I stand down the launch, I cannot afford for you or the Americans to be captured. I will assign my personal guard to escort you across the border into China."

"You speak as if you expect us to leave you behind," said Cho.

"That is exactly what I expect, Daeryeong, which leads me to my second demand …," Kang pointed at Kim, "he must die."

Kim spun around furiously. He looked from one to another. They remained quiet.

He sprung at Kang, wrapping a hand around his neck. It took Mugsy and Scipio to subdue him.

Kim rubbed his throat, "Those are my demands. They are not negotiable."

Cho nodded to Scipio who handed him a ceramic blade, "Since your demands are not reasonable, Taejang, I will fall back on my original objective." He pulled Kang's hand away from his throat and pressed the blade against it.

"My demands are reasonable, Daeryeong. I told you I have no intention of losing my life. I also have no intention of giving up my position and rank. If I abort the launch there will be serious repercussions. Promises were made, promises that will go unfulfilled. And then of course, there is Sojang Kim's treachery."

Kim tried to break from Mugsy and Scipio's grasp, "This is preposterous. Why are you allowing him to continue?" He tried to break free again, but they held him tightly. "I am leaving the country with you. That was my deal with President Park!"

Kang carefully moved the blade away from his throat, "The Sojang simply cannot just disappear. As his commanding officer, I would be saddled with the blame."

"And with Sojang Kim dead?" replied Scipio.

"I will deliver his body to Pyongyang. They will believe I have uncovered a traitor and put a stop to his plot to start a war with the South. And to my allies, I will make the Sojang's betrayal of our cause known. The failure of the attack will hang around the neck of his corpse."

Kim ripped himself free, "I will not listen to anymore of this!"

Kang retreated a few steps, "Have you told your friends how you surrendered and agreed to cooperate?"

The color left Kim's face. He blinked nervously, "I ... had no intention of—"

Kang looked at Cho, "The Sojang had every intention of cooperating. In fact, if you did not step in when you did, you all would have been under arrest by now. The Sojang told me he had a change of heart."

All eyes fell on Kim.

"That is a lie! I never said that!"

Kang pressed, "Then why did you surrender? I will tell you why ... because you are a spineless traitor. First you betrayed me and then you were going to betray them. Isn't that true, Sojang?"

Kim shook his head vigorously. He wiped sweat from his brow as all eyes remained on him.

"The Sojang is nothing more than a traitor and a coward. He deserves his fate. He dies or the missiles launch!"

Cho held the ceramic blade out and pointed it at Kang. The Taejang remained still.

With the blade still pointing at Kang, Cho turned his head to face Kim. The Sojang stared back, oblivious at first, and then in terror.

The smooth weapon snapped out of Cho's hand and soared through the air.

Kim collapsed to his knees with a look of horror on his face, the dagger protruding from his chest.

Mugsy dropped to his side, "Have you lost your mind?!"

"The fate of my country is being decided here, Captain. A missile launch could start a war that leads to the death of hundreds of thousands ... even millions, including American lives." Cho turned to Kang, "Now, Taejang, you will fulfill your side of the agreement."

Kang folded his arms in front of him, "I said dead, Daeryeong. It is believed that a man can survive a knife wound to the heart, as long as the knife is not removed." He pointed at Kim, "Remove the knife and I will comply."

Cho turned back Kim. The Sojang was on his knees, partially supported by Mugsy, with his hands wrapped around the blade.

Mugsy held his hand up, "Don't take a step. Scipio, disarm him."

Scipio remained still.

"Scipio, that's an order!"

"Captain, with respect—"

"I said disarm him!"

Cho spun the machine gun hanging from his shoulder and pointed it at Scipio, "Drop your weapons … both of you … now!"

Scipio held his hands up, "Easy Cho." He placed his rifle on the floor then the other ceramic blade.

Mugsy wiggled the rifle off his shoulder and pushed it away. He pulled his blades and tossed them at Cho's feet.

Cho stepped in front of Kim looking down at him. The Sojang gazed up with pained eyes. He pushed Kim's hands from the knife handle and grasped it himself.

Behind them, Kang slowly stepped backwards towards his desk. Kim let his eyes fall from Cho. He alone saw the Taejang. Using his remaining strength, he pointed, "Stop him …!"

Cho let go of the blade in Kim's chest and spun around. Kang sprung across his desk and reached for something underneath.

Cho dove at him as a spring-loaded steel security wall blasted out of the floor. It slammed against another that descended from the ceiling. The wall separated Cho and Kang from the rest of the room.

The partition that sprung from the floor slammed Cho's legs with enough force to send him into a summersault. He landed hard on his back on the floor in front of the desk.

Kang never looked back. He opened a drawer and withdrew a pistol, but had to rotate himself on the desk to take aim.

Lying on his shoulders with his head cocked, Cho kicked the gun as Kang fired. The bullet chipped the cement ceiling and ricocheted.

Kang tried again to take aim. This time Cho reached up and grabbed Kang's hand, prying it from the pistol grip enough to depress the magazine-eject button. The clip fell onto Cho's stomach as Kang squeezed off the remaining round in the chamber.

The bullet grazed Cho's right cheek, just under his eye. He placed both legs under the front of Kang's desk and pushed up with all his might sending the desk toppling over, with Kang on top of it!

Kang stumbled to his feet still holding the pistol. He couldn't see Cho. He fired at the desk as he backed up to a bookcase next to the far wall. He kept firing until all he heard were the clicks of an empty gun.

Kang tossed the pistol away and pulled a few books down from the bookcase. He hit a button behind them. A motor whirled and the case began to open. He disappeared into the opening.

Cho saw the door beginning to close but had no time to reach it. He kicked Kang's chair at it. The chair thrust forward, rolled, and then fell over. Its back became wedged as the motorized door began to crush it. After a minute of strained whining, the motor finally died out.

Cho heard banging from the other side of the wall. He looked for the switch and found it under the opening of the desk. He threw the switch but nothing happened, so he reached under and ripped the wires from it. He used his teeth to strip them then twisted them together. A spark shot out as the security wall disappeared into its recesses almost as quickly as it appeared.

Mugsy and Scipio entered with their rifles pointed, first in search of Kang, and then at Cho.

Cho raised his hands.

"Kim is dead," yelled Mugsy. "You didn't have to rip the blade from his heart. He died in my arms."

Cho lowered his arms, "Captain, I am sorry Sojang Kim is dead, but—"

"You're sorry? You murdered him in cold blood."

"There was nothing else to be done."

Mugsy lowered his rifle, "Nothing else … you sure about that? We state our demands … Kang states his … one of them is, Kim has to die … and you throw a friggin' dagger into the Sojang's heart?! He says Kim was going to betray us and you took his at his word? How would you know there was nothing else to be done?!"

"I know, Captain. I know Kang. I studied the man. He would not have negotiated. And I did not just take him at his word. I watched the Sojang surrender to Kang, and I know from the guard where they detained him that he had told Kang that he was going to cooperate. That's why Kang didn't have him tortured."

"For all you know, Kim could have been playing him. You don't seem to have the same value for human life as we do, Cho. It's like, kill first, ask questions later with you, isn't it?"

Cho's face filled with anger, "I said before, the fate of my country is in the balance. It still is. We must get to Kang before he can reach his men. The moment the soldiers discover he is not in our custody, they will come barging through the door with guns blazing."

"He's right, Captain," said Scipio. "We have to grab Kang before he reaches his men or all bets are off."

Mugsy stepped close and spoke into Cho's ear, "You murdered that man."

Scipio examined the bookcase. He found the button and hit it. The door opened fully. The three stepped into a dark, narrow tunnel. Scipio shined a small flashlight.

"This tunnel has the same appearance as the other," said Mugsy. "They must meet up at some point."

Cho ran in, "We must move quickly."

CHAPTER 41

ASAN MEDICAL CENTER
POONGNAP-2DONG, SONGPA-GU
SEOUL
SOUTH KOREA
8:55 AM (LOCAL), WEDNESDAY, JUNE 05, 2013

A middle-aged, bespeckled doctor in blue surgical scrubs entered the waiting area and headed towards them. He kept his arms folded, "I am Doctor Sang-Ryong. You are Mr. Cris De Niro?"

De Niro and Michelle stood, "I'm Cris De Niro. This is Michelle Wang."

Dr. Sang-Ryong nodded to her, "I understand that my patient, Mr. John Francis works for you?"

De Niro nodded, "He's also one of my closest friends."

"I understand. Mr. De Niro, you realize that I cannot discuss Mr. Francis's medical condition with anyone other than his closest relative."

Michelle produced a folder from an attaché, "Doctor, this is a certified medical release, signed by Mr. Francis, authorizing any attending physician to discuss Mr. Francis's condition with Mr. De Niro. It stipulates that, upon Mr. Francis's incapacitation and inability to make such decisions on his own, Mr. De Niro is permitted to make medical decisions on his behalf. The folder also contains all of Mr. Francis's medical records."

Dr. Sang-Ryong opened the folder and scanned the contents, "Very well. Mr. De Niro, I am aware of your close association with President Park. Before I came to speak with you, the President personally called me."

"That was very nice of President Park."

"The President explained that your friend received his injuries while acting with the best interest of my country in mind. I would like to express my personal gratitude," he bowed his head.

De Niro nodded, "How is John, Doctor?"

"Mr. Francis's primary injuries were consistent with severe and repeated exposure to electric shock, most probably from normal household current. There were also multiple signs of blunt force trauma. The resulting swelling caused a traumatic brain injury. Emergency surgery became necessary to relieve elevated intracranial pressure."

De Niro blinked from tension, "Is he ... will he be okay?"

"We took further x-rays and a CAT scan. They show two small fragments of bone that have already caused ruptures to blood vessels. In their present location, if left untreated the bone fragments will almost certainly lead to more serious complications ... perhaps even death.

"We will need your authorization to perform another surgical procedure, in order to remove the fragments."

De Niro looked away putting a hand to his forehead. Michelle grasped his arm. He paused before turning to the doctor again, "How risky is the surgery?"

"There are definitely risks anytime surgery is performed on the brain. However, in this case, the risk of leaving those fragments inside his brain outweighs the risks of trying to remove them."

De Niro interlocked his fingers and placed them in front of his mouth. Michelle and Dr. Sang-Ryong could not tell whether he was praying or in deep thought.

Dr. Sang-Ryong cleared this throat, "Mr. De Niro, time is of the essence."

De Niro lowered his hands, "Do what you need to do, Doctor. Save my friend … please."

Dr. Sang-Ryong nodded, "I will have him prepped now."

"Can we see him Doc?"

"He is unconscious. Mr. De Niro, I should also explain that the injury that Mr. Francis sustained to his brain induced a coma. We expect the coma to persist even after successful removal of the skull fragments. If all goes well, Mr. Francis will be put on what is known as … a six-hour watch.

"Patients that lapse into comas for under six hours have typically sustained concussion-type injuries to their brains. The long-term outcome for those individuals is often excellent. However, if the coma lasts longer than six hours … there could be significant brain tissue injury."

De Niro lowered his head.

"Of course, when it comes to the brain, nothing is definitive. For now we need to focus on removing the fragments. Afterwards, we can only wait and see."

"*Pray* and see, Doctor. For me it will be pray and see."

Dr. Sang-Ryong patted his shoulder, "You may sit with him until they prep him for surgery."

De Niro nodded, "Thank you."

"He is in Room 628. I will have visitor's badges brought to you."

＊ ＊ ＊ ＊ ＊

De Niro and Michelle entered Room 628. They found a heavily bandaged man lying unconscious, alone in the darkened room, with an I.V. line inserted into his arm. They had to approach the side of the bed before they could tell it was Francis. Both of his eyes were black and blue and his face swollen and red.

De Niro swallowed hard, "His face …." Tears flowed from his eyes.

Michelle shed tears of her own.

De Niro bowed his head. It took awhile for him to compose himself. He finally looked up at Michelle, "I want you to return to the hotel. Check in with The Watchman and fill in ARCHANGEL. Everyone needs to know."

She wiped her tears away, "Will you be okay?"

He nodded, "I'll be here if you need me."

He waited for her to leave the room before getting to his knees and bowing his head.

CHAPTER 42

ADJUNCT TUNNEL
EAST OF THE MAIN TUNNEL ENTRANCE
HEADQUARTERS OF TAEJANG KANG KUM-SOK
PUNGGYE-RI NUCLEAR TEST SITE
KILJU COUNTY, NORTH HAMGYONG PROVINCE
NORTH KOREA
9:00 AM (LOCAL), WEDNESDAY, JUNE 05, 2013

Scipio increased his pace until he was alongside of Mugsy.

"I thought you had our six?"

Scipio nodded towards Cho, walking 10 meters ahead, "I do, yours and his."

Mugsy glanced back with annoyance, "Your point?"

"Mugs, he made a judgment call for the sake of his country. One you or I often have to make … and *have* made for the sake of ours."

Mugsy stopped in his tracks, "He didn't even attempt to negotiate."

"He said Kim was about to cooperate with Kang. Who knows

what would've happened if we didn't get to him first."

"He said ... and you believe him?"

"Mugs, there's no telling how long we have before those missiles launch and we still don't know the target. We have to trust him to be successful and survive this."

Mugsy started walking. Scipio trailed a step behind.

"He killed Kim, Scipio, and we got nothing in return ... nothing! I was put in charge of this mission. That made me responsible for everyone's well-being, including Kim's. The decision should have been mine, not his."

"Maybe he did you a favor."

Mugsy stopped again. He turned and glared.

"Captain ...." Cho's subdued voice cut through the darkness from up ahead.

They caught up to him. Cho was standing with his back against the tunnel wall where it intersected with a wider tunnel. The wider one had rail tracks running down its center. He thumbed over his shoulder, "That is the main tunnel. Take a look ... we are too late."

Mugsy and Scipio peered around the wall. In the distance, they saw Taejang Kang approaching the well-lit platform. He was calling out. After a moment, two soldiers appeared on the platform.

Scipio aimed his rifle. Mugsy did the same.

Cho put his hands on their shoulders, "What are you doing? They are over 100 meters away."

Mugsy brushed his hand off, "The Captain and I are proficient with AKs. We can down them."

"And if you miss ...? Even if you hit them, every North Korean soldier in this facility will be alerted!"

Mugsy removed his hand, "We'll have to take that chance. Or did you forget ... the fate of your country is at stake."

The soldiers bent to help Kang onto the platform.

"It's now or never," said Scipio. "They haven't radioed for help yet."

"The report of the rifles will echo throughout the entire tunnel," said Cho, "they won't have to!"

"There are three of them, Cho" ordered Mugsy. "Take aim ... on the Taejang. Scip, I'll take the one on the left."

"But we need him alive!"

"Now, Cho …!"

Cho raised his rifle.

Scipio held up his fist, "On my count. Three … two … one … fire!"

The three pulled their triggers together. Their shots rang out as one very loud blast.

The bullets zipped through the darkness. In less than a second both soldiers toppled head-first off of the platform. The Taejang disappeared from sight.

Mugsy and Scipio took off running, "Come on, we have to get to them quickly."

Cho followed.

Mugsy was the first to reach the platform. He found Kang's body lying in a pool of his own blood.

Scipio and Cho caught up.

"Your round sliced through the Taejang's carotid artery. He'll be dead in the next minute or two."

Cho looked down at Kang, "We needed him alive. Now there is no way to stop the launch."

Mugsy faced him, "We had no choice … this time."

"There may be a way," said Scipio, "but first we have to hide these bodies … in a hurry."

Mugsy pointed to the railcar, "How about under the radiation suits?"

Scipio lifted one of the soldiers, "There's so much blood, but it'll have to do. Grab one and follow me."

Each man dumped a body into the back of the railcar. Scipio covered the bodies with the suits and pointed back to the platform, "Cho, soldiers may come to investigate the noise. You're still wearing the captain of the guard credentials."

"But my uniform is stained with the Taejang's blood."

"Tell them there was an explosion deeper in the tunnel and you were hit by flying debris. The radiation there should keep them from investigating right away."

Scipio turned to Mugsy, "We have to ride the railcar back and park it near the intersection with the smaller tunnel."

He turned back to Cho as they took off in the railcar, "Join us back in the Taejang's office as soon as you can."

Cho watched as they rode off into the darkness. Within seconds, soldiers came running onto the platform with rifles pointed.

Cho shouted at them, "Help me up!"

Bewildered, two of the soldiers complied, extending their arms down. Cho grabbed hold and lifted himself onto the platform. He let them all see his name tag and rank.

A Taewi stepped forward and saluted, "Sir, we heard a loud bang."

"There was an explosion near one of the test epicenters."

"Sir, your face is bleeding."

Cho brought his hand up to the gunshot wound to his cheek, "I was hit by flying debris."

"From so far away …?" The Taewi sounded skeptical. He paused, "You should seek medical attention."

"I will."

The Taewi looked around, "Sir, there were guards on duty here. Have you seen them?"

Cho paused before replying, "No, I have not."

"Sir, if I may ask, what were you doing here?"

A voice crackled from a walkie-talkie radio.

A soldier standing behind the Taewi pointed below the platform, "Taewi, it is coming from down there somewhere."

The Taewi gripped his rifle never taking his eyes off of Cho, "Shine your light."

The soldier looked from the Taewi to Cho.

Cho nodded his approval.

The soldier leaned over the edge pointing his flashlight at the dim rails below. The light found a ruddy puddle.

"Taewi … it is blood!"

The soldier's shout distracted the Taewi, making him turn for just an instant. It was all Cho needed. He deflected the Taewi's rifle and delivered a punch to his throat.

Startled, the soldier dropped his flashlight and spun around, raising his rifle. Cho responded by pointing the rifle still in the Taewi's hands and making him pull the trigger.

Their shots rang out in quick succession. The soldier fell backwards off of the platform.

The Taewi struggled with Cho, with one hand holding his throat. The two wrestled to a standstill until Cho pulled a dagger from the scabbard on the Taewi's belt and stabbed him in the heart. With the Taewi still on his feet, he kicked the dying man off the platform.

Dazed, Cho stumbled to the wall and used it to prop himself up. He touched his side then looked at his hand. It was covered in blood. After a deep breath, he jumped down from the platform. His knees buckled.

Cho staggered to his feet and started walking along the rail tracks. He didn't make it 10 meters before he fell on his face.

CHAPTER 43

OFFICE OF THE TAEJANG
PUNGGYE-RI NUCLEAR TEST SITE
KILJU COUNTY, NORTH HAMGYONG PROVINCE
NORTH KOREA
11:00 AM (LOCAL), WEDNESDAY, JUNE 05, 2013

Mugsy continued looking out into the tunnel for several minutes before throwing the switch to close the bookcase door. He returned to the Taejang's desk which had been placed back on its feet. Scipio was kneeling in front of it.

The security wall clanged shut.

Mugsy waited for Scipio to get to his feet, "Any progress?"

Scipio held up a broken flat screen monitor, "This is fried, but I think the hard drive might've survived. I was able to interface with it via double-B, but I'll need Johnny-F's help to tap into the missiles' command and control. The problem is we can't get reception down here." He nodded toward the bookcase, "No sign of the Cho?"

Mugsy frowned shaking his head, "No. Something went wrong. He should've been back here an hour ago. What I can't figure is why they're not breaking down the doors by now."

Scipio pulled a cable from a mini spool built into the bottom of his cell phone and plugged it into the server, "They must not have discovered the Taejang's body yet. The question is … is Cho dead or captured … or …."

"Or …?"

"Or maybe he's wounded and unable to reach us."

Mugsy began pacing and rubbing the back of his neck. He looked up at the security wall, "We're like sardines in here, waiting for the soldiers to pry this can open. Saddle up and take the server with you. We're getting out of here."

Scipio unplugged and recoiled the cable, "Where to?"

Mugsy picked a rifle up. He pulled back on the slide before slinging it over his shoulder, "Our first priority is to stop the launch. We have to contact John, so we need to get to the first floor."

Scipio slung a rifle over his shoulder and picked up the server. "We can take the dead man's trolley back to the platform and look for Cho while we're there. Then we have to find a way back onto the elevator. Any ideas …?"

Mugsy let bandages roll from his hand, "The mummy look worked before."

"That's arguable."

Mugsy began wrapping Scipio's face, "If we can make it upstairs, we'll need to find somewhere you can tap into the internal network and stay awhile."

Scipio winked, "Glad to hear you have all the details worked out."

CHAPTER 44

ASAN MEDICAL CENTER
POONGNAP-2DONG, SONGPA-GU
SEOUL
SOUTH KOREA
12:00 PM (LOCAL), WEDNESDAY, JUNE 05, 2013

Dr. Sang-Ryong walked into Room 628 to De Niro who was sitting in the corner.

No emotion on his face.

"Doctor ... how did it go?"

"We successfully removed the bone fragments before they did any further damage."

De Niro dropped his head and closed his eyes.

Thank you, Father!

What now?"

"There is nothing else to do, except wait to see if the swelling shrinks. You remember what I said about six hours?"

"I do."

"Consider the clock started."

Two orderlies rolled Francis and an I.V. stand into the room. They rolled the gurney next to the bed then transferred his motionless body.

Dr. Sang-Ryong walked over to De Niro, "Your friend will not revive from the anesthesia for awhile. Why don't you get something to eat?"

De Niro stood, "Thank you, Doc … I'm not hungry. I'm grateful for all you've done."

Dr. Sang-Ryong nodded, "I will remain on duty for awhile. Please, have me paged if you need me." He left the room.

De Niro grabbed Francis's hand and bowed his head again.

CHAPTER 45

TUNNEL ENTRANCE
HEADQUARTERS OF TAEJANG KANG KUM-SOK
PUNGGYE-RI NUCLEAR TEST SITE
KILJU COUNTY, NORTH HAMGYONG PROVINCE
NORTH KOREA
12:00 PM (LOCAL), WEDNESDAY, JUNE 05, 2013

Mugsy and Scipio knelt near the tunnel wall. The area around them was pitch-dark.

Mugsy used his index and middle finger to point, "Soldiers … two in front of the platform and one on each side."

"What are the ones in front looking at? Wait, those are bodies."

"Cho …?"

Scipio focused the zoom on his phone's camera, "No way to see from here."

Mugsy crouched and took off, "Let's get closer."

They stopped just short of where the area became illuminated.

Scipio pointed, "Mugs, a body … right there."

Mugsy tilted his head and put his face close to the floor, "That's

Cho."

Scipio continued to scan the platform, "None of the soldiers have gone for help yet and they can't radio from here. We could either wait and let them evac those bodies … and hope they don't return with friends or …."

"We take them down now," Mugsy picked up a stone and tossed it. He hit Cho in the face. He didn't respond.

"Alright, let's draw the soldiers closer … get ready," he picked up another stone and tossed it. It bounced on the ground near Cho's body and had the desired effect. The soldiers turned and looked. One waved the others forward.

Mugsy raised his rifle, "I'll take the ones approaching … you take the one in the rear. Don't shoot until I do."

"Roger that."

The soldiers shined flashlights. Their beams came within inches of Mugsy and Scipio. One of the soldiers came upon Cho. He called to the others.

They huddled around him.

Mugsy took aim and rattled off three rounds. The soldiers' bodies fell around Cho's. The soldier near the platform raised his rifle, but never got off a shot.

Scipio downed him with one round.

Mugsy and Scipio moved in on Cho. Scipio stood watch while Mugsy examined him.

"He's alive, but he's been shot in the gut. The blood isn't dark … usually means his liver isn't damaged. That's a good thing. And he balled his shirt into the wound. That was smart. It stopped some of the bleeding, but the bullet's still inside." Mugsy looked up, "He could make it if we can get him to the infirmary and get a doctor to remove the bullet."

"You're call, Captain."

Mugsy gently cradled Cho and lifted him, "I'll carry him. You lead and do the talking."

* * * * *

Scipio stopped at the door to the infirmary and turned to Mugsy, "I was gonna say we've been lucky, but I know Cris would correct me. We've been blessed ... so far, every soldier we've passed was lower in rank. Once inside, the doctor will outrank Cho. He might not be easy to fool."

"Got it. Let's do this, he's getting heavy."

Scipio threw the door open and spoke in Korean, "Where is the doctor. This man has been injured!"

A balding man wearing a white lab coat appeared from the adjacent room. I am Doctor Seonu, "Who are you?

Scipio approached keeping his hands fixed on his rifle, "This is the Captain of the Guard. He was shot in the tunnels."

The doctor noticed Scipio's hands, "What is the matter with your faces? Who treated you?"

"Doctor, the Captain is seriously wounded."

The doctor stared back as Scipio looked around. He spotted two nurses and one other man in a lab coat.

The doctor pointed to a table, "Lay him up there."

Mugsy set Cho down gently then took a position at the door. The doctor came alongside Cho, "I do not know this man. Who are you people?"

No one replied.

The doctor turned to find his staff with their hands raised in the air. Mugsy covered them.

Scipio motioned to the doctor with his rifle, "You will remove the bullet. If he dies, you all die. Do you understand?"

"Are you the ones that kidnapped the Taejang? Is the Taejang alright?"

Scipio pressed the barrel of the rifle against the doctor's head, "If he dies, all of you die. Do you understand?"

The doctor nodded. He waved his staff over then turned again to Scipio and spoke English, "We need to operate on him immediately. Our surgery is in the next room."

Scipio didn't reply.

"You are obviously the Americans I heard about. Among other duties, I am the Taejang's personal physician. He sort of ... drafted me and had me assigned here for the duration of his stay."

"Where did you learn to speak English?"

"Like I said, I am the Taejang's personal physician. Before he selected me for the position, I was given a Japanese passport and sent to Oxford in England to study medicine."

But, weren't you were already a doctor?"

"Indeed, I was. However, the Taejang considered North Korean doctors inferior to western doctors."

Scipio nodded then motioned to Cho, "Do what you need to do, but remember what I said." Scipio grabbed the doctor by his arm, "How long will this take?"

"I have no idea."

"Give me an estimate."

"I cannot estimate until we scan him and find where the bullet is lodged."

"Do it."

Mugsy checked the hall before locking the door, "What did the doctor say?"

"He can't estimate how long until they find the bullet. He speaks English, by the way. One thing though … he asked if we were the ones that kidnapped the Taejang. He said kidnapped, not murdered."

"So, they still might not have discovered the bodies yet."

Scipio scratched the bandages on his head, "These bandages are making me crazy-itchy. What now, Captain?"

"Now … we sit tight for as long as we can. If they think we're still holding Kang in his office that security door should keep them busy for a long time. The Taejang must have designed it to withstand a tank."

"Let's hope they don't come across the bodies or the adjunct tunnel."

Mugsy nodded, "Meanwhile, see if you can tap into the network from here. Maybe you can get communications out. I'll check to see if there are any scheduled appointments."

* * * * *

Mugsy checked the time on his cell.

4 PM.

He looked over at Scipio, "Any progress?"

"I was able to tap into the network, but negative on communications outside the facility, at least from here."

Dr. Seonu appeared from the surgery in blood-stained scrubs. Mugsy motioned to Scipio to watch the door, before approaching him, "How is he, Doc?"

"The Captain of the Guard … is stable, but still in serious condition. He was very fortunate. The bullet didn't impact any vital organs. It ricocheted off of his rib, fracturing it, but lost a lot of momentum before lodging near one of his kidneys. I was able to remove it without further complications. It was also fortunate you knew his blood type. He required several transfusions."

"Can he be moved?"

"Now …? Absolutely not! He is still unconscious and has sutures both inside and out. He must be monitored in case of hemorrhage."

Mugsy continued to stare.

Dr. Seonu pointed, "If you try to move him now, he will die."

"What's up, Captain," Scipio asked as he approached.

"The Doc says Cho is stable but serious, and can't be moved now." He turned to the doctor, "What's the minimum time until we can move him."

"I do not like to guess, but if you want a best-case scenario, 12 hours."

Scipio laughed, "*Twelve hours* … we might as well enlist in the North Korean army."

There was a knock at the door. Scipio took position at the side of it.

Mugsy faced the others with his index finger to his lips and waved the doctor over to follow him to the door. "Whoever it is, get rid of them."

The doctor pursed his lips, but nodded. He cracked the door open.

They heard the voice of a young man.

Mugsy lifted his chin.

Scipio mouthed the word, "Delivery."

The doctor closed the door with a folder in his hand.

Mugsy took the folder and examined it, "Doc, I want you to put the infirmary on quarantine for the next 12 hours. I don't want anyone else approaching this room."

"What reason can I give?"

"Tell anyone that asks there was an explosion inside the tunnels. Tell them you're treating casualties exposed to high levels of radiation. Also, say the tunnels are flooded with radiation and off limits until further notice."

Dr. Seonu nodded, "Understood."

"Scip, escort the rest of the staff back into the surgery."

Scipio herded everyone into the next room.

Mugsy locked the door.

Twelve hours …

CHAPTER 46

INFIRMARY
HEADQUARTERS OF TAEJANG KANG KUM-SOK
PUNGGYE-RI NUCLEAR TEST SITE
KILJU COUNTY, NORTH HAMGYONG PROVINCE
NORTH KOREA
5:00 AM (LOCAL), THURSDAY, JUNE 06, 2013

Scipio entered the surgery. He found Mugsy standing with his head bowed and eyes closed next to Cho, lying unconscious on a gurney. He waited until Mugsy opened his eyes and turned to him, "What's the status out there?"

"It's starting to hit the fan. They still haven't discovered the Taejang's body, but someone finally took command – a sojwa … equal to a major. With the Taejang, the Sojang, and the Captain of the Guard all gone, there was no command structure. And just before we arrived, Kang issued orders forbidding any communication with anyone outside the facility. That helped us, 'til now."

"Then where'd this sojwa materialize from?"

"I was trying to find that out myself. It seems he was ordered directly by Kang to oversee the movement of a NoDong missile battery."

Mugsy rubbed his chin, "A NoDong missile battery."

"If it's the one we think it is, it's reasonable to assume it's in place and operational now or else the sojwa wouldn't have returned.

"In any case, as soon as the sojwa was brought up to speed on the situation here, he ordered the use of torches to cut through the security wall."

Mugsy exhaled audibly, "How much time do we have?"

Scipio checked his phone, "According to them … 20 minutes. On top of that, the sojwa just called to check on the status of the quarantine. He was about to head down, but the doc convinced him if he did, he'd be quarantined too.

"I think we better get a move on now, Mugs."

"I think so too. I gave Cho an extra hour to rest, but the doc still isn't happy about moving him. Meanwhile, I had the doc administer anesthesia to the rest of the staff. They'll be out for a couple of hours."

Scipio paused, "Mugs, they're cutting through the wall. We have to go with my plan."

"I don't like the idea of leaving you here. We can wait for you deeper in the tunnels. I can stay ahead of them."

"Captain, once I make it upstairs the facility's entire compliment of soldiers will be between us. I'll have a better chance finding my own way out than trying to catch up to you in the tunnels."

"*Once* you make it upstairs? You mean *if*. Scip, trying to fool 'em again with the head bandage is pushing it. Odds are you won't make it onto the elevator."

"Don't worry about that. I have a plan, but I'll need the doctor. Think you can take care of Cho on your own?"

"The doc said there's nothing else to do except make sure he doesn't bounce around too much. I can do that without him."

"Good. You better get a move on then."

Mugsy held out his hand, "Godspeed, Scip."

"You too, Captain. Once I'm clear of the compound, I'll contact you via double-B to coordinate a rendezvous. And Mugs … if it comes down to it …," he peered down at Cho, "save yourself."

Scipio opened the door and checked the corridor, "All clear."

Mugsy pushed Cho's gurney out of the infirmary. They disappeared around a corner, heading in the direction of the tunnel.

Dr. Seonu was sitting next to his sleeping staff. Scipio walked over, "Okay, this is how it's gonna go. If you want to survive this, you're gonna come with me and do *exactly* what I say … nothing more, nothing less. Understood?"

Dr. Seonu nodded.

"Good, now, you have a Geiger counter somewhere, don't you?"

"Yes, we have one, but where are we going?"

"Fetch it and come with me."

* * * * *

Mugsy reached the platform with Cho without running into soldiers.

Between the quarantine and the commotion at Kang's office, there's not a soul in this entire area.

He looked up.

Thanks!

Carefully, he lifted Cho from the gurney and placed him on the platform. Then he lowered the gurney down to the tracks, jumped down, lifted Cho, and placed him back onto it.

Cho opened his eyes. He grabbed Mugsy's arm, "Captain … where …?"

"Easy Cho, you took a bullet. We had a doctor remove it. We're in the tunnels now. It's time we say goodbye to this place."

"Where is Scipio?"

"He's heading to the main floor to try and make contact with our CIO."

Cho squeezed his arm, "Why are we not waiting for him?"

Mugsy removed his hand, "Listen … we don't have much time. The soldiers are cutting through the Taejang's security wall. It's only a matter of time before they find the adjunct tunnel … and us."

Cho tried to sit up but Mugsy pushed him down, "You hate me for what I did to the Sojang, yet you are risking your life to save me?"

"I don't hate you, Cho. What you did to the Sojang … your judgment will come, just like mine. Now, hold on tight 'cause I'm gonna have to race to the railcar."

Mugsy pushed the gurney as fast as the rocky tunnel floor would allow him. Twice he ran over rocks large enough to send Cho's body bouncing, but Cho held on, wincing in pain. When they reached the railcar, with his help, Mugsy lifted him from the gurney.

Mugsy went to the back and dumped the bodies then grabbed two radiation suits. It took him almost ten minutes to place the suit on Cho before donning one himself. When he was done, he looked back at the adjunct tunnel and saw no one. He looked to Heaven and floored the accelerator.

* * * * *

Standing in front of the torched hole cut into the security wall, the burly Sojwa grimaced. He barked to the soldiers inside Taejang Kang's office, "There must be another way out … find it!"

One of the soldiers noticed a broken chair and scratch marks in the bookcase. He investigated and saw overturned books, "Sojwa!"

The Sojwa marched over and reached behind the books. He threw a switch and the door swung open. He drew his pistol, "Follow me!"

Upon reaching the intersection with the main tunnel, the soldiers fanned out. It took only a moment for one of them to cry out, "Sojwa … bodies!"

The Sojwa turned one of the bodies over to see the face, "It is the Taejang. Everyone … quiet!"

He placed his ear to the rail, "They are in a railcar. Quickly, we must contact the depot!"

* * * * *

Scipio adjusted the jury-rigged straps holding the Taejang's server to his back. Approaching the elevator's guard station, he spoke softly into the doctor's ear, "Remember all I told you to say."

Dr. Seonu nodded. He waited until he was sure the guard was watching then began pointing, "Check this entire area. Then we must do the same on the main floor."

With the doctor looking over his shoulder, Scipio fiddled with the controls on the Geiger counter.

The guard approached with a hand on his holster, "What are you doing?"

Neither looked up as the doctor answered, "The explosion in the tunnels released radiation. We must measure the levels here and on the main floor."

The guard eyed his bandaged face with suspicion as Scipio waved the counter's wand from side to side.

The doctor brushed the guard aside, "Please give us room."

"What happened to his face?"

"Radiation burns, quite terrible to behold. We must check the entire facility or others may suffer the same fate."

Scipio held up the Geiger counter and shook his head with emphasis.

The doctor pointed to the elevator, "Apparently, you are safe here. We must check the main floor now."

The guard hesitated, "Doctor, the Sojwa's orders were to let no one onto the elevator."

"The Sojwa is unaware of the radiation leak. I will inform him as soon as we complete our sweep. Now, unless you want to put everyone's life at risk upstairs, I suggest you let us onto the elevator now and give us the key. When we exit, we will have to deactivate it until we are sure the floor is clear."

The guard tried his radio twice with no success.

Dr. Seonu pointed at the radio, "The radiation is also interfering with communication in and out of the compound."

Unsure of what to do, the guard inserted the key and opening the elevator door. Scipio stepped on first, waving the wand in front of him. The doctor followed.

Upon reaching the main floor, Scipio opened a panel, inserted the key, and turned it. The elevator doors remained open. The floor indicator read "EFS."

He led the doctor out and kept his voice low, "I placed it into fire service mode. No one downstairs will be able to access it. Now, I need you to lead me to the Communications Room."

Dr. Seonu following Scipio's directions spoke loudly in case anyone was monitoring them, "Follow me. The radiation leakage is most severe on the east side of the building."

Scipio followed, waving the wand as they went. They drew a few curious eyes, but the doctor ordered everyone back to work as they passed.

They turned a corner at the end of the longest corridor and the doctor pointed to a door. Scipio adjusted the sensitivity on the counter before bursting in. The counter emitted a frantic clicking.

The doctor waved his arms, "Leave this room immediately! There has been a radiation leak."

The room emptied quickly as everyone anxiously scurried into the hall.

Scipio locked the door and turned to the doctor, "I'm surprised that worked so well."

The doctor grinned, "Nothing conjures more fear in a nuclear test site than a radiation leak."

Scipio pointed to a chair, "Sit, Doc, while I do what I need to do."

Scipio examined the equipment. He started throwing switches and pulling wires, "First things first, the only person communicating in or out of this facility will be me."

He set the Taejang's computer on a table then plugged it in. It took a few minutes to establish an internet link.

While he waited, he took his phone out and looked at the reception meter. It was low but registering. He made a call, "Father, it's Scipio."

* * * * *

Everyone on the train gathered around Father Kim, as he held his hand up to quiet them, "Scipio, is everyone okay?"

"Listen Father, I don't have much time. The Captain is heading your way with Cho. Cho is injured, so they could use some help. They should reach the station in about an hour."

"What about you and Sojang Kim?"

"The Sojang is dead. I'll have to meet up with you at the Paegam-Nodongjagu Station. I want you to get underway the moment the Captain and Cho are aboard. I'll contact you as soon as I can to arrange a rendezvous."

* * * * *

Scipio could hear the sadness in the priest's tone, "I understand. Remember though, the westbound train departs from Paegam-Nodongjagu at 9:30 this morning. If we miss it, there is not another until noon."

"I know. I want all of you on that train whether I make it or not, understood?"

Father Kim didn't reply.

"Father, once Captain Ricci gets there he'll be in charge. He understands the need for all of you to be on that train and knows enough not to wait for me. But if he doesn't make it to you, you have to promise to get on that train, okay?"

"Okay, but I pray that will not be necessary."

"One more thing … I shut all communication here down except for mine, but I'm not sure how long it'll remain that way. If it goes back up, the station will be notified of the Captain and Colonel's escape through the tunnel. It's imperative you make contact and help them onto the train. Then take off. Tell the conductor you want him to make the train ready for departure immediately."

"I will. God be with you."

"With you, too, Father."

Scipio made another call.

* * * * *

The Sojwa emerged from the tunnels leading soldiers to the guard station near the elevator. The guard on duty snapped to attention.

The Sojwa ignored his salute and lifted the phone.

The guard spoke up, "Sir, all communication out of the site is down due to radiation leakage."

The Sojwa hung the phone up with a puzzled expression, "What radiation leakage?"

The guard's discomfort became apparent, "Sojwa, the doctor said there was radiation leakage caused by the explosion in the tunnels."

"What explosion?"

"Uh ... sir, the doctor told me there was an explosion deep in the tunnels."

"We just came from the tunnels. We found the Taejang's body along with bodies of soldiers, but no indication of any explosion."

The color left the guard's face, "Sojwa, I am merely relaying the information I was told."

"By the doctor ...."

"Yes, sir, by the doctor."

"And where is the doctor now? I understood he was in the infirmary and the infirmary was under quarantine."

"No sir, the doctor went up to the main floor with an attendant. They were checking for radiation."

The Sojwa's face reddened with anger. He stepped in front of the elevator doors. "Open it."

The guard blinked frantically, "Sir, the doctor took the emergency key. The elevator is in EFS mode now. We cannot access it from down here."

The Sojwa's eyes reddened with fury. He raised his voice, "Call someone upstairs and tell them to send it down!"

"I'm afraid no one can send it down except for the doctor. He has the key."

"Contact the doctor ... now!"

The guard lifted the handset. After several moments he hung it up, "Sojwa ... the phones are dead."

The Sojwa took out his cell phone.

"Sir, our cell phones are useless down here."

The Sojwa's cheeks reddened as much as his eyes.

A soldier came running up the corridor, "Sojwa, we found the doctor's staff unconscious in the infirmary."

"Unconscious …?"

A second soldier ran up from the Captain of the Guard's office, "Sir, we found bodies inside the Captain's office, including the Captain's body."

The Sojwa banged his fist against the elevator door. He thought for a moment then turned to the guard, "I want these doors pried open."

"Sir, the doors are reinforced. If I may suggest, there are stairs leading up to the elevator maintenance room that will give us access to the shaft itself."

"Show us!"

CHAPTER 47

ROOM 628
ASAN MEDICAL CENTER
POONGNAP-2DONG, SONGPA-GU
SEOUL
SOUTH KOREA
6:00 AM (LOCAL), THURSDAY, JUNE 06, 2013

"Cris … don't leave me here."
"I won't, honey, don't worry."
"Why aren't you coming to get me?"
"I'm coming, baby, I'm coming. Just hold on …."
"Oh Cris, I love you."
"I love you too, baby."
"I can't breathe … Cris, there's smoke and fire everywhere."
"Lisa, I'm coming. Don't leave me …."
"I'M BURNING! CRIS, THE BUILDING … IT'S FALLING …
IT'S FALLING!! Kiss the babies for me … I love you …."
"LISA, I'M COMING … DON'T LEAVE ME! LISAAAA!!!"
"Mr. De Niro … wake up, Sir!"

"LIS—" De Niro opened his tear-filled eyes and sprung up.

A nurse stared back at him, her hands on his shoulders, "Mr. De Niro, are you okay, Sir?"

De Niro found himself sitting in a chair next to Johnny-F. He wiped sweat from his forehead and looked over at his sleeping friend.

The nurse persisted, "Are you okay, Mr. De Niro? Can I get you something?"

"No … nothing Nurse, thank you. I'm okay. I must've nodded off. How is my friend?"

"No change. He remains in a coma. I am sorry."

De Niro nodded. He watched the nurse leave the room then got to his feet and stretched. He walked into the bathroom and splashed water on his face. His hands were shaking.

He stared into the mirror at his bloodshot eyes.

Another nightmare … I haven't had one in awhile.

I'm so sorry I couldn't get to you, my love. I miss you so much.

His cell phone rang.

He wiped the tears away, "Hey Michelle."

"Hi Cris. How's John?"

De Niro walked back to the bed, "No change."

"How long has it been?"

He tried to keep his voice steady, "Eighteen hours."

There was a pause, "Any word from Mugsy?"

Lord … I can feel her tension.

"I'm sorry, Michelle, nothing yet."

The line became quiet.

"Michelle, don't lose hope. We'll continue to pray." He changed the subject, "Did you fill everyone in?"

"Yes, I have. They all said they're praying."

Is this the real life? Is this just fantasy?

Queen's Bohemian Rhapsody started blaring from Johnny-F's phone.

Caught in a landslide, No escape from reality.

"Cris, what is that?"

Open your eyes …

"Where's my phone … Does anyone see my phone?"

De Niro let the phone fall from his face, "John …?"

Francis looked over at him, "Cris … that's my phone. Hey, where the heck are we?"

De Niro put his hand on Francis's head, "JOHN!!" he leaned over and kissed his forehead.

Mama, just killed a man, put a gun against his head …

Francis shot him a curious look, "Nice to see you too, Cris. Do me a favor, hand me my phone."

De Niro put his phone back to his ear, "Michelle …."

"Cris, is that John I heard?!"

"It is! He just woke up. Listen, let me go."

"I'll be right there."

The line went dead.

Mama, life had just begun …

But now I've gone and thrown it all away.

De Niro grabbed Francis's phone. He looked at the caller I.D., "Scipio! It's Cris."

"Cris, I was looking for John."

"He's right here. How are you guys?"

"We're okay. Listen, Cris, I'm in a bit of a hurry. I need to speak to John now."

"Scip, John was critically wounded. I'm here with him, in the hospital."

"The hospital … what's his condition?"

De Niro looked down at Francis.

This is going to be news to him too.

"A North Korean operative attacked John in our hotel suite. He tortured him … with electricity then beat him.

"He needed brain surgery. He was in a coma for the last eighteen hours. Your phone call just brought him out of it."

"Can you put him on?"

"Scipio, did you hear what I said?"

"Cris," Francis reached up, "Let me speak to him."

"John, are you sure? I should call the doctor."

"Forget the doctor, I'm hungry. Do me a favor … let me speak to Scipio and get me … get me … what time is it, anyway?"

"It's 6 AM. I'll have some breakfast sent up," he put the phone back to his ear, "Scipio, here's John."

He handed the phone to him. Francis hit the speaker button and set it down next to him.

Scipio's voice crackled through, "John, you up to this?"

Francis tried to sit up, "Hi to you too, Scipio. Apparently, I had a little brain surgery, but I'm good now."

"John, I'm a little pressed for time. Glad you're okay, but I need to know if you're up for this."

Francis waved to De Niro and mouthed the words, "Help me." De Niro helped him sit up, "I guess it depends on what *this* is."

"I'm still inside the Punggye-Ri facility. Cho was injured so Mugsy had to evacuate him. Taejang Kang is dead. Listen John, we were able to take the Musudan missiles out of play, but Kang had another missile battery positioned and ready for launch. We have no idea where it is, or what the target is, and only an estimate of when the launch will take place. I have his desktop computer connected to both the internal network and internet, but the whole thing is locked."

De Niro broke in, "Scipio, Cris, what's the estimate to launch?"

"We believe within the next 24 hours."

Francis gazed at De Niro, "What do you want from me, Scip?"

"I need you to override Kang's password and help me find any intel on that battery."

Francis rubbed his temples. De Niro grabbed him by the shoulders, "Scipio, hold on. John, you okay?"

Francis didn't reply.

"I'm gonna go get the doc—"

Francis grabbed his sleeve, "Cris, I'm alright. I just got dizzy … and I got a headache that could kill a mule. Make sure they bring me some aspirin with my breakfast, will ya?"

"Not a problem."

"Good enough. Sorry about that Scip, I'm back."

"John, I asked if you're up to this. Don't bullshit me. The situation here is tenuous enough. If you can't do it, put me through to someone on your staff."

"You're wasting time. Interface your Double-B with the desktop and let me get to work."

Scipio pulled the wire from his phone and plugged it into the computer. After a moment, Francis saw the link on his phone. He placed the cursor in the password box and tapped an app.

"This could take awhile."

"How long? Give me an estimate."

"I created the decryption algorithms myself. It's never taken longer than 12 hours before."

"John, I don't have 12 hours. I'd be blessed to have one."

"Then all we can do is pray." Francis looked at De Niro, "Isn't that right, Cris?"

De Niro nodded solemnly, "Scipio, can you keep the line open?"

"Affirmative."

"Alright, just holler when you gotta go. Meanwhile, I'll put in a prayer."

"Not sure I'll be able to holler. A whisper may have to do. In any case, prayers are appreciated. In fact, I think I'll say one of my own."

An orderly rolled in a cart of food. Michelle Wang walked in behind him.

Francis rubbed his hands together, "Ah … food! I feel like I haven't eaten in a month. First, let me have those aspirin. Hiya Michelle."

She stared at him from the foot of the bed.

He noticed, "What's the matter with you? You're not exactly catching me at my best, ya know."

She rushed over and kissed his cheek. Her eyes were watery, "I'm so glad to see you're awake. How are you?"

Francis put pills in his mouth and washed them down with water, then lifted the cover off the plate, "As soon as I consume these magnificent eggs and toast, I'll tell you."

De Niro walked over and took her hands, "Michelle … Scipio's on the line. He said Mugsy and he are okay … for now."

Color left Michelle's face. Her knees buckled. De Niro steadied her, "Michelle … here, sit down."

"I'm sorry. I threw up this morning. I guess I'm a little light-headed still."

"Have you eaten?"

"No."

"No …? Stay here," De Niro hurried out of the room and returned with another food tray, "Eat that and drink the apple juice. That's an order."

She nodded, "Where are they?"

"Scipio's still in Punggye-Ri, but he said Mugsy evacuated with Cho already."

"Can we contact him?"

"Let's ask him. Scipio. Michelle just walked in. She wants to know if we can contact Mugsy."

Scipio kept his voice low, "Hi Michelle. No, they're evacuating through a tunnel system. We won't be able to reach 'em until they're out of it."

She let out a deep breath and nodded, "Okay, bring me up to speed."

De Niro handed her the apple juice, "Finish this and I'll fill you in. John's using one of his decryption apps to try and hack into Kang's computer. Scipio said they were successful in neutralizing the Musudan missiles, but Taejang Kang apparently had a contingency plan. He positioned a second missile battery equipped with shorter range, but more accurate missiles … location unknown, target unknown. The missiles are expected to launch within hours. Scipio had to remain at the compound to give us any ability to stop the launch."

"How long does he have?"

"He thinks … no more than an hour."

"An hour …? John, can you gain access in that time?"

Francis had to swallow the food in his mouth before replying, "My app never let me down before."

De Niro took a seat beside her, "All we can do now, is wait." He closed his eyes.

Francis placed his hands together and motioned to Michelle. He nodded towards De Niro.

She understood.

* * * * *

The Sojwa answered his vibrating cell phone.

"Sojwa, we were able to lower ourselves down to the elevator and enter it through its roof. We are sending it to you now."

"Very good."

The doors opened to the elevator and the Sojwa and six other soldiers stepped on. It ascended to the main floor and they stepped off.

The Sojwa made a call, "This is Sojwa Rim, acting commander in charge of Punggye-Ri, pass me through to the station commander immediately."

He waited for the commander, "Sir, this is Sojwa Rim at Punggye-Ri. Sir, Taejang Kang is dead. The men responsible are believed to be heading to Sandone Station via the interconnecting tunnels. They should be arriving there about now. They are armed and dangerous. Yes, sir."

He made another call to the compound's main entrance, "This is Sojwa Rim. Has anyone left the facility in the last hour … perhaps a doctor and a soldier with a bandaged face? Okay, I want you and your men on alert. No one is allowed to come or go until further notice. Is that understood?"

The Sojwa put his phone away and called the soldiers to him, "We have reestablished communication with the outside. Our job now is to find the doctor, and the man accompanying him dressed as a soldier with his face bandaged. I have already confirmed that they have not left the compound. They may still be in this building. I want half of you to fan out to the compound's perimeters and the rest to search every centimeter of this building, now!"

* * * * *

Mugsy brought the railcar to a halt. Ahead, bright daylight blasted into the tunnel entrance. Cho's head was resting on his shoulder. He nudged him.

Cho lifted his head. His cheeks flushed from embarrassment, "I ... must have dozed off."

"Your secret is safe with me." Mugsy stepped out and went around the other side, "Let me help you."

Cho bowed slightly, "Thank you, Captain. I think I can manage to keep up with you now."

The sunshine at the entrance was disturbed by the figures of four men. Mugsy and Cho noticed them at the same time.

Mugsy pulled Cho behind the railcar and aimed his rifle. Cho grabbed his shoulder, "Don't, Captain. If you fire, not even the men on the train will escape this country."

The figures headed in their direction. Two more figures appeared behind them.

Mugsy lowered his weapon and placed it on the floor, "Okay, you up to this?"

Cho extended his arm, "After you."

Both stood and placed hands on their heads.

The first four came into view. They were soldiers. They hurried over with their rifles pointed, two in front, and two behind. Without warning, arms appeared around the necks of the two behind. Their grunts made the soldiers in front turn. Mugsy and Cho kicked the rifles from their hands. They snapped their necks then wrestled the rifles away from the two behind and ended their lives the same way.

Cho fell to his knees.

Father Kim and Song helped Mugsy lift Cho to his feet, "You alright?"

Cho nodded, "I'm alright." He was careful to conceal the blood that seeped from his wound.

Mugsy shook Father Kim's hand, "Good to see you, Father. Glad you showed up when you did." He motioned to the soldiers' bodies, "Do you know if they were just on normal patrol?"

"We do not think so. Song and I received word from Scipio that you would be arriving around now. He told us to tell the conductor to make preparations to leave. He also said there was a chance the station would be alerted. We saw these men scramble from their barracks and head directly here."

"That means others may follow to back them up."

"We thought so too, so Song came up with the idea of setting fire to one of the station's electrical huts."

He saw the looks on Mugsy and Cho's faces.

"Don't worry. He was very good at making it appear to have started accidentally."

Mugsy winked at Song, "Nice work. Alright, I think we've overstayed our welcome here … time to get going. Father, you and Song get us back to the train."

Father Kim pointed to Song to help Cho then stepped in front of Mugsy, "Captain, Scipio told us he would attempt to rendezvous with us somewhere down the line. Do you think … does he have a chance?"

"If anyone does, it's Scipio. I'm convinced the Man upstairs has a soft spot for him."

Father Kim didn't let him pass, "Captain, what happened to Sojang Kim? How did he die?"

Mugsy looked at Cho, "Kang took his life. He died a hero … for his country and yours."

* * * * *

Father Kim held on as the train lurched into motion. He made his way behind Mugsy who was staring out the slightly-ajar boxcar door, "Song gave me his cell phone number so we can remain in contact while he is in the engine. I just called him. He said the conductor is cooperating."

Mugsy didn't turn around, "What about the Cho?"

"I set him down on some cushions and tried to close his wound, but he could be bleeding internally."

Mugsy continued to stare out the door. He didn't reply right away, "Thank you, Father."

"Captain, you are concerned for Scipio?"

Mugsy didn't reply.

"I will pray for him … and for us."

CHAPTER 48

PMB-ALPHA
MIM-104 PATRIOT MISSILE BATTALION
32 KILOMETERS NORTHEAST OF CITY CENTER
SEOUL, SOUTH KOREA
7:00 AM (LOCAL), THURSDAY, JUNE 06, 2013

The technician's white van was waved through PMB-Alpha's security gate. It pulled up next to the Engagement Control Station (ECS), a shelter mounted on the bed of an M927 5-Ton Cargo Truck.

Located in a heavily wooded area, 20 miles northeast of central Seoul, PMB-Alpha was the primary station managing operations of six MIM-104 Patriot surface-to-air missile systems, known as "Line Batteries." Located around the city's perimeter, their primary purpose was protecting the city of Seoul from missile attack.

The technician entered the back of the van and opened a small closet. A woman wearing only an overcoat and heels stepped out. She put her arms around him.

The technician frowned, "Jeong-hwa, I can't believe you talked me into this craziness. I could lose my job, or worse." The woman ignored him, removing his cap and placing it on her head.

She started unbuttoning his shirt. He resisted but was defeated by kisses to his neck. Then she unzipped his trousers and he grabbed her arms, "Jeong-hwa, we mustn't do this here."

She continued to ignore him and started pulling his pants down, but he pushed her away, "I've changed my mind. This was a crazy idea."

"Why are you so uptight? We're already past the guards. It's Memorial Day. You shouldn't even be working today."

"I told you, it's my job to check this installation particularly on holidays. I shouldn't have allowed you to talk me into this."

"I guess you're right," The petite, shapely woman unbuttoned her coat and let it drop to the floor. She stood in front of him wearing only heels, "You shouldn't have let me talk you into this."

The technician swallowed hard before kicking off his shoes and removed his pants, "Okay, but we must hurry."

She put her arms around him and kissed his neck. He closed his eyes and let his hands find her bottom. Softly blowing into his ear, she placed a long, thick plastic wire tie around his neck then let her tongue flick his earlobe as she threaded it. With one violent tug, she tightened it around his throat.

He backed away in shock unsure why he couldn't breathe, and grabbed at his throat. As their eyes locked, he felt the plastic tie and clawed at it with his fingernails. His expression turned to panic. Hers remained devoid of emotion. Unable to even gasp aloud, the technician collapsed to the ground.

Picking up his trousers, Jeong-hwa wasted no time measuring them against her body. Nimbly, she placed adhesive stays to the hems and waist then kicked off her heels and slipped them on. She tucked his baggy shirt in as best she could, but there was little she could do with the length of the sleeves.

Jeong-hwa struggled to place the body inside the same closet in which she had hidden. She removed a case before locking it.

She opened the case to check the brick of C-4 explosive that would act as a deterrent to anyone attempting to deactivate the program once it was running. She also planned to wire the C-4 so it would detonate if anyone attempted to disconnect the splice she would make between the AN/MPQ-65 radar and the AN/MSQ-104 Engagement Control Station (ECS).

She placed the case inside a large tent bag, zipped it then switched the nametag pinned to the shirt. After checking that the tag was visible, she slipped her feet into his shoes. Her feet swam in them.

Jeong-hwa giggled, deciding to put her heels back on, before grabbing the tent bag, a laptop, and a tool case, and heading out of the van.

She noticed the stares from guards as she made her way to the AN/MPQ-65 radar set, a tall oblong housing, mounted to the back of a specially-designed trailer. From it ran three thick cables that fed the radar's data into the AN/MSQ-104 ECS.

Won Jeong-hwa was not a whore. The 39-year-old daughter of a field grade officer, the North recruited her when she was only a teen. Her school grades impressed them, particularly in mathematics and the sciences.

It didn't take her recruitment officer very long to notice she was easy on the eyes, and more so, that she enjoyed the attentions of men. It also didn't take the North Korean National Intelligence Service (NIS) very long to realize her smarts and looks would make her the ideal spy.

Jeong-hwa eventually earned a Masters Degree in electrical engineering. The NIS added weapons-systems expertise to her resume before allowing her to "defect" to the south.

Jeong-hwa was assigned to Taejang Kang six months before. The Taejang only told her that: A.) A missile attack on the south would be conducted on their Memorial Day; B.) The target was somewhere in Seoul; and C.) The success of the attack would depend on her ability to shut down the Patriot missile batteries protecting the city.

What she did not know was that Taejang's plan was not authorized by Pyongyang. Instead, Kang ordered her to go "black." No inbound or outbound communications with anyone, except him.

Other than the radar set and ECM, Jeong-hwa became familiar with every other aspect of the MIM-104 Patriot system including the OE-349 Antenna Mast Group, EPP-III Electric Power Plant, and the M901 Launching Station. She knew though that the heart of the system was the AN/MSQ-104 ECS.

After months of study, in keeping with the Taejang's attack plan, she decided it was impossible to disable any of the subsystems. It came down to the South Korean response time to any system shutdown. They were just too efficient.

She confirmed that with a few careful tests on the missile batteries protecting Pusan, far to the north, and two other coastal cities. In every case, the South Koreans were able to detect and repair the problem within minutes, usually by swapping in a redundant, secondary system which was kept isolated and offline. It would be impossible for her to disable both the primary and secondary systems by herself, so she rethought the problem and devised a novel solution.

Instead of disabling those subsystems, she knew the entire missile defense system depended on the data being fed into the manned ECS from the radar set. The ECS's main sub-components, the Weapons Control Computer (WCC), the Data Link Terminal (DLT), the UHF communications array, the Routing Logic Radio Interface Unit (RLRIU), and the two manstations that served as the system's man-to-machine interface were the system's heart and brain.

Jeong-hwa also knew there was no way to infiltrate the ECS itself. It was reinforced, air-conditioned, pressurized to resist chemical and biological attack, and shielded against electromagnetic pulse (EMP) and interference. Once the data from the radar set made its way into the ECS, there was no way for her to disrupt the operation of the missile battery.

That left her only one real course of action. She needed the ability to alter the data being sent into the ECS. That meant developing a computer program capable of manipulating the "track" data confirmed by the radar set to be an unidentified aircraft. The program would have to alter the unidentified aircraft track so that it appeared inside the ECS as "friendly aircraft." To accomplish that, the data would have to be intercepted after the radar set and before it reached the ECS. That meant Jeong-hwa would have to splice the laptop running the program into the feed between the two.

Jeong-hwa sent the requirements back to Taejang Kang. After a month, she received a laptop loaded with the program, along with the necessary connectors and directions on splicing.

That left penetrating the installation's security. Jeong-hwa knew she not only needed to get inside, but she also needed ample time and access to perform the splice. That problem she decided to solve with her body. All it took was making contact with one of the installation's maintenance staff at a local bar and teasing him out of all reason. Jeong-hwa had long ago honed her expertise at that too.

She giggled aloud walking past the soldiers. The idea of hiding in plain sight aroused her. She knew from experience that it would work.

Try to hide and men can find you, but sashay past them and they become blithering idiots.

Reaching the location, she set down the tent bag, tool case and laptop and noticed an officer heading her way. He looked at her nametag then at her shoes and smiled, "Is there a problem, Miss?"

Jeong-hwa didn't look at him right away. Instead she opened the tool case and removed an RF meter, "Excuse me, who are you?"

The officer smiled, "I am Daewi Po, commander of this battery. I don't know you."

She stood and bowed, "Forgive me, Daewi, I am Won Jeong-hwa. I am a replacement for one of the maintenance technicians that … fell and broke his arm."

"I am unaware of any replacement. Why was I not notified?"

"Daewi, it only happened as the technician was unloading here. With the holiday, none of the other regular technicians were available. I was called at the very last minute to fill in."

Daewi Po looked down at her heels, "That would explain your choice of footwear."

Jeong-hwa looked down and forced a blush, "I am very sorry, Daewi. I was not prepared …."

"Don't be. They are very … becoming. So, may I call you Jeong-hwa?"

She nodded.

"And you may call me Bo-ram. So, Jeong-hwa, is there a

problem?"

Jeong-hwa leaned over and patted the thick cables, "No problem now, but this section of cable is leaking RF. I'll need to perform a splice on it, and run some diagnostics."

The officer's smile disappeared, "Will the feed be down ... should I alert the Jungnyeong?"

The Jungnyeong, equal to an American lieutenant colonel, commanded the entire Patriot battalion of 600 men.

"You may, but the feed will never be down. The splice won't sever the connection and the diagnostics won't interfere with the data flow."

Jeong-hwa could tell the tall officer was still undecided.

That's why I save my smile for last.

She flashed her prettiest grin complete with batting eyelashes, "Bo-ram, may I ask ... what is a girl to do around here on Memorial Day?"

The officer's smile returned, "That depends. When do you get off duty?"

"I have some flexibility. When do you?"

He laughed, "I'm in charge, remember? Besides, I was about to take a little break now. Perhaps you join me for some breakfast?"

"I ...,"

"I could always spend my break here, with you?"

"That would be silly. Of course, I will join you for breakfast. Just give me a minute to stow my things."

The Daewi's eyes lit up, "Very good. Meet me by the mess hall. It's behind the officers' quarters."

Jeong-hwa struck her cutest pose and waved as he walked away. She looked around.

At least the Daewi's attentions have chased away the attentions of the lower ranking guards.

She checked her watch.

I can have breakfast with him and still have enough time.

She looked back at the Daewi.

Men are such fools.

CHAPTER 49

ROOM 628
ASAN MEDICAL CENTER
POONGNAP-2DONG, SONGPA-GU
SEOUL, SOUTH KOREA
7:00 AM (LOCAL), THURSDAY, JUNE 06, 2013

De Niro looked over at Francis. He was barely keeping his eyes open. Michelle had her head resting on his shoulder.

I don't think she's slept since Mugsy left for North Korea.

"Good morning."

"Oh … wow, I didn't mean to—"

De Niro smiled, "Don't forget, you're sleeping for two now."

Her eyes sparkled, "Trust me, I haven't forgotten." She pointed to her belly, "She won't let me."

"She …? So, you think it's a girl?"

She nodded.

"Ya know Lisa used to say that we had boys because God wouldn't give me any more than I could handle."

Michelle burst out laughing.

Francis sat up, "Guys, I'm in … Scipio did you hear me?"

There were a few moments pause, "Affirmative. Do I have access, John?"

"We both do."

"Okay … stand by."

* * * * *

Scipio clicked on a program. Francis could see his screen, "John, can you translate that."

"Give me a minute."

"I will, if they will," Scipio looked over at Dr. Seonu, sitting on a chair in the corner, with his wrists bound to its arms. "How are you, Doc?"

The doctor raised his head, "My wrists hurt. You did not have to bind me. I told you I would not resist."

"Trust me it'll be better for you if you're found that way. Your superiors might consider your lack of resistance as collaboration."

"I am a doctor, not a soldier … and a pragmatist. How much longer will we remain here?"

The screen changed from Korean to English, "One way or the other, not much longer."

Voices could be heard outside the door. Scipio pointed at the Doctor to stay put, "John, we've run out of time. Download the hard drive now."

"Scip, it'll take about 10 minutes to download all the data files for that program."

"Start now … whatever we get, we get."

He went to the door and cracked it open. Three soldiers and an officer were entering the Communications Room across the hall. He closed the door gently.

Dr. Seonu also caught a glimpse of them, "I see now why you made us move into this utility room."

Scipio took a small bottle and a rag from his pocket. He poured the contents of the bottle onto the rag and held it out, "Doc, you know what this is. I'm not gonna hurt you."

The doctor leaned forward and sniffed it, "Halothane. You took it from the infirmary?"

Scipio nodded, "Time for you to take a nap, Doc. I'm leaving."

Scipio brought the rag up.

"Wait …. I wanted to say … thank you … for not killing me."

Scipio nodded and covered his nose and mouth.

* * * * *

Sojwa Rim entered the Communications Room behind two of his soldiers and a technician. The technician sat in front of the main controls and began throwing switches.

The Sojwa stood behind the chair, "What is the trouble?"

"No trouble Sir, it appears someone simply deactivated all communications from this station."

Sojwa Rim looked around and made a twirling motion with his hands, "Start searching this area. Tell the others to converge on this room from wherever they are."

The soldiers hurried from the room, leaving just the technician and the Sojwa. Sojwa Rim tapped the technician's shoulder, "I want you to check the rest of the systems, starting with the security grid."

The technician typed on the keyboard, "Sir, the entire security grid is deactivated and it's been password protected."

The Sojwa banged the back of the chair then realized something sharp was being pressed against his throat.

Scipio spoke into his ear, "Resist and you die."

The technician tried to turn but Scipio prevented him with his foot.

"Tell him to remain seated facing the controls."

The Sojwa hesitated.

Scipio pressed the blade, "Tell him, Sojwa, or you die."

"Remain … seated and face the controls."

The technician nodded.

Voices came from outside the room followed by a knock at the door.

"Sojwa, order your men away from this area."

A voice called out from the hall, "Sojwa, our people are searching and converging as you ordered."

Scipio pressed the blade and drew blood, "Now, Sojwa."

"This is Rim. We have detected a radiation leak. Have everyone clear this floor immediately. I am calling off the search. No personnel are to reenter this area until further notice from me. Is that clear?"

"Sojwa … is everything okay in there?"

Scipio flashed the blade in front of the Sojwa's face then replaced it against his throat.

The Sojwa raised his voice, "Everything is fine, now follow my orders!"

"Yes Sojwa."

They heard the soldier shouting orders. After a minute the hall became quiet.

Scipio looked at a clock on the wall. He took the blade from the Sojwa's neck and kicked the back of his legs, dropping him to his knees.

"Place your hands on your head and don't move."

He opened a drawer, removed a handful of cables, and dumped them on the console in front of the technician, "Struggle and I will kill you. Understood?"

The technician nodded. Scipio used the cables to tie his arms and legs to the chair then removed the technician's tie and used it to gag him.

He motioned for the Sojwa to stand and pushed him to the door, "Let's go."

"Where …?"

Scipio put the ceramic blade to his throat again, "No questions, no resistance. Understood?"

The Sojwa nodded.

Scipio guided them into the utility room and kicked the Sojwa back down to his knees, "Quiet."

He squeezed his throat mic, "Status John."

"Download just completed. We got everything."

Scipio pulled the wire and let it recoil into his phone, "Thanks. Gotta go … and John, glad to know you're okay."

He looked at the time, "Get up Sojwa. Back into the Comm Room."

* * * * *

Francis hit a speed dial and placed the call on speaker.

De Niro gave him a chin-up motion.

"I'm calling my people back at The Watchman."

A voice came on the line.

"Russ, it's John."

"John, are you okay? We heard you were in a coma."

"I got my butt kicked, but yeah, I'm okay. Listen to me … I just uploaded a folder, November-Kilo 130607. The data files inside the folder were encrypted by a proprietary North Korean … it looked like a project management program. It shouldn't be difficult to decrypt, but we're pressed for time. I want you to upload the decrypted files into *November-Kilo 130607-decrypt* a-sap. And Russ, make sure you translate them into English. Got it?"

"I'm on it."

Francis turned to De Niro and Michelle, "Do me a favor guys. I'm still suffering a little double vision. My cell's screen is blurry. Get me a laptop … and hurry."

Michelle headed for the door, "I'll get one, Cris."

De Niro walked over to the bed, "How long will it take to decrypt those files?"

Francis brought his phone close and squinted, "The decrypted files are already being uploaded."

Michelle walked back in with a laptop, "I borrowed one from the office right across from this room. I hope it'll do."

"It will," Francis plugged his phone into the laptop. It took him a few moments for the phone's screen to appear on the laptop monitor.

"I'm opening the first few files."

Documents began appearing on the screen. De Niro and Michelle gathered around.

Francis pointed at a couple, "It looks like many of these files are correspondences ... orders given by Kang."

De Niro moved closer, "Anything about the missiles?"

Francis scrolled faster than De Niro could keep up, "No ... nothing about missiles yet."

"Wait," Michelle pointed to one of the windows, "put that one on top."

She turned the laptop to face her and spent a minute reading, "I think we have something. This is a correspondence from Kang to someone named Won Jeong-hwa. It appears to be information on how to splice into a data feed."

"A data feed," Francis turned the laptop back to face him, "what kind of data feed?" He studied the screen, "Cris, this is bad. This is instructions on how to splice into the output of an AN/MPQ-65 radar set."

De Niro crossed his arms, "John, in English."

"An AN/MPQ-65 radar set is the eyes for a Patriot missile defense system. This is instructions on how to splice into the output that feeds into the AN/MSQ-104 ECS ... the Engagement Control Station. That's the manned control center for the Patriot system."

"What can they do by splicing into that feed?"

"Any number of things ... for one, the feed could be severed."

"That would make no sense," said Michelle. "Why splice into the feed, if your intention was just to sever it?"

Francis studied the rest of the document, "True. Besides, most of this document describes the process of splicing a computer running a program into the feed without disrupting it."

"John, can you tell what kind of program?" asked De Niro.

"No, there's no info on the program itself."

"Can you take an educated guess?"

"All my guesses are educated, you know that."

"John ...."

"Okay, okay. Let me think. The radar set detects flying objects and decides whether they're hostile aircraft or not. It examines the object's size, speed, altitude, heading, and decides whether or not it's a legitimate track or just clutter created by RF interference. If the track is classified as an aircraft it feeds the data into the ECS, where it appears as an unidentified track on the screen of the Patriot operators. They take it from there."

De Niro stepped back and ran his fingers through his hair, "So, the radar decides whether an object is a legitimate threat or not. That right?"

"That's correct."

"Could they just disrupt the feed?" asked Michelle.

"Sure," said Francis, but that would immediately be detected and a backup would be brought online."

De Niro thought, "So then, what if the program alters the attributes of a possible threat ... makes it appear to be friendly? What'd you call it ... the track wouldn't be passed into the ECS then, would it?"

"No, it wouldn't. Cris, that's a very scary scenario."

De Niro turned to Michelle, "Is there any mention of which Patriot system was targeted?"

She turned the laptop back to face her, "No mention of location ... wait. John, there's a reference to SK-MIM-104PMB-ALPHA. Does that mean anything to you?"

"SK ... South Korea. MIM-104PMB-Alpha ... Patriot Missile Battalion, Alpha. It sounds like the South Koreans designed their Patriot System around the U.S. Army's battalion echelon."

"Can you find PMB-Alpha, John?" asked De Niro.

"Patriot batteries are mobile, specifically so you can't locate them ... at least not easily. With that said, my team and I can locate them. The problem is we don't know how many South Korea has and we won't know which one is designated Alpha."

"First things, first ... locate them, John."

"I'll put my team on it now."

Michelle kept reading the screen, "Cris, I think we can narrow the scope. I've found additional messages to this Won Jeong-hwa. What's interesting is that her email address was in her name and in the open."

"Why would Kang correspond with an operative in the open?"

"Actually, that's quite common. Government counter-espionage units are very adept at finding hidden communiqués. But other countries—South Korea included—don't have the ability to monitor the vast ocean of general messages, like our NSA has."

"So you mean this Won Jeong-hwa can be hiding in plain sight."

"Exactly," Michelle started tapping on her Big-Brutha™ phone, "Which also means we might be able to locate her."

Francis turned the laptop so De Niro could see it, "There ... how's that for speed. Actually, my team used more than our map scouring program. I contacted a friend of mine in Germany. The South Koreans purchased second-hand Patriot systems from them. Between my friend's info and our map analysis capabilities, we located 64 Patriot batteries scattered around South Korea."

"Great job John!"

"Cris," Michelle spun around, "I came up with something ... an address for Won Jeong-hwa ... in Seoul."

"Seoul ... John ...?"

"I'm on it. We located four batteries currently surrounding the city."

De Niro studied the screen, "Where is Punggye-Ri on this map?"

Francis entered a marker on the screen.

Michelle stepped behind him as De Niro traced his finger from the marker to Seoul.

"That has to be the one," Michelle pointed to the battery closest to his trace.

"We have to contact the South Korean military," said Francis.

"Cris, that would be a mistake at this point," replied Michelle. "Remember, President Park hasn't disclosed the reason for our presence here."

"So call her," said Francis.

"It won't be that easy. Even if we could reach President Park, and that will be difficult today, it's Memorial Day, remember ... all she could do is contact the battery."

"So, what's wrong with that?" said Francis.

"John, we don't know if Won is working solo or has help on the inside. We have no idea what could happen if she finds out we're on to her. Keep in mind, not only does she have the ability to erase the attributes of a hostile aircraft, if I understood you correctly, that program could also add those attributes to friendly aircraft."

Francis started to reply but De Niro held up his hand, "Michelle, what do you suggest?"

"I need to go to that battery and take a look myself."

"We have no idea when that woman would even try the splice," Francis sat erect, almost knocking the laptop over, "hell Cris, we have no idea if we're even correct about which battery is the target! We have to have President Park notify the military, so they can put all of the batteries on alert."

Both stared at De Niro. He looked between them before turning to Michelle, "Go … but stay in contact."

"I'll need some way to get past the battalion's security."

"I'll contact Karla and see if she can pull that off. Meanwhile, you better get moving."

De Niro tapped the speed dial for The Watchman Agency's Vice President of Government Relations, Karla Matthews.

CHAPTER 50

PMB-ALPHA
MIM-104 PATRIOT MISSILE BATTALION
32 KILOMETERS NORTHEAST OF CITY CENTER
SEOUL, SOUTH KOREA
8:00 AM (LOCAL), THURSDAY, JUNE 06, 2013

Standing in the guard shack, the Sangbyeong, equivalent to an American corporal, hung the phone up and returned to the car with the pretty woman in it, "Ma'am, I just checked with the Jungnyeong's office. No one has called on your behalf. I cannot permit you to enter."

Michelle Wang pursed her lips, "I understand. May I pull over to make a phone call?"

"You may, anywhere outside our gate."

"Thank you," She put the car in reverse and pulled over then pressed a speed dial button.

"Michelle …."

"Cris, I just arrived at PMB-Alpha but I was denied entrance at the gate. Was Karla unsuccessful?"

"Hold on, I'm patching her in now. Let her explain."

De Niro left the line then returned, "Karla, Michelle is on the line. Go ahead and explain to her what you told me."

"Hi Michelle. I've contacted every high-ranking Korean official I could, on such short notice. If it weren't their Memorial Day, any one of them could make a call to secure your entrance. But every military facility in the country is on lockdown today. No unauthorized visitors allowed. It's so frustrating. I can't seem to get you authorized."

"I understand. Thank you for trying, Karla."

"Sorry I couldn't be more help. Cris, what do you want me to do? I can keep trying."

De Niro saw another call on his line. The caller I.D. simply read, *Mugsy.*

"That won't be necessary. I think we may have another way to make it happen. Michelle, hold tight and stay on the line. I have another call."

He switched lines, "Mugs, how are you ... and where are you?"

"I'm fine, Cris. We're an hour out of Sandone Station heading west on the Paektusan Ch'Ongnyon line. Cho was wounded but he's stable now. Cris, Scipio's not with us."

"I know ... he contacted us less than an hour ago."

"An hour ago ... from where, was he still at Punggye-Ri?"

"He was. He enabled John to upload and decrypt Kang's hard drive."

"He should've bugged out then. Do you know if he did?"

"He didn't say, Mugs. Listen, is Cho well enough to talk to me?"

Mugsy looked over at Cho. He was lying with eyes closed.

He looks troubled, even in his sleep. I wonder if it's from the wound, or from the Sojang.

"Hold on, Cris."

He walked over, crouched down and nudged him, "Cho ...."

Cho opened his eyes, "Yes, Captain?"

"Cris De Niro is on the phone. He wants to speak to you." He handed him the phone.

"Mr. De Niro."

"How are you, Cho?"

"I am well, Sir, thank you."

"Daeryeong, one of my people needs to gain access to one of your Patriot batteries."

Cho thought a moment, "Scipio was able to transmit Kang's hard drive?"

"Yes. We found correspondences between him and a woman we believe to be a North Korean spy. The correspondences included instructions on how to splice into the output of a Patriot radar set. We believe Kang's plans included neutralizing one of the Patriot batteries protecting Seoul. Is there some way you can help?"

"Today is Memorial Day. All military facilities will be on lockdown protocol. Only personnel authorized by the battalion commander or Daejang Jeong himself can gain access to a Patriot battery."

"I met Jeong," said De Niro, "we got along. I could contact him."

"That might take some time. He will have a number of meetings and appearances scheduled."

De Niro balled his fist.

I should've thought about calling him sooner.

"Mr. De Niro. Make your attempt now. I will speak to the battalion commander. What is the PMB's designation?"

"Alpha."

"And what is your operative's name?"

"Her name is Michelle Wang. She's Vice President of Intelligence for The Watchman Agency. She's currently parked just outside Alpha's main gate."

"Very good, remain on the line, I will call now."

De Niro motioned to Francis, "John, see if you can get Jeong on the line. Tell him I need to speak to him immediately."

"Got it."

Cho put the call on hold and dialed another number, "This is Daeryeong Cho Jung-woo of NIS. I am in charge of President Park's security detail, Tiger-1. I need to speak to the battalion commander of PMB-Alpha. What is his name, please?

"Thank you. Please tell Jungnyeong Ra I need to speak to him immediately. It is a matter of national security."

It took a minute for the Jungnyeong to get on the line.

"Jungnyeong, you know who I am?"

The Jungnyeong's voice was deep, "We have verified your credentials, Daeryeong Cho. What is this all about, Sir?"

"One of my agents requires access to PMB-Alpha. Her name is Michelle Wang. She is parked outside the main gate."

"Sir, may I ask the reason for this access?"

"It is about the possible breach of your installation, Jungnyeong."

"Possible breach … Daeryeong, if that is true I must go to red status immediately!"

"You cannot do that, Jungnyeong. If you do, we run the risk the infiltrator will also be alerted. She cannot be—"

"She …?"

"Yes, it is a woman, and she could cause immediate harm to the installation. I need you to grant access to my agent now."

The Jungnyeong called to his adjutant, "Are there any women authorized to enter the battery today?"

Cho could hear the reply, "No Jungnyeong. No women are on the list for authorization today."

"Daeryeong Cho, there are no females authorized to enter the battery today. And I will see to it that no females are granted access for the rest of the day."

"Jungnyeong, the woman in question is a North Korean spy, and most likely one of their best. My agent is trained in counter-espionage. Your guards are not."

"With respect Sir, my guards are trained in protecting this installation. There has never been an intruder."

"Ra, I am not questioning the competency of your staff."

"Are you not, Daeryeong?"

Ra, time is short. I need you to grant access now."

"I am not prepared to do that, Sir. First, I do not know you or your agent. And second, I am not prepared to allow access to any individual that has not passed our security screening, including a thorough background check, especially on a day like today."

"Jungnyeong, I will take responsibility."

"That is impossible, Daeryeong, without Daejang Jeong's explicit authorization. I am sure you are aware of that."

"Not in situations involving national security, Jungnyeong. I am invoking my express authority in this matter and ordering you to allow access to—"

"In order to do that, Daeryeong Cho, you must issue the order in person or in writing."

Cho pulled the phone away from his face to cool his temper, "Ra, unless you allow my agent access, Seoul could be at risk today. Please …."

There was no reply.

"Jungnyeong … please."

"Get me the written authorization, Daeryeong. For now, I will put all of the battery's security on high alert."

The line went dead.

Cho punched the wall then grimaced in pain. He switched to the other line, "Mr. De Niro, I tried speaking with the commander in charge of PMB-Alpha. He will not allow Michelle Wang entry unless he gets written authorization. The problem is the authorization will take time to issue through NIS. Many questions will have to be answered first."

"I understand. You did your best. We're still trying to get in touch with Jeong. Put the Captain back on please."

Cho handed the phone back to Mugsy, "Cris, it's me."

"Mugs, we'll keep trying to reach Jeong. In the meantime, do me a favor and contact us as soon as Scipio joins up with you."

"Of course."

"And Mugs … get back in one piece soon or Michelle might declare war on North Korea all by herself."

"Understood. Give her a kiss for me."

De Niro dropped the line and walked over to the bed, "Any progress, John?"

"My people skills stink, Cris, you know that. I reached out to Karla. I'm holding on the line for her."

De Niro checked the time.

8:30 ….

"I have to get going. The ceremony at the cemetery begins in a half hour. I have to change."

"What do you want me to do if Karla can get to Jeong?"

"It's crazy. In 30 minutes I'll be with him." De Niro paced a few steps then stopped at the door, "Contact me immediately the moment Karla reaches Jeong."

He connected the line on hold, "Michelle, it's Cris. Cho attempted to gain access for you, but he was unsuccessful. We're gonna try to get in touch with Jeong. He's the only person now who can get you in."

"So I get to sit and wait while the NK agent is probably already inside taking control of the data flow."

Francis and De Niro's eyes met.

"Just sit tight, Michelle. Karla's still working on it," De Niro put his phone away.

He patted Francis's shoulder, "The moment Karla reaches Jeong, contact me. I gotta go."

* * * * *

Won Jeong-hwa checked her watch, "Thank you for breakfast, Bo-ram. I must get back to my work."

Daewi Po stood, "I will walk you back."

"That really is unnecessary."

"I am the one who says what is necessary here." He smiled, "It is no matter. I have to pass that way anyway."

Jeong-hwa checked her watch again and forced a smile, "Very well."

CHAPTER 51

PMB-ALPHA
MIM-104 PATRIOT MISSILE BATTALION
32 KILOMETERS NORTHEAST OF CITY CENTER
SEOUL, SOUTH KOREA

8:30 AM (LOCAL), THURSDAY, JUNE 06, 2013

Michelle stared at her phone.

This is ridiculous.

She looked over at the gate and began shaking her legs.

And I have to go to the bathroom.

A thought came to her. She got out of the car and walked to the front gate. The same guard met her.

"You remember me, right?"

"I do."

"Has there been any word yet on authorizing my entrance?"

"No ma'am there has not."

"I understand. May I ask a favor? I ... uh ... drank too much tea on the way here. May I use the bathroom please?"

The guard flashed a doubting smiled.

"Listen, I really have to go. You can escort me if you like."

"Ma'am, you will have to be searched."

"Then, please, do that quickly."

* * * * *

Won Jeong-hwa stopped in front of the bags she left near the radar set. She turned and bowed her head, "Once again … thank you Bo-ram. You have been most kind."

"What are in all of those bags?"

"Just my laptop, tools, and an inflatable tent in which to work."

"Inflatable tent … interesting. I will help you set it up."

"I would not want to inconvenience you. You have spent so much time with me already."

"Nonsense. Technically, I should be familiar with everything you bring into my battery. Besides, I like camping."

"Camping …?"

"A tent is a tent, Jeong-hwa."

She shrugged, doing her best to conceal her impatience, "A tent is a tent. Very well, if possible, could you fetch me a folding table and chair?"

"First you turn down my offer of assistance and now you have me fetching things for you. You are quite an interesting woman, Jeong-hwa. If it is alright with you, I will have one of my men do the fetching." Daewi Po turned and started barking orders.

Jeong-hwa moved quickly. She unzipped the tent bag and removed the brushed black metal case containing the C-4. She put it with her tools.

The Daewi turned to her, "Your table and chair are on the way, now how about this tent?"

She removed the tent from the bag, "If you would, please help me roll it out. We will inflate it directly over this section of cable."

He did as she instructed, "What now?"

She handed him a pump, "Now, we inflate it. Place the hose in that inlet."

Within minutes the tent was inflated.

She handed him a dozen sharp metal stakes, "Now, all you have to do is stake the ends of the cords into the ground."

Two soldiers walked over, one with a folding table and the other with a chair. Daewi Po pointed inside the tent, "Place them in there."

Jeong-hwa followed them in with her laptop, tools, and the encased C-4. She waited for the soldiers to leave before placing everything on the table and hurrying to retrieve the tent case.

She placed the black metal box into it as Daewi Po entered. He dropped a couple of stakes onto the table, "These were left over. That was relatively easy. I think I may look into getting one of these."

Having memorized the splicing instructions, Jeong-hwa began slitting the cables open, "You should. It is not terribly expensive."

He watched her work, "Is there something more I can do?"

"Nothing, you have been too kind already, thank you. The rest, I must do."

He walked up close behind her and softly put his hands on her arms, "Then I will leave you to your work. I hope we get the opportunity to see each other again."

She flashed a smile over her shoulder, "I am sure we will. I think I can transfer to the maintenance detail for this battery. That is, if you give a stellar review to my superiors."

"You can count on it," he returned a smile and exited the tent.

Jeong-hwa let out a long breath as she bent down and began attaching the splicing connectors. She didn't see, as much as hear someone reenter the tent.

"I forgot to get the name of the tent," it was Daewi Po's voice. "I will get it from the bag."

She was too slow to her feet. Po reached into the tent bag and drew out the black, metal box. He had his back to her. "What is this?"

Jeong-hwa grabbed a stake from the table and held it behind her back as she approached him.

He turned and held the case out to her, "May I …?"

He is asking out of courtesy, not for permission.

She nodded, "Please be careful though, it is a very sensitive mechanism. You must place it on the ground first."

He squatted and did as she said, as she moved with subtlety behind him.

He flipped the clasp and opened the box.

Jeong-hwa slammed the nine-inch chrome stake into his neck, an inch under his right earlobe. Po fell on his side with a look of shock on his face.

Jeong-hwa wasted no time taking his pistol then sliding the vinyl tent bag over his head and as much of his shoulders as she could manage. She picked up the metal case and left him there writhing.

It took her another five minutes to attach the bomb to her laptop and conceal it amidst the cables, and then to activate the program. She looked back at Daewi Po's legs. They were no longer moving.

She looked at her watch.

Five minutes until the missiles launch then another 12 until they fly over this installation and reach their target ... time for me to leave.

She took out her phone, "It's me. Have the chopper ready to take off as soon as I arrive. I'll be there in two minutes."

* * * * *

The Sangbyeong at the main gate called another guard to escort Michelle to the nearest latrines. She noticed it was located directly across from the ECS shelter. Behind it, she saw the Radar Set.

Excellent.

The guard pointed to the boxlike row of compartments. Michelle bowed her head and entered one. Immediately, she began spooling toilet paper into the tank behind the bowl until the roll was empty then opened the door and stepped out, "There is no toilet paper in here!"

The guard took a look, "Go in the next one."

She entered one adjacent and did the same thing then stepped out, "What is going on? There is no toilet paper in this one too."

The guard checked then walked out, "Use the next one."

"This is ridiculous."

She entered the third and did the same thing, then stepped out raising her voice, "This is completely ridiculous, I need to go now! Please, get me toilet paper!"

The guard hesitated before shrugging his shoulders and hurrying into the next compartment. When he came out, she was gone.

* * * * *

Michelle watched as the guard checked the other stalls and then ran off in the direction of the main gate. She waited until he was out of sight before starting off for the radar set, but had to conceal herself again. An officer and a woman dressed in some sort of uniform appeared in front of it.

Michelle made her way behind the cab of one of the trucks and watched as the two inflated a tent. Behind her, she saw the guard returning with four other soldiers. They fanned out and surrounded the latrines. Two were heading in her direction.

She entered the cab, ducked down, and watched as the two checked all around the truck but didn't bother looking inside.

Just as I thought, the guards are trained to keep people out, not to find anyone once they get in.

She waited for them to pass before exiting the cab, only to see two more soldiers carry a folding table and chair into the now-inflated tent. She continued to watch as, a moment later, the soldiers walked back out followed closely by the uniformed woman. She retrieved something and hurried back inside.

Where's that officer?

Within minutes, the officer stepped out with metal stakes in his hands. He pounded them into the ground around the tent's perimeter then headed back inside.

Michelle exhaled audibly.

Now what?

Minutes passed.

I'll have to chance it.

Michelle stepped out and froze. The woman in the odd uniform hurried out of the tent, but didn't notice her. She headed in the direction of the main gate.

Now, where's the officer? I'm out of time.

Michelle looked around. No one was in sight. She made a beeline for the tent and opened the flap. The glow from a laptop's screen was the only illumination inside. She circled the small table on which it sat and looked at the screen.

Oh no!

She made a call and waited with impatience. John Francis answered. She spoke in a hushed tone, "John, it's Michelle."

"Michelle, where are you?"

"I'm inside PMB-Alpha.

"But how'd you—"

"I snuck in."

"You what …?"

"I snuck in. John, I don't have much time. I found the laptop spliced into the output of the radar set. I'm interfacing with it now. Take a look."

She pulled the cable from her phone and plugged it into the laptop.

"We're plugged in."

"Okay, give me a sec."

Michelle peeked out the flap and saw no one.

"It looks like rudimentary encryption."

"Hurry, John, please."

She continued to look around and spotted a wire running from the laptop to somewhere under the table. She bent down and followed it to a black metal case.

I have a bad feeling about this!

Gently, she opened the latches on the case. It confirmed her fear.

"John, there's a problem. A cable is running from a port on the laptop to a case packed with C-4."

"So that's what that is. I saw it as an unidentified peripheral."

"That peripheral is a pound of plastic explosive, John. Can you shut down the program?"

"I could, but if I'm reading this code correctly, the program is designed to send a command to that unidentified peripheral if it's shut down."

"In other words what …?"

"In other words … boom! The program is also tracking the connection … the splice. If the connection is severed the program will stop and—"

"Boom … I was paying attention. Are there any options?"

"I can try and tweak the program but I'll have to be careful. Whoever created it probably built in other anti-tampering measures. That means I'll have to take it slow. Come to think of it … Michelle, I think you should scram out of there, just in case."

"You're sure you won't need me here for anything?"

"There's nothing else for you to do. Get out of there now."

"Okay, I'll have to leave my phone to keep your connection going though. So, I'll be out of touch. I'm leaving now."

Something caught her eye when she got up from the chair. She approached it then jumped back.

Legs …!

A nylon case covered the rest of the body. She pulled it off.

The officer, I forgot all about him.

Behind her, soldiers entered the tent, the same two. They spotted Michelle next to the Daewi's body and pointed their rifles.

She raised her hands and hollered, "I'm under arrest, John … Contact Cris!"

I hope he's still listening!

She switched to Korean, "You two, there is a woman escaping the installation. She is a North Korean spy. She must be stopped and I need to speak to the Jungnyeong immediately!"

* * * * *

Francis heard Michelle hollering. He picked up the hospital phone and punched a number in, "Cris, it's John."

"What's up?"

"Listen, Michelle broke into the Patriot installation."

"What …?"

"Listen to me. She found the laptop already spliced in with the program running. It can't be disconnected. I'm trying to noodle with it, but I don't think I'll be successful in time."

"Where's Michelle now?"

"That's why I'm calling. I told her to bug out, but before she could I heard her being taken into custody."

"I just arrived at the cemetery. I'll look for Jeong. Call me if you hear from her or if you make progress with the program."

CHAPTER 52

COMMUNICATIONS ROOM
HEADQUARTERS OF TAEJANG KANG KUM-SOK
PUNGGYE-RI NUCLEAR TEST SITE
KILJU COUNTY, NORTH HAMGYONG PROVINCE
NORTH KOREA
8:55 AM (LOCAL), THURSDAY, JUNE 06, 2013

Scipio checked the time. He looked at the North Korean officer he took captive. The man had not uttered a word while they waited.

"The offices open at 9 AM, correct?"

Sojwa Rim nodded.

"Let's go, Sojwa."

The Sojwa stood, but remained quiet.

Scipio extended his arm.

Sojwa Rim proceeded out of the room and into the corridor. The area remained empty.

They exited the building via the main entrance and walked down the stone stairs. A small car was parked by itself right in front.

Scipio pointed to the driver's side, "Get in, you drive."

The brawny man did as he was told. Scipio got in the passenger seat.

Staring out the windshield, Sojwa Rim finally spoke, "What now?"

"Sojwa, may I ask something?"

"You are the one with the weapons."

"You have not attempted to resist or escape?"

He turned to Scipio, "That is because, from the moment I surrendered to you, my life was over. Resistance could possibly endanger others and escape seems pointless."

"Sojwa, I will not harm you if you do as I say."

Sojwa Rim grinned in almost a compassionate way, "I was not speaking of what you might do. My superiors do not tolerate failure. When they discover an American infiltrated this facility and got away, every officer will be condemned to death and their families sent to labor camps."

"Sojwa, do you know why I am here?"

"I would think that is obvious. You are an assassin assigned to murder Taejang Kang."

"But do you know why?"

Rim look at him curiously, "He is in command of our missile defenses. Reason enough for you Americans and the devils to the south."

"Sojwa, the Taejang intends to fire missiles from this installation today. He intends to start a war with the south."

Sojwa Rim glared, "You are lying."

"Am I ...? We will see."

"How will we see?"

"Within the next hour, I expect the Musudan missiles to attempt to launch. If that happens then what I have told you is the truth."

"What do you mean ... attempt to launch?"

"We sabotaged the launch sequence. The missiles will fire while still locked to the launchers."

"How do I know you have not just strapped a bomb to the missiles?"

"If I did, why would I wait? It was impossible to get close enough to place bombs on them."

Rim didn't reply. He stared off in thought.

That made sense to him.

He continued to stare off, "What was the Taejang's target?"

"We think the target of the Musudan missiles was Busan. But while we were here, we learned the Taejang also has other missiles ready to be fired. We do not know their target."

Sojwa Rim's eyes widened, "Other missiles … like NoDong-2 missiles?"

"Yes."

"I … was," Rim shook his head and took a deep breath. "On Saturday, Taejang Kang dispatched me to reposition a battery of NoDong-2 missiles."

Scipio put his hand on Rim's forearm, "How many missiles?"

Rim didn't reply.

"Sojwa, Kang wants to launch the missiles to start a war. Is that what you want?"

"We would be victorious!"

Scipio paused, "Do you have family?"

"I have … a wife and children, and a brother … and my parents are still alive."

"If war comes, what will happen to them?"

Squeezing the steering wheel, Rim continued to stare out the windshield, "Seven. There were seven missiles, and you are correct, they are ready for launch."

"When …?"

"The Taejang said it was merely a test launch of the new GPS guidance systems."

"GPS …? When will they launch?"

They locked eyes, "9 AM."

Scipio checked the time.

A blinding flash emanated from behind them followed closely by an earthquake-like ground shaking. They sprung from the car to see a huge plume of smoke rising from the direction of where the Musudan missiles were located.

"You were right. The Taejang was going to start a war!"

Scipio yelled, "He still may. Get in!"

They jumped back in the car. Scipio returned the key to the ignition, something Rim didn't see him remove.

"What do you want me to do?"

"Drive to the gate, I will tell you on the way."

CHAPTER 53

SEOUL NATIONAL CEMETERY
DONGJAK-GU
SEOUL, SOUTH KOREA
8:55 AM (LOCAL), THURSDAY, JUNE 06, 2013

De Niro hurried to a uniformed guard stationed at the entrance to the backstage area and showed his pass. The guard studied it carefully before allowing him to enter.

Once inside, he approached another guard, "Can you please tell me where I can find Daejang Jeong?"

The guard pointed to a building with a sign reading, *Photographic Exhibition House.*

De Niro walked quickly passing a dozen people who acknowledged him. He presented his pass to several men standing at the door.

They're not wearing uniforms. Black suits and sunglasses with earpieces, the classic look of Secret Service agents everywhere. That could mean that President

Park is inside too, but the General is more important right now.

One of the men took his time examining the pass closely. Finally, he took a lanyard out of his pocket and inserted the pass, "Sir, you are required to wear this around your neck at all times."

De Niro put it on, "Thank you."

He entered into a throng of well-dressed people.

There has to be 200 hundred dignitaries in here – government officials, ambassadors, business magnates, religious leaders … not to mention enough high-ranking military officers to form a company.

He spotted Jeong standing among a small crowd. The Daejang saw him coming, "Ah, Mr. De Niro, it is an honor to see you again. Allow me to introduce you—"

De Niro bowed before everyone, "Daejang, if you don't mind, may I have a word with you in private?"

"Of course."

The General led him into an unoccupied corner. Black-suited guards followed at a distance and formed a perimeter around them.

"What can I do for you?"

"Sir, my people, working alongside Daeryeong Cho, uncovered a plot orchestrated by Taejang Kang to launch missiles at your country. We have reason to believe the launch will happen today, perhaps at any moment."

Jeong's face became serious, "Do you know the target?"

"We believe the target to be somewhere here in Seoul."

Jeong folded his arms, "Mr. De Niro, you understand we have radar technology that would alert us to any missile threats."

"Yes, sir, I am aware. But from the time the missiles launch, you may only have minutes to react … if the missiles are detected by your radar."

"We also have anti-missile capabilities protecting Seoul."

"Sir, I'm also aware of the Patriot batteries surrounding Seoul. However, we recently came across information leading us to believe a North Korean spy is intent on infiltrating one of the installations."

Jeong's face reddened, "How recently? Mr. De Niro, you are very close to my placing you under arrest. Why would you not bring this information to me the moment you became aware of it?"

"Sir, we attempted to reach you as soon as we received the information, but you were unavailable."

The General stared back with a softened expression. He took his phone out, "Which installation?"

"PMB-Alpha …."

"I will send men there now. Then I will contact the battalion commander."

"Sir, one of my people is already there … Michelle Wang, you met her."

"Ms. Wang is at PMB-Alpha now?"

"Yes, sir, but she was denied entry."

Jeong held his finger up, "This is Daejang Jeong. Tell Jungnyeong Ra I want to speak to him immediately."

He placed the call on speaker.

"Daejang, Michelle was—"

A voice on the phone interrupted, "Daejang Jeong, what can I do for you, Sir?"

Jeong held up his finger again, "There is a woman named Michelle Wang that needs to gain entry to the battery."

"Yes, sir. We have Ms. Wang in custody."

"In custody … why?"

"Sir, she entered the installation without authorization and was caught tampering with the cables running from the radar set to the ECS."

Jeong looked at De Niro.

"Daejang that was what I was trying to explain. Michelle wasn't tampering. She snuck into the battery—"

"Snuck into PMB-Alpha?"

"Yes, sir, and discovered the North Korean spy tampering. Daejang, time is essential here. There's not enough of it to explain fully. You need to trust me."

They traded stares.

"Please, Sir."

Jeong cocked his head, "Okay Mr. De Niro, what do you suggest?"

"Speak to Michelle directly."

Jeong nodded, "Jungnyeong, bring Ms. Wang to the phone

immediately."

"Daejang, she is under arrest."

"Then release her and get her on the phone immediately."

Jeong's tone had her to the phone in 30 seconds, "This is Michelle Wang."

"Ms. Wang, this is Daejang Jeong. I am here with Mr. De Niro. He told me there isn't much time and wants you to explain the situation to me."

"Yes, sir. First, there is a North Korean spy—a female dressed as some sort of technician—escaping. Her name is Won Jeong-hwa."

"Is this call on speaker on your side?"

"Yes, sir, it is."

"Jungnyeong, have that woman placed under arrest immediately."

The Jungnyeong could be heard replying, "Yes, sir!"

"Go on Ms. Wang."

"Sir, the North Korean spy has spliced a sophisticated program into the output of the radar set. It cannot be disconnected or shut down without triggering a bomb."

"What is the purpose of the program?"

"Daejang, I conferenced in our Chief Information Officer, John Francis. He can explain better."

"Go on, Mr. Francis."

"Daejang, the program is designed to prevent the ECS from detecting potentially hostile aircraft tracks by the radar set."

Jeong shot an icy stare at De Niro, "And this program has been activated?"

"Yes, sir ... and it cannot be deactivated."

"Is it possible for the spy to shut it down or to instruct us on shutting it down?"

"I don't believe so, Sir. I've taken a look at the code. I can find no trace of override or shut-down commands. I believe the program was designed without them."

"Thank you, Mr. Francis. Jungnyeong Ra ...."

"Yes Daejang?"

Is there any way for us to redirect the radar sets of the other batteries to compensate for PMB-Alpha?"

"It would take a couple of hours and then we would be creating a hole in the grid elsewhere."

Jeong blinked in anger, "Very well, Jungnyeong, please take all necessary steps. You may do so on my authority. I want PMB-Alpha's airspace protected as soon as possible and by whatever means necessary. Have you taken steps to protect against the bomb detonating? I assume you already called for a bomb squad."

"Yes, sir, just before you called. We expect them shortly."

"Very well. Keep me informed, Jungnyeong. Thank you Ms. Wang."

"You're welcome, Sir. Cris, I'm gonna try to pick up Won's trail on my own, in case she's already escaped."

"Okay, but be careful."

Jeong disconnected the line, "I wish you would have entrusted me sooner."

"I do too, Sir."

Jeong covered his fist with his hand, "It appears we will have very little warning and no way to stop the missiles."

"Sir, I still have one agent at the launch site that may be able to tell us the moment the missiles launch."

Jeong stared tight-lipped, "I'm still not sure whether I should place you and your people under arrest. As is the case with most history, your fate will be decided by the outcome."

"I understand, Sir."

Jeong let his stare linger before walking off. After walking a few steps he turned back to De Niro, "Please accompany me. We have to inform President Park immediately."

"Yes, sir."

* * * * *

Michelle entered the tech van parked at the curb in front of the installation's main gate. Soldiers were already tearing it apart. She saw the body of a man being removed from a closet.

She tapped a speed dial, "John, it's Michelle."

"Michelle, are you alright?"

"I'm fine. Listen, I'm trying to track the North Korean spy, Won. She left this installation by the main gate about 10 minutes ago. Think you can help?"

"Hold on ... I'm bringing up satellite imagery. USFK ... United States Forces Korea maintains constant satellite reconnaissance around Seoul, particularly around those Patriot batteries."

"You can hack those satellites?"

"Michelle, hacking is such a 2000-late term. What I'm doing is more akin to inviting myself to have a look ... wait ... got it.

"Only one individual left the installation in the last 10 minutes."

"That has to be Won. Can you tell me where she went?"

"Forward fast ... it looks like ... Michelle, she boarded a helicopter less than a klick east of your location."

"A chopper ... can you track it?"

"I can, but I'll have to invite myself into another satellite ... hold on."

Michelle connected another line, "Cris, it's Michelle. It looks like the North Korean spy, Won boarded a chopper. I'm waiting for John to track it."

De Niro stopped Daejang Jeong, "Sir, hold on. You need to hear this." He placed his phone on speaker.

Jeong motioned for his Secret Service detail to give them space.

Francis came back on the line, "Michelle, I got it. The chopper is heading for Seoul. It's currently less than 13 miles northeast of the center of the city."

"You got that, Cris?"

"I got it, hold on Michelle. Daejang, the North Korean spy is on that chopper."

Jeong waved over another officer, "The commander of Osan Air Base is here. Osan is located only 60 kilometers south of Seoul. I will have him scramble F-16 fighters to compel that chopper to land."

"Cris, it's Michelle. Something's not right."

"You mean the fact Won is heading for Seoul when we believe it to be the target. That bothers me too. Why would she head here?"

"Maybe she thinks it's the last place we'd look for her," said Jeong.

"I don't buy that ... Sir" said Francis. "From the looks of the terrain near PMB-Alpha, if hiding was her goal she could've just as easily dug herself a hole in one of the foothills and remained there."

"I agree," said Michelle.

De Niro broke in, "Alright, both of you remain on the line. I'm going to switch to my earpiece."

A Secret Service Agent whispered in Daejang Jeong's ear. Jeong turned to De Niro, "Mr. De Niro. President Park has already taken the stage."

De Niro checked the time.

9 AM.

CHAPTER 54

INSIDE CAR PARKED IN FRONT OF MAIN ENTRANCE
HEADQUARTERS OF TAEJANG KANG KUM-SOK
PUNGGYE-RI NUCLEAR TEST SITE
KILJU COUNTY, NORTH HAMGYONG PROVINCE
NORTH KOREA
9:00 AM (LOCAL), THURSDAY, JUNE 06, 2013

Sojwa Rim raced the small car straight ahead and skidded in front of the security shack next to the main gate. He jumped out and hollered to the guards who were standing in shock staring at the large firestorm on the other end of the compound.

"Both of you … hurry to the explosion site! They need every man to extinguish the fire before it spreads to the main buildings."

They looked back at the guard shack and didn't move.

Rim approached them and took one of their pistols, "I will watch the gate, NOW GO!"

The soldiers ran off as Scipio exited the car, "Thank you Sojwa.

Now, into the guard shack. I will tie you and leave."

"What is your name?"

"Scipio."

"That is an odd name ... fitting for an odd man."

"Sojwa ... we have little time."

"I have less than you, my friend," Rim turned around with the guard's pistol in hand.

Scipio pulled his.

"That will not be necessary. This is not for you, it's for me. I cannot allow my family to suffer because of my dishonor. My friend, Scipio, if you would do something for me, please remove the gun from my hand ... after."

"No, Sojwa ... wait!"

Rim raised the pistol to his head and pulled the trigger.

Scipio lowered his head. Then he looked up to the sky.

Please ... look after his family.

As the Sojwa requested, Scipio removed the pistol from Rim's hand and tucked it into his waist, then ran to the guard shack and hit the button to open the gate.

He looked around. No one was near. He turned one more time in the direction of the explosion.

That could be downtown Busan, if Kim hadn't done what he done. I won't stand in judgment of Cho, but seeing that blaze makes me understand Mugsy's anger even more.

Scipio jumped in the car and took off down the road. When he lost sight of the gate, he took out his phone,

"Scipio, you okay? Where are you?"

"I'm okay Cris. I just bugged out of Kang's compound. Listen, at exactly 9 AM, seven NoDong-2 missiles launched from one of Punggye-Ri's test sites, just north of the headquarters. We weren't able ... repeat, we were not able to ascertain their target."

"Scipio, I have you on speaker. I'm standing here with Daejang Jeong. We think they're heading for somewhere in Seoul. Jeong is passing your info on now."

"Roger that. How do you know it's Seoul?"

"A lot's happened. Kang employed an NK spy to disable one of the Patriot batteries defending Seoul. We think he did it to allow those missiles to reach their target. That's the working hypothesis anyway."

"Working hypothesis … doesn't exactly sound like your brimming with confidence."

"It's worse than that. The Patriot battery is still down. It can't be brought back online and they won't be able to get another to cover the same airspace in time."

"And Seoul is a big city, Cris. Anyone have an idea what the specific target is?"

"No one does. With Memorial Day, the government and businesses are closed. The entire city has off. One idea is that Kang isn't particularly concerned with the missiles' target. Just the fact that North Korean missiles will explode in Seoul should cause what he wanted … retaliation and escalation."

"I don't think so, Cris. Those missiles are special, equipped with GPS guidance. I think he definitely has a target in mind."

"In any case … we did all we can. Wish we could've done more, but it's up to the South Koreans now. Hey, Mugsy told me you're planning to rendezvous with them?"

"Affirmative, I should be meeting the train in about 30 minutes or so, depending on how I can manage these mountain roads in this little tin can I'm driving."

"Do you expect any trouble along the way?"

"It's hard to say. The compound was out in the middle of nowhere, but I'm heading in the direction of civilization now, at least by North Korean standards."

De Niro noticed high-ranking military officers hurrying past him. He followed.

"Lots of commotion here … I better get going. Take care of yourself Scip, and tell my brother-in-law I want to see you and him back here safely."

"First round's on you, Cris."

* * * * *

Daejang Jeong called all senior officers into a meeting room. He stood at the head of a long conference table with De Niro next to him.

He waited for everyone to be seated before speaking, "As many of you are aware, at exactly 9 AM, seven NoDong-2 missiles launched from one of Punggye-Ri's test sites, just north of the headquarters." He nodded slightly to De Niro. "Our radar just picked up the missiles. As we anticipated, they are on a course that intersects with Seoul. Our fighter jets are already in the air, but they won't be able to fend off the missiles and there is not enough time to evacuate the city. We are notifying President Park now. She just started her speech."

De Niro's phone vibrated. He got up and exited the room, "Cris, I got your message, I was keeping tabs on that chopper. You heard from Scipio?"

"I did. He's okay. He left Kang's compound. He's heading for the train to hook up with Mugsy and the others. John, he said seven NoDong missiles launched at 9 AM."

"God, Cris!"

"We're gonna need God to get through this. Where's that chopper?"

"It just passed your location to the east, heading south."

"Where could she be heading? There's not much south of—"

"Wait a minute," Francis cut him off. "The chopper's changing direction. It's now circling around to the west." He paused, "Cris, it's descending as it's circling and heading in your direction."

De Niro looked out to the eastern horizon.

"They're less than 1,000 feet ... 900 ... 800 ... 700. Continuing to descend ... 500 ... 400 ... 300. Any lower and we could lose it to ground clutter ... 200 feet. Damn, it must be soaring just over the tops of those dense diamond pine trees surrounding the cemetery. I'm losing resolution."

"John, don't lose that chopper."

De Niro headed to the side of the stage and looked out to a crowd of thousands. He saw a Secret Service agent walk up to the President at the podium and whisper into her ear.

She nodded and noticed De Niro at the same time, before facing the crowd, "Ladies and gentlemen, I have just been informed that the city of Seoul is under attack. For security reasons, we must all head indoors. Please follow the instructions of the police and other officials. I know there are many of you in attendance. We will fit as many as possible into the various buildings here. The rest of you must please head home now and remain indoors until the threat has passed."

The President's security detail quickly surrounded and began escorting her from the stage. President Park stopped when she noticed people in the crowd beginning to push and shove. Before they could stop her, she returned to the mic, "Ladies and gentlemen, for everyone's safety, please do not panic. There is still enough time for everyone to evacuate the area."

Many of the people nearest the stage broke through the barriers and started hoisting themselves onto it. The President's detail rushed to the front of the stage and set up a human wall to try and repel them but they were overwhelmed. Hundreds reached the stage and pushed past them. The mob stampeded the President heading for the building behind, as her security detail crowded around her with guns drawn.

"Don't fire your weapons!" shouted President Park.

* * * * *

A couple of scared young men ran past De Niro, "John, I have Michelle on the phone too. Where's that chopper?"

"I found it, but it's fading in and out. It's flying at treetop-level and it changed course again, heading almost due north now. Wait … Cris, it stopped moving."

"Is it landing?"

"No. I think it's just hovering."

Michelle broke in, "Cris, they could be lowering her to the ground."

"John, where is it now?"

"It's a little over 500 yards west of your position."

"500 yards …." De Niro shoved his way through the throng of people continuing to run by him. He looked west and used the camera built into his double-B phone to zoom in.

"John, I see the chopper. It's over a tall stone monument located on the southern perimeter of the cemetery. Can you see anything else?"

"Negative, Cris."

"Why would Won come here?"

De Niro looked over at the Secret Service agents surrounding President Park. They were starting to clear a path back to the building. They formed two lines for her to walk between.

Something bothered him.

He scanned the area and noticed the crowd had totally dispersed. Then he saw what it was. There were no agents behind her. Only the podium blocked the President from the front of the stage and only partially, from her shoulders down.

He let his eyes drift beyond the audience area as a thought crossed his mind.

If anyone dropped onto that monument, the back of the President's head would be in direct line of sight!

He zoomed in and saw someone repelling from the chopper.

"No!"

De Niro took off running, slamming into people before reaching the line of Secret Service agents. They subdued him, but he continued to wrestle with them, "President Park is in danger!"

One of the agents twisted his arms behind his back, while two others placed their pistols against his head.

* * * * *

Standing atop the 50-foot high monolith dedicated to Canadians that fought and died in the Korean War, Won Jeong-hwa unhooked the karabiner from the rope extending from the chopper. The top of the monument was flat. A long, narrow bag was lying on it.

Jeong-hwa unzipped the bag and removed a *Snayperskaya Vintovka Dragunova* (SVD), literally "Dragunov's sniper rifle." The Russian rifle was adopted by the North Koreans. Twenty-four hours before she had placed the weapon there, after doping the scope for exactly 488 meters or the precise distance to where President Park was now standing.

Jeong-hwa ejected the clip, checked it, and then snapped it back into place. She laid flat and assumed the prone position, the most accurate field position for sniping. She scanned the area and realized the timing couldn't be better. President Park was still on stage.

Taejang Kang had told her that this part of his plan was the most tenuous. There was no real way to assure that the President would still be on stage, but the Taejang thought it was worth the risk and Jeong-hwa concurred.

For the supreme leader and my country!

Jeong-hwa brought the back of President Park's head into the crosshairs. Without pausing, she took aim and fired.

* * * * *

With pistols pressing against the sides of his head, and his arms held painfully behind his back, De Niro looked over at President Park. She was standing with her back to the podium waiting for the head of her security detail, a man named HyunBin, to lead her away.

De Niro cried out, "GEUN-HYE!!!"

President Park turned and spotted him, "Cris, is that you?"

The Secret Service agents brought him to the ground, smashing his face against the stage floor. He called out again, "GEUN-HYE … GET DOWN!!!"

The order didn't register instantly with the President but it did with the head of her detail. With enough force to knock a man down twice her size, he tackled her. The round fired by Jeong-hwa zipped over them and slammed into an agent's chest standing just beyond them.

While one agent kept his knee on De Niro's back, the others immediately placed their bodies in a ring surrounding the President.

* * * * *

Jeong-hwa cursed as she realized what happened. For a split-second she thought she was successful, President Park fell, but then she saw the round impact a man behind the President.

Jeong-hwa sprung to her feet and quickly slipped the rifle back into the bag then reattached herself to the rope still dangling from the chopper above. As she was hoisted up, she thought she heard the sounds of jet engines coming from somewhere. She looked up in time to see an AIM-9 Sidewinder, short-range air-to-air missile slice into the helicopter and explode.

Jeong-hwa fell back to the ground, slamming her head hard against the stone. Incapacitated, she screamed in terror as the burning chopper dropped onto her.

CHAPTER 55

SEOUL NATIONAL CEMETERY
DONGJAK-GU
SEOUL, SOUTH KOREA
9:10 AM (LOCAL), THURSDAY, JUNE 06, 2013

After a call of "all clear" rang out from several of her bodyguards, President Park was helped to her feet. With HyunBin in tow, she hurried to De Niro, with his head still pressed against the stage floor. The Secret Service agent subduing him was confused at her approach.

"Help him up."

The agent lifted De Niro to his feet.

"Cris, are you alright? Have you been injured?"

"I'm fine, Ms. President. Are you okay?"

"Yes, thanks to you."

De Niro grabbed her arms, "Your Excellency, there's still a threat. We must get you to a safe shelter immediately."

HyunBin motioned for his detail to surround them, "What threat?"

"Ten minutes ago, seven NoDong missiles were launched from a North Korean nuclear test site. We believe the target to be somewhere in Seoul, possibly here."

"Are they nuclear? Who are you, Sir?"

President Park held her hand up, "Mr. De Niro and his staff have been working under my authority."

"I apologize, Your Excellency. Mr. De Niro, are the missiles equipped with nuclear warheads?"

"We don't believe so, but they could be equipped with high explosive, chemical, or biological warheads … and they are utilizing GPS guidance systems."

HyunBin spoke into his radio, "The building behind us is filled to capacity and not secure. We cannot risk taking the President out of the cemetery. We must choose another place."

De Niro looked at the time, "The missiles will be over the city any minute now."

"I know a place," said President Park. "Call for a car."

"Your car is here, Your Excellency."

"Cris, you will come with me?"

De Niro glanced at HyunBin. He was visibly unhappy. President Park noticed. She grabbed De Niro's hand.

"You will come with me."

They jumped into the back of her limousine, an armored Hyundai Equus VL550. President Park made sure De Niro sat next to her, with HyunBin facing them. Another Secret Service agent sat in the front passenger seat along with the driver.

"Take me to my father's mausoleum."

HyunBin objected, "Your Excellency, the mausoleum is over a kilometer away and there is no shelter there."

"Take me there now!"

HyunBin bowed his head, "Yes, Your Excellency." He banged the separation window behind him and the limo lurched into motion. The heavy vehicle bounced about on the dirt paths leading to the main road, jarring everyone. De Niro held onto the door with one hand, and gently onto President Park's arm with the other.

They made it to the mausoleum in just over a minute. The Presidential resting place of her father was actually an open area, with granite stairs leading up to two stone tombs resting next to each other. A polished onyx monument stood aside them. President Park's mother was laid to rest next to her husband, Park Chung-hee.

President Park exited the car first. Everyone followed her up to the tombs. She sat on the one containing her father's remains.

HyunBin pointed his men to take positions around the perimeter of the area before approaching her with his head bowed, "Your Excellency, this place will not shelter you from harm."

"We have no idea exactly where those missiles will strike. Do we, Mr. De Niro?"

De Niro shook his head, "No, Ms. President, we don't."

"Then this place is as safe as any."

She patted her father's tomb.

De Niro sat next to her.

"My father was a great man ... a great President."

"And his daughter takes after him."

President Park smiled softly.

"Look!" one of the Secret Service agents called out pointing to streaks in the sky. The streaks arched down and slammed into the ground in the direction of the stage. Bright light illuminated from the area followed by the sounds of large explosions.

President Park kneeled between the tombs of her parents, "Pray with me, Cris."

De Niro joined her on her knees. They bowed their heads.

Minutes passed before HyunBin came up behind them, "Your Excellency, I am in contact with our people inside the building behind the stage. The building was hit by one missile, as was the stage. The rest of the missiles fell in the deserted area north of the building.

President Park finished her prayer and opened her eyes. De Niro helped her to her feet.

She faced HyunBin, "Casualties?"

"Yes, Excellency, multiple casualties reported inside the building.

So far, six reported dead and dozens injured, but it is too soon to know the full extent.

President Park bowed her head.

De Niro could feel her anguish, "Ms. President, I've failed you."

She looked up at De Niro and took his hand in hers as her cell phone rang.

After a moment she let out an audible breath, "Daejang Jeong, please hold on, I want to put you on speaker. I am standing here with Mr. De Niro. I want him to hear what you have to say."

She tapped a button.

"Mr. De Niro, this is Daejang Jeong."

"Yes, Daejang, are you alright, Sir?"

"Quite alright, Mr. De Niro thanks to you and your courageous staff. In fact, there are many here who owe their lives to you and your people today, including our President."

De Niro saw President Park smile and nod at him.

"What of the casualties, Daejang?"

"The casualties were unfortunate, but under the circumstances unavoidable. Mr. De Niro, there are over 1,000 people crammed into this building who just minutes before were standing squarely in the main impact zone. There is nothing left of the area in front of the stage and nothing left of the stage itself. You and your staff are heroes to my countrymen today."

De Niro took a moment to steady his voice, "Thank you, Sir."

President Park deactivated the phone speaker, "Daejang, I want our military placed on high alert, but make certain no aggressive moves are made or provocative actions are taken, especially along the border. The attacks that took place here this morning are not actions sanctioned by Pyongyang. Rather, they are the result of a plot by one man, Taejang Kang."

"Yes, Your Excellency, I understand."

"You do?" She glanced at De Niro who smiled back at her. "I am happy to hear that, Daejang. I want you to gather your staff. I will be heading back to the Blue House. As soon as I arrive, I will speak with Kim Jong-Un. I am sure he is already attempting to make contact with me. Please contact my senior staff and let them know that I am okay and of my plans. Thank you Daejang."

De Niro's phone rang. He looked at the caller I.D. and answered it, "Michelle …."

"Cris, I have John on the line, are you alright?"

"I'm okay. I'm with President Park, she's okay too."

Francis spoke up, "Cris we tracked the missiles right to your location. I tried to get a hold of you."

"Not a problem, I was a little busy. Any word from Mugsy or Scipio?"

"Not yet."

"Alright, I'll be heading back over to you, John. Michelle, meet us there."

"I'm already on my way. Cris, how bad was the damage?"

"People died and people were injured, still too early to tell how many. But, many more were saved including the President. I'll see you both soon."

President Park walked De Niro back to the limo, "Is there somewhere we can take you, Cris?"

"Actually, there is, Ms. President, if you don't mind. I took a cab to the ceremony. I'm pretty sure it'll be impossible to hail one from here now."

"Where can we drop you off?"

"Asan Medical Center."

"How is Mr. Francis?"

"You know about … what happened?"

The President led De Niro a few steps away from the car, "I know I said I could not, but I have been trying to keep tabs. I am very sorry for the injuries he sustained. I called to the hospital to make sure they would take the best care of him."

"That was very kind, Your Excellency, but you risked exposure."

"After what happened today, I believe I made the right call. Others will too. I was able to keep track of your activities here in Seoul, but I have not heard anything from Daeryeong Cho. Do you know their status?"

"Actually, I'm heading back to the hospital now. John is well enough to work … at least he says he is. He's been waiting for word from them. The last we knew, Captain Ricci and Cho were aboard the train that will take them west towards China. They're waiting for Scipio."

President Park nodded.

"Ms. President, Cho was injured."

Her eyes filled with concern, "Do you know the extent of his injuries?"

"All we know is that he was shot in the abdomen and that they were able to stabilize his condition."

She paused then placed her hand on his, "It seems many more prayers will be needed to get through this. Please, now that it is okay, keep me informed."

"I will, Your Excellency."

CHAPTER 56

MAIN GATE
HEADQUARTERS OF TAEJANG KANG KUM-SOK
PUNGGYE-RI NUCLEAR TEST SITE
KILJU COUNTY, NORTH HAMGYONG PROVINCE
NORTH KOREA
9:20 AM (LOCAL), THURSDAY, JUNE 06, 2013

A Sojang and his adjutant exited a chopper that landed in front of the main gate. They marched directly to the guard shack.

A Chungwi called for attention and saluted. Behind him, a dozen soldiers did the same.

The Sojang walked past the Chungwi, with only the slightest waving of his hand to return the salute. He stood over the body of Sojwa Rim. Blood was still oozing from his head wound.

"I just flew up from Kilju. What happened here, Chungwi?"

"Sojang ... Sir, the guards that were on duty said the Sojwa drove up to the gate in a car with another man."

"Another man … what other man?"

"They do not know. Sir, the Sojwa relieved the guards and ordered them to go and help put out the fires from the missile accident."

"A Sojwa standing guard at the gate …? I want to know who this other man is and where he is. I want to speak with him."

"Sir, the other man is nowhere to be found. Neither is the Sojwa's car."

"Who found the Sojwa's body?"

"I did, Sir. I work in the control room closest to where the missiles were positioned. I witnessed the explosion and was attempting to help put out the fires when the guards from here reported to me. I asked them why they left their post and they told me that the Sojwa sent them. We were short-handed so I put them to work, but I thought it was my duty to make sure that someone was guarding the gate. I found the Sojwa as you see him."

"And the missile accident, as you call it?"

"Yes, sir."

"Why do you call it an accident?"

"Because they exploded on lift-off, Sir. I saw it with my own eyes. So did many others."

"Lift-off, why were the missiles launching?"

"Taejang Kang scheduled them for a test launch this morning. It appeared that the locking mechanisms never disengaged."

"I was not notified of any test launch. I was told that Taejang Kang was murdered."

"Yes, sir. I do not know all of the details, but from what I was told, Sojang Kim and some other men infiltrated the base and murdered the Taejang."

"Sojang Kim …? Why would Sojang Kim murder Taejang Kang?"

The Chungwi flashed a look of surprise, "Sojang, I thought you would have known. Sojang Kim was labeled a fugitive. The Taejang personally sent out a general order for his arrest on sight."

The Sojang grimaced, "What has been going on here? This is all preposterous! Chungwi, who is in command of this base?"

The Chungwi looked uneasy at the question, "Sojang, with the Taejang, Sojang, and Sojwa all dead-"

"Sojang Kim is dead also?"

"… Yes, sir. I believed he was killed when he attempted to abduct Taejang Kang. Like I said, the soldiers inside know more about what happened in the Taejang's office than I do."

"Go on …."

"With all of our senior officers dead, I believe I am currently the ranking officer on duty, Sir."

"A Chungwi in command of one of our nuclear test sites …?"

"… Yes, sir."

The Sojang stared down at Sojwa Rim's body. He appeared deep in thought then looked up, "First order of business is to find the man that was with the Sojwa in the car."

"Sir, I had these men check. They found one witness arriving at the same time that said he saw a car matching the description of the Sojwa's car. It was leaving the base right after the explosions from the missile accident."

"Very well …," the Sojang turned to his adjutant, "put out a bulletin with the description of the Sojwa's car …." He turned back to the Chungwi, "Did the witness get a look at the man?"

The Chungwi hesitated.

"Chungwi, I asked you if the witness got a look at the man driving the Sojwa's car."

"Yes, sir, but the witness couldn't be sure."

"Sure of what?"

"The witness said that the driver appeared to be … Caucasian."

The Sojang's expression turned dark. He turned to his adjutant again, "Include in the bulletin that the driver may be Caucasian. Make sure the bulletin reaches every base, railroad station and town in a 50-kilometer radius."

The adjutant bowed and made the call.

* * * * *

Scipio checked the bandages on his face before exiting the car. *Glad I held onto the bandages. I had a feeling they'd come in handy again.* He started back on foot to the gas station he had just passed.

It was located in a remote spot with a barren, craggy wasteland sprawled in front and rough hill country behind.

He passed the pumps and headed into the building. There wasn't a car or person in sight.

The uniform should produce just enough fear to pull this off.

He marched to the counter with authority. The man behind it was old and didn't seem as impressed with the uniform as he was curious about the bandages.

"I ran out of gas down the road. I am a courier sent by Taejang Kang at Punggye-Ri, but I have no money to pay."

"And you think I will give you gas for free, just because you say the Taejang sent you? You are mistaken."

Scipio let his hand fall to the pistol tucked into his waistband. The old man noticed but didn't flinch.

Tough old bird ... I should shoot him but that would defeat the purpose.

Scipio turned for the door.

"What happened to your face?"

Scipio stopped, "It was burned."

"Burned ... how?"

Think quick Scipio ...

"A number of us were sent into the tunnels after one of the bomb tests. Most died. The rest were burned like me."

"Come here, I will show you something."

What now?

Scipio returned to the counter. The old man lifted his shirt and pointed to a large area of discolored skin.

"I too was burned in those tunnels after the first test. This is what I was left with ... this and look how old I look. I am probably not much older than you."

Scipio didn't reply.

"I am surprised they allow you to remain in uniform. They drummed me out. I thought they did it so others would not find out how it is in those tunnels. Maybe the Taejang has changed his attitude."

Scipio remained silent.

The man handed him a red gas can, "Go ahead and fill it up. You can pay me when you pass by again."

Scipio bowed his head, "Thank you. May I have a rag with it?"

The former soldier nodded and handed him one.

He exited the building and looked up.

Thanks.

He filled the can, walked back to the car and placed it in the trunk.

Then he took off.

CHAPTER 57

ABOARD TRAIN NKSR H-HYEKIL9-4
PAEGAM-NODONGJAGU STATION
PAEGAM-GUN, RYANGGANG PROVINCE, NORTH
KOREA
9:30 AM (LOCAL), THURSDAY, JUNE 06, 2013

Mugsy returned to the boxcar and crouched next to Cho, "I saw soldiers snooping around the station, so I took a stroll. There's an APC with a squad around it forming a road block just outside of town."

Cho winced as he sat up, "Someone at Punggye-Ri must have called ahead. They must know Scipio is en route."

"I agree. I think it's time we chance a call," Mugsy placed the call on speaker.

"Scipio, where are you?"

"I'm about a klick east of town."

"A squad of soldiers just set up a road block at the town's

entrance, with an APC blocking the road."

Scipio slowed down. He drove until he spotted the roadblock then stopped at the end of a bend in the road. The road straightened from there.

"Scip, are there any other roads you can take?"

"Negative and I can't get off this road. There are hills to one side and a forest to the other, but I have an idea … a contingency in case this happened."

"Scipio, the train is about to leave."

"Mugs, you have to delay it without raising suspicion."

"Copy that. Do what you need to do and get here a-sap."

Mugsy turned back to Cho, "You heard."

Cho called to Song, "We need you and your men to delay the train from departing. We need to buy Scipio some time … a diversion."

Song nodded, "How about a fight in front of the tracks?"

"Do it."

Scipio got out and opened the trunk. He took the gas can and tire jack out then poured the gasoline over the driver's seat, leaving some in the can.

Then, in order, he did the following:

He pulled the full length of the seat belt taut, cut it and—after pointing the wheels straight—tied one end to the steering wheel.

He placed the tire jack between the gas pedal and driver's seat then began pumping it until it applied a small amount of pressure to the pedal.

He stuffed the rag into the gas can allowing one end to stick out like a wick, lit, placed it on the driver's seat, and closed the door. Then he reached in, placed the car in drive, and began running with pistol in hand, first to the tree line to the north of the road, and then in the same direction as the car towards the road block.

The unpiloted car rolled down the road and slowly began to veer. Scipio waited until it reached the shoulder still 200 feet away from the APC, and began firing at the road block. He almost emptied the clip before they began firing back. The car was riddled with bullets then burst into flames.

Scipio didn't stop running towards town as he watched the soldiers approach the flaming vehicle from the road. He ran past them without being detected and jogged the final distance to the boxcar.

Mugsy helped him on, "Everything okay?"

"Everything will be okay if this train starts moving … now!"

Song and his men returned and boarded, "We fought as long as we could, until the engineer threatened to call the police."

"You did well," replied Cho. He turned to Scipio, "Glad you could make it."

Scipio winked, "Not as glad as I am, my friend.

They rolled the door closed as the train jolted into motion.

CHAPTER 58

STATE RECEPTION HOUSE
THE BLUE HOUSE
SEOUL, SOUTH KOREA
9:00 AM (LOCAL), THURSDAY, JUNE 15, 2013

President Park walked with De Niro at the edge of the rolling lawn. The tailored, green blanket stretched out from the ornate reception house on the grounds of the executive office and official residence of the President of the Republic of Korea.

"My country and I owe you and your people an immeasurable debt of gratitude, Cris. If it were not for your combined efforts, the Koreas would be engaged in a terrible conflict, one I fear may have caused the world to choose sides."

"Thank you, Your Excellency."

"Please Cris remember our deal ... Geun-hye."

De Niro nodded and changed the subject, "How do relations with the North stand now?"

"Publicly, the Supreme Leader has taken credit for stopping the plot of the traitor, Taejang Kang. But privately, he was practically begging me to believe that he knew nothing about it."

"I guess that's to be expected."

"I want you also to know that I have spoken to your President, on your behalf. I explained to him that if it weren't for your actions and the actions of your people, the United States would have been drawn into the inevitable conflict.

"I'm afraid to say that, though the President sounded appeased from the result, some on his staff sounded less than appreciative of your efforts."

"I'm afraid that's to be expected. With his counsel, the President made it clear that the U.S. would not investigate the allegations in Sojang Kim's letter."

"Will there be problems for you back home?"

"None that we can't handle. Though the President made the U.S. stance crystal clear to you and his staff, he never specifically ordered me or my agency to stay out of it. The Watchman Agency is a private firm. The United States is our client, not our employer. That gives us much more latitude to act in situations like this one."

"I am glad to hear that."

They stopped walking near marble steps leading down to a small patio on which Mugsy and Michelle were embracing.

President Park smiled, "It is nice to see husband and wife reunited. They appear … quite happy about it."

"Actually, they're not married … yet, but I think my brother-in-law just found out that he's going to be a daddy."

President Park's smile beamed, "That is wonderful. Would it be proper to go down and congratulate them before breakfast? Come to think of it, where are Cho and Scipio? I thought they too were to join us for breakfast."

"Yes … well, Scipio wanted me to apologize on their behalf. According to him, there was still 'unfinished business' that they had to intend to."

"I see."

De Niro held out his arm, "After you, Ms. President."

"Thank you, Mr. De Niro."

De Niro let President Park walk down the stairs and approach them alone. He watched as the head-of-state hugged his brother-in-law and soon-to-be sister-in-law. The happiness on their faces brought back memories of when Lisa first told him that she was pregnant with Richard. Tearfully, he bowed

his head, *Thank you Father, for bringing us through this.*

He blinked the tears away and made a call, "Richard, it's Daddy …"

CHAPTER 59

MEIKAKUKAI SEOUL DOJO
SEODAEMUNGU
SEOUL, SOUTH KOREA
9:00 AM (LOCAL), THURSDAY, JUNE 15, 2013

Dressed in a white gi with black belt, Cho bowed to Scipio. As was his style, Scipio was dressed as he always was … in black street clothes.

"You are a long way from fully healed, my friend."

"My wound is bandaged securely. Besides, it is not my wound that needs protecting."

Scipio raised a brow as Cho reached under his tunic. He untied his pants and let them drop.

He was wearing a cup.

Scipio burst into laughter. Cho joined in.

###

ABOUT THE AUTHOR

Gerard de Marigny is the creator of the #1 *Amazon*-Bestselling Counter-Terrorism & Geopolitical CRIS DE NIRO and ARCHANGEL Thriller series.

For all up-to-date info on Gerard de Marigny please visit:

g's website & blog:
www.GerarddeMarigny.com

g's Facebook:
www.facebook.com/Gerarddem

g's Twitter:
www.Twitter.com/GerarddeMarigny

g's LinkedIn:
www.LinkedIn.com/in/GerarddeMarigny

g's Goodreads:
http://www.goodreads.com/author/show/4607706.Gerard_de_Marigny

g's email:
g@gerarddemarigny.com

BOOK CLUB GUIDE

1.   As the main character, Cris De Niro is unlike other main characters in action & adventure stories (i.e. Thor's Horvath and Flynn's Mitch Rapp). How does he differ?

2.   Which character(s) did you feel aligned with and why?

3.   Do Gerard's plots make you see the world in a different way?

4.   Did this book live up to or exceed your expectations of the author?

5.   What did you like or dislike about the book that hasn't been discussed already? Were you glad you read this book? Would you recommend it to a friend? Do you want to read more work by this author?

(The author would like to hear your views. Please share any/all of them with him by emailing him at: mailto:g@gerarddemarigny.com.)

 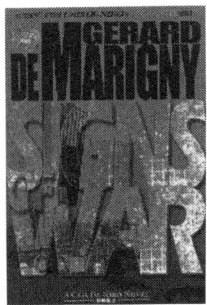  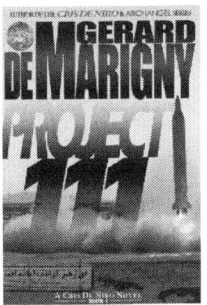

author of the *CRIS DE NIRO* & ~~ARCHANGEL~~ series
GERARD DE MARIGNY
RESCUE FROM SANA'A
MISSION LOG #2
ARCHANGEL

RESCUE FROM SANA'A
Mission Log #2

from master storyteller,
Gerard de Marigny